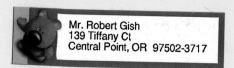

THE
EVOLUTION
OF THOMAS HALL

THE
EVOLUTION
OF THOMAS HALL

KIETH MERRILL

SHADOW
MOUNTAIN

Quotations appearing in the book come from the following sources:

Page 176, from Thomas Jefferson. From a letter written by Thomas Jefferson to William Short, in Thomas Jefferson, *The Jefferson Bible: The Life and Morals of Jesus of Nazareth* (Boston: Beacon Press, 2001), 28.

Pages 212, 214, from Richard Dawkins. Richard Dawkins, *The God Delusion* (New York: Mariner, 2008), 51, 19.

Page 212, from Carl Sagan. Carl Sagan, *Pale Blue Dot: A Vision of the Human Future in Space* (New York: Random House, 1977), 50.

Page 255, from Charles Darwin. Charles Darwin, *On the Origin of Species by Means of Natural Selection* (Norwalk, Connecticut: The Eaton Press, 1976), 445.

Page 261, from C. S. Lewis. C. S. Lewis, *Mere Christianity, Book 1, Right and Wrong as a Clue to the Meaning of the Universe* (New York: HarperCollins, 2003), 1-7.

Page 293, from Saint Augustine. As quoted in William J. Fitzgerald, *One Hundred Cranes: Praying with the Chorus of Creation* (Washington, D.C.: ACTA Publications, 1996), 63.

Pages 437-38, from Charles Darwin. *Autobiography of Charles Darwin,* edited by Francis Darwin (London: Collins, 1958), 26.

Visit us at ShadowMountain.com

Library of Congress Cataloging-in-Publication Data

Merrill, Kieth, author.
　　The evolution of Thomas Hall / Kieth Merrill.
　　　　p. cm.
　　Summary: Artist Thomas Hall comes face to face with his concept of God when he is hired to create two very different murals.
　　ISBN 978-1-60641-836-9 (hardbound : alk. paper)
· 1. Artists—Fiction.　2. Burns and scalds—Patients—Fiction.　3. Conversion—Christianity—Fiction.　I. Title.
　　PS3613.E7762E96 2011
　　813'.6—dc22　　　　　　　　　　　　　　　　　　　　　　　　　　　2011001695

Printed in the United States of America
Worzalla Publishing Co., Stevens Point, WI

10　9　8　7　6　5　4　3　2　1

To Dagny
Being best friends half a century makes spending
eternity together a delicious expectation.

1

Thomas Hall was fascinated by the color of blood. It oozed alizarin crimson from the monster's mouth in a single deft twist of the hog-bristle brush. It dripped from jagged teeth in hues of amaranth and azure. It fell to the stony ground and crusted in a purple scab.

The artist stepped away from the cyclorama that curved into darkness on both sides of the work lights and squinted at the unfinished scene of primitive violence. For a moment he was both inside and outside the painting. His lips mimicked the snarl of the primitive beast unprompted by any conscious thought.

He used a smaller brush for a touch of cadmium yellow. The reflection of fire from the torches of primitive men. A spark of evil in brutish eyes. A glistening wet blaze on the tusk of a feline creature.

Thomas squinted to assess contrast and value. The scene was a depiction of Late Pleistocene. A saber-tooth crouched on the carcass of a mammoth calf. Hunters were trying to drive it away and claim its kill. The hungry Homo sapiens were thick and brutish, animal-like except for the humanoid musculature of perfectly drawn bodies.

As a teenager Thomas had collected the fantasy art of Boris Vallejo—every comic book, poster and graphic novel he could buy, beg, borrow or steal. Vallejo's influence was evident in Thomas's rendering of the ancient prehumans. In spite of shaggy hair, sloping heads and protruding brows, the apelike creatures were drawn with such magnificent physiques they could have appeared just as easily on the cover of *Muscle Magazine* as in a depiction of Cro-Magnon hunters 15,000 years B.C.

The prehistoric cat clawed at the thieves. One brute lay bleeding in the snow, his fur wrap ripped open. Deep gashes clawed across his chest. Thomas stained the snow with blood in a smudge of darkened carmine red.

An adult mammoth charged toward the hunters to protect her fallen young. The monster swung her massive head side to side. Her tusks ripped through the snow and heaved up a foul storm of frost and frozen tundra. The hunters stumbled back in terror.

In the mysterious inner sanctuary where Thomas could visualize whatever his mind could imagine, the men existed. He felt their fear. The beasts were alive. The moment frozen in time by paint on canvas was real. It was a mysterious dimension of his enormous gift.

It was late. The upper pavilion of Pacific Science Museum was deserted. Thomas was alone. But the bellowing of savage beasts and grunts of primitive men echoed in the darkness.

CHAPTER

2

"WHO IS THOMAS HALL?" It was a fair question. Susan Cassidy was recommending the artist to the board of St. Mark's Hospital.

At five foot nine in bare feet Susan Cassidy was impressive. In three-inch heels she was intimidating. She always wore heels.

No one called her Susan anymore. That had ended in second grade when she had crossed her arms, set her jaw and refused to answer roll call. "My name is Cassidy!" she had insisted. By sixth grade she was a rough-and-tumble tomboy everyone called "Cass." The name stuck.

Cass touched a key on her MacBook Pro to answer the question. A picture of Thomas Hall appeared on the screen. A ravishing redhead with a silk bandolier proclaiming her MISS SCOTLAND was kissing him on the cheek. His arms were aloft with a Chesley Award in each hand; his face bore an arrogant smile.

Thomas leaned into the kiss from Miss Scotland with a confident smirk. *The artist's power of observation has been overpowered by his libido,* Cass mused to herself, wondering if the guy had a clue why beauty queens looked so drop-dead gorgeous.

Cass knew. She had run for Miss Palo Alto when she was seventeen and learned all the tricks. Miss Scotland's flaming red hairdo was overdone and extended with a swirl of dyed horsehair. She wore five-inch spikes to make her legs look longer, super-bind control-top pantyhose to keep her stomach flat, duct tape to hoist and enhance her figure, Vaseline on her teeth to insure the endless smile, and WD-40 on her derrière to keep the evening gown from sticking.

Cass's competitive nature clicked through a comparative checklist. Twenty-seven not eighteen. Brunette not redhead. San Francisco not Glasgow. Five nine not five four. Master's degree in communications not a certificate of cosmetology. Cass took smug satisfaction in superior dimensions: 34–25–35. *I never used duct tape,* she thought, then blushed. *Why do I care what Thomas Hall was thinking?* Her eyes shifted from Miss Scotland to the artist. He was grinning at her.

"Mr. Hall won Chesley Awards three years running," Cass said.

"What's a Chesley Award?" It was Clinton Carver again. Cass expected him to pepper her with questions. Carver served as president of the board of St. Mark's Hospital. In real life he was an attorney in a law firm with five names. His wasn't one of them.

"It's like the Academy Award for a style of art Mr. Hall is interested in." *Interested in? Agh! Bad choice of words.*

Cass nodded at Kimberly Johnson, who fluttered her fingers like a first grader asking for permission to go to the bathroom. "I wish we could see something he's done," she said. *Queen of the obvious.* Cass wondered why they kept her on the board.

"What a good idea," Cass said in perfect PR. There were six men and three women on the board. It was a rare occasion when all nine were present. The new Children's Wing was obviously important.

"Who's the girl?" Dr. Barry Bradley asked. The men at the table snickered at the old physician's predictable focus on Miss Scotland. The women put on censorious faces and shook their heads.

"Miss Scotland." Cass smiled at Dr. Bradley. "The photo was taken at the Sixty-third World Science Fiction Convention in Glasgow two years ago. Mr. Hall won the Chesley for both hardcover and magazine illustration."

"I wish we had a way to see his winning entries." Kimberly again.

Cass raised her eyebrows as if the suggestion were an incantation that would magically summon up the winning entries, which were the next image. "What a great idea," she intoned. *How is it possible to be charming and brain-dead at the same time?* The plucky personality that had made Cass the terror of the sixth grade had been in control by the time she got to Stanford University. In the meantime it had won her the high school record in high hurdles and left Leon Pledger with a broken nose and a clear understanding that "no" meant *"NO!"*

She tapped the keyboard. Photographs of Hall's winning entries came up side by side. She galvanized her resolve and braced herself for what she expected next. For the inevitable.

The winning hardcover illustration was for a novel: *Amazon Queen.* The other was the August cover of *Heavy Metal Magazine.* The drone and chatter stopped in stunned silence. *And a hush fell over the crowd.* Cass recited the cliché in her head.

Cass had known that Thomas Hall would be a hard sell. His current genre of fantasy art was different from the modernism of Salvador Canstano, the previous artist, who had quit when he broke both arms.

The silence became leaden. Every eye stared at the eight-foot screen.

The cover art for *Amazon Queen* was on the left: an exotic woman in a tangle of jungle, six foot nine, muscular, perfectly formed body, mostly bare or barely covered by battle-torn fragments of armor. She held a spear in one hand and a chain in the other, with a man-eating tiger in a spiked collar and a giant snake about to strike.

The cover of *Heavy Metal Magazine* was on the right. A bevy of scantily clad biker chicks straddled tricked-out Harleys and sneered in a provocative display of attitude.

An icon of the Chelsey Award, along with the word *WINNER,* was prominent in each.

Dr. Bradley broke the silence. "That ought to get the kids better quick enough." The ripple of laughter eased the tension. *Thank you, Dr. Bradley.*

"Okay," Cass said, "I know what you're thinking: *Cass has lost her mind.*"

"If you're serious, you should be worried about losing your job," Carver snarled and stood up. Cass had no illusions about Carver. She'd been hired by the hospital administrator as director of public relations without board approval, and had inherited the assignment as project director for the new Children's Wing when the assistant administrator had taken an unexpected leave of absence. Carver was outspoken in his opposition, but hiring policies were outside board jurisdiction.

Everyone knew why Carver was opposed to Cass's promotion, but it was one of those delicate situations where common sense got buried by political correctness and so nobody talked about it. Carver did not like women in executive positions.

Bylaws required that there be females on the board. If Carver had his way, the board would be male only. Board meetings would be short. They'd get a few *all-in-favor-say-aye*s out of the way, go to a bar, drink Budweiser, watch the sporting event du jour and argue over draft picks, rankings and coaches in the vocabulary of educated men strangely out of place in the realm of armpits and beer.

Cass concluded that Carver had supported Kimberly's reelection to fill what he called "the girl quota" because she posed no threat. Cass regretted the choice; she considered Kimberly a dough head.

Carver expected a response. Cass felt her face flush. She breathed deep. Shook it off.

"Believe it or not, Mr. Carver, I am willing to put my job on the line if that's what it takes to persuade you . . ." Her confidence hung over the long oval table like an audible ellipsis. " . . . persuade all of you that Thomas Hall is the man who can *rescue* us from the unexpected change in our plans. I feel bad about what happened to Mr. Canstano. That said, I believe it may be the proverbial blessing in disguise." Dr. Bradley nodded his support, so she added, "Some of you shared my belief that he was headed in the wrong direction."

Cass had learned the hard way that there was no place for equivocation when selling. And today's presentation was selling, pure and simple. Most of life was selling. Going halfway or playing it safe rarely cut it at the front end and made no difference in the end. If projected results fell short of expectations, no one remembered the caveats and qualifiers. If you sell and they buy but you fail to deliver and end up flat on your face, no one helps you up, dusts you off, and says, "No worries. We remember you were pessimistic in selling us your crazy idea and committing us to this total disaster. Our fault. We still love you." It never happened that way. If you went down in flames, it was always a solo flight.

Jessica gave Cass the thumbs-up she needed and replenished her power like a kid clicking *RELOAD* in a video game. Jessica was Cass's personal assistant. She was forty-eight years old and as loyal as a Doberman pinscher, and Cass loved her. Since *secretary* was no longer PC and *personal assistant* was woefully inadequate, Cass called her *executive mother.*

In one of those inexplicable flashes of the brain, Jessica's reassuring grin brought Admiral David Glasgow Farragut's words to mind, "*Damn the torpedos. Full speed ahead.*"

"I wanted to show you Mr. Hall's current work because you would see it eventually and I wanted it to be sooner. Get it out of the way."

"What do you mean 'get it out of the way'? It is what it is and it is obviously aaaaa. . . ." Law school had not prepared Carver with a vocabulary to describe the fantasy art of Thomas Hall. "It's so . . ." He sputtered in search of a word more articulate than *junk* and more intelligent than *crap* but evidently didn't find one, so he just stared at the life-sized images on the wall.

A curvaceous, sensuous creature from the legendary race of female warriors in a jungle beyond the edge of the known world.

Bikini-clad biker chicks on hogs.

"Whatever else can be said about this sort of thing," Carver stammered at last, "it is obviously *not* what we want on the walls of the new Children's Wing."

"I agree with you!" Cass said. "It is absolutely NOT what we want!" Carver was disarmed and suddenly suspicious. "This is where Thomas Hall has gone with his art." Cass pointed to the graphic images still on the screen. "Now I want to show you where he came from and why I'm convinced he is the artist you should approve to replace Mr. Canstano."

She smiled at Carver and waited for him to sit down. He did so, then folded his arms, crossed his legs and turned away from Cass. The only thing missing from the belligerent body language was a throbbing neon sign: *No matter what you say, the answer is NO!*

"What you are about to see," Cass intoned in a voice that sounded like recorded narration, "is a sampling of the art created by Thomas Hall during his four years at Buena Vista Art Institute."

Cass touched the remote. The room went dark. Attentions returned to the screen. Carver picked the moment to check messages on his Blackberry and tapped out a text with his thumbs.

Cass could not miss Carver's deliberate slight. *A stubborn adolescent,* she thought. She tried to ignore him but wondered instead whether her zeal to sell a rogue artist was driven by the talent of Thomas Hall or by her need to overpower Carver. *I am hard-selling an artist I've never met. I am putting my reputation on the line for an artist I know almost nothing about.* She inhaled to calm the flutter in her stomach.

"I'm so excited!" Kimberly's exuberance brought scattered chortles and pulled Cass back to the moment. The glow from Carver's Blackberry cast his excessive jowls in pale cerulean and turned him into a ghoul. It made Cass feel better. She touched *PLAY*.

Music rose in the darkness. It played for a few seconds before the first image faded from black. Cass didn't need her master's in communication from Columbia to understand the power of musical underscore.

A single French horn echoed far away. It was herald for the theme from *Crimson Tide*. She loved the movie and the music. Hans Zimmer's haunting composition never failed to lift her from impassive solitude to standing with a hand across her heart.

Cass had organized the fifty-seven images of Hall's art so each piece reflected the mood and spirit of the music. Images appeared then dissolved one into the next. The music continued to grow as other instruments joined the anthem. At forty-three seconds the full orchestra arrived and sixty-five individual instruments blended to become the powerful main theme.

Cass had appreciated Hall's art when she had assembled the slides. Isolated by the darkness with full effects, she saw them again for the first time. They took her breath away.

The first of the images were sketches. Studies of the human form. Figure drawings from life. They grew with the music in complexity and wonder. Several reflected the style of the old masters. Excruciating detail. Mastery of light. Fidelity of color. Extraordinary settings. Expressive gestures. Powerful faces. Some embraced myriad characters, told stories and invited interpretation. Others were glazed until they glowed with a translucent third dimension.

Several large paintings focused on curious objects arranged as still life, textures or fabrics. One was a study in oil of nothing but the endless undulation of falling drapery.

Hall's choice of media was audacious. Oil, acrylic, watercolor, gouache, charcoal, pencil, pen and ink. Some of the pieces were even created with Painter, a software program capable of remarkable digital renderings. But Hall's artworks had two things in common. They tended toward realism. And they were astonishing.

The last of the images arrived as the theme reached "Eternal Father, Strong to Save." Cass glanced at Carver. The cell phone was still in his hand. *A defiant child refusing to give in,* she mused. The swelling music lifted his eyes to the images on the screen. Cass, who had done her homework, relished the moment.

Carver had served in the United States Navy as a younger man. The stirring music rising up from the fabric of Zimmer's score was not a casual decision. The piece was known by every man who ever served at sea as the "Navy Hymn." An all-male choir joined the orchestra, arriving, it seemed, on the gentle undulations of a tranquil sea.

> *Eternal Father, strong to save,*
> *Whose arm hath bound the restless wave,*
> *Who bidd'st the mighty ocean deep,*
> *Its own appointed limits keep.*

A sea battle between two great galleons filled the screen. One was ablaze. Smoke swirled through full sails to mingle with massive storm clouds that billowed above and framed the scene. Long shafts of golden light blazed across the white-capped waves of the turbulent sea.

A Norse king was borne aloft by forlorn subjects to a funeral ship waiting to be pushed out to sea. The elegant Viking caravel was licked by winded flames in the cold twilight of the frozen north. The white-hot yellows and flaming oranges pierced the cold blue of an Arctic winter. For those familiar with Hall's work, the piece was a subtle foreshadow of his current fascination with fantasy.

Waves churned into monsters by a raging storm crashed onto rocks beneath a lonely lighthouse at the edge of night.

Carver's cell phone had gone dark. The seafarer's anthem held him in its emotional grip and riveted his eyes to the screen. Cass could not see his expression. His body language gave her a flicker of optimism before she reminded herself that the emotions of a moment are rarely sufficient to inspire permanent change.

> *Oh, hear us when we cry to Thee,*
> *For those in peril on the sea!*

The choir sang. Soft light from the screen illuminated the faces of the board. The images filling the screen were unlike any they had seen.

First a series of drawings, sketches, and close-up explorations of hands, faces, feet and fabrics. The pencil sketches by Thomas Hall were studies for a major work. It was the final image: a large painting depicting the crucifixion of Christ. It was breathtaking in spite of being unfinished. The man on the cross had no face.

The master work faded to black. The music continued. Cass covered the lens and cast the room into darkness. She wanted to suspend her audience in a black void a moment longer than expected. She wanted their feelings to last and the images to linger in their memories and etch themselves there. The choir finished: "Ahhhhhmen."

Cass walked slowly to the light switch by the door. The silence that had followed the display of the Amazon Queen and Biker Chicks on Motorcycles had come from shock. A scornful silence. The silence that followed the finest art of Thomas Hall came from awe. A silence of wonder.

The only sound Cass heard was from Kimberly. She was sniffling.

3

THE SOUND WAS LIKE THE roar of savage beasts. It ended when the gas tank exploded.

Three minutes earlier the front right fender of Gloria Christensen's 1995 Ford Windstar had slipped under the revolving drum of a ten-wheel McNeilus Bridgemaster. The cement truck had veered into her lane with no blinker, alarm, or warning. Sixty-eight tons of wet concrete drove double duals over the hood and crushed the right front side. The wheel mashed flat. The axle of the Windstar snapped like a piece of cheap plastic.

By the time the truck driver felt his right rear pitch up and over the minivan and realized what was happening, Gloria's fate and the fate of her little girl were cast—*as it were in tragic irony*—in concrete.

When the truck lurched, the driver dropped his cell phone and jerked the steering wheel hard right. Too late. The minivan flipped forward.

Gloria was ejected by the airbag when the minivan landed on its top. The safety lock ruptured and the driver's side door exploded open. Her unfastened seat belt dangled like an executioner's rope.

The concrete pump trailing out behind the cement truck whipped sideways and smashed into the car. The Windstar pirouetted across the pavement, toppled over the embankment, and tumbled to where six-foot waves crashed onto the breakwater below.

The last thing Gloria Christensen saw before she died was Christina spinning away, holding her head with a hand soaked in red crimson and screaming "Mother!"

CHAPTER

4

THOMAS DRAGGED A TWISTED stroke of agony across the face of the fallen hunter. He felt the man's terror. Cocking his head to one side, he looked in the mirror behind him to analyze the composition. Seeing it in reverse forced a critical examination of balance and proportion.

He had learned the technique from Davy Daniels during their year together at Art Institute. Daniels was a gifted artist, the best Thomas knew. He was also the most unhinged human being Thomas had ever met. Daniels had died from AIDS the middle of their second year. Whenever Thomas used the mirror technique he thought of Davy. Such incredible talent. Such a wasted life. Why was such uncommon creativity so often coupled with such ambiguity?

The pantomime of the beast that tightened Thomas's face softened to the satisfied smile of an artist. The figures on the mural were coming to life exactly as he imagined.

He clawed back the tab on a can of Red Bull and let his eyes drift from the painting to his own image in the mirror. The man looking back was most familiar, but not in the way that another man might recognize his own reflection.

Thomas was acquainted with the guy sucking down eight ounces of energy in ways most people never knew themselves. That knowledge came from hours of observing and replicating and evaluating his face—not as a teenage complexion to be picked at or the vanity-filled image of a swaggering rogue in college but as a skull strapped with muscles and covered with skin. As a body constructed with a skeleton connected by tendons, animated by muscle and wrapped in epidermis.

Thomas flexed his jaw. His face was square. In reverse and reflected back, the image floated a few feet away in the strange dimension of a parallel reality. His blond hair was rusted by streaks of chestnut and copper. It was a thick tumble, thrown back and cut long enough to dance along the collar of his shirt. His eyes were Payne's gray invaded by a whisper of cobalt blue.

He had been in second grade when he had discovered that he could replicate reality with a pencil better than any other kid in the room. That was twenty-three years ago. Since then he had sketched, drawn or painted ninety-two self-portraits. All of them had included his face, some of them his upper torso. A few in recent years were head to toe, all six foot two of him.

Thomas loved human anatomy. Freezing the human form without stopping its movement was where mediocre talent tumbled into the chasm and genius learned to fly. Anatomically speaking, every human being was the same but no two people were alike. *The Andrus Paradox.* That's what his favorite professor at Buena Vista Art Institute called it.

Professor Roman Andrus demanded that his students know and draw every muscle perfectly but insisted they never draw a muscle the same way twice. "It's about learning to override your visual autopilot," he would say. "To control a creative aspect of yourself that God intended to keep to Himself but decided to share with a few."

There was always something just behind the gleam of light in Professor Andrus's black eyes that reminded students he knew something incredible he was never going to tell.

"You've got to consciously sever the subconscious associations between language and images," he coached his favored students. "Break the link between words and motor-skill memories." Andrus was convinced that most if not all people could draw better than they imagined but were trapped by their earliest associations between words and objects.

By the time children can understand the idea of art, they have already drawn a circle with five lines to represent the word *hand* a hundred times. The patterns are repeated, neuron memories are imbedded, and *hand* becomes a circle with five lines. When those children become self-aware and discover that a circle with five lines for fingers is not acceptable for seven-year-olds, they abandon art with the only logical conclusion: "I can't draw."

When Thomas discovered he could not only draw hands that looked like hands but create places that never existed, people who never were and creatures wholly beyond reality that seemed believable, he left the legacy of self-portraits to Van Gogh, Picasso and Andy Warhol and plunged into the world of fantasy art.

5

I T WAS A LOVELY DREAM.

Christina's fingers danced across the strings of her violin. She touched each one with grace and confidence. The movement of the bow expressed her love of music. A delicate caress. A fleeting kiss.

She was dazzled by the lights above the stage. Amber. Soft pink. Blue. Halos made of rainbows. Streaks of color splayed out from glittering stars.

Christina was first chair in the violin section. Every eye in the concert hall was on her. Sophisticated women in elegant dresses. Handsome men in long-tailed tuxedos. Every seat occupied to the ninth balcony and above into the darkness where the lights got in your eyes and made seeing the endless tiers impossible.

A Hungarian folk tune by Bartok was a simple piece for such a grand affair, but it was the only piece she had practiced and knew well enough to play in concert. She could play whatever she wanted, though. She was a virtuoso. The child genius. A prodigy. "More gifted than Hilary Hahn," her teacher praised. Her teacher was in the front row. Then standing beside her. Then tapping her finger on the music.

The conductor wore a black coat with long tails that wagged to the music. Dog tails like on Mylo, her black lab. The man's head was a pale yellow prune covered by a tangled bush of white hair. He was Charlie, the man who tuned the piano. That couldn't be. He had no ears. He was a stranger.

The man waved his hand and pointed at her. Time for her solo. Butterflies flew from her stomach with a tickling sensation and winged their way over the music, hiding the notes. Then the butterflies became the notes and fluttered past her nose in allegro exactly the way Mr. Bartok had intended it to be.

She drew the bow across the strings. The sounds of the music emerged as vapors of light, pink, violet, and soft yellow.

NOISE! An explosion in the blackness plunged the hall into darkness. A pain shot through her head. The awful sounds of angry beasts in agony rose up to devour her. The wisps of colored music were writhing snakes. Someone screamed.

Christina looked up at a glimmer of light. The stage lamps were on fire. The ceiling cracked. A heavy blackness fell toward her. She tried to run but could not move. She was strapped to the first chair by a seat belt.

The seat belt was in the backseat of the Windstar minivan. Christina was asleep when a cement truck drove over her mother's car. Her dream became a nightmare but the nightmare was not a dream. Her life was changed forever.

CHAPTER

6

THOMAS LENGTHENED THE TUSKS and lowered the mammoth's head to make the death of the hunters certain.

A cell phone rang in the darkness. The ring tone played several bars of the title music from *Eragon*. Suspended in his altered state with a massive brute about to ravage primal hunters, Thomas heard the music as an underscore to the terror taking place rather than a cell phone ringing. The heroic theme tempted him to give the hunters a chance to wound the beast. Even the odds.

Cymbals crashed. The ring tone started from the top again. The spell was broken.

Thomas turned away from his work and squinnied his eyes to puncture a hole in the din. He was irritated by the interruption. *Why is my phone in here?* he wondered. The upper pavilion of the Science Museum was off-limits. Sacrosanct. Cut off from the world. He never brought his phone.

The ring tone continued. It was the part of Doyle's music Thomas liked the most—the part that allowed him to fly. He made a mental note to order the movie on Blu-ray and watch it again. The thought poked him in the gut with a bony fist of anger.

Thomas had a history with *Eragon*. Stefen Fangmeier, the special effects supervisor, had invited him to work up some sketches for the dragon when he was negotiating to direct the movie. Thomas did, and the sketches were great. Fangmeier got the gig, but when Wolf Kroeger was hired as production designer he brought in his own guys. *They should have had me design their dragon; it would have been better.*

His mouth was sour and the music had become irritating. *Let it go to voice message. Not supposed to be a phone in here anyway.*

He turned from the demons of *Eragon* and Fangmeier to the monsters on the canvas. Another thought. The call might be from Berger with good news on the Heavy Metal Casino project in Vegas. Huge walls of monsters and demons.

Berger was Frank Berger: agent, manager, friend and confidant. Heavy Metal Inc. was building a themed hotel and casino in Las Vegas with plans to decorate the entry and vaulted atrium with enormous figures of fantasy art. Thomas was one of three artists being considered. *Gotta be Berger. Who else has this number?* He laid his palette aside.

He found his iPhone on the workbench. There was a note attached with blue tape: *YOU LEFT THIS AT SECURITY.* He ripped the note away and checked the caller ID.

OAKRIDGE MANOR

He canceled the call and crumpled the note.

CHAPTER

7

THE OLD MAN HELD THE PHONE with a trembling hand. He covered his left ear and strained to hear with the other. "Leave a message after the tone." A shaft of dusty sunlight fell through the French window and danced across his shoulders, igniting a celestial fire that rimmed his face in a halo of white.

The tone ended.

"Hello, Tommy. It's your father." His voice was weak, stammering. "I've been trying to reach you. Left a message yesterday and the day before. Hope you're all right. Wanted to remind you my birthday is a week from Friday. They want to give me a party. Eighty-one candles." He laughed softly. "Probably burn the place down 'fore I blow 'em out, but . . ." A burning in his throat forced him to cough. "I'd sure like it if you could come." His lips moved but no sound came. Alexander Hall caught a tear with the back of his hand before it could trickle to his chin. "Or call me. I know you're busy."

The burning came again. He swallowed hard. It got worse. He coughed, and a pain hacked up from deep inside, where it seem to crush his lungs. He moved the phone away. His shoulders hunched forward and the coughing caused him to shudder. He kept his breaths shallow to avoid another bout.

"Sorry, I've picked up a . . . you've got the number here I think but just in case." He held the wireless handset close to his face and bobbed his head to position bifocal lenses in search of the telephone number. It was written in pencil, smudged and difficult to decipher. "Sorry, Tommy, I can't read the—"

The number appeared in bold, dark numerals only inches from his eyes. The Post-it note was suspended from long, delicate fingers, each adorned with one or more extravagant rings.

Alexander's eyes swept upward from the brace of bangles to a frail arm not much more than bones wrapped in translucent skin. The muslin shawl on the woman's shoulders gathered the light from the window and bounced it onto her face. It softened the wrinkles and filled the shallow recesses of her eyes. It accentuated the high cheekbones that were surely a hallmark of her beauty as a younger woman. She was lovely still in a way even a younger man could appreciate. She was smiling.

Patricia Benning was eighty-eight. She had been the first to welcome Alexander to Oakridge Manor Assisted Living when he had arrived eighteen months before. She was tall and carried herself erect. Her sense of fashion was frozen in time but she plied the feminine arts with care. Her eyes were light blue at the outer edge and darker toward the middle. She did not need glasses and was zealous in sharing the secret of her eye exercises with anyone willing to believe they were responsible for her 20/20 vision. Alexander faithfully practiced his eye exercises whenever he saw her coming.

"Ah, wait a minute, Tommy. I've got it now." Alexander nodded thank you to Mrs. Benning. In the time he had known her he had never felt comfortable calling her Patricia. She never suggested he should. "Mrs. Benning" it was.

He read the number slowly into the phone, taking a tiny breath between every digit. "9 2 5 9 0 6 0 5 7 9." He paused, as if there were one more thing to say. Whatever it might have been it didn't come. "Good-bye, Tommy. Call me. If you can."

CHAPTER

8

CHRISTINA AWAKENED FROM her dream, but the nightmare didn't end. Her head slammed into the rear window of the minivan. Tempered glass shattered into worthless diamonds.

A shrill cacophony. Ripping metal and grinding steel. Her ears were bleeding. She cried out for her mother. The ear-piercing explosion of the concrete pump smashing into the car punctuated the brutal jolt like thunder follows lightning.

The car plunged down the rocky ledge toward the waves. Christina whirled through darkness. Her limbs and head thrashed violently from the constraint of the seat belt. Each crash of sound was followed by an eerie silence as the car caromed off one boulder and floated free until striking the next. The final drop took less than 1.7 seconds, but Christina experienced an elongation of time. She gripped her seat belt and moved in slow motion. She had what seemed like hours to anticipate her death.

• • •

Sergeant Ray Evans hit the lights and emergency switch and stomped on the brakes all at once. His California Highway Patrol cruiser skidded to a stop. Headlights, taillights and the emergency light bar on the roof lit up like the Fourth of July. Red, white and blue.

Evans barked into his radio. "Code three. PCH. Two clicks south of Cliff House." *Emergency. Pacific Coast Highway. Landmark for location.*

Evans spoke in the aural code of CHP as easily as he discussed Monday night football with his teenage son.

The Windstar landed on its nose in the tumble of breakwater boulders at the bottom of the cliff. It jacked over on its top and teetered precariously above the waves. The sidebar buckled and the headrest of the front seat slammed into Christina's chest.

Evans was in the outside lane three car lengths behind Gloria Christensen's Windstar when the cement truck ended her life. He saw it happen. Adrenaline surged into his system as it always did.

Vehicular homicide. He was writing the report in his subconscious. The truck driver's life had also changed in a fleeting moment of neglect. A split second of stupidity.

Evans was trained to stay calm in emergency situations. EMT courses emphasized emotional detachment. It was easy to discuss the psychology of "calm" in a class of men and women studying to be emergency medical technicians. When you were suddenly ringside to horror, "emotional detachment" was no longer an intellectual abstraction.

The disaster on the road in front of Evans was not his first rodeo. That was his way of referring to his significant experience in handling emergencies without sounding like a braggart. He was a Gulf War veteran, a firefighter for Marin County, and a trained paramedic. He had applied to the CHP Academy when he met Marty; she persuaded him to follow his boyhood dream. He married her the day he took the oath as an officer in the California Highway Patrol.

Evans moved quickly and deliberately. He summarized the details of the accident to Dispatch as he pulled his emergency kit from the trunk of the cruiser. "We've got a major 11–80. Need an 11–41."

He sprinted to where the vehicle had disappeared over the edge of the escarpment. He picked his way down the tumble of boulders, his boots slipping on the seaweed slime and mossy rocks. Twice he almost fell. The beam of his mag light found the minivan wedged top down in the ragged rocks along the ocean's edge.

"Get a Life Flight chopper out here!"

"You got survivors?" Dispatch came back.

"Not likely, but just in case."

"Roger that."

He saw the orange flicker of light below the crushed hood. Fire!

"Tell 'em to get here ten minutes ago!"

• • •

Christina's limp body hung upside down from her seat belt. The grating agony of metal on rock was replaced by the roar of waves. A light punched a hole in the darkness. It was filtered red by the blood she blinked back from her eyes. It appeared for a moment and then the darkness returned.

The door was missing. Her mother was gone. Pain shot through her chest every time she inhaled. She imagined she'd been skewered by a splintered wooden stake or something worse.

• • •

The flame licked its way along a rubber hose and spread to the residue of sludge on the bottom of the engine that was downside up.

Evans's calm gave way to a surge of panic. He knew from experience that the overturned vehicle was about to explode. Even if the gas tank was not ruptured, there was enough leakage from gas lines to turn an already tragic accident into a flaming catastrophe.

Evans increased his pace, pushing caution aside. His boot skidded on a slimy rock that angled steeply downward. He twisted to catch himself but landed on his hip and tumbled forward. He clawed at the rock for purchase, ripping the ends of his fingers. He slammed into a vertical slab of stone that seemed placed there to stop his slide. His elbow cracked on the sharp upper edge; his lower arm went numb. The mag light skidded away and fell into a tide pool ten feet below.

He gauged the spreading flames. With no hesitation he jumped into the water and retrieved the torch. He crossed the last few yards of slimy rock and probed what was left of the Windstar with the flashlight. His beam of light washed across Christina.

• • •

The light came back. It was brighter and closer than before. It wobbled as it moved toward her but stayed pointed in her eyes. The flame crawled into the fractured oil pan. The flash of fire from below illuminated a dark form in an eerie half-light. It was a man in a uniform. He ducked down to enter the inverted doorway. There was an explosion of orange light and awful heat.

· · ·

Evans was blown back by the rolling ball of flame that erupted below and enveloped the interior of the Windstar. He bolted back toward the opening, desperate to get the girl out, but was blocked by a wall of flame.

Instinct told Evans that the explosion was too small. *Puddle of gas from a ruptured fuel line.* He knew it was only a matter of seconds before the fire ignited the main tank. Neither of them would survive the second explosion.

He had no time to get the child out before she was burned alive. The daunting reality reached him with the merciless scream of a child on fire. It was already too late. His only chance of survival was to get away from the car and find protection among the rocks from the inevitable blast.

· · ·

The pain of the shaft of slivers in her side was overpowered by the scorching heat from the fire. She struggled to climb away from the flames. She was losing consciousness and her mind floated elsewhere. Then suddenly she was moving again. The whole car was moving.

· · ·

Evans got a firm grip on the luggage rack and drove his shoulder into the twisted frame. The polyester and wool serge jacket offered little protection from the hot metal that seared into his shoulder. The smell of his uniform on fire etched itself in memory, but it was only later that he would realize the source of the fetor.

He lifted and shoved with all his strength. The fire slithered upward like an amorphous living creature resolute on reaching the ruptured tank before Evans could topple the car. Evans found better footing and heaved again. He cried out for God to help him save the child. The flaming vehicle moved slightly. Christina's screaming stopped.

She was gone. *Save yourself. Go now!* He ignored the impulse. He tightened his grip and heaved upward with the full strength of his legs, back, shoulder and arms.

Was that a whimper? It came again. It was the girl. She was still alive. "God, don't let this child die!" Evans shouted aloud and threw himself against the sizzling metal with total abandon.

There was an agonizing groan as five thousand pounds of twisted metal broke the grip of pockmarked lava. The Windstar toppled into the surf. Unwilling to let go or stop pushing lest the car teeter back, Evans was dragged over and thrown forward. The Windstar rolled once and settled on its side in three feet of water.

Evans floundered through the surging water to reach the still-burning minivan. He had scarcely gained footing on the broken shoal when he was hit by an enormous wave. The wall of water swept over him and slammed into a wall of rock. "The wave from God," it would be called when his great-great-grandchildren would hear about what happened on that day. The story of his heroism would live that long at least.

Like an answer to his breathless prayer, the wave baptized the Windstar, extinguished the fire and retreated into the darkness, allowing Evans access to the child.

• • •

Christina hovered in a dreamlike trance of semiconsciousness. Existence was a swirl of vague impressions. Fleeting glimpses of shapes and sounds and colors. Most of it without meaning. The ethereal realms of the mind between life and death.

She sensed the urgency of Evans's arm around her. His knife cutting the seat belt. Being lifted from the overturned Windstar and carried through the water to the rocks. Evans moved swiftly, but in her dark place of pain it seemed to happen over hours, not minutes. When his arms went around her, she imagined the splinters breaking from the shaft and piercing her insides.

The synthetic fibers of the seat belt had been stubborn against the sawing of the blade. One by one they lost their will and set her free. The arm and leg that dangled in the flame felt cut off from her body. Then the pain came and the blackened limbs were the only part of her body her brain could focus about.

The man spoke softly. His tone was reassuring but the words were unintelligible and far away. His voice retreated into the darkness until the words were no more than hollow echoes from a bottomless well. When she was conscious of the husky angel in his badly burned uniform, the pain was unbearable. When he went away, retreating to the other place became enticing. There was no pain there, only a sense of peace. *I'm going to die.* It was her last conscious thought before she was engulfed in the darkness and the other light appeared.

• • •

Evans broke emergency medical rule number one. He had no choice. There was high risk moving an accident victim with a possible neck injury. Waves coming in with the rising tides had saved her from death by fire. Leaving her in the car would insure her death by drowning.

If she was still alive. She had no pulse. She was not breathing.

Evans lifted the girl, taking care to protect her neck the best he could. He held her head with one hand and used the straightness of his forearm as a headboard, stabilizing her cervical spine from the top of her head to her shoulder blades. He wrapped the other arm around the small of her back and lifted her by the lumbar spine. He made every move with maximum care. The girl was limp, and that made moving her safely a bit easier. There was nothing else good about the situation.

Once the child was safe from fire and flood, Evans placed her on a flat rock and covered her with what was left of his jacket. He administered emergency CPR. She didn't respond. The night seemed to swallow them. Evans did the only other thing he knew might save the child. He prayed.

• • •

A pulse. A breath. She was alive. Evans turned his attention to her condition and injuries. Most of her clothing had been burned or ripped away. The tibia poked from a ragged hole in her left leg. The right leg was so badly bruised by blood beneath the skin he suspected a fracture of the femur. Both legs were badly burned. In a curious twist of fate—*or faith, as Evans would later profess*—the fire had cauterized some of the superficial arteries in the open wound of the compound fracture. Otherwise the loss of blood may have been fatal. Half her hair was singed away, but the laceration in her scalp continued to bleed. Evans covered it with a pad of absorbent gauze and applied pressure to stop the blood.

Evans knew that bones would mend and heads would heal. There were more urgent matters. *Airway. Breathing. Circulation.* He used his finger to check for obstruction. Her airway was clear but her breathing was torturous.

Christina gasped for breath and for a moment seemed to regain consciousness. She made a pitiful gurgling sound. Evans shouted into his voice-activated radio, hoping it had survived the seawater: "What's the ETA on Life Flight?"

"Six minutes out," came the reply.

Christina tried to breathe and couldn't. Her little body arched up from the rock. *On her way to respiratory failure. Blunt trauma to the chest. Probable hemothorax.*

Evans walked his fingers down the child's rib cage. They stepped into a depression. Two ribs were badly broken. One of them was likely sticking into her lungs. That meant the sack between the lung and chest wall was filling with blood and air and would soon put pressure on the intact lung, preventing it from expanding.

It had been a while since he had stuck a chest tube in anybody, but it was like riding a bike, the old doc who taught him had promised—once you got it, you could always do it. He pulled a chest tube from his emergency bag. It looked like an expensive soda straw with a sharp, hollow needle on the end. Evans located a space in the mid-thorax vertebrae. With a deft thrust he inserted the tube into the pleural cavity. Blood flowed from the open end. The child's breathing eased but the gurgling continued. *Blood in the lungs as well.* Evans's emergency pack made his patrol car wager-worthy of being named the most fully stocked CHP cruiser in Northern California. Even so, he was not equipped to intubate the girl.

He changed the pressure bandage on her head and wrapped her badly burned limbs. He checked her pulse. It was getting weaker. Her eyes fluttered open but seemed unable to focus. She quivered with a wave of pain and then lay perfectly still.

She had a smile on her face. It worried him. He cradled her head in his hands and looked into the night sky as if doing so would quicken the arrival of Life Flight. He talked to God just one more time.

CHAPTER

9

THE RED AND WHITE Agusta AW 109 hovered with one wheel pressed against a boulder. The wind was erratic along the rocky shore. Sudden updrafts were frequent and unpredictable. Holding the lightweight, twin-engine helicopter stable on the precarious perch was difficult. The blast of air from the prop wash was disquieting and dangerous.

The rescue plan was a risky trade-off for the precious minutes it would take to carry the girl up the cliff by stretcher or deploy the sling and hoist to get her aboard.

Evans sat with the girl's head cradled in his lap. He knew most of the EMTs with Life Flight, but the two men clambering across the rocks toward him were strangers. The first one to arrive shook Evans's hand with obvious respect. The name tag over the button-down pocket said *WILLIAMS*. "How's she doing?" he asked.

Evans looked at him with a bewildered smile. Brushing a clump of blood-crusted hair from the girl's face, he said, "She's alive."

The second EMT, a kid named Jenkins, was already at work on the child. Evans clung to her; Jenkins pushed him away. "I got her. I got her. You okay?" He glanced at Williams as he said it, his eyes telegraphing: *Shock?*

"Yeah. I'm fine." Evans looked at the child. "I think . . . I think she is going to be okay."

"Let's hope. Doesn't look good."

Evans smiled and nodded. "She'll make it."

Christina was strapped to a body board and wrapped in a blanket. Two large bore needles were thrust into the largest patent veins Jenkins could find and snapped to a portable field IV heavy with Lactated Ringer's solution.

"Run the fluids wide open," Williams said as they bagged her with oxygen and put a pulse oximeter on her index finger.

Jenkins looked at the numbers. "Her O_2 sat is 79."

"We've got to get her on board and intubate her!" Williams motioned for Jenkins to pick up the body board. He cranked his head left and pressed his mouth against the small microphone fastened to the epaulet on his shoulder. "This is Life Flight One to St. Mark's Emergency."

"St. Mark's Emergency. This is Rosemary. What's up?" The voice crackled in from the rubber bud jammed in Williams's ear and connected to his radio by a coil of wire that disappeared into the collar of his shirt. Evans helped Williams and Jenkins move Christina on the body board across the slick rocks to the hovering helicopter.

"Hey, Rosemary. It's Nick Williams."

"Someone told me you got fired."

"Listen up! We've got an eight- to ten-year-old Caucasian female. Status post MVA in respiratory failure and third-degree burns. We'll intubate en route. I need to speak to the doc."

"The doctor is busy. What's your ETA?"

"Will you please get the doc on the phone?"

"He's reducing a fractured hip right now."

"Get me the doc!"

"Just tell me what you need. I can help."

"There's no time for your 'wanna-be-a-doctor' claptrap, Rosemary! Get the doc on the phone *now!*"

"I've been in ER twenty-five years and know more than most of these—"

"This little girl is going to lose her arm and probably her life if I don't get a REAL doctor on the phone and I mean STAT!"

Evans held the body board in place as Williams and Jenkins scrambled from the rock to the open door of the 109. They pulled the board and child into a mobile emergency room that had once been a passenger cabin for eight.

"Don't get your buns in squeegee!"

Williams was irritated. He looked at Evans and shook his head. "You doing good?" he mouthed. Evans nodded.

Jenkins fastened the last of the safety straps. Evans stood on the rock with one hand on the open frame of the helicopter. His other arm hung limp.

"Why don't you come along?" Williams said. "We need to take care of that arm." It was the first time since the fire that Evans had thought about his badly burned arm.

"There's still a mess on top," he said. "You guys get out of here. I'll be all right." Williams tapped the pilot on the shoulder and yelled over the whine of the twin engines as the pilot increased the RPMs.

"Don't put it off," warned Williams. "Get an infection in that thing and you could lose your arm." Evans nodded and waved them away. He was certified as a burn specialist with the Marin County Fire Department and knew the danger.

Not my first rodeo, he thought and knew he'd be okay. Was it instinct or something else? He shrugged the question away.

The 109 shuddered as it left its parlous perch and turned into the offshore wind. Evans watched as it rose swiftly in a graceful arc and in less than sixty seconds was nothing but blinking lights moving 184 miles per hour in the direction of St. Mark's Hospital.

As Evans climbed to the road, his head was in the chopper with the little girl. He knew Williams was on the radio to the ER doc. It ran like an old recording he'd heard a hundred times.

A little girl. Nine or ten years old. Caucasian female. Status post MVA. Respiratory failure, orthopedic injury, bilateral compound fractures to both lower extremities and head laceration. Blunt chest trauma; fractured rib with pneumo/hemothorax—chest is in place, not yet sutured in. Thirty percent surface area burns. Severe third-degree burns left upper extremity and left thorax. Second-degree burns on lower left face and legs.

Under similarly extreme circumstances the conclusive statement would be, "Not likely the child will survive the night." The circumstances of the accident were extreme—but so was what happened in the eighteen minutes it took Life Flight to arrive. Officer Evans had heard about such things, even imagined they might be true. But nothing could have prepared him for what actually happened at the bottom of the cliff.

CHAPTER

10

T HEY LOOK MORE LIKE APES than men." The voice startled Thomas. He turned to discover a tall man standing where the circle of light fell into darkness. The man's face was in shadow.

"What'd you say? Thomas squinted to adjust his eyes to the gloom. The stranger's face was obscure in the dim light. "Can I help you?" A rush of apprehension squiggled up his spine from the reservoir of his dark imagination. "This area's off-limits during the renovation."

There was movement in the darkness. The man stared at the mural. "SIR!" Thomas added a threatening edge to his voice. "This whole area is off-limits. No one is allowed up here!"

The man moved forward until the glow from the canvas added shape to his face. His hand fluttered toward Thomas in a gesture that both ac-knowledged and dismissed him. He stepped closer to the painting and into the light.

Thomas took inventory. Etched the man in memory. It was the way Thomas saw human beings. Anatomy. Textures. Lines. Shapes. Color. Values. Also the superficial. Style. Fashion. Symbols. A replicated image. A composition. Everything a visual metaphor of fantasy. It was part of the gift.

The visitor was older than Thomas by fifteen years and taller by an inch, maybe two. He was lean but sturdy in an athletic sort of way. The expensive suit hung perfectly on broad shoulders. It was black with a subtle pinstripe. *William Fioravanti or Savile Row?* Thomas knew fine clothes and wondered. The shirt was white. The necktie, pure silk. Antique pink. *Ninety dollars. Probably Forzieri. A symbol of success.* The man's hair was several subtle shades of gray, worn long and touching his collar. *Robert Redford on a perfect hair day.* His tennis tan obscured the creases in his forehead. The corrugated furrow between wide-set brows deepened as he studied the canvas. He looked vaguely familiar, but nothing came to mind.

The man lifted a leather case from the inside pocket of his coat without loosening the button. He put on an expensive pair of glasses and took a closer look at the images on the wall.

"Cro-Magnon was the final step in evolution before the emergence of modern man," the stranger said. It didn't sound like a criticism of the artwork. It sounded like an eternal truth from the Greek god Hermes. "He didn't look like that."

Thomas scrutinized the alpha male figure at the center of his composition. His face was ferocious, the jowls large and drooling, the forehead pitched back until it was lost beneath a shaggy mane. Exaggeration was a vital element in the creative magic that gave Thomas Hall's art an elusive dimension of breathtaking hyper-reality.

"They look too healthy," the man went on. "Cro-Magnon's whole existence was about finding food. Staying alive. Survival." He moved to his left. "These people look like they lived on Big Macs and fries." The criticism focused Thomas's attention on his artwork rather than the identity of the stranger denigrating his brilliance.

"It's mostly their faces, I think." The man continued, studying the images more closely. "They look too . . . too . . . I don't know. Primitive. More Neanderthal than Cro-Magnon. That's it. That's what you've got wrong."

"Did Frank Berger give you permission to be up here?"

Thomas hated anyone to see his work before it was finished. He insisted that Berger include restricted access in his contract. Lawyers tagged it the "paranoia provision" but refused to exclude museum management from looking over his shoulder. In the middle of the night, with the intimidating stranger looking down his aquiline nose and asking moronic questions, Thomas was angry that his agent-manager was not protecting him.

"Permission?" The man removed his glasses and gave Thomas a quiz-zical smile. "You don't know who I am?" He was obviously annoyed.

"I don't care who you are or who you think you are. You are not al-lowed up here. You've got about ten seconds to leave before I call security."

"Maxine didn't tell you I was meeting you here tonight?"

"Who's Maxine?

"The museum secretary." The name meant nothing. "The older, plumpish woman in Hamilton's old office." An exaggerated caricature of a plumpish woman sitting coyly cross-legged on the former director's desk flitted into Thomas's mind, making him smile.

"The only people allowed up here have to be cleared by my manager, Frank Berger." He smiled again to soften the irresistible insult. "Keeps me from wasting time getting advice from people who don't know the differ-ence between Homo erectus and Michael Jackson."

The tall man removed his glasses. A flush of irritation and a wry smile arrived in the same moment. "The infamous *paranoid provision*," he said.

The comment jolted Thomas. *How does this clown know what's in my contract?*

"I heard about it. What was it you finally 'allowed' to the people who sign your check?" His tone was sardonic. "Meaningful consultation?"

Angst tickled the back of Thomas's neck. "Who are you?"

"If neither my people nor yours gave you warning, Mr. Hall, I apologize. When I saw you working late, I assumed you knew about our meeting."

"I work late for total seclusion. So nobody bugs me."

"I didn't mean to invade your sanctum sanctorum without your per-mission." The man extended his hand. "I'm Silas Hawker."

At six years old, Thomas had stolen a box of Snickers bars from the Food Mart at the Chevron station. He and Bobby Van Fleet had hidden in the culvert that allowed Steed Creek to flow under Robinson Ranch Road. They were one bite into bars five and six when the woman from the counter and a deputy sheriff appeared at the end of the tunnel. The claw that had gripped his little-boy stomach in the culvert that day now clenched him again.

"*The* Silas Hawker?" Thomas gasped and his mouth remained open. It was a rhetorical question because he knew the name and now realized why the face was familiar. The man's picture had been in the paper and his face on local TV. Silas Hawker was the new director of the museum.

Thomas felt as if he were standing on one foot about to fall on his head. He managed to close his mouth and shake Silas Hawker's hand with both his own.

"What a pleasure to meet you, sir. Sorry I didn't . . ."

"Looks like we better fire Maxine and your man Berger both?" Hawker sniggered.

"I'm Thomas Hall. Well, I guess you knew that."

"I haven't had a chance to get up here and meet you since taking over."

Thomas swept his hand in a wide arc that took in the pavilion as well as the mural. "Quite a project you've inherited."

"*Rescued* would be a better word, Mr. Hall."

"*Thomas* is good. I prefer that to *Tom* or *Tommy* and it's certainly better than *Mr. Hall.* And you? Silas?"

"I prefer the formality of surnames in a business relationship." Perfectly manicured fingers tightened the pink tie. "*Mr. Hawker* suits me best, if you don't mind. In my experience, craftspeople too often mistake informality for a personal rather than professional relationship."

Dr. Silas Hawker had been headhunted from the famed Chicago Science Center to take over the renovation of the Pacific Science Museum. The abrupt dismissal of the former director, Dr. Dennis Hamilton, was rife with conflicting rumors.

The *San Francisco Chronicle* described Hawker as "an irrepressible intellectual, visionary, innovator and brilliant scientist in his own right. A seasoned executive whose hallmark is hands-on leadership."

The article made "hands-on leadership" such an ennobling quality, it conjured up for Thomas an image of Hawker in a soiled apron helping an apprentice assemble broken fragments of Yani Indian pottery. He would soon discover what it really meant.

Berger had assured Thomas that the change of directors changed nothing as far as his project and contract were concerned. Thomas assumed Frank was right. Frank usually was. But in his first few minutes with Silas Hawker, Thomas worried that this time Frank might be wrong. Very wrong.

CHAPTER

11

THE FORMER MUSEUM DIRECTOR, Dr. Dennis Hamilton, had picked Thomas to create a mural for the Descent of Man exhibit in the museum's third-floor pavilion. After three presentations, a bundle of sketches, and twenty-four completed drawings, Thomas was awarded the commission.

Thomas had met Dr. Hamilton at the first presentation. The man's grip was firm, his reactions complimentary. Hamilton locked eyes and listened to what the artist said. It was impossible not to like the wizened old scientist.

Hamilton's hair was a neglected tousle of white that covered half his head. He wore large, horn-rimmed glasses with bifocal inserts that magnified the wrinkled bags beneath his eyes. He had on a blue shirt with the top button undone and hiding beneath the fat knot of a tie Thomas would come to recognize as one of the two ties the director always wore. His tweed sport coat had leather elbow patches and gave him the appearance of a college professor. His face was perpetually pleasant with the impish look of an adolescent snitching cookies.

Berger had been informed that his client had won the commission—subject to an interview with Hamilton. The artist and director met at seven o'clock the following morning.

Hamilton's office was in the oldest part of the museum's original wing. It preserved the architectural elegance from the turn of the century. Thick walls. Ornate moldings. High ceilings. Dark walnut bookshelves. Window seats with fat, fringed cushions. Tall windows with true divided light panels of blown glass.

Every flat surface was piled with books and magazines. Shelves were cluttered with artifacts and curiosities. A suit of armor stood watch in one corner. A dangling skeleton hung from a rod in the other.

A sap-green leather couch with spiderweb cracks separated the room from a steel examination table. Thomas thought it an odd anachronism, given the setting. The table was littered with bones, fragments of pottery, dried flora, jars floating ghastly little creatures in dirty yellow liquid and, of course, microscopes, glass plates, probes, magnifying glasses, tape measures, recording instruments and myriad notebooks, scraps and scribbles. In the center of it all there was a bright tin can painted with colorful flowers and filled with pencils, pens and markers. *Gift from a grandchild,* Thomas decided.

A neglected broadleaf dieffenbachia next to the couch needed water. Dry leaves had already fallen to the burnt sienna hardwood.

Black-and-white photographs documenting the museum's history covered a single panel between the bookcases. Prominent among them was a shot of the museum following the earthquake of 1906.

Hamilton's desk was a hand-carved mahogany antique. A small work area with a MacBook Pro was surrounded by a barricade of periodicals, reference books and a clutter of letters Thomas imagined was neglected correspondence.

The order of the exhibits in the museum was a curious juxtaposition to the chaos in the inner sanctum of the man in charge. On the other hand, Thomas understood the power of a singular creative passion that rendered everything else bothersome. Amidst Hamilton's chaos—and to a large degree because of it—Thomas understood the man.

"I'm delighted you are willing to give our old mural a new face." Hamilton grinned. "It's so faded you can hardly tell the monkeys from the men." There was rich significance hidden behind the sly humor. Only when the trouble started would Thomas begin to understand what it was.

They met all morning and for lunch the following day. Thomas had heard of John's Grill on Ellis but had never eaten there. It had risen from the ashes of the '06 quake and not closed since. A bar of polished brass and hardwood wrapped around a corner near the back. The walls were dark panels of oak cluttered with sepia photos of San Francisco's famous and infamous: gamblers and gangsters, cops and politicians, broadcasters and bishops, actors and artists, gigolos and the girls of Broadway.

Hamilton ordered a Cobb but was so eager to discuss his ideas with Thomas he hardly ate any of it. Thomas ordered the Jack LaLanne Salad. He had no idea who Jack LaLanne was, but the selection showed up under "Hearty Salads" with a little heart, which implied that menu selections without a little heart might kill you. The salad came with crab and sourdough bread.

Dr. Hamilton was the final word on the exhibits. The decision maker. It was exciting for Thomas to anticipate a project without the usual scrutiny by corporate committee that smothered creativity and made it hard to breathe.

Thomas was determined to give Hamilton what he wanted. On the last day of class their senior year, Professor Andrus had made his students raise their hands and pledge to always give 100 percent of their talent regardless of how large or small the assignment.

Thomas felt certain this lunch with Hamilton was an ongoing part of the qualifying interview. Thomas knew, *It ain't a done deal 'til the check clears the bank.* Berger might have originated the cliché, he used it so often.

Only twelve artists had been invited to propose on the Science Museum project. How they were selected and by whom was never known. An arts and entertainment writer at the *Chronicle* tagged candidates "The Dazzling Dozen" once they were announced. The prestige of being on that list was significant.

As the choreographer of Thomas's career, Berger had pointed out that winning the Science Museum commission would add significant cachet to their bid for the Heavy Metal Hotel and Casino in Las Vegas. *Both ends against the middle,* Berger had mused. The Science Museum was sophisticated, highbrow and a good piece of business. Fantasy art in the vaulted atrium of the spectacular Heavy Metal Hotel and Casino was the breakout-beaucoup-bucks bonanza.

Thomas made sketches on the paper tablecloth as Hamilton talked. Swirling lines with his pencil. Quick bites of salad. More lines. Two hours later there was nothing left of Jack LaLanne and the tabletop was a mosaic of Hamilton's ideas in Thomas's graphic shorthand.

The headwaiter at John's Grill collected graphic novels and knew the art of Thomas Hall. He asked Thomas to sign the tablecloth and give them permission to hang it on the wall. Hamilton wagged a finger and folded it up for himself. That was the moment Thomas knew he'd closed the deal.

Thomas spent nine days working on a design. Hamilton assigned a research assistant to help. Felix Edgers was a dissertation shy of his PhD in paleoanthropology and by any standard an intelligent, single-minded nerd. In their few days together Edgers gave Thomas a crash course on the Descent of Man mural on the wall in the pavilion, which had been painted for the opening of the west wing in 1927.

Edgers also gave Thomas a tour of the puzzling process of cultural anthropology. What was known and what was not. The science and the search. The mysterious missing pieces and the infamous missing link. They joked about that. By midnight of their final day together Thomas had a monstrous headache.

The project was announced to the media at a press conference held in the pavilion. The Descent of Man was backdrop to the podium. Hamilton talked about renovating the museum and modernizing the exhibits, with an emphasis on his commitment to "preserve the historical integrity of the building and classic character of the exhibits." He skirted questions that required specific answers. Hamilton had a gift for what he jokingly called "linguistic dexterity." He had mastered the art of ambiguity necessary to navigate the shark-infested waters of publicly funded entities.

Thomas applauded with the rest. He had no idea of the battle ahead in a war that would challenge him in ways he couldn't imagine.

CHAPTER

12

Hawker turned the halogen work light to the left, leaving the Cro-Magnon hunters to face danger and death in the darkness. The light spilled across the length of the curved canvas wall. It was covered with elaborate drawings that receded in time through the steps of human evolution until they reached Australopithecus on the far left side.

The light cast a twisted shadow across the canvas as Thomas followed Hawker to where a family of Neanderthals were gathered about a fire. Two females nursed a stricken adolescent. One burly male stood watch. The others huddled about the fire, gnawing strips of fleshy hides.

Hawker massaged his chin and shook his head. "These are supposed to be Neanderthal?"

"Did you or Maxine talk to Frank about how this is supposed to work? About setting an appointment if there's something you need to discuss?"

Half of Hawker's face was in shadow and merged with the blackness. The look was chilling. Hawker was evidently a veteran of the games at hand. A doyen of intimidation. His pause exceeded the interval of expectation. *He who speaks first loses.* Thomas knew better than to break the silence, but Hawker's silent stare was debilitating.

"They're not finished," he said, gesturing toward the sketches of the Neanderthals, "and no one is going to be this close." He was rambling. "I'm working out the composition. Details make a big difference. Hard to judge until . . ." He caught himself apologizing. It made him angry. *Who the hell are you to challenge me? It's a black-and-white sketch in charcoal, you idiot!*

"Why did you leave so much space in between?" Hawker asked, pointing to the wide swath of canvas between Cro-Magnon and Neanderthal. There was a scrawl of charcoal lines and shapes, the rudimentary blocking for half a dozen figures in what appeared to be a rock shelter of some kind.

"Haven't you seen the design drawings?" Thomas asked, quickly regretting his cynical tone. The feeling of intimidation unnerved him.

"A quick glance," Hawker said. It was clearly not the truth and red flags went up. "I'm curious to know what you think goes between Neanderthal man and . . . are you following the fossil record or evolution?"

"You obviously didn't look at the design sketches!" Thomas said it with the tone of an indictment. He traced the figure hiding in the swirl of lines as if Hawker had to be blind not to see it. "That's Louis Lartet in the cave at Les Eyzies digging up the bones." Thomas kept drawing with his finger. "Lartet is just lifting the female skull." The skull was an oval of swirling gray charcoal.

"The *discovery* of Cro-Magnon man?"

"Exactly. For each of the stages of human evolution." Irritation melted in a rush of creative enthusiasm. "It's the same all the way across. It's a whole other layer. Between each of the classic stages I've put a scene that shows when and where it was discovered and who dug it up. It puts it all in context. Adds the paleoanthropological dimension. The location and date will be written right here." Thomas marked out a square at the lower right corner. "Les Eyzies, France, 1868."

"Was this your idea or Hamilton's?"

"Hamilton's. It's going to be great. Here, I'll show you." Thomas rolled out a six-foot strip of butcher paper with a miniature sketch of the completed mural and taped it to the canvas. "Dr. Hamilton calls it the 'discovery layer.' It is only roughed in on the canvas, but on the layout you can see what the sections look like. I'm doing them in a whole different style from the primary figures. In sepia, like old photographs. I'll be doing them last."

Hawker narrowed his eyes and adjusted his glasses. He made a sound in his throat without opening his mouth.

Thomas pointed to a figure left of the Neanderthal family. "This is Philippe-Charles Schmerling with the first Neanderthal skull at Engis, Belgium, and . . ." Hawker was not looking at the well-drawn paleo-anthropologist holding the partial skull of a child. He had moved right and was staring at the drawings on the other side of Cro-Magnon man.

"What is this supposed to be?"

"Piltdown man," Thomas said with a light chuckle.

"You're joking! Piltdown man? That was a ridiculous hoax."

"No, no, of course. That's the way I'm portraying it." He used his finger to point as he spoke. "That's Charles Dawson, the collector who perpetrated the fraud. That's Oakley, Weiner, and Sir Wilfrid Clark, who exposed him, and if you look closer . . . " He tapped two other strange and ugly "men" castigating the humiliated Dawson. "When it's full scale on the wall, of course, you'll see them perfectly." He waited a moment for Hawker to get the joke and laugh. The director remained silent. "That's the orangutan and chimpanzee whose bones Dawson used," Thomas grinned. He was about to claim the idea but Hawker clenched his jaw and shook his head.

"Piltdown man was a complete fraud. An embarrassment to science!"

"That was Dr. Hamilton's whole point. Piltdown man was accepted as absolute scientific fact for forty years. It was proclaimed by paleoanthropologists as a 'hitherto unknown stage in human evolution,' the infamous missing link."

"Pure stupidity!"

"Not in the broader perspective. Not through the eyes of a seventh grader trying to sort it all out. Hamilton put Piltdown man here as a reminder that science is ultimately about human beings, and human beings are not omniscient. They make mistakes. Knowledge is a process. That was the whole idea. He thought it would be fun if—"

"Fun! This isn't some pettifogging amusement park, it's a science museum!" Hawker pulled the drawings from the wall. The paper ripped in half. Then he seemed to catch himself. He fumed in silence a few seconds before his demeanor changed.

"I should have taken time to look at the original drawings when I first arrived. I regret you've wasted so much time going the wrong direction." The concession was offered like a string of glass beads to an aboriginal whose village had just been burned to the ground.

"My purpose in meeting you tonight was to tell you what I am planning for this space and how you might fit in if we can agree on a way forward." *Might fit in? If we can agree?* Hawker's choice of words jammed a spike in Thomas's stomach.

"You said, '*If* we can agree on a way forward.' I'm not sure what you mean. I'm sure my contract requires that . . ."

Hawker put his hand on Thomas's shoulder. Thomas felt like a fifth grader in the principal's office. In the few seconds that followed, Thomas discovered why Silas Hawker was a leader whom people were willing to follow. Even if it was over a cliff.

"Let's not make this about your contract. We'll get that sorted out. Let's make it about the most important piece of art you will ever create. Let's make it about a turning point in your career. I've seen your work. I know the type of thing you do."

He took his hand away. "I believe in being frank, and I can tell you I would not have chosen you for the project. Don't get me wrong. I recognize you have significant talent." *The tyrant giveth and the tyrant taketh away.*

"You should probably be talking to Frank," Thomas said, but if Hawker heard him or even knew who Frank was, he showed no sign of it.

"I think you're better than this." He tapped the ripped drawings in Thomas's hand and glanced at the mural. "I've known Dennis Hamilton a long time," he continued. "We haven't always . . ." The memory took him away and whatever he was about to say was swallowed up. He looked at the swirling sketches stretching into the darkness, then back at Thomas.

"For you to do what I need you to do, you must understand one very important fact. This is a science museum, not a comic book. If you work for me, you will be governed by science, not imagination. You will be influenced by the finest minds of science, not apologists. By experts, not amateurs." Hawker walked the length of the canvas and turned on the work lights one at a time.

"I *have* talked to experts," Thomas said as he followed Hawker. His voice was hollow under the empty dome.

"Really?"

"Every so-called expert on the Neanderthal I talked to told me the last expert I had talked to was an idiot." Hawker chuckled as Thomas's rant continued. "Same with all of them. Cro-Magnon, Homo erectus, Rhodesian man, take your pick. Nobody agrees with anybody."

Following his three-day crash course with Edgers, Thomas had spent an additional five days of research on the phone and Internet and used e-mail to contact notable experts who specialized in each of the classifications of humanoids. All were celebrated academicians, according to their credentials. Besides a persistent headache from overtaxing the left side of his brain, Thomas had found the adventure a little like tumbling down a rabbit hole.

He caught up as Hawker reached on the far end of the canvas and switched on the last of the lights. The pavilion glowed with a soft ambience bounced back from the white canvas.

"When I told Dr. Rosen at Berkeley I had been talking to Stanford about Neanderthal man, he said the whole paleoanthropology department at Stanford were Neanderthals." Hawker's laugh revealed his acquaintance with the eccentric Dr. Rosen. "Hamilton didn't agree with either of them, so—"

Hawker cut him off. "You don't work for Hamilton!" The director took Thomas by the arm and walked him to the center of the hall. "You have a unique talent," Hawker said in a way that made Thomas want to trust him. He circled the room. "I'm changing all of this," he said. "It's incredible to me that Hamilton intended to leave so much of this antiquated junk." He pointed to a clan of three-quarter scale mannequins with wooden spears and molting hides huddled in a display of Early Man. It was being dismantled. "They've been here fifty years collecting dust and rotting away. Much of it is out-of-date and no longer consistent with the latest discoveries."

"Dr. Hamilton was taking that out, I think. Are you keeping any of his exhibits?"

Hawker treated the question with more gravity than Thomas

expected. "Denny Hamilton and I met briefly at the University of the Witwatersrand in Johannesburg. We were young. He taught there for a year while I was attending the Institute for Human Evolution." Hawker shook his head slowly, as if coaxing a dead memory from its crypt. "Denny was one of the best and brightest. Maybe THE brightest." Humility did not come gracefully to Hawker. "It will forever baffle me how he drifted over the years into . . . into a kind of scientific no-man's-land. How he allowed nostalgia or fear . . ." Hawker paused with the thought, then continued, ". . . whatever it was that overpowered his scientific integrity."

"Is that why he got fired?"

"Hamilton resigned," Hawker snapped. One noun. One verb. Two words. It sounded memorized. "He wanted to spend more time with his family and a chance to pursue personal projects." The line had been written, approved and rehearsed.

"What did you mean, 'scientific no-man's-land?'" Thomas could tell Hawker was tempted to eviscerate the credentials of the former director. He resisted, and the moment passed.

"It's not important." Hawker laughed. "Hamilton is history. It's going forward that matters, and from here on, everything changes."

Hawker stopped in a circle of light directly below the center of the dome. He spoke in reverent tones. "I am dedicating this entire hall to the life and times of Charles Darwin. This will be DARWIN PAVILION." He gave the pronouncement the gravity of a prophet announcing the promised land.

He took a few steps toward the mural. "I want you to start over. Redo the whole thing as Darwin himself would have done it. Conform perfectly to his writings rather than the splintered opinions of some breed of scholars arrogant enough to presume they can add one jot or tittle to his genius."

In Thomas's fertile imagination Hawker was John Malkovich playing a villainous megalomaniac in a scene from one of those bizarre horror films no one ever understood. When Thomas's imagination escaped the Malkovich set, he worried he'd missed something.

"Start over? The whole thing?" Thomas looked at his Cro-Magnon hunters and felt a sense of loss. "What about—"

"The contractor is refacing the wall with canvas. On this side you will paint Darwin's *Descent of Man* and on the other side a mural illustrating his *Origin of Species*."

Whatever else Hawker said, the only thing Thomas heard was *Expanded project. Change order. Revisions to the contract. More money. MORE MONEY!*

Thomas walked to the wall of dismantling displays as if he were already visualizing the Hawker masterpiece. Life was selling. "I'll need one hundred percent Belgian linen."

"Whatever you want."

"Acrylic titanium double-primed with acid-free smooth ground."

"Write your specifications and give them to Maxine." Hawker watched with pleasure as his artist visualized a mural to honor his god.

Thomas's left hand floated upward as if he were already sketching images on the wall. It was a grand performance. Hawker bought it, but the image in Thomas's head was not that of a slithering creature wobbling on fin flipper legs from the tepid soup of a primordial stew. It was the sleek sailboat sitting at Sausalito Harbor with a sign that said For Sale.

Berger can double the contract at least. Don't blow this. He was speaking to himself in Berger's voice.

Thomas skewed his face into a studied expression of profound appreciation and turned to Hawker. The performance continued. He was Moses coming from Mount Sinai with whitened hair and face aflame. His countenance let Hawker know he had seen the divine. The thought amused him. *Divine Darwinism? The ultimate oxymoron.*

Curious metaphors came often and easily. Good ones rarely did. Moses seeing God in a burning bush was decidedly not the right metaphor to represent an artist seeing creatures evolving from lower forms with no intelligent design. That it bubbled up at all tickled him. Until Hamilton had asked Thomas to repaint the Descent of Man, the origins of humankind had hardly crossed his mind. Hawker's question brought him back.

"Have you read Darwin?"

"In college. Not all of it. CliffsNotes."

Hawker steepled his fingers, tapped them together, then placed them under his nose in a ritual that measured the depth of his contemplation. "Do you believe in the concept of God?"

The question startled Thomas. *Why is he asking me THAT? Was it my Moses face? Do I believe in God? Like God, capital 'G'?* The question fluttered in his head like a gypsy moth avoiding a flame. Berger's voice was still there: *Don't blow this.*

"Isn't that an illegal question?" Thomas grinned broadly to reduce the sting. It bought him a few seconds. "God" was not something he thought about very often.

He didn't consider himself a Christian. Not anymore. Perhaps he never had been. In college he had decided nothing was really known or could be known about anything beyond the material world. Least of all a "higher power." If he couldn't see it, hear it, touch it—or create it on canvas—it couldn't be known. When conversations drifted to religion, God or Jesus, he opted to be agnostic. Arguing with believers was a waste of time.

Hawker was amused rather than put off by Thomas's glib answer. "It's an important question under the circumstances, wouldn't you say?" Hawker studied his reaction. Thomas shrugged agreement. "Obviously we need an artist who believes in what he is painting. Otherwise you can't avoid the taint of fantasy. Hmmm?"

Give him the answer he wants, the Berger voice said. Thomas imagined the sailboat adrift. Before he could pull it to shore, Hawker asked, "Are you a Christian, Mr. Hall?"

"No! No. Not really. I might have, you know, been baptized as an infant, but no. I don't believe Jesus was God, if that's what you mean." *Stop rambling.*

A sudden uneasiness shuddered through him. Something deep and forgotten. He wasn't a Christian by any standard, but denying Jesus out loud was discomforting. "I'm agnostic," Thomas declared. His stomach hurt. Leaving the door to God ajar seemed prudent.

"Agnostic?" Hawker spat the word like he'd taken a bite of dandelion. His face went cold. "Really?"

Wrong answer? Thomas's thoughts collided. *He can't want me to be a Christian.*

"Agnosticism is the religion of intellectual cowards!" Hawker sneered.

Thomas was surprised. He assumed agnosticism was a short hop from Darwin and a giant leap from God. The scorn on Hawker's face made it clear he was wrong. Machiavellian instincts rushed to the rescue.

"Not agnostic, exactly. In the classic sense. What I mean is . . ."

Hawker raised a hand to stop his backpedaling. "The man who lacks the guts to believe in God or the courage to admit there's no such thing is the most pathetic creature of all!"

"What I meant was—"

Hawker wasn't finished. "I have more respect for a televangelist with fake eyelashes and big hair bilking money from widows if they really believe than a milksop, namby-pamby who doesn't want the guilt that comes with God but is too scared to offend him just on the off chance there is such a thing."

"You're right. I never—"

"'Because thou art neither cold nor hot, I will spew thee out of my mouth,'" Hawker's rant continued. "You know who said that?"

Thomas shook his head. "I don't."

"Jesus. Even the greatest of all charlatans had no time for intellectual cowards."

Hawker crossed to a stack of boxes near the entrance to the hall. He sliced one open and brought Thomas a set of books. They were bound in antique leather and embossed with gold. Heavier than Thomas expected. "Replicas of Darwin's classic works," Hawker said. Thomas opened the cover and read the title page.

ON
THE ORIGIN OF SPECIES

BY MEANS OF NATURAL SELECTION,

OR THE

PRESERVATION OF FAVOURED RACES
IN THE STRUGGLE FOR LIFE

By CHARLES DARWIN, M.A.

THE DESCENT OF MAN AND SELECTION
IN RELATION TO SEX

"You're right, by the way," Hawker said. "It is illegal to ask you about your race, color, age, sex, sexual preference, national origin or religious belief. If you're serious about politically correct poppycock, I suggest you memorize chapter and verse. It's Title Seven of the Civil Rights Act. Absurd, isn't it? I've no right to ask who you are or what you believe and yet I'm expected to entrust you with responsibility, introduce you to my colleagues, put my reputation in your hands and pay you money. There is a chasm between discrimination and discernment."

"I wasn't being completely serious."

"Good. What you believe matters to me. It matters a great deal because of what we need to do here. What I'm trusting YOU to do." His demeanor changed. He put his hand on Thomas's shoulder.

"More important than what you believe is that you understand and accept the reality of your life on earth. Floating about in some agnostic fairyland deprives you of ultimate truth. There's no moment in life more liberating than when you shed the illusion of God, embrace the law of nature and accept your place in it."

The exchange with Hawker was disturbing. Just when he thought he had skirted the issue of personal belief, here it was again. The flip side of the same question, this time as fatherly advice. He wanted Hawker's approval. He wanted the project. He felt like he was floating. He had come face-to-face with what he believed and realized he didn't have a clue.

He believed in art. Most of the time he believed in himself. He believed his life was blessed. *Does "blessed" mean I acknowledge a higher power? Maybe there is a God. Maybe my great-great-grandpa was an ape. I am what my genes have made me.* That was enough. Calm came again. Then Berger was back. *Tell Hawker whatever he wants to hear. Get the job. Get the money!*

"I believe in what I paint, Dr. Hawker, and no one can paint the genius of Charles Darwin better than I can." His declaration hung in the semidarkness like the last drop of water quivering from the canteen of a man dying in the desert.

"Fair enough," Hawker said and laid his hand on *Origin of Species* in Thomas's grip like a witness swearing to tell the truth, the whole truth and nothing but the truth. His voice was reverent. "This is your Bible. I want you to read it. Open yourself to it. Allow Darwin to influence you to the highest level of your talent. Immerse yourself in all that he wrote."

Hawker patted the book with affection. "See it as he saw it. The mural must illustrate in a clear and powerful way that modern men are the modified descendants of some preexisting form. You need to illustrate how the bodily structure of modern man shows plain traces of his descent from those forms."

He waved a dismissive hand toward Thomas's sketch of an erect ape-like creature at the far left side of the mural. "For goodness sake, let's not begin with Australopithecus so it looks like we copied it from a textbook. Go all the way back. Beyond Pliopithecus, if there's enough room."

He turned to the other wall. "Maybe you should take it all the way around to the primal forms of life, the first single-cell bacterium. Our common ancestor. Depict the sublime truth of evolution as it's never been seen before."

Hawker locked eyes with Thomas. "What do want from your life, Thomas?" Hawker's use of his given name in the shadow of his earlier comment was not lost. "This is your time. What is your life going to be about?"

"Creating a mural to celebrate the genius of Charles Darwin that will outlive us both." The answer seemed to please Hawker even more than Thomas had hoped. He was back on his game.

"Perfect."

"You, sir, are standing in the Sistine Chapel of the natural world." The artist and scientist considered one another for a long, silent moment. Hawker extended his hand. Thomas clasped it with a hardy grip and hoped the sailboat was still for sale.

CHAPTER

13

Thomas released the control line from its cleat and spun the chrome tiller to the right. The sail fluttered without purpose for a few seconds as the boom hinged at the gooseneck and skimmed across the roof of the cabin. It filled with air again as the sloop came around and headed downwind.

"This is the part that makes it worth every dollar, my friend." Archie Granger was the quintessential image of yachting. White pants, deck shoes, open-collared shirt exposing a tanned chest the color of raw sienna. The perfect touch of white and gray on his chest matched the coarse mane flowing from the edges of a captain's hat that had gold laurel-leaf scrambles embroidered on the bill. He sold boats for a living.

Archie unfurled the spinnaker as the sleek sailboat swept an arc from a reaching course until the wind was 160 degrees off the bow. The colorful nylon caught the wind. It shuddered as the guy line went taut against the tack on the windward side. It billowed open with an audible pop as slack in the sheet was gone. The leading edges curled in. With the spinnaker in full camber the colors unfolded to reveal a magnificent phoenix.

Thomas could feel the acceleration of the forty-five-foot yacht as the stiff wind blowing under the Golden Gate Bridge filled the wings of the mythical bird that could burn and be born again and sent them flying toward Alcatraz Island.

It was still early and the sun over the Richmond Hills played peek-a-boo with Thomas through the spinnaker. The nylon glowed in the backlight and the great bird seemed ablaze.

The wind pushed the mainsail north. Thomas caught the tiller as it spun free. Momentum sagged for a moment before he corrected their course to the right. He would learn the art of sailing. He'd get better. His life was defined by his imagination. He could feel the pride he knew would come when he rubbed shoulders with the elite fraternity of yachters at the historic club.

Archie gave Thomas a thumbs-up grin from the bow of the boat. Thomas answered with both thumbs held high. He'd just bought himself a boat and life was good!

CHAPTER

14

THE MARBLE FACE OF JESUS watched Cass and Dr. Bradley strolling
in the garden of St. Mark's. The statue stood on a block of black granite
in the center of an inner court. A stone wall breached by a gated arch
finished the enclosure.

The statue of Jesus was created by Jens Andersen in 1926. Andersen
studied at *Det Kongelige Danske Kunstakademi* (The Royal Danish
Academy of Art) in Copenhagen, Denmark. Andersen was inspired by
Bertel Thorvaldsen's colossal Christus and Twelve Apostles commissioned
for the rebuilding of *Vor Frue Kirke* in Copenhagen in the early part of
the nineteenth century. The statue was given to St. Mark's in 1956 by
Andersen's estate. It was placed in the garden during the renovation of the
hospital in 1968.

As director of public relations, Cass was working on a history of the
hospital. She'd found the history of the statue in the archives.

Cass was Christian, though not Catholic. She found it interesting that
the centerpiece of a Catholic hospital was nothing like the sorrowful, ef-
feminate figure of a tortured man with bleeding heart so common among
the icons of Catholicism.

The Jesus that smiled down on Cass and Dr. Bradley was a powerful
masculine personage with a gentle face and piercing eyes. It was the image
Cass saw when she prayed. He cradled a lamb in the crook of his left arm.
His right reached out in an invitation to come near. The Savior's words
from Matthew 11:28 were etched on the face of the rock: "Come unto
me, all ye that labour and are heavy laden, and I will give you rest."

Cass was one of the few people who knew the complete history of St. Mark's. Clinton Carver didn't. In a conversation about the statue, she had discovered that Carver knew almost nothing about the hospital's history and traditions. She also realized he was patently ignorant about Catholic beliefs in spite of his pious lip service to the "Virgin Mary" and "Holy Mother Church."

As an employee of a Catholic institution, Cass wanted to learn all she could and be conversant with the history, doctrine, and dogma of the Catholic tradition. In one casual discussion she had corrected Carver on a point of doctrine. He had reacted as if she had hit him in the head with a sacred relic. It was only the beginning of the conflict between them, and now he was opposing her effort to engage Thomas Hall.

"Your presentation went fine," Bradley assured her.

"What about the artwork?"

"You are so gorgeous to look at I wasn't paying attention to the art," the old doctor teased. Cass scolded him with her eyes but the smile gave her away. Bradley settled his heavy frame on a stone bench in the shade of the marble Jesus.

"Sally Rogers told me the board is split," Cass said.

"So you lure me into the garden with your beguiling charms, eh?"

She cocked her hip and conjured up her idea of a sultry woman. "Come into my parlor, said the spider to the fly," she purred.

Cass pretending to be a vamp was so out of character that Bradley laughed until he coughed. "Oh, to be young again," he sighed.

"Thomas Hall will create something extraordinary. I'm sure of it."

"Carver is adamant that he beat you on this one."

"Carver would vote no if I showed up with Michelangelo."

"Is he available?" They shared a laugh.

Cass went on: "Hall's professor at Art Institute told me, 'Given the time and discipline, he could be in league with Michelangelo and DaVinci.'"

"That's not all he had to say."

"You talked to him?"

"I'm in a profession that values second opinions."

"And?"

"Andrus knows your Mr. Hall very well."

Cass knew where Bradley was going. Her stomach knotted up.

"One of things that troubled me about Canstano was his attitude," Bradley said. "He was rather . . ."

Conceited. Egotistical. Arrogant. Haughty. The adjectives Andrus had likely used to describe Thomas Hall tumbled through Cass's head. Whatever the doctor's reticence had been about Canstano, Hall was a times-ten.

Bradley drew a thoughtful breath while he found the right word. "Immodest," he said finally. "He didn't seem to have much humility about him."

"Hall doesn't lack confidence, if that's your point," Cass said. *Why am I so committed to Thomas Hall?* she wondered and continued on the offensive. "It could be that he is *so* good and *so* talented that from a practical standpoint his confidence is a measure of humility," she said, then wished she hadn't.

Bradley's face puckered. He leaned forward with a hand on each knee. "Talent is one thing. Being able to listen, working with other people and understanding that no one has a corner on creativity are qualities that, well . . ." Bradley had been told about patches of scorched earth Thomas Hall had left behind. "Andrus's final word to me was, 'Be cautious.'"

Cass sagged to the bench beside him. Bradley patted her arm. "I've never been cautious," he said.

"You're a surgeon."

He laughed. "The joy of being my age is that you've finally conquered all of those ugly fears we allow to define our lives. You wanna know why?"

"Sure." Cass feigned hunger for his philosophical insights, still hoping to persuade him.

"Because you finally believe what you've heard your whole life and read a hundred times in those self-help books you keep around." Cass blushed. "You finally realize it's not at all about what others think or say or do or believe. It's only about the man in the mirror."

"I'm a woman."

"That, sweetheart, is an understatement worthy of a felony charge."

"Soooo. Who's in the mirror? You or me? Do I get your vote or not?"

He laughed, and the look he gave her made her feel like a little girl who didn't understand a story problem.

"No," he said.

"But—"

"You bring your Mr. Hall to meet the board. Make sure he dazzles us with his talent and—"

Cass stood up. "Carver won't change his mind no matter who shows up."

"You didn't let me finish." Cass sat back down. "You bring Mr. Hall and make a presentation to the board. Tell him to impress us with his character as well as his talent."

"His humility?"

"Win our hearts."

"Carver's heart? Does he have one?"

Bradley chuckled. Cass inhaled through clenched teeth and let it out slow.

"There are some things you don't know about St. Mark's, my young friend. Not many people do. Not everything is buried in the archives. There is one person more influential in selecting the artist for the mural than Carver. You lured this old fly into your parlor to get my vote, but sitting here with Jesus listening, I promise you this. If you persuade your Mr. Hall to meet with the board, I will bring you something better than my vote."

CHAPTER

15

I HAVE ZERO INTEREST IN painting a mural for some stupid hospital," Thomas said flatly. Mystical patterns of light and shadow flickered over the Mercedes SLK 350. The top was down. The air was crisp. The last of the morning fog lingered in damp pockets, but the sky was bright. Sunlight fluttered over his face in a game of peekaboo as he drove the roadster beneath an arching corridor of eucalyptus.

He turned his head to look at Frank Berger. The agent was strapped in the sculpted seat next to him. The supple leather was the color of creamed coffee.

"You're not at a point where you can turn down work," Berger said.

"Are you deaf, man? Haven't you heard anything I've told you? The gig at the Science Museum is a whole new deal. You can double what they're paying me. At least."

"They haven't paid us anything yet, and you've been working on it for over two months."

"Yeah, but this Hawker character wants me to turn the whole place into a mural."

"Maybe he does and maybe he doesn't."

"You can milk some big bucks out of this deal. You're the man, Frank!"

Berger sighed. "It ain't a done deal 'til—"

"Yeah, yeah, 'til the check clears the bank. I swear, you must have that tattooed on your brain."

"Well, buying a boat just because some guy's good at yappin' without even—" Berger's face got red.

Thomas cut him off. "You still whining about the boat?'"

"I'm just saying you should talk to the man who gets you work, manages your money, runs your life and wipes your nose before you jump out of a plane without a parachute."

"Archie made me too good a deal, man! Sweetest forty-five-foot sloop you've ever seen, and he said there's a way to write off the payments so costwise it's a wash. Costs me nothing in real dollars."

"Now, there's brilliant estate planning. Get tax advice from a guy who sells boats." Berger was out of patience. He shook his head. "Even if you could write it off—which you can't—tax write-offs only help if you make a LOT OF MONEY!" Berger's yardstick of life was marked with dollars and cents rather than feet and inches. As he took a deep breath to continue his lecture on fiscal responsibility, a congregation of gnats swirled into his mouth. He spat them out like a bugler triple-tonguing a string of semiquaver notes.

Driving with the top down irritated Berger. It was too noisy, too windy and too chilly for San Francisco on all but the best summer days. Inhaling bugs and being bugged about the boat got tangled in some cosmic hoax and made it tough for him to keep the aggravation to himself. He managed. Again.

Berger kept petty annoyances pent up. Managing clients, coddling creative temperaments and keeping egocentric artists happy demanded a special skill set. Mothers came by these gifts naturally. Approval. Appreciation. Admiration. Adoration. Empathy. Understanding. Persistent assurance.

Berger had been mothering for twenty years. Pampering without patronizing. It was a balancing act worthy of Ringling Brothers, Barnum and Bailey. Berger was the ringmaster.

He was older than Thomas by thirteen years. Under a navy jacket, he wore a Tony Bahama shirt tucked into charcoal slacks. Black with a floral print in grays and shades of muted white. The belt was hidden by a twenty-pound overlap he'd had since the eighth grade. *Not fat, just thick,* he quantified.

His cheeks were dappled by the remnant of teenage acne. His hair was long, but not in a holdover-hippie way. More like he thought of himself as Jeff Bridges before he'd shaved his head to play Obadiah Stane in *Iron Man*. Berger wore a beard trimmed short. It was starting to show gray.

"Did Archie have you take the yachter's exam?" Berger said.

"Yachter's exam?" His puzzled look let Berger know Thomas had not heard the old joke.

"Yeah, you know. Find out if you really want a sailboat? Make sure you'll love owning a yacht as much as you imagine?" He teased Thomas with a pause long enough to make sure he had him.

"Never heard of it."

"You take a pair of scissors and cut holes in your raincoat. You put it on, stand in a freezing cold shower and stuff hundred-dollar bills down the drain as fast as you can for six hours." Berger's ability to tell jokes rivaled his ability to coddle clients. "If you enjoy that, you'll love owning a boat."

The punch line apparently caught Thomas off guard and he laughed out loud. Driving south on Twenty-Fifth to Fulton Street, he turned left at Golden Gate Park, then right onto Crossover Drive. He passed through the sculpted portals erected for the World's Fair in 1915 and wound across the lush oasis that marked the middle of San Francisco.

"I can't believe you conned me into a meeting for a project I wouldn't do if I was starving to death." Thomas's tone was irritated as he came back to the core conversation.

"It's not a meeting. It's a presentation, and you were supposed to work up some sketches."

Thomas gave Frank the evil eye and shook his head. "I brought some stuff."

"Good. That's good."

"How'd you ever talk me into this?"

"Guilt. Redemption. It was easy."

"Why do I put up with you?"

Berger looked at Thomas to be reassured the question was light-hearted. "You want a real answer or we just spittin' in the wind here?"

"Lot of agents in the world," Thomas shrugged.

"Lots more artists."

"Not with my talent." Thomas grinned but he sounded arrogant just the same.

"And I see talent in you that you don't even know about yourself," Berger said. Thomas offered him a fist of bones. Their knuckles touched.

"That's it? That's why I put up with you?"

"No. It's because God gave you more talent than you deserve and it needs looking after."

"God has nothing to do with it." Cynicism colored the comment an ugly gray. Berger wondered why.

The Mercedes swept through a wide turn without the slightest sway and followed the jogging path through the center of the park. Two long-legged girls in serious running togs were jogging in the opposite direction. They followed the car with their eyes until they had to look over their shoulders.

Thomas adjusted his Foster Grants and acknowledged their obviously good taste in cool cars and gorgeous guys with a modest nod.

CHAPTER

16

Her heart rate pounded up to 112 the moment she locked the office door. Cass was surprised how anxious she felt. She went into the closet and uncovered the antique wooden chest she'd hidden there.

Getting it up from the basement had been difficult. It was heavy and had no handles. It was two feet square and thirteen inches high. Made of hardwood—oak, Cass guessed—the chest was fastened with metal straps and had brass corners that resembled the claws of a falcon. She carried it from the closet to her desk.

The padlock appeared to be nickel over brass. It was small and worn smooth with a hinged hasp. *Polhem Lock Company* was stamped in raised letters but barely readable.

Cass had discovered the chest when she was searching the archives for the history of the hospital she was compiling. It was in an alcove off the original archive in the lower basement, buried over the years beneath crushed boxes of outdated patient files.

She wrote an e-mail to the hospital administrator with a copy to Carver asking permission to break the lock and open the box. She imagined a treasure trove of hospital history. A nanosecond before her finger touched SEND she changed her mind and deleted it.

Easier to ask forgiveness than get permission. For all of Rear Admiral Grace Hopper's incredible accomplishments in developing the first computer programming languages, it was her famous quip that Cass remembered best. She had written a paper on Grace Hopper for her computer science class her sophomore year at Stanford, becoming one of the thousands of young women for whom "Amazing Grace" was an inspiration for what women can accomplish.

Grace Murray Hopper would have opened the chest and asked forgiveness later. So would Susan "Cass" Cassidy.

She pulled the cordless Makita drill from her backpack, fitted the high-speed steel bit into the jaws and tightened the keyless chuck. A guy named Bill at Ace Hardware had told her what she needed to drill a lock. His instructions ran through her head with the cadence of spy music playing in the background as she prepared her assault on the mysterious box.

"HSS better 'n the cobalt or tungsten. Don't break so easy. You'll wanna take yer time and drill her slow. Keep the heat down. Best to use a lubricant. Lower the friction. Oil or even water make it easier. Rivets on the plate be easier 'n the lock if you can get at 'em."

When he'd handed her the bag, he'd asked, "So what'ja doin anyway, darlin'? Robbin' a bank?" Cass realized the music in her subconscious was the theme from a James Bond movie. She'd seen all twenty-four of them. What was she doing? *Cold sweat* was a cliché until now.

She picked up the drill and scrubbed away the grime on the plate in search of the rivets. "Easier 'n the lock if you can get at 'em," Bill had said. As the grime and corrosion gave way to a persistent thumb, a name appeared, engraved in Victorian script just above the lock.

J. Winston Von Horn

KNOCK. KNOCK! Cass dropped the drill. It hit the floor with a dull thud. *I've been found out! I should have gotten permission!* Getting caught had a curious way of engendering instant remorse. The knock came again.

"Cass? Cass? Are you in there? Hello?" It was Jessica. Cass breathed again.

"Yes, just a second." Jessica was her confidante in most things but even Jessica did not know her plan to break into the treasure box of history. Cass threw a coat over the chest and opened the door.

"They need you in the Burn Center stat." Like most of the people who worked at the hospital, Jessica had adopted the day-to-day medical vernacular. Cass knew *stat* meant "urgent." She didn't know the term came from the Latin word *statim,* meaning "immediate." She did know a stat call to the Burn Center couldn't be good.

CHAPTER

17

THE MAN ON THE CORNER held a piece of cardboard with a message scrawled in red marker.

Poisoned by the Government.
Can't work. Please help.
God bless you.

The man's posture was pathetic. His camouflage fatigues were stained and faded. The left knee of his dirty jeans was worn away and frayed. He wore a field jacket from Vietnam and a tattered scarf wrapped twice around his neck. The original color of the fabric was indeterminable. His mismatched layers blended into the broken light of oleander bushes that spilled onto the sidewalk at the corner of Lincoln and Seventh Avenue.

Thomas stopped at the red light without seeing the homeless man. He twisted in his seat to pull the sample sketches from a zippered leather portfolio at Berger's request. The agent checked his watch. Twenty minutes from now Thomas would dazzle a woman named Susan Cassidy and the board of St. Mark's Hospital.

The homeless man crossed to the Mercedes with aggressive strides. Thomas's head was still between the seats. Berger saw him coming.

"Bogey on your left," Berger cautioned. The disheveled man stuck his hand into the open Mercedes.

"Hey, brother. Can ya help a vet?" His throat was full of gravel.

Thomas whirled at the sound and cracked his elbow on the steering wheel. The stench was palpable. Fetid breath. Rotten cheese. Dirty socks in the bottom of a warm locker.

"Company D, 38th Infantry. Staff Sergeant Jake Demeanus," the man said and offered a card printed at Kinko's with his unit, name, rank and places he'd served. "Nine years, man. Your country and mine. I ain't lying."

"You should have stayed in," Thomas said, opting to breathe through his mouth rather than endure the smell.

"Too shot up, man!" He pulled the ragged jacket aside and lifted a handful of shirt to reveal ugly lumps of skin. "Just need some bread for some bread, brother," the man asked humbly and smiled.

"You mean booze?" Thomas scoffed. He pushed the hand away. The card fell in Thomas's lap.

During his first year at college Thomas had made a decision about the street people of San Francisco. *Don't give them money.* He made it a rule. Panhandlers in San Francisco were part of the culture. A booby trap for tourists and suckers. He kept his rule. *No handouts—ever!* Today would be no exception.

Thomas eyed the traffic light and eased the front wheels into the crosswalk. He held the brake and revved the engine to 2000 RPMs. In seconds he'd get a green, kick the 300 horses under the hood and end the unpleasant encounter. *Five point three seconds zero to sixty and you are history, pal!*

"I haven't eaten for two days," Staff Sergeant Demeanus begged.

That is such a lie. Thomas was tempted to spit the words in the beggar's face but set his jaw and ignored the poor man completely.

"I'm telling you the truth, man. The government took my—"

Thomas's contempt for useless freeloaders erupted. "Go get a job!" he barked as if panhandling were a game both players understood and being rude was acceptable.

"I'm trying to get work, man."

"Get your hand the hell off of my car!" That was outside the rules of the game. The beggar's eyes floated over the graceful lines of the Mercedes.

"Okay. Okay. I'm cool." The man withdrew his outstretched palm and backed away. "Looks like God already blessed you good enough, man. No need to be castin' more bread on the water helpin' a guy like me. Cool."

Thomas looked at the man but refused to see him. Not the way he usually saw. Then, without warning, the artist inside took over and he sketched the man in his mind.

His hair was long and curled under at his shoulders. His scraggly beard and gaunt face made him older than he was. *What terrible choices brought you to this?* A rush to judgment trampled a flicker of compassion.

He wanted to look away, but Staff Sergeant Jake Demeanus's intense stare caught his eyes, and he couldn't. You can never afford to make eye contact in the game. People learn soon enough it is safest to go through life without eye contact—particularly with strangers. Thomas knew that but it was too late.

The man's eyes were dark blue-violet, almost black, with tiny flaws of green and gray. For a moment Thomas had the strange sensation that he had met the man before. It was disquieting. He felt a sudden urge to draw that face. At first the man had seemed vacuous, inexpressive, even witless. Then he saw the flicker of a mysterious passion behind his eyes.

Berger reached in front of Thomas with a five-dollar bill between his fingers. Every line on the leather-brown face wrinkled into a smile.

"God bless you, brother." The light turned green and the spell was broken.

Thomas punched the accelerator and jammed right onto Seventh. The Michelins squealed through the turn.

"Giving that guy money is like poking a blind man in the eye to help him see again," Thomas scolded. "You're not helping him. You're making it worse!"

"Hard not to feel sorry for him."

"You don't think he has choices?"

"Maybe."

"Not maybe! He brought it on himself."

"Some of them, maybe. But come on, Thomas, some of these people—"

"A con working the streets can make fifty thousand a year from compassionate suckers like you." Thomas shared what he remembered from an article in the *Chronicle* about the city's plague of professional panhandlers. "I'll bet you that . . ." He glanced at the Kinko's card. "A, the guy was never in Vietnam; B, he has a decent place to live; C, he gets up in the morning, sucks down a Starbucks, puts on his rag costume and goes to work. He probably belongs to Actor's Workshop."

"You never make exceptions?"

Thomas thought about it and had to smile. "One time." Berger waited expectantly. "I gave ten bucks to a guy with a sign that said, 'Please help. My wife has been kidnapped. I need two dollars for the ransom and eight bucks for some beer.'"

Berger scrunched his face and waited for the punch line. There wasn't one. "So why that guy?" he asked.

"Creativity, man! I was entertained. Big difference between entertained and ripped off!"

Berger cranked his head to catch a final glimpse of the man who had served his country for nine years.

CHAPTER

18

THE BURN CENTER WAS NEXT to the Children's Ward on the third floor. Cass took the stairs. Stat meant *now.* The elevators were closer but old and slow and always in use. She opted to avoid an anxious wait pushing the button repeatedly. Cass tended toward impatience and always pushed the elevator button more than once, whether she was in a hurry or not. On Friday she had been waiting with one of the custodians. After she had pushed the down button at least twelve times, the man said, "It doesn't know you're doing that. It's a machine." *The guy should be promoted,* Cass mused, blushing.

Burn Center STAT! Cass knew without being told that the crisis was Christina. In the seven minutes it took to navigate the maze to the stairwell, climb to the third floor and cross to the Burn Center she contemplated what she knew about Christina Christensen.

• • •

Life Flight One landed on the helipad marked by a circle of lights at the edge of the parking lot. An ER team moved Christina onto a gurney before the twin rotors began to wind down.

The Emergency Room at St. Mark's was crowded, as in every inner city hospital. Confusing. Within minutes of Life Flight's arrival, Christina had been wheeled next to a bed in the open bay of the ER and surrounded by half a dozen medical professionals, each determined to save her life.

The ER doctor was at the top of the gurney attending to her head and neck injuries. The tag on his green tunic said *Dr. Jeffrey Hill*. He looked young enough to be a freshman in college. Except for his eyes. They were old and seasoned and left no doubt that he knew exactly what he was doing.

There was a nurse on each side and a second ER doc at Christina's feet.

"On the count of three," Dr. Hill said with urgent calm. "One, two, three!" Christina was lifted from the gurney to the bed in a smooth arc. She'd been bagged on the way to the hospital but was hurriedly switched to a portable mechanical vent.

There was a bright light. She thought for a moment she had gone back and she wondered about her mother but the light was blocked by amorphous gray forms that smeared her vision with a blur of white floating over and around her and then she felt strong hands on her head and neck and shoulders and back and she was turning.

They rolled Christina to her side and removed the straps of the backboard.

Dr. Hill examined the laceration on the girl's head and the fracture of the skull beneath. He removed the neck brace and checked the cervical spine. He ran his hand down the vertebral column on either side of her backbone looking for step-offs and checked for bruised signs of occult bleeding.

Airway. Breathing. Circulation. He ran the checklist again. Dr. Hill was driven by a single goal. Rule out what might kill her and work backwards.

The blinding light was touching one eye. The other one was dark. Christina tried to close it out but her lids were stretched open and held there by a rubber hand. The light moved to the other eye and she floated backwards into semiconsciousness, only faintly aware of where she was and what was happening.

"Pupilary reflex good. Intracranial hemorrhage less likely. But we will need to get a head CT scan to rule out subdural/epidural hemorrhage."

There were voices, vague and far away. Sounds. Nonsensical. Slurred and blurred as the figures that floated in and out of the light.

"Thank God." The voice of a gray angel. Christina thanked God too.

"Get me a CT of the head, chest and abdomen."

The gauze compression on her head went away. Her head was

scrubbed with something that burned all the way to the back of her skull. A bigger bandage came. Pressure replaced pain. "Just hold it for now. We'll sew it up later. Anyone know her tetanus status? Let's give her a booster just in case."

A needled pierced her arm. A quick point of pain. Cold running inside. Her fingers on the strings of her violin. Her mother smiling. The dark man coming at her through the flames. Blackness.

"Chest tube in place," a nurse reported.

"Get it stable. What are the O₂ stats? Come on, people. I need numbers," Hill snapped.

The nurse peeled the paper off the buttons and stuck them to the child's chest, hips and wrists, then snapped the EKG leads into place. "EKG leads on."

"Where's plastics? The burns on her hands and legs are ferocious."

"I called him ten minutes ago. He's on his way. Should be here by now. Orthopedics just got here."

"How's she doing?" Dr. Mary Matthews joined the circle of saviors and went straight to Christina's broken legs. Matthews's at-rest face was pleasant so she had to work at looking angry. She had been in surgery when the call came and was still in blue surgical scrubs.

"I need that portable X-ray here now!" The familiar calm and urgent voice of Dr. Hill reached Christina in waves of light that pulsated through the blackness. *Chest tube. Hemothorax. Gargling blood. Bad news.*

Somewhere in the darkness Christina heard a woman's voice. Mother?

"I need to get her into the operating room and get this pinned like yesterday!" Matthews was looking at the bone poking through the skin.

"She can't be moved!"

"It's bad, Jeff. We need to get her to OR and pin it."

"I need some imaging done first."

"What she needs, if we want her to walk again, is to get to the OR ASAP."

"I'm almost finished," the X-ray tech said, taking invisible pictures on her portable machine.

"The massive bruising on the other leg worries me more than the open fracture," Matthews said. "The other femur's likely broken under there and ripping havoc with the tissue." She turned to the tech. "Give me a shot of the right femur when you're finished there. I bet we're going to have to pin that one as well."

The burn surgeon swaggered in like a movie star late for call. *Top Gun coming to the flight line. Prima donna making a second bow.* Dr. Emile W. Durant was middle-aged, tanned, and dusted gray at the temples. He wore a green golf shirt with a logo that said *MASTERS 2009* tucked into tan slacks that fit perfectly in spite of a middle-age paunch, thanks to elasticized expanders hidden on either side. He snapped the second surgical glove in place as he entered.

"'Bout time, Tiger," Hill said. Durant ignored the ER doc's barb. His passion for golf had tagged him 'Tiger' among the staff. Given recent scandals, he now considered it a slur. He looked at the girl's legs, pulling away burned fragments of cloth.

"Not as bad as you said, Jeff." He talked down to younger physicians no matter who they were. "Not much worse than second degree, and those burns on the face look superficial."

"Look at her hand," Hill said. Christina's left hand was covered. Durant pulled the wrap away. His arrogance was replaced by sudden concern.

"What antibiotic is she on?"

"Rocephin and Gentamycin."

"My apologies. She's got a full-thickness burn. What do you have her on for MRSA?"

"Nothing adequate yet," Hill said with a hint of exasperation. "You see what I'm dealing with here."

Durant nodded. "Give me some Vancomycin stat." Then, to the nurse in charge of IV access, "Check the lines. I want maximum flow."

Nurses scribbled down the doctor's instructions. Nurses' assistants scampered to get whatever they needed.

• • •

Cass met Christina Christensen the following day. The administrator had asked her to come to the Emergency Room. She didn't know why.

The ER was a perpetual public relations nightmare but usually *after* the bleeding stopped.

There was a problem. The girl admitted the night before had no next of kin that anyone could find. Family services had searched all night and most of the morning without finding a relative.

When Cass arrived in the ER there was a war going on between Mavis Parnell from administration and the medical team.

Mavis Parnell was director of social and family services. In her case the title was a euphemism for "*CZAR OF ADMISSIONS, INSURANCE AND MAKING DAMN SURE THE HOSPITAL GETS PAID!*" She stood with her feet planted like poplar trees and her arms folded across her abundant bosom. Mavis was black, brilliant and at 285 pounds a formidable foe if you happened to favor anything she was against. Her friends called her Sugar.

Doctors Hill, Matthews, and Durant were shoulder to shoulder in the opposing skirmish line. Mavis listened to the doctors rant for a few moments before cutting them off. "I understand, but the policy is clear. She can't leave ER until we find her next of kin or guardian so somebody signs off on who pays the bills."

"Look around!" Dr. Hill raised his voice. "We're out of room and Durant needs to get her upstairs now." Mavis refused to look at the patients on gurneys in the hallways.

"I don't make the rules, Dr. Hill, but this hospital stays solvent because I follow them. Without exception."

"We're supposed to be saving lives, not following rules," Durant demanded. "This is unbelievable. If she were indigent or illegal we wouldn't be having this conversation! What the hell is wrong with you people?"

"Don't you raise your voice at me." Mavis's folded fat arms came unraveled to allow one finger to wag. The other hand became a fist planted on what would have been a hip if the woman had had a waist.

"Over at General they would have put her into surgery last night," Durant scolded, unimpressed by Parnell's scolding.

"What can I do to help?" Cass asked as she stepped into the breach between Mavis and the medical team.

"Oh, there you are, sweetie," Mavis said and picked up a clipboard from the counter. "We got a patient with no family or next of kin and hoped you folks up in public relations might be able to find a responsible party so the good doctors here can get on with what they like to do."

"We can't wait for that!" Durant appealed to Cass as if she were suddenly empowered to arbitrate. "She was supposed to be in the OR being prepped by the time I got here this morning but the pencil pushers came wallowing in and—"

Cass cut him off before he inflamed the situation more. She turned to Mavis with a broad smile. "This hospital would fall apart without you, Sugar. Everybody knows that. Even they know that." She smiled at the stern circle of faces. "There must be some way for them to go ahead with what they need to do while we help find the girl's family and . . ."

Mavis started shaking her head at *there must be some way.* "You get the board to change the policy, sweetie, and I'll do whatever they say. Be nice if everything was perfect but for the sake of a day or two they can do what they need to do right here until I get a responsible party." Mavis tapped the clipboard. "Other choice is California Child Protective Services. Turn the girl over to them."

"That's a nightmare!" Dr. Matthews said. "Don't even think about that."

"It's up to Cass, then. Find me a guardian or next of kin. Till then, the girl stays where she is."

"That child is going to lose her hand because of you." Durant ripped off his sterile gloves and stomped away.

"Wait!" Cass shouted. Durant looked back. Cass took the clipboard from Mavis. "Give me your pen." The woman snagged it from where it was parked in deep cleavage. Cass signed her name at the bottom of the form.

"You're not her family!" The big woman looked puzzled.

"You said she has no family." Cass handed the clipboard to Mavis. "You've got your responsible party," she said and nodded at the doctors. "Do what you need to do."

Matthews and Durant barked orders on the move and within seconds Christina was wheeling past Cass on her way to the OR. Matthews stopped the gurney for a moment.

"This is Christina," Dr. Matthews said. The child looked at Cass through a foggy filter of the medication. "Christina, this is Susan Cassidy, your new best friend."

"Nice to meet you," Cass said. A tiny movement of the child's mouth and twitch of a finger were greeting enough. Dr. Hill gave Cass a hug. The unexpected embrace made her blush. "They need to make you president," he said and went back to caring for strangers whose lives depended on him.

Cass caught up with Dr. Durant as he scrubbed up for surgery. "Is she going to be okay?"

"I've performed bigger miracles."

"Which means . . . ?" Cass let the question hang. Durant glanced up, then soaped and scrubbed again.

"There is severe necrotic tissue with no pulse. Her radial pulse is weak. The tops of her fingers are cold and discolored. The two reasons a burn victim loses a limb are compromised blood flow and destruction of the nerves," he said as he raised his hands for the nurse's aide to put on his sterile surgical gloves.

"She had no reflexes when she came in, which means the nerves are badly damaged. The most severe area of the burn is right over the carpal tunnel." Cass furrowed her brow. "The band of fibrous tissue that overlies the median nerve and flexor tendons, which control most of the fingers."

"You've 'performed bigger miracles'?" she quoted him hopefully.

He nodded. "We'll see. I need to release that compartment. Open it up to make sure there is good blood supply, and while I'm in there I'll find out if there is anything left of the median nerve. It's a very bad burn and I'm also worried about the ulnar nerve."

"Ulnar? I'm sorry I forget that . . ."

"Controls the ring finger and pinky." Durant drew a diagram on his own hand and wrist with a finger made deathly gray by sterile latex. "There are two main nerves that control the majority of functions in your fingers. On the palm side it is the ulnar and median nerves. Ulnar on the outside. Median goes right down the center of the wrist and under the carpal tunnel."

The aide tied the mask over his face and he walked toward the double doors of the operatory. "If we can get enough blood to her hand she won't lose it. Whether she uses it again depends on what we find. If the nerves are compromised and the flexor muscles that control the fingers have been too badly burned, her hand will be a claw."

He bumped the doors with his hip and disappeared.

Cass walked back to her office and recounted her adventures of the last forty minutes to Jessica. Her executive mother made her repeat three times the part about grabbing the clipboard from big Sugar and signing her life away. "It's only until we find the next of kin, and I'm making that *your* job," Cass grinned.

The nurse called when Christina came out of surgery and was moved to the Burn Center. Even though Cass was a member of the hospital administrative staff she needed a pass to enter the ICU. The visitor's pass said *GUARDIAN*. The implications of her rash decision overwhelmed her with a sudden rush of responsibility. She spent all night at the side of the child's bed.

CHAPTER

19

CASS HURRIED TOWARD THE Burn Center. She still had the pass. She'd used it to visit Christina so many times since the surgery that it no longer stuck so she attached it with a safety pin.

Dr. Durant was waiting at the main desk. He wore a beige sweater vest over a striped orange golf shirt with green khaki slacks that were the color-wheel complement to the shirt. He was talking to a man Cass had never seen. *Intern,* she supposed. He was Asian, Chinese perhaps. He wore a white physician's jacket with a stethoscope around his neck.

"Is Christina all right?" she asked the moment she saw him.

"She's fine."

"Why the stat?"

"I've got a tee time in twenty minutes," Durant confided with a grin. Cass remembered why she considered the surgeon his own peculiar variant of Dr. Jekyll and Mr. Hyde. "I wanted you to meet Dr. Namkung."

Cass glanced at the Asian doctor's name tag. It was perfectly aligned with the top of the pocket and written in both English and Hangul.

"Korean," Namkung smiled when he saw her staring at the characters. Cass hated to confess she couldn't distinguish between Chinese and Korean, or Japanese, for that matter. The blessing and curse of growing up white Protestant Christian in a community without much ethnic diversity.

Namkung had a broad, flat chin and high cheekbones. His lips were full, the upper larger than the lower. The epicanthic fold typical in Northeast Asians gave his black eyes the shape of almonds. Cass had never thought of Asian men as handsome until today.

"Dr. Namkung is taking over as primary care physician," Durant said. "I'll look in from time to time, but you and Christina are in his hands now." He turned to the doctor. "This is Susan Cassidy, the woman I told you about."

"Cass," she said and extended her hand. "Pleasure to meet you."

"Remarkable thing you did," Namkung said with the drop shadow of an accent that made his English sound sophisticated and the doctor seem brilliant.

"How is she today?" Cass asked, deflecting the compliment.

"She's asleep. She's been having a lot of pain in spite of the medication, so I increased the level."

"Morphine?"

"Fentanyl. Faster acting. It's a synthetic primary mu-opioid agonist. She'll sleep a lot until we step it back. I understand you've still not found any family."

"Not yet."

"Well, I'm off," Durant said. "Eight handicap and twenty bucks a hole. Gotta focus."

Cass shook Dr. Durant's hand. "Thank you for all you've done," she said.

"Call me if you need me," Durant said and waved over his shoulder on his way out the door.

"If you have a few minutes, I'd like to discuss the girl's future," Namkung said. Cold, formal. "California Child Protective Services have been notified of the girl's situation and want to arrange a meeting."

"That's unnecessary, Dr. Namkung," Cass said, suddenly defensive. "I have signed off to be the responsible party for the hospital, and Christina is still *in* the hospital. I'll be happy to discuss her future with you at some point, but right now I've got an important meeting with the artist who will be doing our mural in the Healing Place."

CHAPTER

20

THOMAS SLOWED WITHOUT COMING to a full stop.

"We need to talk about the boat," Berger said, "but right now I want you to stay focused on landing a contract with these people. Work your magic."

"I'll do the dance because you promised, but . . ." The thought struck like a winning Bingo card. "Is your committing me to a presentation without asking me anything like me buying a boat without asking you? Or should I ask the man who wipes my nose?" Berger ignored him. "Come on, Frank! I don't need some cheesy gig at a hospital. We're doubling the deal at the Science Museum, and Friday you're in Vegas to close the Heavy Metal Casino deal. That's ten months right there. We add one more project, you gotta find a way to clone me."

"Don't I wish?"

"Huh-uh! There it is. You'd do it, too! Greed! It's your most endearing quality."

"You can't spear fish in a barrel until they're in the barrel."

"That's the point. Darwin and Las Vegas are in the barrel." Then Thomas was struck by a funny thought. "The beginning and end of evolution."

Frank's laugh was halfhearted and Thomas felt a twinge of doubt. "You agree we've got them?" he pressed.

Berger shrugged. "Yeah, of course."

"Both of 'em?"

"No worries, man. We're good. But let's get this one just in case. A backup plan is never a bad idea. Besides, this Susan Cassidy, whoever she is, would not take no for an answer."

"Saying no to stupid projects is part of your job, Frank."

"Until this car is paid for and you get rid of the boat, *no* is not in my vocabulary. Tack up that fact in your creative cranium." Berger tapped him on the forehead.

Thomas gripped his finger and pulled it down. "I am not getting rid of the boat, and you really need to manage your expectations on this hospital thing. Comprende, mi amigo?"

"Sounded to me like this Susan Cassidy is your biggest fan in the world."

Thomas searched Frank's face for sarcasm. Found none.

A Buick the color of red wine backed from a slot as Thomas turned into the parking lot of St. Mark's Hospital. The sun found a hole in the gathering fog and flashed a writhing highlight across the hood of the LaCrosse. *Vinaceous.* The color registered in his head, as colors always did.

The visitor's parking was full except for the hole left by the Buick. Thomas goosed the Mercedes, looped around, and headed for the open space. A two-tone Volkswagen bus with a faded chartreuse bottom and pus yellow top waited for the Buick on the other side. Its blinker was flashing.

The Buick backed out in front of the VW. Thomas punched the gas and swung the Mercedes into the empty spot. The driver of the VW was a shaggy fellow trapped in the seventies. He bleeped his horn and spoke to Thomas in the universal language of the middle finger on his left hand.

Thomas responded with a shrug that said, *Life's tough.* He tapped his wrist even though he didn't wear a watch to let the loser in the parking wars know he was in a hurry and significantly more important than anybody who would drive a VW bus.

• • •

Cass exited the building as Thomas and Berger ascended the seven broad steps to the main entrance.

"I'm Susan Cassidy," she said, extending her hand. "I spoke with you on the phone, Mr. Berger." She knew who was who even though Berger looked more like a stereotypic artist than Thomas.

"Yeah. Hi. Great to meet you too." Berger's Bible was *How to Win Friends and Influence People.* It had become required reading for Thomas the day Berger had signed him on.

"This is Thomas Hall," Berger said.

"Of course I know who this is," Cass said. "It is a real honor to meet you, Mr. Hall. I am a huge fan of your work."

Thomas was immediately attracted to this woman. "Then I'm a huge fan of your good taste," he smiled, and somewhere in the exchange of cordialities he took her hand.

"Sorry you were delayed. I was so hoping to give you a quick tour before your presentation. We'll do it right after." He was still holding her hand.

Thomas had dated very little during his years at Art Institute. He attended a variety of social events. He enjoyed conversations with engaging women. "Engaging" in his mind equated to an inquisitive interest in art.

Juanita Villanueva came closest to being a girlfriend. She was a design student from San Diego and an outspoken commentator on his work. She was animated, witty and candid in her critique. Thomas loved to spend long hours listening to her analysis of his latest creation. He called her *hermana* and loved to roll the *r.*

For Juanita the "friendship" was sixteen months of unrequited love, patience and suffering in silence. It ended in an explosive eruption of Latin passion that caught Thomas off guard.

They were eating pizza at a funky hole-in-the-wall joint. Thomas had just finished a four-hour advanced figure drawing class with a nude model and Juanita was looking at his sketch pad. Thomas waited for her glowing praise. She pushed the pad aside and picked up a slice of pizza instead.

Halfway through the pepperoni and double cheese she asked, "How has a gorgeous man like you escaped getting involved with one of these exotic women in your life?" She shoved the sketch pad across the table.

He laughed and tried to explain that a woman posing as a model— nude or otherwise—was an *objet d'art,* an abstraction, not a human being per se to whom there was some other connection.

Then he answered the other part of her question. "I want to focus on my art. There's always time to find Miss Right." He chomped into the Hawaiian pineapple and ham. She rolled her eyes, took a drink of her Coke, and crunched the ice with her teeth.

"Such a liar," she accused.

"What is it they say? 'To every thing there is a season, and a time to every purpose.'"

"I thought you never read the Bible."

"I don't."

"You're quoting it."

"No. That's Shakespeare, isn't it?"

"Ecclesiastes, and you left out 'under the heaven.'"

"This is the only time I'll be able to immerse myself without distraction. Become a master of my talent and learn all there is to know," Thomas concluded.

"Everything about art and nothing about life," she scolded.

Thomas could have done worse than Juanita. It was only after she was gone that he understood why she had asked the question and what she was saying when she continued the quotation from Ecclesiastes: "A time to embrace, and a time to refrain from embracing; a time to get, and a time to lose; a time to keep, and a time to cast away."

Thomas discovered that being a commercial artist was more isolating than being a student. Lest his client become a hermit, Berger forced him to attend cultural events and participate in social causes.

Being part of the San Francisco art community had advantages. There was also a worrisome downside. Berger made sure Thomas appeared at social occasions with a female companion. A good-looking woman on your arm in San Francisco was the answer to the question so often unasked but always present. For Berger it was business. For Thomas it was about picking trophies, not soul mates. Thomas didn't believe in soul mates. Why would he? He didn't believe in souls.

He selected his dates by two criteria. One: Appearance. Always gorgeous. Two: Composition. Design and balance. The right woman for the right occasion.

Catrina Lindley was first choice when swimsuits were appropriate.

Patricia Livingston was top of the list for highbrow culture. Unfortunately, after seven nights at Civic Light Opera in a single season without a hint of romance, she had figured him out.

Mandy Frost was the perfect date for the invitational luncheon at the yacht club where Thomas was being considered for membership. Besides being one of the few women who'd crewed in America's Cup, Mandy Frost happened to be the great-granddaughter of Captain James Yarlborough Frost. Grandpa Frost had founded the yacht club and built the marina right after the earthquake of 1906.

Mandy Frost broke her leg rock climbing. On short notice, he called Patricia and invited her to the yacht club luncheon.

"Why, Thomas!" Patricia cooed in her Wellesley College English. "The yacht club? Whatever makes you imagine your *objet d'art* for opera can possibly meet your yacht club expectation?"

He made some vague stab at connecting her love of Verdi's *La Traviata* with Dennis Conner's *Stars and Stripes*. "Tell Mandy I hope she breaks her other leg!" she yelled, slamming down the phone.

All the women in Thomas Hall's life knew his scandalous modus operandi. Well, all of them but Catrina Lindley. Her mental acuity was as limited as her body was boundless.

There was adequate attention and affection in his life, but Thomas missed the kind of friendship he'd had with Juanita and wished their relationship had not ended.

If another woman comes along who . . .

Thomas always ejected the thought before the seed could sprout.

CHAPTER

21

CLINTON CARVER WAS HUDDLED with Dr. Bradley by the window at the far end of the boardroom when Cass arrived with Frank Berger and Thomas Hall. Carver was animated. Aggressive. Bradley's head wagged like a bobble-head doll, but his arms were wrapped tight across his chest. Carver became more animated. *Demanding his support?* Cass wondered.

Bradley glanced past the board president to the door. It was evident he was expecting someone. Cass glanced around the room to find the missing party. All present and accounted for. *Who, then?*

Members of the board babbled profound insights to one another, creating a dissonant drone.

Kimberly Johnson picked cashews from a bowl of mixed nuts and used three bites to nibble each.

Carver acknowledged Cass with a condescending smile.

Bradley stepped into the hall and tapped a number into his cell phone. He moved ghostlike beyond the frosted glass.

Thomas was curious and watched him. After a minute the old doctor returned to the room and took his seat.

"Thank you for coming on short notice," Carver began. He pitched his voice lower when he spoke in his official capacity. It made him sound pretentious and self-important. "Since this is not a regular board meeting I didn't ask for an agenda, but—"

Kimberly raised her hand with the enthusiasm of a third grader who had the answer to a question and spoke at the same time. "I prepared an agenda." Tittering around the table. "There is only one order of business, but I thought it would be helpful." She held up a sample agenda. Flame orange, hundred-pound card stock. There were four lines. "You should each have one. Hold them up so I can see." Orange agendas went up like autumn leaves in a dust devil.

"Ms. Cassidy couldn't wait nine days, so don't blame me for missing the football game." He intended humor but the subtext was biting. There were murmurs but no laughter. "She's the one who insisted we meet off-calendar. Your meeting, Suzanne."

Suzanne! Her face bloomed pink at the deliberate mispronunciation of her name. *Such a jerk!* Her discomfort met Carver's expectation. He held the smug smile to make sure she saw it, then settled into the leather wingback at the head of the table.

He knows it's not Suzanne! He knows I prefer Cass. He calls me everything but what I've asked, lest I forget where I stand in the pecking order. Calm. Take a deep breath. Calm. This is too important. You can do this! Cass inhaled deeply and regained composure. Her voice was that of a patient mother with an errant child.

"It's Cass, Clinton."

"Oh, of course. *Caa-yassss.* Sorry." He pronounced it with two syllables, emphasizing the second. Kimberly giggled. Cass took a second deep breath and began.

"You've been introduced to the work of Thomas Hall. Today you meet him in person. Hear his ideas. Ask him questions."

Whatever thought came into her mind at that moment, it changed her. She was suddenly informal. Vulnerable. A friend.

She laughed softly and leaned forward into a shaft of dusty sunlight that sliced through the high windows on the south side of the room. Her head drifted in and out of the sunshine, giving her an intermittent halo of backlight.

It seemed to Thomas that the flashes of light punctuated her presentation. Gave it emphasis. Added confirmation. *God rays showing divine approval.* It was the way his mind's eye worked.

God rays was the name artists and photographers gave to those dramatic shafts of light seen in nature when clouds obscure the sun and the light illuminates moist air in long, glorious shafts from heaven to earth. Thomas's fantasy art was filled with them.

"I hope after you meet him you will understand why Mr. Hall is my recommendation to paint the mural in the Healing Place."

The Healing Place? Berger obviously kept a few surprises up his sleeve.

"Mr. Hall is here with Mr. Frank Berger, his a—" Cass did not want to say agent or manager. Too much like watchdog or go-between. She knew that the secret of selling Thomas to the board was accessibility. "His business associate," Cass finished.

Thomas and Berger swapped glances. *Business associate? Yeah, right.* Thomas mused. *As in cutthroat agent who will tell you I will do this even when I won't and persuade you to pay us something even when I don't.*

Cass leaned into the light again. Her hair was a gossamer fire. Thomas rehearsed his invitation for this woman to go out with him on his boat. The thought caused him to drift into that place. Her words floated out of range and were swallowed up by the ambient hum of the air conditioning.

"It is my pleasure to introduce to you Thomas Hall," Cass concluded. "Artist extraordinaire." Kimberly's hands slapped together seven times before she realized no one else was applauding. The solo ovation brought Thomas back from sea, sun and sailing under the Golden Gate Bridge with his new girlfriend.

Thomas had no interest in doing a project for the hospital but he liked to pitch. He enjoyed selling himself. Beneath the eccentric reclusive artist persona Berger worked hard to promote, Thomas was a performer. It was a talent that distinguished him from fellow artists. He turned on his charm.

He knew only what Berger had told him, and it wasn't much. They were building a new Children's Wing. Cass called it the Healing Place. That spawned a few ideas. They wanted a mural.

The other artist had broken his arm or his leg, or maybe it was both arms and both legs. Funny he couldn't remember a story like that. Details must have been lost in a moment of distraction. Being second choice did not sit well with his ego. He added it to his list of reasons not to do the mural.

On the other hand. He was here now, and Susan Cassidy was a babe.

Whoops. He smiled at the thought. *In a PC world that would be "gorgeous person."* He rehearsed their conversation after the presentation. Patricia Livingston, the former first pick for high-class dates, needed to be replaced.

There was a fourteen-foot run of white butcher paper tacked up along the wall. Berger had suggested it to Cass on the phone. "In case he gets in the mood to sketch," he explained, knowing his client could hardly talk without a pencil in his hand.

Coming up with ideas, pitching in real time and thinking on his feet were all skills tucked away in Thomas Hall's bag of tricks. Ideas, images and finished art presented themselves faster than Thomas could recite, write, paint or explain. Berger often chided Thomas for his lack of preparation. But he never complained. He recognized that Thomas's ability to make it up on the fly was one more talent distinguishing Hall from the other artists he represented.

Today was no different. By the time Thomas stepped to the butcher paper the mural was already finished in his head. Five minutes into the pitch Berger realized Thomas was putting on a one-man show for Susan Cassidy and didn't give a hoot about the hospital.

"I see children," Thomas said and allowed the image to form in his mind. He drew swift sketches of children. "At the outer edge on either side," he said as he turned his words into impressions of beauty in a swirl of colored markers, "are fields of flowers and as the hills roll toward the center, the living, growing things of the earth become children." He switched colors so quickly and so often he seemed more juggler than artist.

"White kids, yellow kids, red, black and seven shades of brown," he said. Rudimentary sketches of children with quick indications of ethnicity and familiar icons of culture appeared on the mockup mural. Some were remarkable. Some only scribbles.

Thomas stepped back, squinted, cocked his head side to side, then added crutches, wheelchairs and one child helping another. "So, the idea," Thomas said as he continued to draw, "is sick kids. Children from everywhere, suffering with everything, coming to . . ." the idea appeared a nanosecond before he spoke but he described it as if he'd worked on it for months. "To a grand castle. A wonderful fairy-tale castle full of magic and joy, a place where all your dreams come true and you live happily ever after."

He traded a blue marker for dark brown. His left arm began drawing in the air before the felt tip touched the paper. When it did, a flurry of disjointed lines and shapes appeared.

Kimberly was emotional. She whispered to the woman beside her, "He's drawing a castle." Thomas switched to lavender, purple and pink. Blocks of color connected. Skeleton lines were suddenly shapes and the shapes a first cousin to King Ludwig's famous Neuschwanstein castle.

"They're going to Disneyland?" Kimberly wondered aloud. A commotion at the door saved her from complete humiliation. Thomas turned toward the disturbance at the back.

A tall, dark man of mixed ethnic origin stepped into the room. Carver rocked forward in the wingback. "Whoa. Excuse me! We're in the middle of a board meeting here." The man paid Carver no mind. He was dressed in a plain black suit. Something you could buy at Nordstrom Rack. He wore a white shirt and narrow tie. His hair was short and almost black, two shades darker than his skin. His jaw was wider than the span of his temples. He wore dark glasses.

Carver stood up. "Sir?" The man continued to ignore him.

The tall man reminded Thomas of a character he had created for Dark Horse comics. The barrier between reality and imagination was tissue thin. *He's carrying. The lump at the small of his back is a piece. Glock 9mm?* Drawing weapons for his fantasy art gave Thomas a cold-steel intimacy with the dark and dangerous that was hard to explain.

The man pushed the door against the wall. He slipped the lock on the pneumatic cylinder and set it in place. Carver was red in the face. "We've booked the room! Did you understand what I said? Do you speak English?"

"It's all right," Dr. Bradley said. He had struggled from his chair and was on his way around the table. By the time he reached the door, the tall man had stepped into the hall and returned with a wheelchair bearing an old woman.

The cause of her invalidism was not apparent. She sat erect in spite of a hump between her shoulders.

Osteoporosis and compression fractures in the vertebrae, Thomas remembered. If he drew something once, it stayed forever in his mind. An enlightened dean at Art Institute had persuaded a professor from UC Medical School to teach anatomy to students of art. Memorizing bones and muscles and learning to draw them was easy. Studying the impact of different pathologies offered artists—particularly those like Thomas, whose passion was the human figure—an invaluable archive of abnormal anatomy.

Macabre as it seemed to some, the study of deformity and debilitating pathologies enabled Thomas to create creatures that retained believable human characteristics. It made them all the more terrifying. The best of his beasts devolved from nature gone wrong.

The old woman offered a frail hand to Dr. Bradley. He took it between his own and clasped it warmly. Her face was majestic. Her brows were raised in an arc of optimism. The wrinkles earned over a lifetime were etched like a map of memories and trapped in a permanent smile. Her hair was white without a fleck of gray and mostly hidden by the black hat whose broad brim cast a subtle shadow across the bridge of her delicate nose. She had passed the time when age was easily determined. The distance between seventy-five and ninety-five is another lifetime. She might have been either. Bradley moved a chair aside and the visitor was wheeled to a sunny spot near the window. She lifted the veil. Her eyes were dark, almost black, but liquid and highlighted with a spark of light that seem to come from within rather than from the window.

"I'm sorry to arrive late," she said in a voice surprisingly husky for her petite stature. The wrinkles moved all at once and her face brightened into a smile.

To everyone but Thomas she was dressed in black. He saw subtle shades of gray. The pattern in the sweater. The hatband a tone lighter and different hue from the hat itself. The veil that partially covered her face was the nearest thing to real black. She wore a cashmere coat the color of charcoal. The collar was real animal fur, not seen much anymore. It was

black to all appearances even with a glossy shimmer of sunlight at the
crest.

Thomas didn't believe in black. He never used black pigment on his
palette. As long as light was present, there was no such thing as black. It
had no place in his art. Black didn't occur in nature.

Black is the absence of light.

Few ideas had revolutionized his perception more than that statement
tacked to his easel by Professor Andrus his first year at Art Institute.

As these thoughts fluttered aimlessly through his mind, he could not
have imagined how the true separation of light and dark was about to
change his life.

"Please go on," the old woman said, rolling long, graceful fingers toward Thomas like a benevolent monarch. Carver scowled at Cass and
looked to Bradley in search of an explanation.

"Since the new wing is dedicated to children," Thomas began again,
"I thought the motif of sick children from—"

"If you'll excuse me just a moment, Mr. Hall," Dr. Bradley interrupted. He stood beside the wheelchair. "Before we continue, I would like
to introduce our special guest. She is someone all of you know but none
of you has met."

He paused for a moment, then explained, "You know her as 'anonymous donor.'" A tangible magnetism gathered the energy in the room and
converged on the old woman. An audible gasp of wonder and appreciation swept around the table.

"I have known Miss Lucy Von Horn since our senior year in high
school."

Cass gasped. Von Horn. The old case. The founding family.

Miss Von Horn lifted the veil from her face and smiled at Dr. Bradley.
Long past but never forgotten memories flashed behind her dark eyes.

"I promised Miss Von Horn that her generosity in donating the
money to build the new Children's Wing would remain confidential," her
old friend continued, "but it was important she be here today to meet all
of you. Outside this room she wishes to remain anonymous."

Kimberly jumped up and clapped her hands. Cass joined the applause and felt a rush of relief that she had not succeeded in breaking into the locked box of Von Horn family treasures.

Carver acknowledged Miss Von Horn with an affirming nod and likewise put his hands together. Moments later the room was standing. Everyone applauding. Miss Von Horn waved a frail hand to stop them but the ovation continued. She bowed her head modestly.

Cass tried to constrain the emotions swelling up from her heart. They were impossible to stop. The generosity of this woman's gift would bring healing and health to thousands of children from generation to generation long after she was gone. *To a marvelous reward in the presence of God,* Cass thought to herself, knowing it was true. *Spend your life for something that outlasts it.* Cass remembered one of her grandfather's favorite sayings as the impact of this woman's charity filled her eyes with tears.

Thomas watched Cass. The vision of the woman in a halo of light with tears in her eyes contradicted his previous fantasy of sun and sea and Susan Cassidy in a scanty two-piece.

Miss Von Horn motioned again for the board to desist in their praises. "Oh no, no, please," she said at last. "Stop clapping and sit down." They didn't. She bowed her head and graciously acknowledged their acclamation. The clapping finally stopped and members of the board settled in their seats.

"Thank you so much. How embarrassing. Thank you. I certainly didn't come for that! Giving money is the easy part," she smiled. "It is the good we can do with the money that matters. What you've done here and all that's left to do is what will make a difference." She turned and spoke directly to Thomas. "Barry told me good things about you, Mr. Hall. The mural to be painted in the Healing Place is of very special importance to me. He suggested I should meet you myself."

Bradley shrugged his shoulders and grinned at Cass. It was suddenly perfectly clear to her. *There is only one person more powerful and influential in selecting the artist for the mural than Carver.* She thanked him with a kind of spiritual telepathy that she knew he understood and a smile he couldn't mistake. *The person more powerful than Carver is sitting in a wheelchair at the end of the room.*

"I am honored to meet you," Thomas said. "It's impressive what you've done here." The words did not come with accustomed ease. *Eye contact creates credibility.* Thomas had read that in Berger's "Bible." Oddly, he found himself shifting his eyes. He had the uneasy feeling that locking eyes with this old woman would give her access to his thoughts.

"Of all the good things that will happen here," Miss Von Horn said in reverent tones, "what happens in the Healing Place is closest to my heart. I am so anxious about that special wall, about what you propose to put there. When Barry told me you were coming today to share your vision of what it can be, I had to agree I needed to be here."

Thomas could usually lighten a conversation with a glib remark or a terse bit of humor. Nothing bubbled from his brain or danced to the end of his tongue.

"You saw the Healing Place," she asked, but it wasn't a question.

"We got here a little late," Thomas said, suddenly feeling guilty that she was visibly disappointed.

"Please go on," she said, and the tall man wheeled her closer to the banner of butcher paper.

Berger gave him a sly thumbs-up. The agent had moved to a hard-back chair against the opposite wall. Berger's encouragement boosted confidence and brought Thomas back. He turned to the swirling sketches.

"The new wing is dedicated to kids." A wrinkle furrowed the pale skin between the old woman's brows at his choice of words. "Children," Thomas corrected himself. "Children . . ." he said again and waited for the surge of spontaneous creativity. "Children are universal . . ." The fantasy came in an unexplainable rush. "So are sickness, disease, accidents and injuries. Children may be our greatest single source of joy."

"Do you have children, Mr. Hall?" Miss Von Horn's question nudged him off course. *Terse question or interrogation?* he wondered.

"Not . . . exactly."

"There is nothing ambiguous about fatherhood, Mr. Hall." She said it kindly, and some laughed softly. "You are a daddy or you aren't."

"What I mean is I have no children of my own." He held up an empty ring finger on his left hand and scrambled to get back on his game. "Not married." For some reason his eyes darted to Cass. She was looking straight at him. Their eyes locked for a fleeting moment.

"I've worked with a ton of kids in my studio. As models. My sister has kids." Miss Von Horn waited. "I'm a favorite uncle," he smiled and winked at Miss Von Horn. Cass closed her eyes and prayed. The uncle line was a serious stretch of the truth and Cass knew it. In her due diligence checking out the artist, she knew about his strained relationship with his sister.

Thomas missed her reaction. The wink put him back on a roll. Berger started breathing again.

"Children not only bring delight into our lives, they are the hope in the future." The 'favorite uncle' spewed the cliché with the conviction of a father of ten. "Sickness and disease threaten that future. They are the enemies of happiness. The dark lords of evil on a mission of destruction." The fanciful vision blossomed in his mind and he enhanced his rudimentary drawings.

The artist's ego, his pride and the challenge of the pitch shoved aside his earlier lack of interest in the project. Whether he would ever do it was no longer the issue. The skeptical old Miss Von Horn was there to test him. Game on! New challenge. Winning Miss Von Horn's heart and impressing the alluring woman by the window became the new goals. He ramped up his enthusiasm. His imagination soared. He would have the woman in the wheelchair eating out of his hand and the woman by the window dying to go on his boat.

The spontaneous creation continued. The children became warriors. Sickness was personified as dark lords of evil. The infirmities of youth were dragons with fire spewing from their nostrils. The castle became the fortress of St. Mark's. As Thomas sketched out his fantasy, he animated the story with expressive hands and broad dramatic gestures.

Berger read the faces of the board members. Some were enthralled. Others confused. Carver was focused on Miss Von Horn's reaction. His anxious look made it obvious that her opinion was the only one that mattered.

Miss Von Horn looked impressed but puzzled in the same expression. Berger tried to warn Thomas with a silent signal. It was too late. Thomas had crossed the mysterious bridge of his imagination. Not only was he immersed in the fanciful world transmogrifying on the wall, he believed in the brilliance of his creation.

"The whole mural is a grand depiction of the universal conflict between sickness and health," Thomas said with conviction. "Life and death. Joy and sorrow. Good and evil. All present. All represented in visual metaphor. All in the graphic language of children. Healthy children and children who are sick." He paused as a new idea took shape. "Over here we will add . . ." He sketched like he was projected at eighteen frames a second.

Kimberly Johnson clearly didn't have the slightest notion what Thomas Hall was talking about. Carver scowled at Cass as if reminding her that Hall was not HIS guy, she was the one dangling on the hook and *life has consequences.*

Miss Von Horn looked at Dr. Bradley. Her face puckered in an anxious expression. The old doctor raised one unruly brow and passed the ruffled look to Cass, who was staring at the fantasy epic emerging from the swirls of charcoal on the butcher paper stretching the width of the room.

An army of child warriors faced the dark forces of sickness and dragons of disease in a battle that seethed from opposite sides of the long paper mural. They overran the former flower children and collided where King Ludwig's castle fortress, with no resemblance to St. Mark's, rose from the edge of a rocky precipice in the center of what was clearly the rough layout for a remarkable piece of fantasy art. The evolution had been stunning.

Thomas backed away from the drawing. It was part of the show. He retreated to the farthest corner of the room and studied the sketch. He squinted his eyes. Everyone watched. No one doubted they were observing a genius at work. He bounced forward to the board. In a dozen deft strokes he added color, lines and shapes that brought a sense of movement to the coarse drawing.

It was not what Cass had expected but she recognized it was astounding. Thomas handed the markers to Cass and waited for an utterance of amazed admiration. She was rather more like the proverbial deer in the headlights.

He shifted his gaze to Miss Von Horn. Her expression was polite but cold and restrained. There was a long awkward moment. She shook her head disapprovingly. Like a bolt from the crossbow of a child warrior fighting evil lords behind him, something sharp jabbed his stomach. He waved dismissively at the rambling sketches. Apologetically. "It's one idea. More than I expected to share in a first meeting." He said it without a glimmer of humility.

"I'm sorry you didn't have time to visit the Healing Place," Miss Von Horn said. Her face was a frown of disappointment.

"I'm taking him to see it the moment we've finished," Cass said, choosing to interpret Miss Von Horn's comment as a tenuous approval.

"The idea of a Healing Place is brilliant," Thomas said, then turned from Miss Von Horn to those assembled. "Does anyone have a question? Any suggestions?" His eyes came back to Miss Von Horn.

The tall man rolled her closer to the drawings. The only sound was the purr of wire spokes brushing over the hem of the cashmere coat. The old woman narrowed her eyes and studied the fanciful creation.

People are programmed with a sense of how long certain intervals should last. The interval between a traffic light turning green and the driver in the car behind blasting his horn is less than three nanoseconds. In a movie, the interval of darkness between a fade to black and new image is practically embedded in our DNA. If the interval exceeds expectations by even a few seconds, people crane their necks to see if there is anyone in the projection booth.

No one knows how many floors two strangers in an elevator must pass before they exceed the interval of expectation between staring at the floor indicator light above the door in silence and feeling obligated to acknowledge the presence of another human being by speaking. If the elevator jerks to a stop between floors and the emergency light flashes red, the interval of expectation is probably less than two seconds.

The interval of silence a performer is allowed to take a breath or turn a page or find a note or regain composure has each its own precise allotted time. If silence or darkness or floundering or crying or searching or waiting exceeds the interval of expectation by even a second, the audience becomes uncomfortable. They buzz. Then chortle. The party to such a lapse in private conversation experiences a kind of emotional paralysis.

As far as anyone can tell, all of it is governed by some mystical cosmic clock that science cannot find. One thing is understood: In the delicate art of communication, the length of a pause before responding to a question is clue to the answer.

Miss Von Horn's contemplation continued. She exceeded the interval of expectation between a person looking at an artist's work and making a positive comment about it. The cosmic clock ticked. The deadline arrived, teetered on the brink of hope, then passed. Thomas waited with rose-colored angst. Berger's reassuring nod was predictable but did not soothe the artist.

The silence thickened. Breathing in the crowd became shallow lest any person be the one to breach Miss Von Horn's reverie.

"It's hard to catch the overall vision." Thomas was rarely so contrite but the silence was becoming visceral. "Up close like this it is just lines but—" Miss Von Horn's trembling hand cut him off. She lowered the lace across her face.

"Thank you for coming, Mr. Hall." The tall man turned the chair and started from the room. Cass crossed quickly and walked beside her.

"Today was only about exploring ideas," she said. "As Mr. Hall mentioned, he went a little farther today than any of us expected." The look she hurled at Thomas was a fireball from the catapult of the evil lords. "He agreed to come on short notice and has not had the benefit of our thinking. Your vision."

Miss Von Horn gripped the wheels and turned the chair around. She removed her hat and brushed a wild strand of white from her forehead. "You're obviously a brilliant artist, Mr. Hall. I loved comic books when I was a child. But you don't seem to understand what it is we are doing here. The new wing is dedicated to children. Sick children, crippled children, injured children and those dear children who need healing in their minds and hearts. St. Mark's is a Christian hospital for a reason." She rolled forward until the foot plates of the chair were over the toes of his shoes and pressed against his shin bones.

"Jesus healed the sick, but He also gives us hope. The Healing Place is a room filled with light. It is a place for children to get well, of course, but most of all to give them hope. He was the Light of the World, you know." The thought hung in the silence. "It seems to me a mural in a room filled with light and healing and hope should have something to do with Jesus."

Thomas suffered a stupor of thought. He felt paralyzed. Berger came over the hill in the nick of time like the cavalry in a John Wayne movie. His artist had been brilliant, as always, but this time he had pulled the wrong rabbit from the hat.

"That's a fantastic idea," Berger exuded. "That's exactly the vision Thomas needed to understand. It's perfect!" He dropped to one knee so Miss Von Horn did not need to look up. "Thomas can do that. To tell you the truth, he suggested we go that way," Berger lied. "I was the one who pushed the fantasy theme, so you shouldn't blame him."

The old woman's expression didn't even twitch.

Berger stammered on. "I thought, you know, with the stuff kids are into these days . . . but Jesus and healing the blind people. I mean. That's terrific! Nobody can paint Jesus like Thomas Hall." Berger opened the portfolio to examples of Thomas's pre-fantasy work from Art Institute. Two were photos of paintings inspired by the Dutch masters.

"I represent fourteen artists, Miss Von Horn, and I assure you Mr. Hall is the best. His mural for your Healing Place will be exactly right."

Cass noticed both she and Berger were looming over the tiny woman like vultures over roadkill. She stepped back and tugged on Berger's shoulder. Miss Von Horn continued to penetrate Thomas's soul. She seemed certain he had one even if he didn't know it.

"Do you believe in Jesus, Mr. Hall?" The interval between the question and Carver leaping to his feet was well within the limit of expectation.

"Whoa, whoa! Wait, we're not allowed to ask that kind of question. I'm sorry, Miss Von Horn, we just have to be so careful these days, but look . . ." His voice modulated to its authoritative timbre. "If Cass thinks this can work, let's have Mr. Hall put together a formal proposal. Illustrations along the line of . . ." the pause reflected his indifference to the historic Christian convention of St. Mark's, "something a little more Jesus-centered."

"That works," Berger said. "A development phase works for us."

Miss Von Horn had not taken her eyes from Thomas since her

pointed question. He avoided eye contact. He did not want this woman divining his thoughts. Miss Von Horn motioned for Thomas to lean down so their faces were close. The mystical point of light in her dark eyes cast a spell.

"Some call Jesus the 'Great Physician' because he healed the sick." Her voice was weak but unwavering. "It is a mistaken notion. Jesus was not a physician. He did not heal with medicine or herbs or surgery. He healed by the power of faith. Faith is what I want our children to find in the Healing Place. If children find faith, they will also find hope. Faith and hope, Mr. Hall, are what our mural needs to be about."

A memory beckoned from the windows or a silent voice called her name. She turned away. A splash of sunlight danced across her face. She closed her eyes for a moment, then looked back and smiled. "Can you do that?"

Every eye was focused on Thomas. He rose slowly. Her face followed him upward. Emotions collided. His mouth moved but no words came.

Berger put an arm around Thomas. "He can do that. There is no one who can paint Jesus better than Thomas Hall."

The old woman smiled and was about to go when a final thought animated the lines of her face. "Even if we have become so unsure of who we are that we cannot ask a man what he believes, you can be sure I will get the answer to my question when I see your drawings of our Lord and Savior."

CHAPTER

22

St. Mark's burned to the ground in the fire of 1906. It survived as an institution because the doctors and nurses were incredible. Patients were moved to private homes while the hospital was rebuilt. Can you even imagine? We've been expanding ever since." Cass narrated the history of the hospital as they passed through the long corridor that connected the boardroom with the new wing.

Thomas walked beside Cass. Berger followed a few steps behind. "It is more than three times the original size, and with the new Children's Wing it will be—" The history tour was interrupted by a nurse's assistant who pushed through the double-hinged doors with a woman on a gurney.

"So how long have you been at the hospital? Are you from here?" Thomas shifted his interest from history to historian.

"No. Indiana. It's been almost two years."

"Have you sailed under the Golden Gate yet?" Thomas asked.

Cass laughed softly. "I haven't even taken the tour of Alcatraz."

"There's a city ordinance that requires newcomers to sail under the bridge, you know." He tried to say it earnestly enough to make Cass think, at least for a fleeting moment, that he was serious. But then his poker face broke and his grin gave it away. "I know a guy with a brand-new boat. You're a law-abiding citizen, right?" She brushed his flirtation aside with a clumsy laugh and continued the tour.

"As I started to explain, the hospital is much bigger now than the original and today of course St. Mark's is considered one of the finest facilities of its kind west of Mayo Clinic. Even better than Stanford, we think." She added the comment about Stanford with a clandestine twinkle that made it sound like the passing of top-secret information. "Makes me feel like a traitor."

Thomas had come prepared to dislike this woman and discount the project. The first part wasn't working.

"Put these on, please," Cass said as she pulled three fluorescent orange safety helmets from a shelf. "The official construction zone begins with the break in the old wall. The new wing is connected by the sky bridge. You can see it there." She pointed through a window in the old wall. "OSHA requires hard hats once we cross this line." There was a fat yellow line painted on the floor. Cass stepped across and fastened the strap to her safety helmet in one graceful move.

Berger's helmet was too small and rode high on his head like a clown's joke. He looked ridiculous. He followed Cass across the line.

Thomas dangled the bright orange hat from a finger. "Whoever picked this color should be put in front of a firing squad," he said.

"Put it on anyway," Cass giggled. Her laugh was melodic and mostly in her throat. "I'm excited for you to see the Healing Place. You'll be surprised." She let the promise of something unexpected hang. "There's a lot I didn't explain to Mr. Berger."

"*Mr.* Berger? Do I seem that old? Just call me Frank. Please."

Thomas stood with the hat dangling at the end of the chin strap. "I'm afraid I don't have time for a tour right now."

"We got plenty of time," Berger encouraged. "We're in the same car. Put your hat on."

"It will only take few minutes," Cass promised. "We don't need to tour the whole wing. I just want you to see the wall in the Healing Place and get a feel for what's possible."

Thomas rolled the hard hat between his fingers like a basketball—or cannon ball—and stared at the yellow line. In his ever-active imagination he thought of William Travis at the Alamo and the line drawn in the sand. *Those willing to stay and die step across the line.*

"Look. I appreciate your confidence in me and in my art, but, uh . . ." He searched for a credible cool way to say it. There wasn't one. "I'm going to pass on this project."

"Pass? What do you mean 'pass'?" Cass's tone suggested she knew what it meant but hoped she was wrong.

"I'm not the right artist for your project."

"What are you talking about?" Berger said, stepping back across the line. "You're perfect for it."

"I'm not. It's just not a project I'm interested in doing."

"You don't know that! It's not what you thought! All they're asking for right now is a few sketches."

Thomas hung the fluorescent helmet on a stub of rebar sticking out from the wall.

"If it's about budget . . ." Cass turned to Berger. "The numbers we discussed on the phone were ballpark. I'm sure we can make adjustments."

"It's not about that," Thomas said. "Not for me, at least." He fired a dart at Berger, who was at the moment a self-serving traitor. "There are a bunch of guys I know who can do a project like this. Piece of cake."

"None of them can do what you can do. I took three months sorting through your 'bunch of guys' and . . . you heard Miss Von Horn. We need a masterpiece."

"How do you know that I'll be able to . . . ?" Thomas wanted to skip the dance. Not possible.

"Before today I was going by pure instinct. Then I saw what you—"

"You're wrong. Trust me when I tell you: I am not the guy for your healing room."

"At least let me show you the Healing Place," she implored. Cass was tall and elegant in the half-light of the window. Thomas was not thinking about a room for sick kids. He was wondering how he was going to untangle the tension, get her back on his side, and get her out on his boat. His daydream melted when Cass gave away her secret. "The wall is ninety feet wide."

"Now you tempt me."

"It will last five hundred years."

"Unless there's another fire." *Clever line.* "Let's talk about sailing under the Golden Gate Bridge."

Her expression turned stormy. "If you had any idea what I've gone through to persuade the board to even consider a fantasy artist." She bit down hard on the word *fantasy.*

"I don't think the board has anything to say about it."

"I didn't know about Miss Von Horn until today."

Berger saw the breach and jumped in. "That makes it easier, Tommy. Good grief, man! Way better for us. You make the old gal happy with a few sketches and she'll give you carte blanche. At that point I negotiate a killer deal and you knock it out in a couple of months."

Thomas patted his heart. "Art has to come from here, man." He pounded his stomach with a clenched fist. "And here." He fluttered the fingers on both hands. "These guys have to be anxious beyond my control."

Cass grew ashen and spoke to Berger with her hands as much as her mouth. "When we talked you promised me you would deliver the artist if I was able to—"

"I know. I know."

"On the strength of that promise I put my job on the line." She looked at Berger but was speaking to Thomas. "That's how much I believe in the talent of Thomas Hall."

"How long have you two been talking about this?" Thomas asked. Neither answered.

"I expect you to keep that commitment," Cass said. Her words teetered on the edge of a threat.

"We're good. Don't worry. It'll be fine," Berger replied. "Tommy and I just need to talk. We'll sort it out." Berger handed Cass his clown hat and tugged Thomas toward the door. Thomas offered his hand to Cass. She shook it but he held onto her hand as he spoke.

"You understand, I hope, any promises that were made were made without me. Agents forget we have brains of our own. They prefer trained monkeys as clients, but the market for monkeys that paint is small." Cass smiled. Thomas felt a subtle release of tension. "In any event, look, I am sorry he's put you in a thorny situation."

"It's only 'thorny' if you turn me down."

"I've already turned you down." He intended glib humor. Cass pulled her hand away. "I'm guessing this is not the best time to invite you out on my boat?"

Her face flushed crimson. "You have unusual talent, Mr. Hall."

"Is that a 'maybe' you'll go on my boat?"

"You're wasting your talent on most of what you do."

"You're the expert on what I do?"

"You might be surprised how well I know what you do. I know your work well enough to know you're not as good as you think you are or ought to be because you've coasted since you left Art Institute."

"Why doesn't that sound like a compliment?"

"I don't think you've begun to plumb the depths of your real capacity."

His instincts cried, *Slice her in small pieces.* His libido said, *Stay cool.* Thomas watched the tension rising in her face. Small blue veins bulged on the side of her neck and marked her pulse. The more agitated she became, the more attractive she seemed.

"This project needs the kind of classic art you were doing before you finished at Art Institute. Before you . . ." she picked the words deliberately, "before you sold out to the whole commercial quick and dirty."

"You sound like one of my professors."

"I share Dr. Andrus's disappointment." Thomas was startled that Cass knew the name of his former professor. There was a wooden plaque on the wall of the art room with a quote from *Hamlet*. It came to mind in the moment.

"'To thine own self be true,'" Thomas grinned, knowing that in truth he rarely was. He had read the crib notes, not the play. The rest of Shakespeare's famous line could not wallow free of murky memory.

"'And it must follow as the night the day, Thou canst not then be false to any man,'" Cass finished it.

"If you're already disappointed, seems to me no harm, no foul." Thomas saluted with a single finger and walked away.

"Do you believe in destiny, Mr. Hall?" Thomas turned and looked back when Cass said it. "I can't explain why I'm so sure you are supposed to do this. Right now it is the frankly the *last* thing I would look forward to, but . . ." she paused to think it through, "I believe things happen for a reason. Have you considered the possibility you might be passing up the one project that will define who you are? Who you are destined to be?"

Thomas felt a fanciful urge to walk over to Cass, put his arms around her, and say, "As you wish," as if he were Westley and she were Buttercup and the moment had morphed into a scene from *The Princess Bride.* The fantasy passed and he turned to go.

"Have you considered this is something God wants you to do?" Cass asked.

For all your due diligence, Ms. Cassidy, it's obvious you don't know Thomas Hall at all. The thought went with him as he stepped through the portal and disappeared.

Berger gave Cass a reassuring wave and followed Thomas. "No worries. I'll talk to him. It's going to be okay." He held a thumb to his ear and pinky to his lips and mouthed the words, *I'll call you.*

CHAPTER

23

I'M DONE."

"Good riddance."

"I mean it!"

"So do I!"

"You don't want an agent, you want a damned Irish Setter!"

Thomas scowled at Berger when he looked right for oncoming traffic before swinging south on Pacific Coast Highway. It was not their first fight.

"I spend three cockeyed weeks thrashing through briars and thistles to find you a gig, hold it in place, set you up like a kid with a canary in a cage, and you waltz in and shoot the damn bird." Berger's face puffed up in reddish splotches whenever he was angry.

Nouns made pictures in Thomas's head. Berger's metaphor conjured up a curious composition. "You are almost poetic."

"I'm serious, Tommy! I've had it! That was total betrayal! You never turn on your agent in front of a client. What the hell were you thinking?"

"You dragged me into this deal totally blind. You didn't tell me squat about what they really wanted. Jesus? Give me a break!"

"The old woman surprised everybody. Even Cass."

"Really? You scheduled a presentation and all but signed a contract before you had any real fix on what it was about!"

"You want to wallow in the details? Do you? You hate details. You want me to call you every ten minutes and get permission to find you work? It bugs you when I call." Berger swiped a hand across his forehead and squeezed the bridge of his nose as if willing away a headache. "Whenever I *have* to talk to you and try to schedule time, you whine about me violating your precious 'creative seclusion.' No! This time . . . this time I mean it. I'm done!"

Thomas stepped on the brake.

Berger's jeremiad was upstaged by a plump woman with skin the color and texture of old boots. She stood in the road and waved a hand-held stop sign. She wore scuffed-up Wolverines that matched her face and a DOT standard-issue reflective vest. Vivid chartreuse with fluorescent orange stripes. Thomas stopped the Mercedes.

"What's the holdup?"

"Puttin' up a temporary guardrail. Some idiot went over the side a few days back. Ripped out a whole section."

"Why temporary?"

"They ain't been able to get the car up yet."

Thomas arched up in his seat to get a glimpse of the activity going on. He imagined the wreckage at the bottom.

"How long will it be?"

"Pilot truck already left the other end."

"You wanna know the other reason I'm dropping you as a client?" Berger said, oblivious to the woman. Thomas came back from the bottom of the cliff.

"Shhhh, I'm in creative seclusion." Thomas slipped the car into park and took a deep breath.

"You are such a jackass!"

A sailboat just outside the Golden Gate rode up and over a rolling swell. Thomas watched as the lithe little craft tacked hard into the wind. He closed his eyes and let his head fall back against the soft leather of the headrest.

"Scale of ten, Frank. My chance of getting Susan Cassidy out on my boat?"

"The boat is the other damn thing. You cannot afford that boat!"

"Payments don't start for ninety days and by then you'll have closed the Heavy Metal Casino deal in Vegas." Berger shook his head and looked out to sea. "Come on. You said it yourself!"

"It's never done until it's done. Never done 'til the check clears the bank."

"You said 'good as done.'"

"I said 'reasonably good.'"

"You said they loved my sketches and that my ideas for the ceiling in the rotunda blew Harvey's mind."

"Harvey thinks you walk on water."

"So it's a done deal!" Thomas slapped his shoulder.

"Even with the Vegas project, and even if you can afford to make the payments, that's not the point."

"So what is 'the point,' Frank?" Thomas found the conversation irksome and couldn't resist baiting him.

"You moan because I don't yap to you about every little conversation; then you go off and buy a sailboat without saying boo."

"I talked to you."

"You said you were looking at sailboats."

"You always hear what you want to hear," Thomas grinned, then, mimicking the nasal twang of a medical professional, "Selective hearing is a gift, Mr. Hall."

Berger opened the door and got out of the car.

"Stay in your car, sir." It was the woman with boot leather for skin.

"What are you doing?" Thomas laughed.

Berger put both hands on the top of the door and leaned in like a lawyer making a closing argument in a murder trial. "I am your agent-slash-manager. That's what you wanted. That's what you needed. That was our agreement! What does a manager do, Tommy? Hmmm? What?"

"If the manager doesn't get back in the car, he is going to be walking twenty-six miles home." Thomas grinned. Boot Face walked toward Berger holding her stop sign in both hands like a medieval beheading axe. Berger got back in the car.

"The role of a manager is to manage! You're the artist. You're the creative guy. You're the radiant star. The guy who earns the money. The magician who works the magic. Yeah! Okay. Fine, but you don't have a single blasted brain cell in the left side of your head. Zippo, nada, empty, nothing! That's why you need a manager."

"You believe that right-brain, left-brain nonsense?"

"You and I are the best evidence in the world." Berger took a breath. "Logic. Facts. Order. Numbers. Reality. That's what I do. It's right in the contract. I find the work. I negotiate the deals. I manage the money, and all you have to do is paint the damn pictures."

Berger had crossed the line. His tirade was no longer amusing.

"ALL I have to do?" Thomas's frustration level was rising.

"I'm not saying left is better. The thing that makes you brilliant as an artist is what makes you so hair-brained when it comes to money."

Whatever mysterious neurology gave Thomas a fantasy kingdom inside his head where he could go whenever he wanted, it engaged and beamed him up. He tuned Berger out. What little there was of Thomas's left brain shut down and a daydream appeared on the other side of the midline.

He pushed the tiller to starboard. He was just outside the Golden Gate. The sloop turned into an offshore breeze and headed south. Susan Cassidy lounged on the bow deck. For a fleeting moment she wore a bikini. A flash of sunlight. They passed through a fog and it was not a swimsuit at all. No bikini, two piece or one piece. The woman wore a baggy sweat suit with a hood hiding all her beauty, charm and figure. Just enough of her face showed so he could see her confident smirk. Who controlled a man's daydream anyway? Didn't seem right.

"Hey." The voice was punctuated by a slap on the right front fender. The gorgeous girl in the sweat suit was the woman in the DOT vest flaunting colors that did not occur in nature. "You need to go! Get moving." In the same instant the driver behind him punched the horn. He was past the interval of expectation by almost two seconds. *Courteous driver.*

Thomas slipped the Mercedes into gear and accelerated between two rows of orange cones. "You weren't even listening!" Berger griped.

Thomas smiled. Being with Cass on his sailboat had put him in a good mood. "Of course I was."

"That's another thing. You do that to me all the time."

"Well, you quit, so now you don't have to worry about it."

"You know I'm not quitting. At least not until I convince you that you have got to do the St. Mark's project."

"I'm not going to do it."

"I gave my word, Tommy!" Berger emphasized his frustration by swearing loudly.

The profane use of the Lord's name in conversation had always been to Thomas just one of fifty-five hundred other words in the average vocabulary. Berger used it all the time and Thomas never noticed. Until now. The irreverence assaulted his ears. The name, spoken as an expletive, hung in the air as if the sound waves had solidified. An image of the word etched itself on the back of his brain in blazing red letters.

"Yeah! That's exactly my point," Thomas said. "I am the last guy they should want to paint a picture of . . . of Him."

Berger was confused. The word had slipped from his lips with such habit he didn't make the connection. The religious aspect of the project had never crossed the agent's mind.

"There's nothing in the universe, real or imagined, that you can't paint."

"Yeah. Remember? It's ALL I do."

"I didn't mean that the way it sounded."

Thomas and Berger couldn't count how many times Berger had dropped Thomas as a client or Thomas had fired Berger as his "agent-slash-manager." Each loved and loathed the other, depending on the time and circumstance. They were tethered in a unity of opposition.

Thomas let Berger's almost-apology slip by without comment. Miss Von Horn was in his head and looking for his soul, asking him if he believed in Jesus. Thomas rolled his neck until it cracked. "Can you imagine where I could go with a character like Jesus?" he mused.

Berger's face brightened. The partition between his anger and laughter was always gossamer thin. "He'd probably end up looking a lot like Captain Marvel," Berger chortled.

"At least."

"SHAZAM! Sparks from the ends of his fingers and some crippled guy chucks his crutches and does a Michael Jackson moon walk!" Berger could be comical on rare occasions. Thomas saw a comic book cover in his head. Their laughter got louder and the lunacy of Jesus as superhero escalated in a banter of irreverent quips and sacrilegious humor.

"Okay, look. Here's what I'll do," Thomas said as he accelerated across the double yellow to pass a banged-up Camaro moving slowly so surfers could check out the waves. "I am NOT going to do the project, so don't even go there, but I will throw together a few token sketches. Get you off the hook. Fair enough?"

"You won't sabotage it with crummy stuff?"

"You want me to recite the Andrus pledge again?" he grinned.

"Just don't close the door on St. Mark's, Tommy. Okay?"

"It's already closed but I'll leave it unlocked."

"The one thing I've learned in fourteen years of representing artists, Tommy, is you NEVER turn anything down. Things happen. People change."

"Tastes evolve." Thomas finished the familiar speech. "That makes a hundred and one."

"She could be right, you know."

"About what?" He scanned the earlier conversation. "You mean God wants me to do this?" Repeating the words troubled him.

"No, no. Not that. The St. Mark's project could be a milestone for your career. The best projects are always the toughest to land."

"You've landed me some good ones, buddy. I'll give you that," Thomas admitted.

"You have no idea what it takes or what I've gone through to get us to where we are with this St. Mark's thing."

"You're the best. What can I say?"

Berger chuckled to himself with a kind of modest arrogance. "They ought to put me in the *Guinness Book of World Records*." Berger stayed so focused on his clients that Thomas liked it when he allowed a rare moment to talk about himself. "I mean, think about it! I'm a Jew who sold an agnostic artist to a coddle of Christians to paint a picture of Jesus."

"You told them I was agnostic?"

"Of course not."

"Frank?" *Timing is the secret of humor.* "You're Jewish?"

"Total jackass!"

CHAPTER

24

CASS SAT BESIDE CHRISTINA'S bed and held her good hand. The girl was asleep.

Cass had spent the morning with Miss Von Horn. The old woman was more excited to open the curious old trunk than Cass had been. J. Winston Von Horn was her grandfather and the founder of St. Mark's. They tittered like schoolgirls from a Nancy Drew adventure as they watched the Tall Man drill the lock. The lock fell away and he opened the box.

Everything was perfectly preserved. On top was a stack of photographs from the turn of the century. The city. The hospital. Winston on his world travels. Miss Von Horn's father as a boy, and the grandmother she had never seen. There were bound bundles of building plans, contracts, letters and newspaper clippings. At the bottom they found the personal journal of J. Winston Von Horn.

His granddaughter lifted it from the box with reverence. "We knew he kept a journal of his adventures," she said, "but we thought it had been lost." Without warning she embraced Cass, who was sitting beside her. "Thank you," she said.

Whatever the importance of the discovery for the history she was writing for St. Mark's, in the days to come Cass would discover that the real treasure of the long-lost chest was the friendship forged with Miss Von Horn.

. . .

The child's eyes fluttered open. Dr. Namkung had finally lowered the pain medication, so Cass's daily visits involved more than sitting by the girl while she slept.

"You doing good today?" Cass asked. Christina nodded. They talked for a while. The pain. The casts on both her legs. The peeling skin. Bandages. Hospital food. Their secret stash of treats. The stuffed animal Cass had bought in the gift boutique and given her the day before. Cass was relieved to see Christina out of the medicated fog that usually enveloped her.

"Her name is Gloria."

"That's a perfect name," Cass said, not knowing why. "I'll bring you a surprise tomorrow. What would you like?"

"If I say, it won't be a surprise."

"Oh. That's right." Christina lifted Gloria and looked at her a long time.

"Have you seen my violin?" Christina asked. Her voice seemed stronger than it had been since Cass began her visits. Since Cass became the only family the child had as far as anyone could discover.

"Your violin?" Cass didn't know what she was talking about.

"It's my mother's."

"Where is it, sweetie?"

"In the car." A reminder of the horror that would forever twist this child's dreams into nightmares cracked Cass's heart.

"I'm not sure what they did with it, but I'll find out, okay?"

"Okay." Christina turned her head toward the window, revealing scar tissue Cass had not seen before.

The duty nurse came in. "Time for your bath, darlin'. Visitors out!" She winked at Cass and ejected her with a jerk of a thumb over her shoulder.

"Does she have to go?"

"I'll be back. I'd rather stay with you all day, but I've got to do my job some of the time."

"Will you pray with me before you go?"

The duty nurse raised drawn-on brows and backed through the swinging door so they could be alone.

CHAPTER

25

Thomas dropped Berger in Burlingame and drove back to Marin County. The sun was a softly glowing circle in the swirl of fog that slithered under the Golden Gate like a mischievous wraith. Their skirmish had ended well, as they usually did.

Thomas saw the smoke from the outside northbound lane of the Golden Gate Bridge. It twisted skyward in a smudge of gray peppered with firefly embers and swirling black particles of debris.

At the bottom of the Sausalito exit he turned right onto Bird Haven and was blown off the road by the blast of dual-powered air horns only twenty yards behind. He swerved to the shoulder and jammed the brakes. The car skidded in the gravel as the fire engine blew past him at sixty miles an hour.

The truck careened over the abandoned railroad spur and turned right on Harbor Road. Bony fingers gripped Thomas's stomach. There were only three buildings on the south end of Harbor Road. His studio was one of them.

A pumper truck, fire-engine red with a *WHOP, WHOP* siren like Italian police, was right behind. It looked like the adult version of a toy Thomas had played with as a kid. Before blood had taken its place as his favorite color in the family of crimson hues, he had loved fire-engine red.

He hit the accelerator and swung in behind the emergency vehicles. Past the yacht club and over Bayshore Drive.

A police car pulled across the road as the emergency vehicle passed. Thomas stopped. The rooftop bar flashed yellow and blue. A female officer stepped from the car. She wore a black uniform and sunglasses even though the light was almost gone. She waved Thomas to an unpaved road on the right.

"I need to get through!" he cried.

"Pull to the right, sir!"

"Where's the fire? My place is—"

"They've got it covered, sir. Now please move your vehicle. We've got an ambulance coming in."

Thomas stood on the seat of the open Mercedes but still wasn't tall enough to see over the clutter of buildings that blocked his view of the fire. The policewoman pointed to a patch of gravel leading to the right. She was close enough that he could read her tag. Nancy Webber.

"Officer Webber, my name is Thomas Hall and I—"

"Move your car now, sir. NOW! Or I will have it pushed out of the way." Thomas imagined the SLK-350 being pushed sideways by the angry steel snout protruding from Webber's cruiser.

"What's on fire?" An intuitive sense of dread shrieked louder than the yelping siren of the ambulance that was airborne as it hurdled the hump of abandoned track. "Is it all the way to the end?"

The sound of the ambulance injected Nancy Webber with 91 octane. She was screeching. "MOVE YOUR CAR!"

"You've gotta let me through. I think it's my place that's burning."

Webber slapped the windshield of the SLK-350 with a black leather hand. When she scowled, her too-big-for-her-face reflective Ray Ban Aviators made her look like a bug.

The service road ran back across the rail spur to a fenced yard behind Blue Haven Boat Repair. *Officious jerk,* Thomas mumbled to himself and smoked all four Michelins in a three-point turn. He powered the Mercedes onto the muddy road, bottoming out when he crossed the rails. He skidded to a stop on the other side, bounded from the car and scrambled up the hump of crushed rock undergirding the abandoned rail spur. He checked to make sure his nemesis was out of sight. She was abusing her authority on the next poor sap desperate to get past.

Thomas sprinted south. He mumbled a description of the female cop in words he hadn't thought of since the locker room in high school. The rush of angry expletives relieved the rising anxiety.

He set his stride and landed on every other railroad tie. The ties were slick with oozing creosote. He slipped and almost fell. When he reached the row of warehouses that fronted Harbor Road he dropped into the hollow between the tracks and the bank of landfill.

A finger of fog enticed by the stagnant damp slithered inland. It broke in frantic swirls and grabbed at his ankles as he sloshed across the hollow. He used his hands as claws to ascend the steep bank on the opposite side.

The row of condemned buildings blocked his view of the flames, but he knew the fire was dangerously close to the studio. The air was thick with the acrid stench of burning coal tar.

In the few seconds it took Thomas to get from the drainage slough to the front of the warehouses, he was consumed by an inner pleading. In his angst he had no time to wonder to whom he was begging that the disaster might not be.

He stumbled through a cluttered gap between the rusted-steel buildings. The gloom thickened, making it hard to see. Near the end of the alley his left leg smacked into an engine block hidden in a tangle of weeds. His other foot flew forward and landed on an L-shape flange of three-quarter-inch plate that flipped under and away. His ankle twisted. His legs collapsed. As he was thrust forward, he reached out to break the fall. His hand ripped open on a ragged edge of corroded iron and he landed on his side in a mound of rusted junk. His head struck the right-side wall of corrugated steel.

Scrambling up again, Thomas limped to the opening between the buildings. The pain in his head and hand was numbed by the rush of adrenaline. Dusk had yielded to night. In a slow-motion dream Thomas saw the reflection of flames on wet pavement as he hobbled the last few steps.

It was what he'd imagined in his darkest dread. The shock of the burning reality was indescribable. His studio was on fire!

· · ·

The structure on the waterfront had been built in 1931 as a processing plant for fish. It was small for the purpose but thrived as a business over three generations by the hard work and sacrifice of a single family.

Tony DeMillos had immigrated to California in 1922. He worked as a fisherman for nine years, living on his boat and saving every penny. His third son was born the year he opened his business. The company continued until the early seventies, when it was targeted by a militant group of environmentalists opposed to everything human. The battle went on for a decade. In the end the DeMillos family lost. The business was closed and the building shut down.

The Fish Cannery, as it was known, was a particularly sensitive site. The north wall rested on a foundation of pilings pounded into the harbor floor. The water lapped against the outer wall, allowing boats direct access to the lower level. The channel passed through a set of grated iron doors that rolled open on a track running along the top.

Such convenient access to the bay was no longer allowed. Two different entrepreneurs proposed innovative ideas for redevelopment, but both plans were blocked by environmentalists and rejected by the planning commission. The building was used for storage until 1999.

A new generation of activists arrived: SAVE THE SEALS. The latest breed of zealots were opposed to trucks moving goods in and out of the warehouse and staged demonstrations demanding that the building be condemned. They succeeded on a frail technicality over electrical codes. The Fish Cannery sat empty and abandoned for twelve years.

The timing of Thomas's move to Sausalito was serendipitous. Good luck, good karma and Thomas's irrational sense of entitlement converged. Pure and simple.

Two grizzled harridans from the days of Haight-Ashbury sat on the city council as self-appointed guardians of the kind of insane decisions that enabled SAVE THE SEALS to oppose everything. When those two were finally defeated, the waterfront was approved for redevelopment on an angrily protested initiative that slipped by on a vote of five to four.

For all the other troubles and disappointments of his childhood, in all things related to his art and talent Thomas felt unbelievably lucky. Destined to live a charmed life. He gave no thought to *by whom* or to what purpose—if there were a purpose. He had talent. He felt gifted, lucky and entitled.

He was nine years old when he realized he had a talent that made him different and gave him an advantage over other kids his age. "All men may be created equal," he quipped at one press conference, "but some can draw WAY better than others!" He embraced acclaim as inevitable; "the will of the gods" was his waggish answer to questions about his talent. Thomas never paused to considered which "gods" had singled him out for such beneficence.

• • •

A light rain was falling. The gusting wind from the north bay was uncomfortably cold. Floodlights on scissor arms above the fire trucks painted the scene in white shapes and black shadows with splashes of retroreflective yellow.

Thomas watched as firefighters soaked a ruin of smoldering timbers. He stared at the ragged black hole in the west side of his studio and shuddered with a disquieting sense of uncertainty. For the first time since he had left home as a teenager, he felt vulnerable. Violated. Like the gods of his cosmic destiny had been asleep at the switch. *How could this happen?*

"You're lucky!" The buoyant optimism of the voice was oddly out of place. The firefighter removed his helmet and pushed the Nomex Hood to a clump at the nape of his neck. He wiped his forehead with a red bandanna and said, "Electric spark in these old wooden buildings like lighting a newspaper with a blowtorch," he grinned.

"I'm so careful about that. I don't understand how . . ."

"You're lucky. We don't save 'em very often. Not these old ones."

"I'm grateful. Thank you."

The man acknowledged the appreciation with a nod and chuckled. "Yeah, well, that's what they pay us for. Guy you oughtta thank is the jogger who called it in. She musta run past a couple minutes after whoever it was lit it up."

"What do you mean 'lit it up'?"

The firefighter looked flustered for a moment, as if it were not his place to explain, but he finally said, "It was arson."

"Arson! What? No. Who would . . . are you sure?"

"I'll show you." Thomas followed the firefighter along the blackened side of the building. "You just get divorced?"

"No. I've never been married. Why? What do you mean?"

"Guy last week lost his house. Dumped his wife for some young hottie, and his ex-mother-in-law set his house on fire. Middle of the night. Gone. Burned to the ground."

The firefighter unbuttoned his insulated canvas coat. A chain of D-ring carabiners jingled in rhythm with his stride. He stopped at a thick clump of charred oleanders not far from the edge of the burned-out hole. He pushed sooty branches aside and nudged a gas can with the steel toe of his insulated rubber boot.

"That's unbelievable," Thomas exclaimed.

"Yeah. Funny thing is, looks like they want to be sure you know this ain't no accident."

Thomas squatted and poked at the can with a stick.

"No, no. Need to leave that for the inspector."

Thomas felt paralyzed.

"So," the firefighter went on, "if you ain't got an ex-mother-in-law, who do you know that hates you?"

CHAPTER

26

THOMAS HAD MADE AN OFFER to lease the abandoned Fish Cannery with an option to buy. It was accepted by the trustees of the DeMillos estate. He submitted a plan to convert the old factory into an art studio with an apartment attached. He applied for a building permit and trouble began.

He had expected opposition from the environmental activists called SAVE THE SEALS. But he had underestimated their radical passion to keep human beings away from harbor seals and other creatures and crustaceans living along the shoreline. Their goal to reestablish the primitive shoreline of Richardson Bay was absurd. Beginning with Sausalito Harbor, they wanted no human habitation within fifty yards of the water.

The day Thomas filed for his building permit, soldiers from SAVE THE SEALS found a dead sea lion caught in the grated doors of the boat channel under the Fish Cannery. He became a target. STS activists passed out flyers condemning him as "the man who murders seals."

The permitting process took fourteen months. Thomas appeared repeatedly before the city planners. Approvals hung on a citizen's complaint about the skylight that opened the loft to north light.

The planning commission had accepted the skylight as planned and sent it back to the city council for final approval. There was standing room only on the day of the hearing. Thomas was in the front row. Berger had promised to be there but was in preliminary discussions with the Science Museum about the planned renovation.

The hysterical objection came from Ada Kanster. Kanster spoke to the mayor and six members of the city council from the speaker's podium that faced them. She wept as she explained how Thomas Hall's project would destroy her life. Kanster lived in a house on the hills west of the harbor. She argued that the skylight on the proposed studio was going to reflect "blinding sunlight" into her bedroom, disrupt "the rhythm of her life" and cause life-threatening health problems. Kanster was an active member of SAVE THE SEALS.

The council listened respectfully. One woman covered her mouth to hide a smile over Kanster's ludicrous quarrel. The plastic nameplate tagged the councilman next to the mayor as Phillip Marston. He weighed 320 pounds bone dry and had been on the council since Gaspar de Portola had discovered San Francisco Bay. At least it seemed that long. He held eye contact with Kanster for her entire rant. She ended it in tears.

"I'm not sure I understand why sunlight is so troublesome during the day," Marston said.

The woman looked toward the SAVE THE SEALS activists for support. She twisted her face in a sorrowful wrench to make her twisting of the truth less evident. "I have a job working swing shift and need to sleep during the day."

Marston pinched a chunk of chocolate doughnut from a box of Krispy Kremes and put it in his mouth. The fat man savored the wad of sugared dough as if tasting fine wine, then sent a clog of cholesterol to his great aorta in a single gulp. Thomas wondered if Marston's girth and lack of personal discipline made it hard for members of the council to take him seriously. Would his interrogating Kanster skew them in her favor?

Marston held up a book with a picture of a solar explosion taken by the Hubble telescope on the cover. It looked like an effects shot from a Michael Bay movie. The book's title, *Helio Astronomy*, was printed in bright blue.

"Are you familiar with helio astronomy, Mrs. Kanster?"

"*MS.* Kanster!" The woman scowled. "I've asked you a thousand times to call me Ms. I am NOT a MRS. anything!"

"MS. Kanster." Marston grinned without disguising his distaste for the Kanster ilk of women still clinging to the feminism of the nineties. Marston glanced at Thomas. *Did he just wink? I love this guy!* Marston's thick fingers scooped off another lump of donut. It went into his mouth as the words came out.

"Helio astronomy is the study of the sun," Marston continued. Kanster's tongue flicked across her thin lip. A straggle of hair escaped her rubber-band bound ponytail. She pushed it behind her ear. It was the color of river mud.

Marston waved the book. "The relative position of the earth's axis in relationship to the sun changes every day. It seems to us the sun is moving, but of course we're the ones wobbling around." He licked a residue of sugar from his index finger as if Ms. Kanster needed a moment to follow his brilliant discourse.

She didn't. She was almost yelling. "You have a responsibility to make sure that permissions granted one person do not impinge on the rights of another. It seems to me—it seems to all of us . . ." Kanster's arm swept over the gaggle of protestors to her left. A hammock of fat hanging where a triceps should have been wobbled like the planet off its axis. Marston shuffled his notes, found the one he wanted and interrupted.

"You're missing my point, Ms. Kanster. The angle of light coming from the sun moves. Point 1287 degrees a day, to be exact. Even if Mr. Hall were determined to torture you by beaming sunlight into your bedroom, he could do it only once a year for thirty-nine hours, nine days before the September equinox. And historically," Marston waved a photocopy of what Thomas assumed was a page from an almanac, "those days are overcast 54 percent of the time."

The plans with the skylight were approved on a vote of 6–1. *The will of the gods.* The victory affirmed his sense of entitlement rather than a notion of humility or gratitude. He thanked Marston and promised to support his reelection. *Quid pro quo. The way of the world.*

"It's got nothing to do with your windows," Marston said. "They don't want you there at all. Just more of the same old crap these SAVE THE SEALS idiots been trying to pull forever. Worry about seals and slugs and to hell with people."

Kanster was waiting for Thomas at the bottom of the stairs. Protestors wearing SAVE THE SEALS T-shirts clogged the hallway from the stairs to the exit, bearing signs that proclaimed: *SEALS WERE HERE FIRST.*

The security guard at the main door cast a cautious eye as Thomas came down the steps and was forced to push a pathway through the swarm. Protestors bumped, jostled and intimidated him.

At the end of the gauntlet Kanster blocked his way. Standing at the podium with an unsympathetic council glaring down on her, she had seemed weak. Even frightened. Face-to-face she was menacing. Her head was narrow, her jawbone longer than it should have been. From a distance her tanned face appeared smooth. Nine inches from her nose Thomas could see it was dry and cracked like the surface of an old painting. *Not something you'd hang in the main gallery. Most likely kept in storage. Maybe the garage.*

"You think you've won, but this is a long way from over," she hissed. "That building should not be there in the first place." She stepped aside to let Thomas pass but added in a hoarse whisper, "I wouldn't spend a lot of money fixing it up if I were you."

CHAPTER

27

THE DAMAGE LOOKED WORSE than it was. By midnight the hole in the west wall was covered by construction-grade plastic. The flame had not reached the loft or burned any art. Smoke damage could not be assessed immediately but the rain stopped, the wind shifted and the acrid stench of wet smoke was carried out to sea. *Perhaps his gods had only been distracted. Perhaps they were back.*

The confrontation with Kanster had happened seven months ago. The thought of her came back and gave him a stomachache. In the first weeks of construction he had thought about her warning. By the second month, the excitement of the new studio had put Kanster in the forget-about-it box in the back of his head. Now she was back. *Or was she? Would she wait so long to carry out her threat? Perhaps it wasn't her at all. Then who?*

The construction plastic slapped softly against the timbers. It was the only sound. He turned on every light and climbed to the loft. The blood on his head had dried. The puncture in his hand began to ache. He took a hot shower, soaped and scrubbed the wounds in head and hand. He bandaged both and stood at the rail of the loft.

As he looked at the painstaking detail that made this place so personal, recollections of what it had taken to get the space from what it had been to what it was now returned. Memories came not in a rush or all at once but like old friends dropping in at a reception as his eyes drifted through the space.

Converting the Fish Cannery to an art studio was not only an enormous challenge, it was very expensive. Thomas had done much of the work himself. His awards and recognition in Scotland had given the bank sufficient confidence to make him a sizable loan. Monthly payments on the debt were significant.

Where others saw an abandoned factory, Thomas saw the perfect studio. He exposed the original bricks on the inside walls. He sandblasted through four layers of paint. Ultramarine blue. Hooker green. Gold ochre. *What were they thinking?* The top coat was a Byzantine purple put there twenty years before. The color made the place look more like a Victorian bordello than a location for eviscerating fish and putting them in cans. People saw a single wall the color of used brick. Thomas saw a thousand individually fired blocks of clay and a plethora of color.

I wouldn't spent a lot of money fixing it up if I were you. Kanster's menacing words swirled up from the blackened wound in the wall. It was only the wind in the plastic. He gripped the rail and a spike of pain shot through his arm from the ragged hole in his hand.

Thomas hated Kanster. He hated SAVE THE SEALS. He hated whoever had torched his studio. He shuddered and ejected the negative thoughts. *Think positive. This too shall pass. I am predestined to good fortune.* Again the man of unusual gifts was sustained by the will of the gods.

CHAPTER

28

Thomas called from the car on his drive into the city. Berger reacted to the news of the arson with predictable commiseration. He asked Thomas who he suspected would do such a thing. Thomas said nothing about Kanster's threat or his suspicion of SAVE THE SEALS. He wasn't sure why.

Berger offered, "Any way that I can help, buddy, just name it." Thomas took advantage of Berger's obligatory offer and asked him to make sure the place got cleaned up. "Too much for me to deal with in the middle of everything else," he reasoned. "Be great if you'd make sure it all got put back the way it was."

Quid pro quo. Berger took advantage of Thomas's desperation and used the moment to point out another instance of *selfless service as manager.* "Beyond the call of duty," he added, then grumbled about his 15 percent fee being a pittance for all he did. Some issues were never resolved.

Thomas decided to stay at the Marriott Courtyard for the nine days Berger needed to clean up and repair the damage from the fire. It was within walking distance of the Science Museum. Security gave him a PIN to open the doors and manage the alarm on the upper floors. His hours were erratic. He started early and stayed late, working on the revised layout for Hawker's vision of the mural. It was frustrating. Second-guessing was crippling.

The ideas that usually came easily were crowded out. *Kanster. SAVE THE SEALS. Who set fire to the building?* He was annoyed by the pain of drawing with a wounded hand.

He decided to stop speculating about Kanster's evil conspiracy with SAVE THE SEALS to burn him out. Withhold judgment until the fire inspector finished the investigation. Clear his head. It didn't work. Why was it taking the fire inspector so long? Was the fire inspector a member of SAVE THE SEALS? Conspiracy. Cover-up. The forces of darkness combining against Thomas to hedge up the way. *STOP!* He shuddered it all away.

Even Susan Cassidy was out of mind until he decided to take his boat on its maiden voyage come Sunday. He tried to imagine her on the deck, but she wasn't on the boat. She was standing in the half-light of the hospital corridor with a scowl on her face. *Have you considered the possibility you might be passing up the one project that will define who you are? Who you are destined to be? Have you considered this is something God wants you to do?*

He escaped the demons that loomed in the dark forest of imagination. At night he fed his body from the room service menu and his mind by reading *Origin of Species* and *The Descent of Man.* Every page filled his head with ideas, and his sketch pad full of drawings grew fat. Whether his ideas or his sketches were connected to reality slipped through the cracks of what seemed important.

He changed the bandage on his hand. The discomfort of drawing had becoming a throbbing pain. He worried about infection. He opened the wound with cotton swabs and endured excruciating pain as he scrubbed it raw with hydrogen peroxide.

Thomas spent the days in a strange suspension of time and space impossible to describe to one who'd never been there. He had learned as a child that the euphoria of creation was the process, not the result. As a teenager he had discovered the intoxication of putting pencil to paper and brush to canvas. It was better than the rush he got the one time he'd tried pot.

A faction of students at Art Institute had tried to persuade him that hallucinogenic drugs put artists in touch with their inner selves, heightened creativity and make them brilliant. It was nonsense. Idiocy. In those experimental years, Thomas's imagination produced "hallucinations" more outrageous and creative than those of any of his buddies popping pills. Why his colleagues swallowed, sniffed, injected or inhaled toxic substances in search of self-expression baffled Thomas. Made him disappointed in them.

There were exemptions. Thomas excluded Red Bull from his tirade against the use of substances to enhance performance. He always kept a can or case close by. Taurine, vitamin B, two kinds of sugar and eighty milligrams of caffeine sustained concentration and gave him extra hours at the wall.

The statue of Charles Darwin was moved into place on Wednesday. It was larger than Thomas had imagined when Hawker had described it on the night they met. The twelve-foot colossus was created in clay and cast in bronze using the lost-wax process. It was assembled one piece at a time in the annex of the third floor. It was too massive to get there any other way.

For its short journey from the annex to pavilion, the piece was swaddled in foam and wrapped top to bottom with four-inch packing tape. That wasn't necessary, but Hawker preferred that no one see the piece before the opening. Thomas was working when workers rolled it into the pavilion. He imagined a grotesque mummy with protruding limbs that had petrified before they shredded their way through the swaddle of death. The massive statue was moved on rollers to the center of the room, where the tape and foam were removed.

Reading Darwin's masterworks made Thomas curious about the man who had written them. Watching him emerge from the protective wrap as if being born again was a strange introduction to the English naturalist who changed the world. *Powerful. Inspiring. Frightful. Frozen in bronze.*

The statue depicted Charles Darwin in his later years. The famous naturalist sat, legs crossed, in an elegant armchair adorned with scallop shells. He was bearded and bald. He held his place among the papers on his lap and gazed into space. *Still searching for the missing link, Charlie?* Thomas amused himself with the thought. Workers took a break while they waited for Hawker to position the statue in the pavilion.

Two workers sauntered to where Thomas was at his easel working on sketches. They stood an acceptable distance behind him and watched in fascination. Simple lines evolved to lifelike creatures in a fluid swirl of arms and hands, brushes and paint. His hand was feeling better and the scab on his head had fallen away.

Hawker entered the hall in long, excited strides. It was the first Thomas had seen of him since the night they had met. He thought it curious. He had pinned the sketches to the wall, left messages with Maxine and waited. Berger had also called but gotten no response and heard nothing more about additional work or changes in the contract.

Two men entered the pavilion with Hawker. They looked very much alike. *Father and son?* Thomas wondered. The younger man carried a fat roll of blueprints. *Architects for the renovation,* he guessed. The architects showed interest in the sketches pinned to the wall behind Thomas. He stepped forward and extended his hand. *These guys are artists. They love what they see. Hawker needs to appreciate how fantastic the mural is going to be.*

"I'm Thomas Hall."

"Oh, sorry," Hawker said with a furtive glance. "McCobie and Sons. The architects." Young McCobie reached out to shake Thomas's hand but Hawker ushered him away before their fingers touched.

The thought struck Thomas with such humiliation that he would remember for the rest of his life where he was standing when *the gods* let him know his rank in the hierarchy of the cosmos. *The artists who carved the sphinx were never friends with the pharaoh. They were nothing more than means to the pharaoh's ends of glory.* Having seen Darwin wrapped like a mummy, he found Egyptian metaphors springing easily to mind. *To the pharaohs of the world—to men of power like Silas Hawker—artists are dross, tradesmen, tools to be used and cast away. Slaves. Trained monkeys. Bring in the clowns.*

Where Darwin sat in the pavilion was important to Hawker. He stood the architects before his twelve-foot god in bronze sitting beneath the dome of heaven with its fiber-optic stars and asked for their opinion. The workers waited for instructions as they circled the statue.

Hawker examined the bronze giant from every perspective and spoke in reverent tones. "This is a replica of the Darwin bronze created by Horace Montford in 1897 for the Shrewsbury Library," he said with pride. "Except for the polished black granite pedestal. Too much weight

for this old building. Darwin attended Shrewsbury school as a boy,"
Hawker continued, circling the sculpture all the while. "He was a mediocre student. Called his time at Shrewsbury 'nothing but a blank' when he
wrote of it years later." He seemed to be listening to what the bronze god
whispered to its favored disciple. His footfalls of leather on marble echoed
in the chamber. The only sound.

"Darwin is the classic story of genius," Hawker began again. "As a
child he seemed to care about nothing but shooting his gun, playing with
dogs and catching rats. To his 'deep mortification,' as he said later, his
father told him he would be a disgrace to his family and himself."

Hawker stood in front of the statue and looked up at the enormous
bearded face. "Now this. Truly one of the greatest men who ever lived."

CHAPTER

29

ALOT OF PEOPLE THINK he was the greatest man who ever lived."

"A lot of people think he was God!" Thomas was on the headset of his iPhone talking to Berger. They were not talking about Charles Darwin.

Thomas polished the railing that crossed the stern behind the cockpit of his new sailboat. The chrome could not have been cleaner or shone more. Apple earbuds put Berger's voice dead center in his head.

"It doesn't matter what you believe. You promised me some sketches for the Jesus piece and I've seen *ZILCH!*"

"I'm the wrong guy! These people want the reincarnation of Gustave Doré or somebody. I do fantasy, Frank!"

"It is fantasy!"

"Not to them."

"Why are you getting all tangled up on what's true and what isn't all of a sudden? They want you to paint a picture, not get baptized! It's a piece of art! What difference does it make?" Berger punctuated his rant as he often did by taking the Lord's name in vain.

"You should stop saying that all the time!"

"What?"

"That name." Thomas paused. "Jesus' name." He spoke the words with a reverence that surprised even him. "You shouldn't use it like that."

"I thought you didn't believe in Jesus."

"That's not the point. Using his name like a four-letter word is a big deal with Christians."

"You're starting to sound like a Sunday school teacher!" Berger's quip gurgled out in a sardonic chuckle.

"I'm just saying it's offensive when you say his name all the time without really talking about him."

"We are talking about him."

"You know what I mean."

"Yeah. Okay. Fine. I won't say his name if you'll go draw some sketches of him like we promised. Deal?"

Thomas shook his head. "I'm the wrong guy, Frank. Jesus and his miracles are like . . . it's all so real for them, you know." He picked the next words thoughtfully. "To them it's precious, sacrosanct. Holy. I don't know. I just can't get my head around coming up with what I know they're going to expect when I don't believe all that stuff."

"You don't believe in dragons or men who can fly or creatures spawned by the devil, but you create them just the same," Berger pointed out. "Brilliantly. Bigger than life. Fiction or fact. Folklore or fantasy. In the end, everything you create is real."

"It's about expectations. Respect, I guess."

"What's so different between Jesus and Zorazaman, or whatever you called that character you created for Dark Castle?"

"For starters, people don't pray to superheroes."

"But you made him real. Totally believable. You made him *true,* Tommy!"

"Do Jews believe in Zorazaman?" Thomas grinned.

"This Jew does. I believe in everything you paint."

"Maybe I don't pay you enough."

"Just merge your old masters stuff with fantasy and come up with something. Okay?"

Thomas put his hand on the railing and stopped to polish away the invisible fingerprints. Frank's banter had become boring. "What makes you think I don't believe in dragons?"

"Just do the sketches!"

"Keep tomorrow afternoon open, all right? I want to take you out on the boat. And bring somebody." He imagined Frank with a Vegas show-girl. Skimpy costume. Toothy smile. Synthetic body.

"Not sure I'll be back," Frank said.

"Where are you now?"

"Just headed into the meeting with Harvey and the Heavy Metal Casino guys."

"They moved it up a day," Thomas noted. "You spared me the details again. What time you flyin' back? I'll pick you up and we'll celebrate."

"Probably won't be tonight."

"Everything on track? Still a slam-dunk deal?"

"Yeah, yeah. Couple of things have come up I've got to work through. I'll worry about that. You worry about drawing some pictures of Jesus."

Thomas tapped *END CALL*. A twinge of uncertainty rippled through him. *Couple of things have come up?* The hand of fate jerked the ratchet on his gut. *Of all my troubles great and small, the things that never happened were the greatest of them all.* The axiom was taped to his bathroom mirror. He summoned the pithy aphorism whenever the innate insecurity of his artistic temperament rattled out of control. So far it was the truth.

He called Susan Cassidy to invite her on the maiden voyage, then chickened out and ended the call before she picked up. The maiden voyage of his new boat was trophy date time. He called Catrina and left a message on her voice mail. Catrina spent two hours a day at the gym and in a bikini looked like one of the fantasy women Thomas drew for the covers of graphic novels. She was unabashed about wearing only what was legally essential and glistened with suntan oil. He imagined the old guys who fished for perch off the end of the pier gawking at Catrina laid out on the nose of his boat as he cruised out of the harbor on Sunday.

"'Bout here okay?" The voice startled him out of his luscious daydream. He peered forward over the railing. The voice was bigger than the girl who stood there. She was skinny in a hard, sinewy sort of way. Her hair was seven shades of brown tangled with streaks of bleached blonde, pulled back into a rubber-banded ponytail. Her eyebrows were dark and too thick for her narrow face. She had a ring in her lip. Several silver studs trimmed the pinna of her left ear. Her lavender tank top hung loose over bony shoulders. There was a tattoo with flowers over her heart: *JESUS LOVES ME*. A small silver cross dangled from her neck. She was standing at the bow and pointing to where the hull began its sweep inward.

"I'm sorry, what'd you say?" Thomas asked.

"The name? Where'd you want me to paint the name of your boat?"

"Oh, you're the painter Archie sent over?" He recalled the quick con-versation from a few days before. *We'll even paint the name on her for you.* Slick Archie's promise came to mind. *Generous,* Thomas thought, not considering the reality that painting a name on a new boat would negate the seventy-two-hour right-of-recision clause in the purchase agreement.

A souvenir shop hangs out a warning sign: *YOU BREAK IT, YOU BUY IT.* There were no signs when you bought a boat, but there should have been: *YOU PAINT YOUR NAME ON THIS BOAT, YOU CAN'T GIVE IT BACK.* You could sell it to someone else, of course, but the name made it "used" and you took the big hit.

"I'm the artist Archie hired, if that's what you mean." There was a bitter edge to her retort. "Here okay?" She slapped the hull. Thomas's ir-repressible inner artist was already making a sketch of the angular girl. His left hand swirled unconsciously. Her lanky form was an S-curve accentu-ated by the way she cocked her hip to offset the weight of the green metal paint box in her right hand.

"What are you staring at?" she said, annoyance filling her voice. "Don't get any creepy ideas."

"No, no, no, I was just—"

She cut him off. "You want a name on your boat or not, sport?"

"I do. Yes, I forgot that was part of my deal. Haven't given it much thought. I've got a lot going on."

"Course ya do. Big-time boat owner." It dripped with sarcasm. "You good with putting it right here?" Her hand lay flat on the hull. Light danced from the water onto her face.

"Should either go right here," she said, "or in the back across the stern." Thomas ran a hand over the stubble on his face. He'd stopped shaving when he bought the seaman's hat. He was Captain Nemo until the girl punctured his fantasy: "It's kind of small to put the name on the stern."

• • •

By the time Chastity went to work, Thomas knew her name. She sat cross-legged on the dock. He squatted beside her. She had written *Da Vinci* on rice paper and taped it on the hull where she said it ought to go.

"A bit lower and to the left." Thomas's sense of composition was neither cognitive nor learned. It was intuitive, in place from the moment he was born.

"Really! You think it should be lower?" She said it with disdain. For a fleeting instant he mistook the smudge of paint on her tank top as the logo of SAVE THE SEALS, a wounded seal with a bandage on its head and a broken flipper. *Is this girl capable of burning me out?* He laughed at his paranoia and inhaled the salty air. *She makes a living painting names on boats.* The wounded seal returned to being a colorful blotch.

"That's awful far down," she was saying.

"Try it." It was perfect in his mind. She stripped the paper in a way that let Thomas know she thought him an ignorant fool. She put it back lower and to the left.

"Half again as big and it'll be perfect," Thomas said. The girl rose straight up on scissor-lift legs and walked to the other side of the dock. She crossed her arms and massaged the cross at her neck between a thumb and forefinger. She cocked her head and squinted at the boat.

"Works better, don't you think," Thomas nudged. It was a statement, not a question.

"Whatever. You don't care what I think." She walked back. "You want it to look ugly, fine! No skin off my nose. Archie pays me either way."

"If you don't believe in what you're doing I'd rather you not do it at all."

She scowled at him. "Really? Okay. I believe," she oozed with sarcasm. She ripped the paper away, picked up a marker and wrote the name freehand.

"You're very good at that!"

"Believe it or not, I could do this without your help."

"Can you match the cobalt blue of the trim?" She ignored him, her countenance so indignant that Thomas had to smile.

"I took a calligraphy class once," he went on, "but I could never do what you do."

"You can't 'learn' art. You're either an artist or you're not."

Pride poked his ego with a rusty pin. He started to tell her who he was, but this harbor was the STS war zone and common sense said *keep your mouth shut.*

"*Da Vinci*'s a funny name for a boat."

"You think?"

"Where'd you come up with it?"

"Da Vinci?" *You think you're an artist and you don't know Da Vinci?* "Leonardo Da Vinci," Thomas said. "You've never heard of him?"

"Duh! Of course I know who he is! He painted *Mona Lisa,* but it's not like he was Columbus or somebody." Her sarcasm was endearing. "I meant, of all the artists, why him?"

"Because he was so much more than an artist. He was an inventor, intellectual, philosopher, visionary. Probably the most diversely talented man who ever lived."

"He was left-handed," she said with a little smirk that smacked of pride, then rested the ball end of her mahlstick on the surface of the hull and steadied her left hand against it. She held a 00 MACK Sword Striper brush. She exhaled, stopped breathing and dragged a long, graceful line, then breathed again. "Know the best name for a boat?"

"Tell me."

"*Poseidon.*"

"Why *Poseidon?*"

"God of the sea." She turned to refill the brush with paint. "If you name your boat in honor of the gods, you'll always be safe on the water." Thomas realized she was serious.

The sun struck the cross that swung at her neck. A spike of white light caught Thomas in the eye. It seemed to punctuate the promise of the mariner's myth.

She worked without speaking for what seemed a long time. Thomas was impressed by the near-perfect lines drawn with her freehand brush. He tried to reconcile Chastity's unexpected talent with a frail girl who could pass for homeless and get quarters in a cup. *Wonder if she knows Sergeant Jake Demeanus?* It struck Thomas as odd that the beggar's name came to mind.

He didn't disturb her during the concentrated strokes. He spoke when she lifted her brush and reoxygenated her lungs.

"What about *Neptune?*" Thomas felt inclined to make a friend of the curious girl and find a way to tell her who he was.

"What about him?"

"The Romans thought HE was god of the sea."

"Really? Well, a lot of people name their boats *Neptune.* Probably for the same reason."

"Fear and superstition?"

She stopped painting and looked at him. "There's only one other reason a person puts a name on a boat."

"Only one?"

She nodded. "Let somebody know that you love them."

Thomas felt awkward and changed the mood. "Lot of people name their boat *Gone Fishin',*" he said. She gave him a puzzled look. "Gotta be some of us brave enough to go sailing without the protection of the gods." Thomas chortled. The girl didn't.

"If I ever owned a boat I'd name it *Jesus.*"

CHAPTER

30

By the time Chastity finished painting *Da Vinci* on the sailboat, the sun was an orange ball sinking behind the Marin Hills. The harbor was suspended in a warm twilight as the last full rays of the sun turned Tiburon to gold and reflected west.

Thomas left another message for Frank and put his iPhone on the roof of the cabin. He had polished every chrome railing, brass fitting and glass surface he could reach. He stood on the deck holding the cloth.

Cymbals crashed. The theme from *Eragon* enveloped the sailboat. The incoming call bounced from the iPhone to the Parrot Bluetooth and the ring tone played over the boat's 5.1 surround sound system. This time the music was rich and full and made flying seem possible.

He assumed the call was from Berger. He punched the Parrot's green button and answered from the back of the boat without picking up the phone to check caller ID.

"Give me some good news, buddy!"

"Tommy?" If it was Berger, one wild night in Vegas had aged him thirty years.

"Frank? Who is this?"

"Hello, Tommy, it's your father." The old man's voice played in 5.1 surround. Chastity looked up from the green box as she put away her tools and paint. Thomas tightened the muscles of his face.

"What line are you calling me on?"

"Oh, they got a new one here. It's in the room where—"

Thomas cut him off. "What do you need? He turned off the Parrot and picked up the phone. The speakers went dead. The conversation went private.

"Nothing. I don't need anything. I was just wondering if you were coming on Friday."

"No, I told you, remember? I told you last week."

"You didn't call last week."

"Well, whenever it was. Maybe I just told Mary. I can't be there."

"It's my birthday Friday. You probably forgot, but I thought that—"

"I can't be there! Okay? Is Mary there? Let me talk to Mary."

It was only a few seconds, but the silence on both ends exceeded the interval of expectation.

"Did you hear me?" Thomas spoke louder. Impatient. "Alex? Put Mary on the phone."

"All done," Chastity intoned in the background as she patted the hull with enough slap to insure Thomas could hear although he was still on the phone. He smiled at Chastity and held up a finger. *Just a second.* He turned away.

"He doesn't remember anything I say, so you can call it whatever you want. I canceled the private line to keep him from calling twice a day." Thomas continued to hold his "wait a minute" finger aloft for Chastity as he listened and bobbed his head. "Yeah, I know, Mary, but he forgets. Trust me! Anyway, that's why we pay you people. To take care of these things."

Chastity gazed at the harbor as if attempting to distance herself from the awkward conversation.

"Great. Thank you, Mary. Good-bye." Thomas ended the call.

"You like it?" Chastity pointed to the swirling *Da Vinci* on the bow.

"Looks great." He did not look up from the phone. He was scrolling through *Missed Calls* looking for Berger.

"You see around corners?"

"What?" He looked up.

"Never mind. See ya around. Try not to drown yourself." The girl snagged her heavy paint box and headed down the dock.

"No, wait! Sorry. I was just . . ." He scrambled over the railing and hurried to where he could see her handiwork. "I've been expecting an important call. Sorry."

She turned to wait for him. Her left hand clutched the triceps of her other arm. It was a gesture of displeasure more than any real need to assist with the weight of the green metal paint box. Thomas stepped to the edge of the dock opposite *Da Vinci*.

"Whoa. I do like it. Wow! You did a great job!" Thomas pulled out his wallet and danced his fingers across a sheaf of bills.

"It's paid for already."

"Yeah, I know, but I wanted to give you a tip. I really like what—"

"Don't be lame. You 'tip' people who carry your bags and shine your shoes. I mean, it's like, 'Thanks for the brain surgery; here's a twenty'!" The muscles of her face contorted. "For a guy with a boat named *Da Vinci*, you are obviously clueless when it comes to artists." She shook her head and started again for the parking lot.

Thomas was chagrined. He berated himself for missing the chance to tell her who he was. "An artist's artist" was what the art critic of the *San Francisco Chronicle* had written of Thomas when Hamilton had hired him for the Science Museum project. He was irritated that the girl assumed he was just one more wealthy yuppie with a boat slip in the harbor. *Obviously clueless when it comes to artists.* Too much. He followed the girl with the green metal paint box.

By the time he caught up, Chastity had reached her 89 VW. Her talents were displayed in the decorative paint job that covered the entire Beetle. She was parked closer to the boats than the NO VEHICLES BEYOND THIS POINT sign allowed. She turned as he slowed and caught a breath.

"Hey, sorry about offering the tip, okay?" In one deep breath his breathing returned to normal. "You did a great job. I just wanted to make sure you knew I appreciated it."

"If you change your mind? I can repaint it with *Gone Fishin'.*"

He laughed. "No. I wanted to give you my card. No special reason, you know. Just in case I can ever be helpful." His wallet was out and the business card extended before he finished. She put her paint box on the seat and took the card. She pulled her car keys from a tight rear pocket before she looked at it.

Thomas anticipated recognition. A rush of adoration. There was only a glimmer of disbelief.

"You're Thomas Hall?"

He nodded modestly and held out his hand. She didn't take it. A gust of wind hurled hair across her face like a hand with flowing tendrils instead of fingers.

"The guy redoing the old Fish Cannery?" He nodded. "The artist?"

"Some of my stuff is on the website there," he pointed to the card. "If you ever wanted to see my studio, you know, I would—"

Thomas's phone quivered, Patrick Doyle's music replaced by vibration. Caller ID came up. He held up a finger. "Gotta take this." He tucked buds in both ears. "Frank!"

Chastity circled the front of the VW, climbed in and started the engine. "Where you been, man? The meeting go that long or you just kick up your heels in Vegas? Hang on a second, Frank."

Thomas stuck his head through the passenger window of Chastity's VW. "Thank you. Really. Drop by and I'll show you around the studio," he whispered and gave her a thumbs-up.

"Not likely," she said. The words hit his face like barbs of frost blown over glacial ice.

"Who you talking to?" Berger asked. Thomas was stopped cold before he could answer. Eyes staring up from the green metal box numbed his brain. Big, wet sorrowful eyes. The eyes of a wounded seal with a bandaged head and its flipper in a sling. SAVE THE SEALS decal. He backed from the window with the look of a convicted felon caught with his hand in the cookie jar. His last impression of the girl was her glaring disdain.

"Thomas?" Berger's voice in the center of his head.

"Yeah." The VW wheeled away. A rank of wounded seals across the rear bumper wept for Thomas until they vanished in a choke of black exhaust. The spike of adrenaline was replaced by a rush of good humor. He grinned at the irony and headed back down the dock toward his boat.

"You hear me okay?" Berger asked.

"Yeah. Better now. Where are you? How'd the meeting go?"

"Can you pick me up?" Berger's request competed with static, noise and the crackling of an airport PA.

"Sounds like you're at the airport?"

"I leave here in half an hour."

"So you'll get here at what? Like eight o'clock?"

"Yeah. I've only got carry-on so meet me at the curb at ten after. Southwest."

"So tell me what happened," Thomas urged.

"We'll talk when I get there."

"It went okay, didn't it?" The pause was too long. So much of life is measured by expectations. "Frank?"

"I'll fill you in when I get there." A jackpot bell went off in the background, tinny and compressed but clearly the sound of someone's lucky day.

"Frank?"

The noise filled the silence. A woman screeched. Her voice was a dissonant harmonic with the clanging jackpot bell.

"Too noisy here," Frank insisted.

An eruption of squawking birds pulled Thomas from the phone. A man stood on the deck of the houseboat next to him, ripping a sandwich into chunks and throwing them to the hovering squadron of insatiable gulls. He was marked with a tattoo that crawled up his arm and spread across his shoulders like an evil weed.

"There wasn't a problem with the contract, was there?" Thomas's heart sank as the clatter of gaming in the airport was the only sound cackling from his phone.

"Pick me up. We'll talk then."

CHAPTER

31

I T WAS RAINING BY THE TIME Thomas got to the airport. He was in a foul mood. Traffic was slow going south on the 101, giving Thomas time to suffer through a list of worst-case scenarios. Each gave him a jolt of adrenaline. Each was more ominous than the one before. *Of all my troubles great and small, the things that never happened were the greatest of them all.* He repeated the aphorism. It didn't help. *I'll fill you in when I get there,* Frank had said on the phone. What had happened in Las Vegas that he wouldn't talk about? It was not like Frank to spare good news.

Thomas got to the curb ten minutes late. He searched for Frank in the crush of passengers exiting the baggage area. An airport cop tapped on the window of the Mercedes. Her uniform was a size too small without the bulletproof vest. Her chest was cursed with more than its share of extra weight. Thomas touched the control and the window dropped, opening a portal to an alien world. A gust of wet air blew in as an airport bus blew by. "He'll be right here," Thomas smiled with practiced charm.

"No waiting," the large woman grunted, avoiding eye contact. The corners of her mouth drooped. Her name tag said *BERTHA. That's gotta be a joke,* Thomas thought. Bertha pointed her stick forward as if Thomas didn't know it was the only way out. *Why does a person directing traffic at an airport need a bulletproof vest?* It gave him an idea for a sketch for his friend at Dark Castle.

"You've got quite a responsibility trying to keep this mess untangled," Thomas said, flashing his best smile in hopes of distracting the woman with blithe conversation, stalling her long enough for Frank to show up.

"Move your car, sir, and go around."

"He's right there," Thomas lied, pointing through the windows in front of the baggage carousels. "Two minutes," he smiled. The large woman stuffed the nightstick into her armpit. She lifted a ticket book from a back pocket and walked to the rear of the car. Thomas watched her in his mirror as she copied the number from his license plate.

His first assessment of weight distribution had been wrong. The woman's caboose packed more than its fair share. *A hundred pounds of derrière.* "Wait, wait, wait. I'll go around. It's ridiculous!" A flash of teenage rebellion swept over him. The urge to jam the accelerator, peel out, smoke the tires and choke his nemesis in a cloud of exhaust was almost irresistible. Some small measure of maturity saved him.

He drove fifteen miles an hour faster than allowed and exited the terminal area. He was so focused on rehashing what he should have said to the woman in the bulletproof vest that he got into the wrong lane and missed the shortcut RETURN TO AIRPORT.

The rain got worse. His mistake spewed him out on the 101 freeway headed north. He took the first exit, looped over the freeway and made his way back to the airport. He cut off a Yellow Cab and stopped at the curb.

Big Bertha lumbered toward him from the left. There was no mistaking her intent. He pulled from the curb and this time smoked the tires. He circled the airport again and again and again and again before Frank finally showed up. The traffic, the rain, the fat black woman, and the seven circuits around the airport had put him in no mood to hear bad news—and it was very bad news.

CHAPTER

32

"IT WAS A DONE DEAL!"

"It's never done until the check clears the bank! How many times do I—"

"Harvey loved the sketches. How could you mess it up?"

"Yeah, well . . ." It was true but not the time for a manager to say *I told you so*. Berger stayed quiet.

"I trust you with my career! With my whole freakin' life, for that matter, and this is what I get?"

The Mercedes swerved lane to lane as Thomas threaded his way south on 101 at ninety-two miles an hour. Berger glanced at the airbag indicator and let Thomas vent. He had tried to anticipate this conversation during the ninety-minute flight from McCarran Field. It was worse than he had imagined.

They stopped at Knuckles Historical Sports Bar in Burlingame. Berger needed a drink and intended to have more than one. He knew that what had happened at the meetings in Las Vegas was more serious than laying blame and pointing fingers. Without the Heavy Metal Hotel and Casino project, Thomas was facing serious financial troubles. *Studio lease, Mercedes and now the boat.* There was another reason Berger insisted on Knuckles. It was within walking distance from his apartment. A long walk, but Berger had no intention of getting back in the Mercedes.

"Why don't you go ahead and have a drink," Berger suggested, hoping to lubricate Thomas's brain for the inevitable conflict ahead.

Thomas waved the offer away, saying, "What a pathetic way to escape."

Berger ordered him a gin anyway. "It'll calm you down," he promised.

"Will it keep me from ripping your head off?"

"A little slow gin be good for you right now. Trust a man who knows."

"Trust you? What, are you trying to be my mother?"

"I'm trying to be your friend."

"*Slam dunk. Can't miss.* You promise to come back with a $258,000 contract and a check for $86,000 and now you tell me you not only lost the deal but they've stolen all my sketches?"

"Ever try Drank?"

Thomas glanced up to the voice. A cocktail waitress who looked like she should be at the library doing her homework offered him a purple can. "Slow your roll," she smiled, "and no alcohol." She pulled the tab and poured it down the side of a glass like it was Budweiser.

The curious mixture of melatonin, valerian root and rose hips did what the label promised. Thomas relaxed. His rant ended. He became quiet. Stoic. Borderline morose.

Berger reminded Thomas that they had argued about front money when Thomas was invited to submit sketches for the new Heavy Metal Casino on the Vegas strip. Thomas had needed cash. The conversion of the old fish cannery was costing more and taking longer than imagined. Thomas remembered the argument but wished he couldn't.

He had asked Berger to negotiate money up front for development. "Like in a Hollywood movie deal," he said.

"Bad idea, Tommy. They pay for the drawings, they own them. They can go with a different artist and use your stuff."

"That'd never happen," Thomas laughed. "Once they see my ideas there's no way they're going with somebody else."

• • •

Harvey Liakovitch rejected Berger's initial proposal to pay Thomas for developing characters and design ideas. A young attorney at Green & Trask, just out of St. Francis Law School, sent Harvey a note.

Mr. Liakovitch,

There are a couple of reasons you may be better served paying for development and may want to take advantage of the artist's need for cash.

Give me a call.

Daenen

They met for lunch and Daenen explained it in simple terms. Harvey told Green to have the new guy draft the agreement.

Thomas scanned the forty-six-page development agreement. He missed the provision tucked away in a paragraph of 10-point legalese on page 39. It was the one that worried Berger.

1. E (h) In the event HMC does not go forward with Artist under the terms and conditions of this agreement, all right title and interest in and to development as defined hereinafter, including all original sketches, plans, drawings and characters shall become the exclusive property of HMC.

The development budget was $25,000. Berger tried to talk Thomas out of taking the money. He failed. He tried to talk Thomas into reserving some of the best ideas until they nailed the contract. He failed.

Thomas went to work creating characters and a conceptual design for the enormous atrium. Harvey loved all of it. He fawned over every drawing and made sure the exotic girls on his Las Vegas team fawned over Thomas. Thomas got rock-star treatment when he went to Vegas. Flattery enticed him beyond the requirements of the agreement. He extended the fantasy-scape to the domed ceiling. "The Sistine ceiling of Vegas," Harvey told Thomas. "Brilliant." *All in good faith. Not to worry.* Harvey's assurances were gold.

One week after Thomas finished the drawings, went to a private dinner at Caesar's Palace with Harvey, had a blind date with a showgirl of stunning proportion, enjoyed front-row seats to Cirque du Soleil and flew home in Harvey's Cessna Citation, three top students from Art Center College of Design in Pasadena were hired to replicate exactly what

Thomas had created. The $258,000 Thomas Hall contract cost Harvey less than $90,000, including meals and accommodations at the off-strip Platinum Hotel where he put all three guys in a single room.

The young attorney from Green & Trask received a basket of fruit, bread, cheese and chocolate with two vintage bottles of Chateau Haut Brion pessac-Lognan, 1982. There were four tickets for ringside seats to the heavyweight championship fight the following Friday and keys to a new BMW. And there was a card:

> Daenen,
>
> We're even.
>
> Harv.

Berger learned the awful truth at the bad-news meeting in Las Vegas. The kids from Art Center were already constructing the scaffolds when Berger met with Harvey. Berger could not get Harvey to understand that even with Thomas's sketches, other artists could never duplicate the mystical quality of a Thomas Hall original.

Harvey slipped a Gurkha in the left side of his mouth and reached for a silver lighter monogrammed with his initials. "There are only two things people remember about an experience," Harvey said like a professor of psychology at Harvard instead of a showman in Las Vegas, "what they feel at the peak and what they feel at the end. That's it. Eyeballs, guts and feathers." He stopped long enough to allow the flame to fully ignite the $750 cigar. "What we paint on the walls is not the high point and it's certainly not the end."

"Using Thomas's ideas and characters without using him is like . . . like . . ." No adequately vindictive comparison came to mind.

Harvey puffed a mouthful of smoke and rotated the cigar. "His ideas? Well, we agree that's important. Your boy is brilliant. I love what he's done. I always have, you know that. But in the end it's just decoration. Wallpaper. Once we got the idea right, who paints it can't be that important."

· · ·

In spite of the soothing affect of the Drank, Thomas lambasted Berger for the disastrous turn of events. Berger downed one too many vodka tonics. It was going to end badly. Berger finally blamed Thomas with, "You should have listened," and "I told you so."

Thomas turned sullen. His woes seemed overwhelming. The boat—first payment due on Friday. The Mercedes—monthly payments of $1,239. Lease on the studio—$3,800 a month and two months behind. No money from the Science Museum since Hawker showed up.

By his sixth vodka tonic Berger had enough liquid courage to give Thomas more bad news. The cost of the repairs to the studio was $57,000. Arson was excluded from the fire insurance policies on wooden buildings built before 1926 in the historic dock district.

Thomas fired Berger. Berger quit. Thomas described Berger with words he hadn't used since high school. The vodka gave Berger the intrepidity to do what he had wanted to do a hundred times. He slapped Thomas in the face and walked out of the bar.

Six hours earlier Thomas had been polishing chrome and daydreaming about Catrina Lindley in her bikini under the Golden Gate Bridge. His cosmic destiny had changed. The thought sent a chill down his spine. As he watched Berger slam the door, he could hear the gods laughing.

CHAPTER

33

THOMAS AWAKENED FROM A fitful sleep. In spite of the two Tylenol PM he had taken at 2:30 in the morning when he'd gotten got back to the studio, it had been a night of demons and dark dreams. He had not slept long enough to exhaust the drizzle of diphenhydramine HCl, so on top of a debilitating focus on the loss of Heavy Metal Casino, his breakup with Berger and a stomach aching over serious money problems, he was groggy and felt lousy.

The landline phone woke him up. It rang four times and went to message. Thomas sat at the edge of his bed and stared at the blinking red light. *Might be Berger with an apology.* It was an oddly pleasant thought in spite of what had happened at Knuckles.

It wasn't Berger.

"Mr. Hall. This is Linda James from Oakridge Manor. You are listed as the responsible party on the account for Alexander Hall and I wondered if you were aware we've not received a payment for two months? Would you call me, please, at 929-453-3483. Thank you."

He stretched the fingers of his injured hand and massaged the palm with his thumb. It was still sore. The way he felt, he half expected blood poisoning. His impulse was to call Berger. Dumping problems on Berger always solved the problems. Not this time. The thought of Berger jabbed another knife in his gut. *How did Berger get everything so screwed up so quickly?*

He unwrapped the cord to the skylight and opened the blinds. Soft light from the northern sky filled the loft. The morning fog was almost gone. Patches of blue and twisted strands of cirrus clouds were only blurry shapes of color through the frosted glass. Thomas enjoyed the effect of the light as it moved across the room, struck his easel and bounced to fill dark corners. He started to feel better.

Adjusting the blinds with the dangling cord brought memories of lowering the American flag at school when he was eleven. He'd wanted to be a Cub Scout like Bobby Van Fleet and Ronny Assenberg. They had blue shirts with emblems on the pockets and gold neckerchiefs with navy trim. Bobby had a neckerchief slide with a wolf face on it. His dad had carved it from a pine knot for his eleventh birthday. At Bobby's birthday party, most of the boys had worn their Cub Scout uniforms. Thomas never was a Cub Scout and couldn't remember ever having a birthday party.

• • •

Jim Harris was more of a handyman than a builder. He had a contractor's license but only worked on little jobs. Berger had found him working on a houseboat at the other end of the wharf. Harris was ripping away charred wood with a wrecking bar when Thomas came down. He introduced himself to Harris, said a few things had changed and told him he was having second thoughts about the best way to finish the ruined wall and wanted to hold off a while. Labor and materials to date came to $3,240. Thomas gave Harris a check and asked him to hold it for a few days.

"Everything's all right?" Harris asked with concern, massaging the check between his fingers as if checking it for rubber.

"Fine. Good. Yup," Thomas assured him. "Just need to move few things around in my investment portfolio. Get the insurance sorted out." Thomas had too much pride to flatout tell the man he had no money.

Harris wanted a date certain the check would clear. "Friday," Thomas said without a clue how that was going to happen.

• • •

Thomas ascended the circular stairs to the studio loft. They were made of wrought iron and reflected the tastes of San Francisco's Victorian past. They had been created to connect servants' quarters to kitchen in one of Nob Hill's imposing mansions, a grand old house that was damaged in the infamous earthquake of 1906 and never rebuilt. The stairs were put into a restaurant that flourished near Haight-Ashbury in the days of the flower children; it closed in 1989. They were bought by an antique dealer and rusted in his yard for twenty years waiting for Thomas to find them.

Most mornings he experienced euphoria as his eyes swept over his studio. A dream come true. A soft blue light fell from the skylight to his easel. The promise of destiny. No magic on this morning. He roamed his world with an anxious heart like a child clinging to a toy that might be lost. His mind was muddled. His head hurt. His palm was in pain again and the knot in his stomach was getting bigger.

Everything seemed precious. Paintings in progress and projects left unfinished. A platform for live models. Costumes hung haphazardly on rolling racks. Double-jointed mannequins watching without faces from a dark corner. Scarlet drapes slung over a Black Forest chair. A hat from the French Revolution on a peg protruding from a post. A cyclorama laid against one wall. Armor, helmets and shields. Medieval weapons racked between thick columns dividing the space. Two-handed claymores. Basket-hilted broadswords. Military flails with swinging balls of spiked iron. War hammers, lances, flanged mace, clubs and bludgeons. A Lochaber axe, halberd and two crossbows. Weapons of war. Toys of delight. Contraptions of history. Contrivances of fantasy. Perfectly proportioned females. Males in padded muscle suits with armor and plumed helmets still in place. They watched with large, unblinking eyes as Thomas walked through the studio.

• • •

The outer wall of the shower was mostly window. It offered a view of water, sailboats, harbor seals (alive and well) and, on a clear day, the isle of Tiburon. Only a determined voyeur with a boat and binoculars could invade his privacy.

Thomas closed his eyes and let the hot water pour over his head.

He was an optimist by nature. Three shelves of his library were crowded with self-help and popular psychology books. The collection had started by accident when Berger had insisted he read Dale Carnegie's *How to Win Friends and Influence People*. The book had come in a three-volume bundle of classics: *As a Man Thinketh* by James Allen and *The Power of Positive Thinking* by Norman Vincent Peale were the others included.

Napoleon Hill had trapped him by putting *Grow Rich* in the titles of his books. He'd ordered a copy of *Think and Grow Rich* from Amazon for Berger's birthday and ended up with twenty pages of "Customers Who Bought This Item Also Bought." The list of self-help books in print was longer than he imagined existed.

By the time he read his way through the original mentors like Dale Carnegie, W. Clement Stone and Maxwell Maltz and got to guys like Anthony Robbins, Stephen R. Covey and Joseph Murphy and cheeky knockoffs like *Who Moved My Cheese?* he realized that thousands of pages had been written and publishing fortunes made by repacking a few fundamental principles.

Positive ideas poured into his mind as if put there by the hot water pounding on his head. His problems evolved into challenges to be conquered, transformed by positive affirmations. *I will not allow Berger's failure or Harvey's betrayal or Kanster's intimidation or this bloody hole in my hand to defeat me. As of this moment, everything is okay. Nothing great and awful has happened yet. As a person thinks, feels and believes, so is the condition of his mind, body and circumstances.*

For all his hubris, Thomas, like most artists, was thin-skinned and insecure. In their war of words at Knuckles, Berger had convinced him that what had happened with the Vegas project was about duplicity and underhandedness and not a reflection on his talent or a personal rejection.

"On the contrary," Berger had reminded him, "they liked your ideas so much they stole them."

Berger had tried hard to convince Thomas that the only consequence of losing Vegas was money. Not getting more on the one hand. Having spent most of what he had on the other. *He had to jab me with that.*

Thomas felt run over by a train of worst-case scenarios. Something Professor Andrus used to say came to mind: "Life is about solving problems. There is opposition in everything you do. Some problems are real. Most are only imagined. If your problem is money, it is not a real problem."

There was a whole philosophical paradigm behind the old professor's statement that didn't accompany the memory or even seem important, but the thought encouraged Thomas in a rush of optimism. *If your problem is money, it is not a real problem.* Thomas took it further: *The world is full of money and I only need a smidgen. I should write my own self-help book,* he mused, and with the thought came a powerful impression.

Call Susan Cassidy and tell her you've changed your mind.

34

A REPTILIAN BEAST WITH razor claws reached out for a woman chained to an ancient altar made of stones. Fire spewed from volcanic rock. The creature was sweating and drooling blood. Fierce eyes burned with lust and hunger. The voluptuous woman writhed in terror. Her clothes hung in shreds. Her body was scratched and bleeding. *Call Susan Cassidy.* The thought persisted as Thomas worked to finish a spec piece for Dark Castle that might lead to a gig creating covers. *First things first.*

The sensuous woman twisting away from the beast was only a charcoal sketch, but Thomas could already feel her fear. She was a graceful swirl of lines on her way into existence as a piece of fantasy art. In the mysterious inner sanctuary where Thomas found the visual inspiration for whatever his mind could think up, the woman and beast existed in the twilight beyond mere imagination. There were no problems here, only creative ecstasy. *Call Susan Cassidy.* He was surprised that the prompting kept finding its way into his world. He set the brushes aside.

• • •

Thomas keyed 411 and asked for the main number at St. Mark's Hospital. "Press one for the number or stay on the line and I'll connect you at no additional charge." It was a computer with a woman's voice. He rehearsed his lines while he waited to be connected. He anticipated Susan Cassidy's first question: *How are the sketches?* He tapped END. There was something he needed to do before he spoke with the woman

who wondered if God was the one who wanted him to paint a mural for
St. Mark's.

Thomas sat with a Bristol drawing pad and began to sketch. His love
affair with yellow-gold 2B Ticonderoga wood-case six-sided pencils had
begun in the first grade and never ended. Within a few minutes the page
was covered with sketches. They were less confident and fluid than the
one of the terrified woman and ravishing beast. His strokes were tentative
and uncertain. The figures reflected what Thomas had seen of Christian
art and stored away in visual memory. The first of the sketches were in the
realms of fantasy. The last few began to emerge; they were more refined,
realistic and true to life. Now he was ready. *Call Susan Cassidy.*

· · ·

"One moment, please. I'll transfer you to Miss Cassidy's extension."
Thomas carved up the pages of his sketch pad with an X-Acto blade
and hung the drawings on the wall as he waited. Sound buds in his ears.
iPhone in his shirt pocket.

He was still rehearsing his dialogue. *I've been working on the preliminary sketches like you and Berger agreed.* Some neglected part of his inner
soul made it difficult for him to say he was working on the sketches if it
wasn't true. That was why he'd waited. One sketch only qualified as working. Two or more were "sketches," plural, and made it true.

Rehearsal continued. *It is a great project, and your ideas and Miss Von
Horn's ideas are very exciting. I've thought about what you said and I've decided to do the project.*

Writing lines and rehearsing them made eating crow easier. *I'd like to
meet early next week to go over the preliminary sketches.* Thomas knew he
needed time to come up with a batch of sketches that looked like they
were drawn by Miss Von Horn's alter ego.

What he would not confess to Susan Cassidy was the real reason
behind his sudden change of heart. *Let's get face-to-face and talk about
money.*

Thomas started a new sketch while he waited. A blind man on his
knees holding up his arms. A child beside him looking up to a figure

whose face could not be seen. Carl Bloch had been a favorite study of his at Art Institute. Images from the artist's masterwork returned from his unusually vivid memory—eidetic, one researcher had called it.

"Hospital relations." The voice shut off the awful music that had filled the long interlude.

"Hi, Susan. It's Thomas Hall. I've been working on the preliminary sketches like you and Berger agreed and—"

"This is not Susan Cassidy. I'm her assistant. She is away from her desk at the moment."

"Oh, I'm sorry. You sounded just like her."

"I'll take that as a compliment. May I help?"

"When do you think I could speak with her? Directly? It's important. It's a follow-up to our meeting a week or so ago."

"What was your name again?"

"Hall. Thomas Hall."

"Oh, Mr. Hall! The artist?" Thomas took a breath, his first since the conversation began. *Back in the game.*

"Yes, yes. The artist."

"I'm sure she'll want to speak with you. I know how disappointed she is that you are not doing the mural for us."

"Well, I think Frank Berger talked to her since and arranged for me to do some sketches. Frank is . . . was . . . my—uh—manager at the time."

"Oh, really? Hmm. I know she's been meeting with another artist, so I just assumed that—"

"Another artist?"

"Yes, from Europe. A friend of Mr. Carver, I believe. She's wonderful from what I hear."

"Is Susan—uh—Ms. Cassidy there now?"

"No. They're meeting with the architects this afternoon."

"They?" Thomas asked.

"Ms. Cassidy and the artist."

"Will you please try to reach her and have her call me when she can?"

"This number?"

"Yes. And make sure she knows I've been working on the sketches. They're great. Tell her they're exactly what she wants."

"I'll bet they're wonderful."

He looked at the sketches on the wall. None of them were very good. "You know my work?"

"I was at the presentation when she sold you to the board. She was brilliant." She giggled, then almost whispered in a happy little devilish sort of way, "They're a stiff bunch, if you know what I mean. I think that's why she was so disappointed when you turned her down."

"She's talked to Berger since then, hasn't she?"

"I don't think so. I got the impression you weren't involved anymore."

"Well, I am and I need to have her call me back ASAP. Okay?" Thomas pictured the voice as a young woman and found it hard not to sound condescending.

"If I were you, I would come over and meet with her." When Thomas didn't respond immediately she added in a conspiratorial tone, "People do better with Cass face-to-face. You know what I mean?"

Code. She's sending code.

"Has Ms. Cassidy signed a contract with the Europe woman?" The interval of silence went over the threshold. "Are you still there?"

"If it were me, I would be here at eight-thirty tomorrow morning."

"Tomorrow!" *I've got seven crummy sketches!* "What about early next week? Give me a couple of days to clean up a few of the sketches?"

"That's up to you. I'm just saying, if it were me . . ."

Code deciphered.

"Tomorrow's good. Does a little later work?"

"She's got meetings starting at nine o'clock." Another too-long pause was punctuated by an audible sigh. "I would love to see you do the mural, Mr. Hall, but it's certainly not up to me." *Seven crummy sketches!* "Shall I pencil you in for eight-thirty?"

"I'll be there at eight-fifteen in case she can start early."

"Wonderful. I'll let her know. And, by the way, you'll do better if you call her Cass. She does not like *Susan*. Little heads-up?"

"I owe you."

"No worries."

"Tell me your name."

"Jessica."

"Thanks, Jessica."

"Good luck."

. . .

Thomas typed "Holy Bible" into Google Search and hit *RETURN*. He glanced at the old-fashioned clock on the wall: 11:25. *Nineteen hours and thirty-five minutes to come up with something that will save my professional life.*

The second hand stopped ticking and the lights went out. The power was gone and so was Thomas's plan to find Jesus on the Internet. *Nineteen hours and thirty-three minutes.*

CHAPTER

35

ALEXANDER SAT ALONE ON the patio staring out into the garden. Mrs. Benning arrived with a pot of tea and two cups on a tray.

"I'm about to have a cup of tea; would you like some?" Her hair was the color of polished steel, accented by stubborn streaks of blonde and highlights of pure white. She kept it piled on top of her head, held there by a pair of carved ivory combs that she had acquired long before importing such things was forbidden.

"I'm sorry, what did you say?" Alexander cupped his left hand behind his good ear and turned it toward her.

She spoke a little louder. "Tea? Would you like some tea?

"Oh, thank you, thank you, yes."

"It's herbal."

"I'm not too fussy. Thank you."

As she poured she purred, "I think I would have loved to grow up in England now that I've taken to drinking tea instead of coffee." She handed him the cup. "Have you ever been in England?'

"Thank you. No. I was in Germany a while. Never England."

Mrs. Benning crossed a remarkably well-preserved right leg over her left and sat erect on the edge of her chair. She blew across the top of her cup. A tiny spiral of steam spun away. She took a sip and smiled at Alexander. "Are you worried about your son?"

The question took him by surprise. He couldn't remember ever mentioning his son to the other residents at Oakridge Manor. He slurped half a mouthful of tea and decided she had overheard his message to Tommy the day she'd given him the number.

"Talking about what troubles us helps sometimes." Her sympathetic smile disappeared behind her cup as she took another dainty sip.

"I haven't seen Tommy in a long while."

"It's been a long while?" she asked. Mrs. Benning was a classic conversationalist. She sustained a dialogue by repeating the other person's comment as a question. She was a master at it and kept their discussion going all afternoon. Had she not channeled her energies into becoming such a gifted musician, she might easily have been a successful psychologist. By the time the call came for dinner, Mrs. Benning knew all there was to know about Alexander and his son.

· · ·

Alexander had spent his life at the edge of the medical profession. He was a corpsman during his short tour of duty with the United States Army—after that, an ambulance driver and paramedic. In the early years he aspired to be a real doctor. That demanded that he unravel some bad decisions and finish college. He underestimated the difficulty to qualify for medical school.

For years he imagined he would find a way to become a physician. He longed to be considered one among the men he admired so much. It never happened. There was always a good excuse. A legitimate reason. An acceptable cause to procrastinate. Get more money in the savings account. Put it off a semester. Get started in the spring.

Meanwhile, he settled into a job "pushing drugs." It was his jocular way to say he worked for Eli Lilly Pharmaceuticals. He took pride in knowing more about the latest drugs than most doctors. Too much pride. He presumed to make diagnoses and recommend treatments. His know-it-all approach created resentment among physicians and poor results for Eli Lilly.

Alexander married at thirty-eight and had a little girl named Andrea. He and his wife were divorced when Andrea was eight. Six years later he remarried a woman fourteen years younger and Thomas was born. When Thomas was two Andrea came to live with them. She was seventeen.

Alexander became the regional sales manager for a company that produced a line of new age medical devices. His employer persuaded him to invest most of what he had managed to save into the startup company. None of the devices obtained FDA approval and the company failed. It was a difficult time for Alexander. When he finally accepted the reality of his life he became depressed. He drank. Twelve steps saved him but by then he had made the biggest mistake of his life.

. . .

Once Alexander opened the door of his memory for Mrs. Benning, he started to remember things he wished he'd forgotten. "I wasn't much of a father to Thomas," he said. Mrs. Benning's sympathetic nod encouraged him to continue. "I was too old to have a little boy. He was raised by his mother, really."

"By his mother?"

"She was the one, you know. All the soccer and the baseball. Took him to school. Helped him with his homework. Even took him to church a few times." He chortled softly. "She covered one whole wall of the kitchen with his artwork. He liked to draw pictures and she was always . . ." The old man pushed a trembling hand through the thin white hair as if brushing away a memory he no longer wished to keep. "She was a good, good woman."

Mrs. Benning laid a hand on his shoulder. "She's still a good woman." The comment gave him a tiny surge of joy.

"So many things I wish I'd a done, wish I could have . . ." The words faded away. "I was gone most of the time. Trying to recover." He covered a cough with his hand. "I had lost so much." He looked at Mrs. Benning and without knowing why wanted her to forgive him for being less of a father than he should have been. The hand on his shoulder patted him gently. It was enough.

"She died when Tommy was eleven and there I was. I hardly knew the boy. I mean, to him I was an old man who came on weekends." The memory of sitting on a hard bench with a dozen young parents amused him for some reason. The humor in the smile dissolved to pathos. "I was sixty-three years old and he's playing Little League. By then Andrea was off to college, so it was just him and me. Just as well. He never got along with Andrea. Big difference in their ages. Step-siblings and all."

"So there were just the two of you?"

"It was hard on Tommy. I felt like he blamed me for his mother's death." A familiar fist tightened around his heart. "I did the best I could. I did what I thought a father needed to do. I was too late and never understood him, you know. Never considered what he needed. Who he was." As the memory darkened, Alexander picked up the teacup, knowing it was empty. Like his life.

Mrs. Benning lifted the teapot. "I'm afraid it's cold. I can get some more."

He put the cup back. Shook his head.

"When he was fourteen I told him to stop wasting all of his time drawing stupid pictures and make something of himself. I'd tell him to do his homework and he'd draw pictures instead. He'd hide from me and make his pictures. I understand now, goodness knows years and years after it's too late, I understand. I was trying to live my life over in him. I wanted him to be important. Respected. I was on him all the time about being a doctor, you know, telling him to study harder because I wanted him to be what I never was."

Alexander was suddenly embarrassed. He hardly knew the woman who had opened his soul. He stood up and shuffled down the steps from the patio to the garden. "You're kind to listen to an old man's lament. I must be boring you to death." He waved his hand dismissively.

Mrs. Benning remained seated but raised her voice to make sure he could hear. "Did you help him become what he is?"

Her question stopped Alexander at the bottom of the steps. He steadied himself on a stone post. A shock of white fluttered across his furrowed brow.

"I burned his sketch books! All of them! I tore down his pictures!" Mrs. Benning stopped breathing. "He failed biology and I was drunk!" The old man smiled, his face contrite. Allowing his confession to hang in the still air of the quiet garden gave him the relief that comes from finally exposing the darkest recesses of one's heart. "When I woke up the next morning, I was on the floor where I had fallen. Thomas was gone. I never saw him again until I suffered the stroke two years ago. He came to the hospital with Andrea. She lives in Florida."

"I'm sorry," Mrs. Benning said. Alexander didn't move. He stared down at the stones of the path, which were mortared with moss. Mrs. Benning plucked a withered brown leaf from a potted plant and twirled it between her fingers.

"He pays for this." Alex's lips quivered and he teetered slightly as he swept his arm across the luxurious surroundings of Oakridge Manor. "My son, Thomas, is the only reason I am able to be here." Mrs. Benning's eyes did not move from him. "He wants nothing to do with me."

"I'm sure that's not true. What's Thomas doing now?"

"The very thing I tried to destroy."

CHAPTER

36

W HICH BIBLE DO YOU WANT?" The woman spoke in a throaty whisper. She seemed impatient.

"Just—you know—the Holy Bible."

"Shhhhhh! Not so loud." She raised a finger to thin lips painted fat with lipstick. The woman glaring at Thomas over the checkout desk of the Sausalito Public Library on Litho Street reminded him of Miss Walsh. He felt like he was back in second grade.

The tag pinned to her pocket said *LIBRARY VOLUNTEER— WILMA HARCORT.* Her gray hair was tortured into a tight bun at the nape of her neck. Her glasses clung to the tip of her nose and magnified her eyes, accentuating the scowl on her face. He whispered so she wouldn't send him to the principal's office. "The stories of Jesus?" He didn't intend to make it a question; it just came out that way.

The woman pushed her owl-eye lenses up the ridge of her nose and rolled her eyes. "Every Bible has the story of Jesus, but there are many different versions. Different translations." She tapped a few keys on the computer and read from the screen. "The New American Standard. God's Word Translation. King James. Douay-Rheims Bible. And there's one called the *Weymouth New Testament in Modern Speech* if it's only Jesus you're looking for."

"Mostly Jesus."

"We don't have them all. And many of the ones we do have are in our special collections, so I need to know which one you want."

"King James, I guess. I've heard of that one."

Wilma cut him off. "Heard of it? You've never read the Bible?"

Thomas had an uncomfortable sensation of neglecting his homework. *Still in the second grade. Sorry, Miss Walsh.* He shook his head.

"The language of the King James is elegant. It was translated into beautiful, literary English. It's practically poetry but certainly not the language we speak anymore. It's hard to understand, in my view."

"I'll go with whatever you recommend, Wilma," Thomas said as he glanced from her name tag to the clock on the wall behind. 12:20. *Eighteen hours and forty minutes.*

"If you are reading the Bible for the first time, I suggest the New English Standard Version."

"Perfect." Thomas grinned and drummed his fingers to let her know he was in a rush.

Wilma looked in the computer. "Both our copies are out at the moment."

"Whichever one you've got will be fine."

She scanned the list and shook her head. "Tell you what you need to do. I know a man who buys copies of the New English Standard Version Bibles by the box full. Sells them or gives them away. I'm not sure, but if it's Jesus you're looking for, he's a man you should meet anyway."

One-on-one with a Bible expert'll get me what I need without wasting hours flipping pages. The thought relieved his rising stress. The library volunteer scribbled an address and handed it to Thomas.

"You're kidding."

"I'm sorry?"

"This is the marina."

"He lives on a houseboat."

"It's right next to where I live."

"God moves in a mysterious way." The woman beamed with the satisfaction of Christian service.

• • •

The houseboat rocked as Thomas stepped aboard. The address from Wilma Harcort was the floating domicile of the Tattooed Man who fed the seagulls. They had spoken only a couple of times when Thomas was working on his boat and the man was serving dinner to the gulls. Never more than frivolous comments on the weather.

He pulled the strap to the bell bolted above the door. It was loud. "Who is it?"

He was surprised by a woman's voice. He had never seen a woman on or around the houseboat in slip 64. "Thomas Hall," he answered.

"Who?" Thomas and the Tattooed Man had never traded names. In California it was common if not expected to live next door to someone for twenty years and never know the person's name.

With SAVE THE SEALS spies everywhere, Thomas wondered how much to say. *People living in a houseboat could not be opposed to human beings sharing the harbor with other living things,* Thomas mused. *Probably not SAVE THE SEALS folks. Probably not opposed to my studio.*

"The guy fixing up the old fish cannery," Thomas answered. A squawk of gulls fluttered into formation above him.

The woman who opened the door had black hair and dark eyes. Her skin was the color of red mahogany. Her mixed ethnicity was indiscernible. *Vietnamese. Filipina. Some Chinese. Probably an American father.*

"What you want?" She spoke with an accent. Her question dangled on a string of suspicion.

"Sorry to bother you," Thomas said. "I was looking for your husband." He caught himself too late. It was risky to assume that two people living together in Sausalito, regardless of age, ethnicity or gender, were married. He made a quick correction by glancing at Wilma's note. "Is there a Reverend Mike who lives here?"

She looked to the upper deck of the two-story houseboat. Her fleeting glance told Thomas the Tattooed Man was there. The woman said nothing. Thomas filled the awkward silence by glancing at the ravenous gulls just overhead. "He feeds the seagulls all the time?" he asked. She nodded. "They think I'm him." The woman studied him. "They're looking for lunch."

"Did you have an appointment?" she finally said.

"No. I just . . ." *Appointment?* He waved Wilma's note. "The woman at the library told me that you . . . or he . . ." The lunacy of his errand interrupted his train of thought. He started at the top.

"I'm looking for a New English Standard Version of the Bible. I need it for a project I'm working on—that I just found out about—and . . ." *Just found out about it? More like just decided to eat humble pie for Susan Cassidy and beg her to give me a job.* "It's an art project. Scenes from the Bible. A woman named Wilma told me I might be able to get one here. *Buy* one!"

"Please. One minute." She closed the door. A gull landed on the ship's bell. Thomas had lived at the harbor long enough to know better than to stand under a perched seagull. He took a few steps back and scrutinized the houseboat.

It was a two-story house on a floating platform constructed from remnants of other structures. The walls were lemon yellow. The trims and railings were painted a color Thomas presumed was intended to be sky blue. The deck, roof and sides were cluttered with a hodgepodge of attachments, railings, walkways, ladders and canopies.

The door opened. The Tattooed Man held out his hand. "Come in, come in," the man said, pulling Thomas inside as they shook hands. "Please sit down."

"I don't want to interrupt anything. I just wondered if—"

"No, no, no. Sit down. Sit, sit." The man's demeanor was a baffling contradiction to his rugged physique, tattooed body and shaven head. The woman cleared away an untidy jumble of yarn and macrame projects from the sofa. She was younger than her housemate by ten years. Maybe more.

Thomas's eyes adjusted to the din. Cotton curtains were drawn across the windows. Sunlight was filtered by colorful floral patterns and glowed a soft yellow-orange.

The interior of the houseboat was a cluttered version of the decks outside. The walls were crowded with shelves. The shelves were crowded with books in a variety of titles, shapes, sizes and colors. Thomas noted they tended toward reference rather than fiction.

There were stacks of magazines, notebooks and binders and piles of papers clipped or stapled together. Planted pots hung in macrame slings from eightpenny nails hammered into the ceiling. Curios, novelties and trinkets were tucked wherever the books allowed. The coffee table was barely visible beneath a layer of newspapers, magazines and pamphlets.

There were no electric lights burning. *The power is still off. How do I work through the night with no light?*

In different circumstances Thomas would have taken time to appreciate the eclectic accumulation. "Junk as art" was always fascinating to him. Not today. His mind was on Susan Cassidy, not a collection of bibelots and baubles.

The digital clock next to the stairs ran on battery. Red LED numbers floated in a sea of Tyrian purple. When the 1 changed to 2 Thomas felt the painful importance of making his way back into St. Mark's and the good graces of Susan Cassidy. Cass! *Sixteen hours and fifty-seven minutes.*

"Go grab one of those Bibles, Jing-Wei. Open a new box if you have to." The woman left the room. "I love the Bible," the Tattooed Man said. "Read it cover to cover eleven times. Wanna beer?"

37

Thomas passed on the Michelob. The Tattooed Man had drunk a six-pack plus two by the time Thomas left with his marked-up New English Standard Version of the Bible under his arm.

"Yours to keep. No charge, neighbor," Reverend Mike said as Thomas crossed the short plank to the wharf. "Think about what I said." Thomas sprinted the short distance to his studio. Their hour together had been unexpected. Strange and ordinary. Entertaining and disturbing. Had it not been for the ticking clock, Thomas might have accepted Jing-Wei's invitation to stay for an early dinner.

• • •

The Tattooed Man introduced himself as Reverend Mike. He and Jing-Wei were pastors of a congregation that met in a church in the redwoods once a month. When Thomas rang the bell in search of a Bible, it was for them an unmistakable sign he had been "called" to join their congregation.

Thomas explained the project at St. Mark's and persuaded them that it was desperation and not a supernatural manifestation that had brought him to their door. From that point forward the conversation became increasingly interesting. Even enlightening. It was difficult for Thomas to think of the Tattooed Man as "Reverend Mike."

His name was Michael Landerman. He was a retired vet with twenty-six years of active duty with the navy. He met Jing-Wei in the

Philippines and married her. She was raised Catholic in Baguio City, where she was taught by fervid nuns in the local School of Our Sacred Lady. Corporal punishment was a painful part of her being taught to fear God. She didn't fear God nearly as much as she did the God-fearing sisters in black and white hoods who considered everything she did a sin. In later years Jing-Wei learned the church was taking steps to eliminate the abuse of children in the Catholic-run schools of the Philippines. She wept.

If Mike was anything, he was a Baptist. His most memorable religious experience was the year he spent with his stepmother's parents in Wilmer, Alabama. Nine days after his dad married a woman the boy had never met, Mike was put on a bus going south. "'Cause you're the devil's child" was the only reason his new mother ever gave for sending him away.

His step-granny was Southern Baptist. She took him to the white church on the north end of Wilmer every Sunday. In October she found out he was sneaking out of Sunday School and smoking cigars behind the auto repair garage with Denny Garrett. She had Gramps beat his butt with a belt until it bled. He lied about his age and joined the navy. He served with honor.

Reverend Mike said religion played no part in their life together until they moved to Marin County. "Then God spoke to me," he told Thomas with about as much reverence as he might say, "I bumped into Bob at the game and he bought me a beer." Such casualness for sacred things clashed with an obviously profound commitment to what Mike and Jing-Wei now believed. And what the two believed was not always the same, Thomas soon discovered.

Mike and Jing-Wei attended a Unitarian Universalist congregation on a whim. They were attracted by the absence of a formal creed. "To experience the transcending mystery and wonder of it all in our own way," the Tattooed Man explained. "To be open to the forces that create and uphold life. It was an epiphany for us. We realized the meaning of life was to find our own spiritual path."

The anxiety over what Thomas had to accomplish in a few hours pushed his patience. When Reverend Mike escalated into sermon mode his voice toned up half an octave. Thomas wanted to take the Bible and run but he had no idea where to begin. He presumed the stories of Jesus and the miracles were in the New Testament but didn't know where. It made sense that a man who had read the Bible eleven times and called himself Reverend Mike could save Thomas precious time. He kept an eye on the digital clock.

Mike and Jing-Wei's "own spiritual path" prompted them to start their own church in a redwood forest. They named it God's Place. They were granted 501(c)(3) status by the IRS and within a few months had a congregation that was of respectable size if not thoroughly respectable in other particulars.

The creed of the church of God's Place evolved week to week in the sermons written and expounded by the Tattooed Preacher. The doctrines were an interesting mixture of Mike's conclusions about life and hours of speculation with Jing-Wei about the mysteries of the universe. They dredged up fragments of their Christian childhood—both good and bad—and mismatched chunks borrowed from the Unitarian Universalists. Only a few of the UU Principles and Sources of Faith survived without being twisted to fit what Mike and Jing-Wei wanted to believe. They seemed eager to share those beliefs with Thomas whether destiny had brought him to their floating door or not.

Reverend Mike preached his humanist precepts on reason and the results of science side by side with biblical verses about faith and the duplicity of man. He quoted verses from the Bible to validate his ideas. Reverend Mike's concoction of philosophy and scripture sustained the cynicism that allowed Thomas a sense of intellectual superiority in his choice to be agnostic.

Thomas knew enough people in Marin County to understand why Reverend Mike's earth-centered sermons on going green, celebrating mother earth and embracing "the sacred circle of life" generated significant donations. The profundities he invoked positioned God's Place in harmony with the rhythms of nature and, thus, the existential rhythms of Marin County. Though less accepting than its Unitarian Universalist birth mother, God's Place had become a home for humanists, agnostics and even atheists who had a need to worship something as long as it wasn't called Allah, God or Jesus.

Agnostic lit up in Thomas's mind like a flashing neon sign. He felt like an observer on the outside looking in. "What about the Bible?" he asked.

The Tattooed Man patted a tattered Bible lying on the coffee table. "Some see the Bible as a single chapter in a vast collection of religious texts. At God's Place it is our most valued source of inspiration and reflection."

The longer Thomas listened, the less confident he was that the Tattooed Man was the right one to give him a crash course on Jesus. His mind drifted away. The voice receded as the man droned on. "Jewish and Christian teachings don't necessarily have to be the 'word of God' to call us to respond to God's love by loving our neighbors as ourselves."

Thomas's eyes traced the intricate black swirls that wound up the man's muscular arm. At close range he could see the pattern was a twisted vine of thorns. A few of them "pierced" the skin, and blood tattooed with crimson ink oozed from the wounds. A black snake slithered upward through the thorns and disappeared beneath the sleeve of Reverend Mike's T-shirt. The serpent reappeared and crawled higher around his neck, exposing dripping fangs just below the preacher's ear.

Jing-Wei returned with a box sealed in the original shrink-wrap cover. She handed it to Reverend Mike. He sliced the polymer plastic film with a bone-handled switchblade that appeared from nowhere. He opened the lid and handed the hardbound book to Thomas.

"It's brand-new," Thomas noted.

"We buy fifty at a time and keep them on hand for people who come to the church."

"Twenty-eight dollars," Jing-Wei smiled. She pronounced *dollars* without the *r*. Thomas reached for his wallet. His hand hit the empty back pocket of his jeans. He flushed with embarrassment.

The Tattooed Man stopped him with a reassuring hand. "No, no." He tapped the Bible in Thomas's hand. "Luke six, thirty. Give to everyone who asks you, and if anyone takes what belongs to you, do not demand it back."

"I'll go get some cash. Sorry I . . ."

"No worries. Anytime is good. When you're finished. You may just want to bring it back."

Why Thomas felt the need to impress a tattooed preacher living in a houseboat with a woman half his age that he wasn't a complete moron where the Bible was concerned, he could not explain. He just did. "The stories of Jesus are in the last half of the Bible. Right? The New Testament?"

"Nah. The NT is hardly half. More like twenty percent." Thomas considered the Bible a history at best or a collection of folk stories at least. Even so, the man's reference to the New Testament as "the NT" seemed irreverent.

"What can you tell me about Jesus and his miracles?" Thomas didn't mean to smile but couldn't help himself the way his words came out. "Where does Jesus and all of that stuff fit in over at God's Place?"

Reverend Mike took the question seriously. "We believe the words and deeds of prophetic women and men should challenge us to confront powers and structures of evil with justice, compassion and the transforming power of love." It was one of the few tenets of Unitarian Universalism that had survived the transition to God's Place almost in one piece. "Jesus was without question the greatest prophet who ever lived."

"But he wasn't God?" Thomas asked cautiously.

Jing-Wei's eyes darted to the Reverend as she said, "I'll make some tea." She left the room. It was clear to Thomas she did not agree with whatever the Reverend was about to say.

"We seek to experience the transcending mystery of God each in our own way," he said, looking after Jing-Wei with a hint of weary disappointment. "Some find it comforting to think of Jesus as more than a mortal."

Each in our own way—except your wife. You expect her to believe what you believe. The thought angered Thomas for some reason. He brushed it away.

"What I really need to get my head around are the stories about Jesus healing people. I'm embarrassed to say I've never read the Bible so I need a crash course on all the healing stuff."

"The emphasis needs to be on the teachings of Jesus, not on a few miraculous anecdotes."

Thomas sensed a sudden alliance with the Tattooed Man. "As far as I'm concerned, the whole thing is an anecdote," he smiled.

He had apparently misjudged their kinship.

Reverend Mike twisted his head to the left, then pushed up on his chin with his left hand. His neck cracked in a staccato burst of gas from the synovial fluid. *The barking hiss of a viper.* "You can be sure about one thing," he said, his eyes burrowing into Thomas's own. "Jesus is real. The man you propose to paint on the wall is a man who really lived." He allowed time for his words to settle. "The historical Jesus has been established beyond any uncertainty. His followers' claims to his divinity, of course, never can be."

"I didn't mean that . . ." Thomas started the sentence without knowing where it was headed. He needed the crash course. *I'll be whoever this Tattooed Man needs me to be until I get the information I need to do what I've got to do.* He glanced at the clock. Half an hour had passed.

"We can never know Jesus completely, of course," Reverend Mike continued. "That is why the myths about him linger on. Every Gospel fragment that turns up, every ancient scroll we uncover, every simple inscription on some ancient ossuary will affirm there was a man called Jesus. A teacher. An oracle. A prophet. But God?" He shook his head.

Thomas nodded in agreement, not caring whether Jesus was real or not. Whether he lived or didn't. "He was controversial and largely misunderstood," Reverend Mike continued. "He confounded the people who knew him during his lifetime. The power of personality and the authority of his sayings created a legacy that has lasted over two thousand years. Why should we be surprised he remains so confounding and continues to be so controversial?"

Research was a critical first step in any art project. It was why Thomas needed a Bible. Why he lingered and probed his unexpected neighbors for information. Attention to detail distinguished great from good in the world of commercial art. It added an immeasurable dimension of authenticity. It grounded fantasy in what Thomas liked to call the "obscurely familiar," thus making it seem real.

The angst of getting to the core of Jesus, his miracles and the essence of whatever it was that Susan Cassidy and the old woman were looking for was getting worse, not better. Thomas had never read the New Testament, but he knew something of Jesus. Like sex and Santa Claus,

Jesus was something you picked up at the playground whether adults told you the facts of life or not. What he knew of Jesus and miracles from hanging out with kids who went to Sunday School was startlingly simplistic compared to what he was hearing on the houseboat.

In most projects the epiphany came early in the research. Not this time. The opposite was happening. Thomas felt adrift. *Reading the Bible myself would be easier than sorting through what this guy is saying. Reverend Mike's Jesus would likely be a stranger to Miss Von Horn. Gotta stick to the Bible.*

"I'm sure you think I'm brain-dead when it comes to all of this," Thomas said with a self-deprecating chuckle. "I appreciate your help." He opened the Bible. "Where are the stories about Jesus? Be helpful if I could mark the pages."

"All the way through the New Testament," Jing-Wei said, coming down the curved wooden stairs with a tray of peppermint tea.

"Are the miracles indexed under 'healing' or—"

"You want to make sure you put your emphasis on the sayings, the platitudes and parables. Not the mythology of the miracles," Reverend Mike said, and Thomas sensed the man might have a short fuse.

"Mythology? So even though you're a minister you don't believe that—"

"I can show you," Jing-Wei said, crossing the room. "I know where the miracles are and I believe in them." She scowled at the man with the snake on his neck and put the tray down without clearing a space in the clutter. She took the Bible from Thomas and sat cross-legged on the floor next to the coffee table. The Tattooed Man poured a cup of tea for Thomas and one for himself and settled in his overstuffed chair with a frown on his face.

"I'll mark all of them for you." Jing-Wei leafed through the New Testament with such familiarity it was evident she had been there many times before. She bookmarked pages with strips of paper ripped from a discarded envelope. She colored a passage with a yellow marker and put an *H* in the margin. "There were different kinds of miracles. I'll mark healings with an *H*," she said, moving from one to the next without hesitation.

The tea cooled a few degrees below the temperature of scalded tongue. Thomas blew across the surface. Steam swirled away in a graceful pirouette as he sipped it slowly. The taste was unfamiliar.

"There are many passages that document the miracles of Jesus," Jing-Wei said without looking up from marking the pages.

"Nothing in the Bible 'documents' anything," Reverend Mike said. "Least of all Jesus." He spoke to Thomas but was challenging Jing-Wei. "I treasure the Bible, like I said, but it's not a history book."

Don't judge a book by its cover. The cliché from childhood—perhaps from a kid on the playground—came to mind as Thomas realized he had underestimated the intellect of the man who fed the seagulls.

"Let me show you something," Reverend Mike said. "You'll enjoy this." He stepped to the shelves, scanned the cluttered stacks and found the volume he sought. It was dog-eared and marked with clips and Post-it notes. He shuffled through the pages to where a green piece of paper marked the spot. "Thomas Jefferson decided the only way to discover the real Jesus was to cut up the Bible and paste what he believed to be accurate in a notebook." He read a block of text highlighted in yellow marker.

> Among the sayings and discourses imputed to Jesus by his biographers, I find many passages of fine imagination, correct morality, and of the most lovely benevolence; and others again of so much ignorance, so much absurdity, so much untruth, charlatanism, and imposture, as to pronounce it impossible that such contradictions should have proceeded from the same being. I separate therefore the gold from the dross; restore to him the former and leave the latter to the stupidity of some and roguery of others of his disciples.

"Thomas Jefferson? Wow." Thomas said. Reverend Mike put the volume on the floor beside his chair. Next to it were other books: *The Five Gospels: The Search for the Authentic Words of Jesus. The Jesus Seminar.* Thomas glanced up from the pile of books. He wanted to get back on track. *Keep it simple. Find the stories. Make some sketches. Pay for my boat.*

"History is warped by tradition, parables and folk stories." Reverend

Mike sounded apologetic. "The morality tales are mostly myth or metaphor and have nothing to do with the facts of the stories themselves. Like Jefferson says, 'dross.'" He smiled. Jing-Wei shook her head in what Thomas discerned was frustrated resignation. The Jesus of the man with the angry snake under his ear was obviously very different from the Jesus Jing-Wei loved. *Confusing. Which of them is right? Or are they both wrong?*

"Just mark the stories you like the best," Thomas said.

"I like them all," Jing-Wei replied. "Some are more interesting than others, of course. Leprosy and blindness are the most well-known, probably because the overarching message of the miracles intended by Jesus is easier to grasp there. With only a couple of exceptions, each of those healed suffered from a different illness or condition. Persons near death, high fever, paralysis, crippled legs, withered limbs, lifelong sickness, maybe even birth defects, hemorrhages, deafness and edema."

"Edema?"

"Fluid in the tissues and body cavities. It was called dropsy in Jesus' time." The images taking shape in Thomas's mind were dark, grotesque and frightening. They were not images that would bring hope to a room full of sick children.

"Depending on the way you look at it, there are fifteen or sixteen stories of Jesus healing people in the Gospels. It's hard to separate healing per se from some of the other miracles."

"Make your picture about the sayings of Jesus, man! Don't perpetuate the supernatural mythology like everybody else." The fangs swelled up with a vein in Reverend Mike's neck and the snake was alive. Jing-Wei ignored him.

"You can divide the miracles into four categories," Jing-Wei continued, "not counting his birth and resurrection or his appearance to the disciples after the crucifixion." She held up her fingers one at a time as she ticked them off. "Healing the sick, of course. Raising the dead. The 'metaphysical miracles'—at least, that's what I call them. And casting out demons and evil spirits."

"Exorcism is the one thing Jesus might have done," Reverend Mike said, sounding angry.

Exorcism. Thomas's mind was splattered by hordes of evil wraiths, demons and the creatures of fantasy art that lived in his head.

"Exorcism is not a miracle!" Mike stacked the teacups with such vigor that one shattered in his hand. Tension was tangible. The Reverend's demeanor was for the first time consistent with his physical presence and the snake tattoo. He picked up the tray and carried it to the circular staircase.

Jing-Wei spoke softly. "Don't mind him; he has . . ." Whatever she had been about to divulge about her partner, she changed her mind. "There are five accounts of Jesus healing people possessed by demons." She marked another page. "Two of them were children."

"But they are not miracles!" The Tattooed Man raised his voice as he returned from the kitchen. "I'll tell you why! Exorcism was practiced among the Jews a long time before Jesus arrived. There were all kinds of dark arts and soothsayers. Most of the supernatural stories about Jesus are folktales dreamed up by his followers to support the notion of his divinity. I suspect there's some historical basis for Jesus' involvement with demonic possession and exorcisms, but that doesn't make them miracles."

Reverend Mike picked up fragments of the broken cup and placed them in his other palm. "Exorcists are not divine! They may not even be religious. It is not unreasonable to imagine that a mystic, a prophet or even a rabbi with the influence of Jesus might have possessed that special ability to cast out evil spirits." He put the fragments in an ashtray.

"Do the stories in the Bible give descriptions of the—uh . . . " Thomas paused to disguise his incredulity, " . . . demons and evil spirits?" He wanted to look them straight in the face and ask them flatout if they REALLY believed there was such a thing. He reminded himself that what they believed was even less important than what he believed, and what he believed didn't matter at all.

"You don't believe there's such a thing as evil spirits?" Jing-Wei asked. Thomas shrugged without committing. *Am I so transparent?* The incredulous expressions of Mike and Jing-Wei were the same. In at least one thing the two agreed: Evil spirits were real and demons had the power to possess human bodies.

Thomas had the creepy feeling that not believing in evil spirits—if there really were such things—made him vulnerable to their influence.

A prickle scurried up his spine like a spider wearing cleats. He had felt it before. It came often when the demons, fiends and devils of imagination came to life with the touch of a pencil, wand or surge of painted blood. The blessing and curse of creativity.

"Exorcism is still going on. The gift was not unique to Jesus, so expelling evil spirits does not qualify as miraculous. There are natural laws involved."

"They were miracles," Jing-Wei said and returned to marking her favorite passages.

"Josephus recorded exorcisms that used poisonous root extracts. Some required various kinds of sacrifices. Exorcisms of demons even show up in the Dead Sea Scrolls. They were hardly considered miracles," Reverend Mike persisted.

"Josephus?" Thomas asked.

"You've never heard of Josephus?" He pointed to a volume on the shelf. It was disquieting for Thomas to be reminded how ignorant he was about religion and how ill prepared he was to propose anything to Susan Cassidy based on the Bible. He glanced at the clock. Almost an hour had passed.

"Brain-dead about all things biblical. Like I said."

"He's not in the Bible. He was a first-century Jewish historian. Born a few years after Jesus was killed."

"He recorded that Jesus was a 'doer of wonderful works,'" Jing-Wei said with a wry smile clearly intended to provoke the Tattooed Man. Thomas wondered if their relationship had been forged by religious combat.

"That doesn't mean miracles," Mike snapped.

Jing-wei quoted Josephus from memory: "'He was the Christ and he appeared to them alive again the third day; as the divine prophets had foretold these and ten thousand other wonderful things concerning him.' Doesn't that sound miraculous to you, Mr. Hall?"

"Josephus was a historian?" Thomas asked.

She nodded. "'Metaphysical miracles' is what I call the things Jesus did that transcended the physical world."

"Ahhhh." It was a weary groan of aggravation. The Tattooed Man sat forward and hooked his tailbone on the edge of the chair to keep him there.

Jing-Wei answered the question on Thomas's face. "Changing the water into wine at the wedding. Feeding the five thousand with a single basket of bread and fishes. Calming a storm. Walking on the water. Things that seem to transcend the laws of nature in our limited understanding."

"You can't 'transcend the laws of nature'!" the Tattooed Man groaned. "Everything we know about anything confirms the immutable, unalterable character of natural law. Science has demonstrated it repeatedly. The laws of nature cannot be changed! If a so-called miracle violates a natural law, you can be sure it didn't happen."

"OR be sure we lack the humility to admit we don't know everything and accept the fact that miracles DO obey the laws of nature and the immutable laws of God," Jing-Wei said.

"Miracle or myth. Doesn't really matter for what I need," Thomas said. "It's just one more painting depicting a Christian tradition, so . . ."

"That's my beef with miracles," Reverend Mike said. "They dominate the stage in a religious dialogue and distract us from understanding who Jesus really was. The mythology of miracles was obviously conjured up by his followers to make him 'divine.'"

"It was not 'conjured up,'" Jing-Wei scolded. "Jesus WAS divine. He was the Son of God!" It was an old argument restaged for a new audience of one.

"No! Making him 'divine' distracts us from the importance of his teachings. It diminishes the power of his example. If he was a man, then doing what he did was incredible. If he had godly powers, then no big deal. If he was a man, he was the greatest man who ever lived. If he was a god, he was the most paltry god there ever was. Don't you see? The miracles obscure the brilliance of Jesus' true identity. His magnificent humanity."

There it was. The schism between them. *Jesus as man or Jesus as God.* Thomas was eager to hack a path through the tangle of philosophical debris before he lost his way and had to read the whole New Testament in search of a few great visual ideas. He had a job to do and he was running out of time. "I just need to get my head around which of the miracles or the so-called miracles are going to be the most visual on a mural."

Jing-Wei turned a page and continued a fat yellow line. "Raising Lazarus from the dead was the best described and certainly most spectacular miracle."

"The most outrageous folk story of them all," the Tattooed Man quipped.

"It was a healing in one way, but restoring life obviously transcends the laws of nature—at least to the extent of our understanding."

"I've heard that story. Jesus goes into a cave where a man is buried or something?"

"A tomb. Lazarus was the brother of a woman who followed Jesus."

"The woman was there?" An image emerged in his mind.

"Yes."

"You marked the page for that one, right? That could be very visual."

"You want kids to think they can die and come back to life?" The question was tinged with humor in spite of the harshness in Reverend Mike's voice. Thomas worried the rising conflict might derail Jing-Wei before he got what he needed. She just shook her head. "However that story got started, obviously Jesus did not bring a dead person back to life!"

Jing-Wei highlighted the story of Lazarus with the yellow marker. "There were witnesses," she said without looking up.

"The witnesses lied!"

"You are so sure you're right you wouldn't recognize the truth if an angel came down and hit you in the head!"

"If the story is based on a real event, it is far more probable that the witnesses lied than that a dead man came back to life. Think about it!"

"Why would they lie?" Thomas asked and found himself focused on the snake crawling up the man's arm and biting him on the neck.

"We have to assume they were deluded or lying because no one has ever SEEN a miracle that violates the natural law. Bringing a person back to life after they were dead has never been documented in any age, in any country, ever! This guy was supposedly dead four days!" Reverend Mike had worked himself into a frenzy.

Jing-Wei handed the Bible to Thomas. "I've marked the best of them. Should give you a start." She stood up.

"Thank you. This is great." He started for the door.

Reverend Mike blocked the way. "Nothing transcends the natural law!"

"Makes sense, but it's not about what I believe or don't believe. It's about what the clients want." *Susan Cassidy watched him from the warm half-light of the colored curtains with her arms folded tightly across her chest.* "They want a mural about Jesus. Something to give the kids hope."

"You don't you see anything twisted about giving innocent kids false hope? Covering a wall with miracles when there's no such thing except up here?" He pressed a finger to his bald head just above his ear. Thomas expected the snake to sink the dripping fangs into his wrist.

"It's a painting. It's a job. It's what I do." *Who Jesus was or wasn't makes no difference to me.* A shiver of fear passed through him, then disappeared.

When his mother died, Thomas had decided there was no god. Life was what he saw and heard and touched. The only reality was the moment he was in. He had wrapped the notion up and tucked it away, hardly thinking of it again until he met Silas Hawker. It had never mattered until the old woman had looked into his soul. *Do you believe in Jesus, Mr. Hall?*

She was there now. In her wheelchair on the houseboat. Her face was covered by the shadow of the black veil falling from the brim of her hat. Her piercing eyes penetrated the privacy of his thoughts. She was waiting for an answer. Thomas brushed the illusion away.

And in that moment the electrical power came back on.

CHAPTER

38

THOMAS GULPED A TURKEY POT PIE and went upstairs. It was 3:49 P.M. He had fifteen hours and eleven minutes before he had to head south across the Golden Gate Bridge to make his 8:30 A.M. appointment with Susan Cassidy.

He opened the Bible to the first torn scrap of envelope. It was the eighth chapter in the book of Matthew. The entire page was marked in yellow. From the outside looking in, the moment amused him. *Thomas Hall is reading the Bible.* It was a preposterous quest to visualize the man called Jesus he didn't know for a painting he didn't want to do.

After reading for thirty seconds Thomas realized the stories of Jesus doing miracles were not stories at all. They were cryptic little snippets of text broken into numbered verses with no description or visual detail at all. The New Testament was not what he expected. He was amazed that so much art had been inspired by such feeble stories, meager detail and wispy text.

It took Thomas three minutes and forty seconds to read the entire chapter. To his surprise, the block of yellow contained six different miracle stories. He read it again, this time more slowly, and scribbled notes at the edge of his sketch pad.

The first miracle gave him almost nothing. Four verses. Less than a hundred words. No details. A leper. No age. No gender. No physical description. *What does leprosy look like? Start with Jesus.* Thomas resisted the predictable iconic image of Jesus that came to mind.

If the famous Thomas Hall is going to paint a picture of Jesus, it is going to be a Jesus no one has ever seen. Thomas had come back to the St. Mark's project for the money but his creative ego made it impossible not to care. Jesus had been painted a million times. Whatever other results there might be, Thomas was determined to capture the bigger-than-life character in a way others had not. A way that would distinguish him as bold, innovative and original.

The only action in the vignette was, "He put forth his hand." There were three lines of dialogue.

"Make me clean." The leper.

"I will. Be thou clean." Jesus.

"Don't tell anybody." The wrap-up.

He saw the "story" as three frames in a comic book with silly caricatures and little balloons of dialogue. It made Thomas smile. It also worried him.

He worked his way through the eighth chapter again. This time he doodled in the sketch book as pictures presented themselves.

The story of the centurion was interesting. It reminded him of the cover he had created for *Gladiator King,* a graphic novel published in the wake of Frank Miller's enormously successful *300.* One problem. The centurion's servant got well without ever seeing Jesus. *How visual is that?* Thomas wondered.

Peter's mother-in-law got up and fixed dinner when Jesus touched her hand.

In thirteen words, mostly nouns and verbs, Jesus ejected "many devils" and "healed all." Not a scrap of detail. No description. Not a single color. Nothing fresh. His artistic ego refused to default to classic Christian art. Anxiety rose to mild panic.

Verse 28 caught his attention. *Two possessed with devils. Living among the tombs. Fierce and terrifying. People afraid to come too close. Exciting, stirring stuff.* He was encouraged. He picked up his pad and began to draw. The "two possessed" came into being as women. Matthew hadn't recorded the gender of the sufferers, and women possessed, it seemed to Thomas, were the epitome of terror. His angst subsided as the tombs of Matthew took shape on the drawing tablet.

The sparsity of detail meant visualizing everything. *The challenge is tougher than imagined.* The good news struck Thomas in the same moment: *The challenge to interpret the cryptic words of scriptures into detailed artistic depictions allows me—requires of me—a significant degree of artistic freedom.*

The questions came like a flock of frightened pigeons from the belfry of a church. *What is my responsibility to Christian tradition? What is Miss Von Horn's expectation?* The thoughts tumbled about in his head as he sketched out the first of the miracles for the presentation to Susan Cassidy. *How can I do this in less than fifteen hours?*

How authentic do I have to be? Are Christian icons authentic? How could they be authentic? Was Jesus a god masquerading as a man?

Thomas didn't doubt that Jesus was a historical figure. The Reverend Mike affirmed it. *If I can't trust a man with a snake tattoo who started a church in a redwood forest called God's Place, who can I trust?* He laughed at the thought. Jing-Wei was zealous in her belief that Jesus was the Son of God. A god himself.

Agnostics suspended the question of God in some amorphous ambiguity like a clump of crushed pineapple in green Jell-O. *The religion of intellectual cowards.* Hawker had handed him Darwin, and Darwin was tugging him toward Hawker's doctrine of the universe.

. . .

The sketch of the Jewish Rabbi in a dialogue with devils wasn't working. Thomas reworked the lines of his posture. His arm thrust out. His hand a clenched fist. It was barely blocked in. A few quick lines, but it felt very wrong.

Thomas dropped his sketch pad on the floor to give him perspective. He hovered over it, then shook his head. He used the art gum eraser to eliminate his first attempt to draw Jesus.

The rest of the drawing worked well. The women were wretched, frightening creatures tortured by the devils within. Evil wraiths inhabiting the tombs were there tormenting them. The swineherds struggled to control their pack of pigs. Some broke away and plunged toward the river. The pieces of the drawing flowed together.

His ability to visualize Jesus was clouded by a stupor of thought. It was an odd experience he'd never had before—not that he recalled, at least. He was determined to avoid the classic Jesus everyone had seen a thousand times. He wanted his creation of the famous figure to be uniquely his own. Bring something unexpected to who Jesus was and what he did. *I'm the only one who can.* A man who could discount Jesus' divinity brought a cold objectivity to the enigmatic figure few artists ever had.

He checked the clock. Susan Cassidy was expecting him in her office in twelve hours. The only thing that mattered was dazzling her socks off.

Then it came! The breakthrough idea. Not a flash or jolting epiphany, but in a surge of reassuring warmth. A feeling of clarity, tranquillity and confidence. A swelling. There was no other way to describe it. He had a distinct sense that it came from a source outside himself.

. . .

Frank Berger called at eleven o'clock. Thomas saw the agent's name on caller ID. He turned the iPhone off and tossed it onto the Black Forest chair draped in velvet.

Thomas worked through the night. At 2:15 in the morning he chased two No-Doz maximum strength with a twelve-ounce can of Red Bull. Five hundred twenty milligrams of caffeine gave him wings in a rushing headwind of creative energy.

He read the thirty-four blocks of scripture highlighted by Jing-Wei. He was surprised to find that some of the stories were told more than once. He was disappointed to discover Mark's "*man* with an unclean spirit dwelling among the tombs" and Luke's "*certain man* which had devils, wore no clothes and abode in the tombs." He considered his finished sketch of tormented women and drowning swine from his reading of Matthew 8. He left it alone. *Susan Cassidy's a woman. She's gotta love it.*

By 3:30 A.M., with only three and a half hours to go, IFI gave way to reality. *IFI* was an acronym for "Impulsive First Impressions," one of Professor Andrus's pet theories. "It's like a flash point in your brain," Andrus explained. "It comes in that millisecond when you feed the right brain an idea you wish to create. IFI is faster than conscious awareness," the old professor said. "You must train your mind to recognize it and your memory to capture it. It is more like a dream than a cognitive thought, but in some miraculous way the entire piece is already finished in your mind. Unfortunately, when you go to work the left brain does its best to scrub those illogical impressions clean."

Thomas was out of time. He took out his art books of old masters and turned on his Mac. He hurried to the pages of classic Christian art. He borrowed ideas, authenticated details and embellished his sketches.

He pulled up pictures from Google Images. He compared his sketches with Christian art spread across five hundred years. He was troubled that even artistically inferior works had an emotional quality he had not captured.

By 6:45 A.M. the wind had died and the wings were drooping. He ate a power bar, drank another Red Bull and headed for San Francisco to dazzle Susan Cassidy.

CHAPTER

39

Your meeting with Ms. Cassidy was set for eight-thirty."

"I'm sorry. The traffic on the bridge was murder."

"You should have left earlier."

"I know. Look. A car got stalled on the bridge and . . ." Thomas was out of breath. He had sprinted from visitor parking, gone in the wrong door, been lost for four precious minutes and finally found Administration.

The woman at the reception desk was unsympathetic. "It's ten to nine."

"Yeah, I know. I'm sorry I'm late. I called, but no one . . . I left a voice message."

The woman nodded at the roll under his arm. "Those blueprints for her? You can leave 'em here and I'll send 'em up later." *Those blueprints* was a 1/6 scale composite of the sketches scanned into Photoshop and printed as a single banner on the Canon Prograf printer leased for the Vegas project. It was in effect the proposed mural in miniature, twenty-four inches wide and twelve feet long.

"I've still got ten minutes. I'll give it to her in person."

"She's not in her office. Take a seat."

"She has a meeting at nine!"

"Just take a seat, please." She seemed bent on displaying her irritation.

"Are you Jessica?"

"Excuse me?"

"Was it you I talked to yesterday?"

"No."

. . .

Thomas had left Sausalito in plenty of time to be at St. Mark's by eight-fifteen. He had even given himself an extra twenty minutes in case morning traffic was slower than usual over the Golden Gate.

He was seven cars behind a late-model Chevrolet when it stopped midspan and blocked the number-three lane, sparking a chain reaction of jammed brakes and blinking lights. Four of the six lanes were allocated for southbound commuters. Thomas cut off a woman in a Honda and sliced right into lane number four. She hit her brake and her horn and showed Thomas the middle finger of her left hand.

The driver of the Chevy got out of his car and darted across both outside lanes of traffic until he was on the narrow raised ledge between the pavement and the railing on the west side of the bridge. Wind from the ocean pushed him back but he seemed determined and he pulled himself forward.

Thomas glanced at the digital display, unaware of the drama ahead. His lane moved slowly but at least it was moving. Even with a short delay he would still be okay.

He rehearsed his opening lines. *Charm Susan Cassidy in the first two minutes.* He glanced up and saw the man on the bridge. He was struggling over the railing. *The guy is going to jump.*

The traffic in his lane inched forward until he was directly across from the man committed to suicide. *A few short steps to rescue.* In the dark days ahead, the moment would return to haunt him. The memory would ask why no part of him was prompted to leap from the car, grab the poor fellow and drag him from the railing.

Thomas sat among the morning commuters and watched the man who was determined to die. The wind moaned through the cables that hung the bridge and helped the jumper pull himself over the edge. His foot slipped and he fell to the walkway but pulled himself up and thrust his left leg over the high railing.

A white Ford utility truck two cars ahead slammed its brakes and stopped. Thomas almost rear-ended the BMW between them.

The doors of the Ford truck flew open, and two men in white coveralls ran toward the man struggling to get over the railing. He had one leg over the rounded cap, still sticky with a fresh coat of vermilion orange paint. The fellow was over the railing and perched on the pipe that ran along the edge of the girder sixteen inches below.

Thomas pushed the button on the smartTOP Remote and watched the drama with macabre fascination. The soft top of the Mercedes lifted up, retracted and disappeared. Thomas checked his watch and placed a call to St. Mark's.

Marin commuters knew the history of suicides from the Golden Gate Bridge. People driving north slowed to rubberneck or stopped to gawk. Twenty-five people a year jumped off the bridge. It was an unspoken rite of passage for a Marin commuter to see at least one attempt. A grim reward for the banality of a daily commute.

Thomas had gotten the history his first week in San Francisco on the compulsory stroll across the bridge with other students from out of state. For people determined to kill themselves by jumping, the Golden Gate Bridge was the number-one choice. It was 245 feet to the water. It took jumpers four seconds to travel the distance, and by the time they got there they were falling at seventy-six miles an hour. At that speed, water reacted more like a solid than a liquid. Most jumpers were killed by the impact. The few who survived the initial collision died from hypothermia in the frigid water or drowned.

Swift currents often carried bodies out to sea before they could be recovered. As a result, no one knew for sure the real tally of people who had leapt to their deaths from the bridge. Known suicides and suicide attempts, including people stopped by the highway patrol or official bridge watchers—*or good Samaritans, like the two guys in white coveralls*—totaled more than fifteen hundred. Twenty-six people were known to have survived. Thomas had met a man working as a janitor at Art Institute who claimed to be one of them.

The angels in white coveralls reached the man at the last possible second. The taller of the two wrapped his arms around the would-be jumper and hung on. The other straddled the railing, put an arm around the man's shoulder and talked to him. Eventually they coaxed him back across the railing. He collapsed into the outside lane.

It was twenty minutes before the CHP navigated the tangle of automobiles, trucks and buses. The man was helped into the cruiser and sat on the backseat talking to the officer and the coverall angels. It was impossible to hear what was being said, but it was taking forever to get the traffic moving again, and Thomas was in agony. *Let the idiot jump if he still wants to jump,* Thomas thought. It made him angry that people with important things to do and places to be were being stuck in traffic all because of some . . . *some manic-depressive loser from the edge of society.*

The traffic started to move. Thomas passed the CHP cruiser and caught a glimpse of the would-be jumper. His face was smudged by grime and tears and vermilion orange. He reminded Thomas of the refugees from some war-torn country he'd seen on CNN. Or was it a natural disaster? He couldn't remember. It was all the same. The diet of death and destruction had become an abstraction. There was no choice. Separating one's own life from the endless tragedies of others came in a rush of emotional self-preservation.

Thomas was unable to take his eyes off that face. The man stared back without expression, his eyes vacant. *How does a person get to the point where obliteration seems better than life, difficult as life can be?* He checked the time. *I might find out.*

Thomas was late for a critical appointment.

CHAPTER

40

THE DIGITAL CLOCK ON THE wall above the woman who told Thomas to sit down changed to 8:56 A.M. He was back at the desk.

"I think I'll go wait in her office."

"St. Mark's Hospital. How may I direct your call?" The receptionist shook her head at Thomas and wagged a finger. "One moment, please; I'll see if he's available."

Thomas felt the vibration of the iPhone in his pocket. It was a text message from Hawker, all in caps.

WHERE ARE YOU?

YOU'RE SUPPOSED TO BE HERE!

WE NEED TO TALK!

DR. HAWKER.

His gut wrenched. He glanced at the clock. 8:57.

"Dr. Melville has a call on line one." The woman who relished her authority pointed toward the chairs in the reception area and waved Thomas away. *Three minutes!* He walked around her desk and pushed through the double doors marked AUTHORIZED HOSPITAL ADMINISTRATIVE PERSONNEL ONLY.

"Sir, you can't," The woman called after him. "Sir!" She jumped up to stop him, but the wire on her headset was clipped to the collar of her dress. "Stop! The administrative offices are off-limits to—" The doors swooshed shut, cutting off her voice as if it had been snipped with a pair of surgical scissors.

She pushed the microphone against her lips. "Security to Administration."

. . .

"Security to Administration" boomed through the corridor. Thomas hurried forward in long, bounding strides. A large map at the first intersection of the main hall showed the location of every department. Public Relations was on the second floor in the oldest part of the building. It was at the end of a short hall on the east side, just off the main corridor.

Jessica stood up as Thomas opened the door. "Hello, Mr. Hall," she said.

"You're Jessica?" Her smile said yes. *Older than her voice,* he thought. She had an oval face and wide eyes framed by tortoiseshell horn-rim glasses. Her hair was dark red, straight and cut short. She wore earrings that dangled with green stones. *Perfect color complement to her hair.* Her eyebrows went up with the corners of her mouth when Thomas came in and neither came down again. She was so upbeat and buoyant, he wondered if they ever did.

"You didn't make it," she said.

"I know. I'm so sorry. Some guy tried to jump off the bridge."

"That's funny. I've heard some good excuses, but—"

"No, there really was."

"Oh! That's awful!" The man's anguished face flashed in Thomas's head. *Eidetic memory. A blessing and a curse.*

"Sad," he said and realized he meant it. "Is there any chance she'll have time to see me?"

"Well, she's got a nine o'clock."

"You told me. Can I just wait here? See her for just a minute, maybe?"

"They called Security when you came up without a pass, so—"

His iPhone buzzed again.

CONFIRM RECEIPT OF MESSAGE.

DR. HAWKER.

Jessica read the stress on his face. "Bad news?"

"Just another project I'm working on." *Crazy guy!* Thomas used both thumbs to key in a return message.

Bad traffic. On my way.

The sound of boots moving with purpose echoed down the corridor. Thomas stepped to the door with a shrug of resignation.

"Wait a minute." Jessica scribbled on a form. "Sign this," she said and pushed a temporary visitor's pass across the desk. She picked a lanyard and plastic ID window from a basket on the desk and put the pass inside.

"This'll keep me out of jail?" Thomas grinned.

"Cass went to ICU. They called her ten minutes ago, and since you weren't here . . . you might get a few minutes with her if she's still there."

Two men wearing the black-and-gray uniforms of St. Mark's Security entered the short hall. "Go out that way." Jessica pointed to a door behind her. "Through Cass's office, right to the main corridor, then all the way down and take the elevator to the third floor." She hung the lanyard around his neck. "This'll get you in."

"You're better than a fairy godmother!"

"Sometimes," she grinned. "Hurry up and good luck."

CHAPTER

41

WHEN THOMAS REACHED ICU, the duty nurse confirmed that Susan Cassidy was visiting Christina. Access to ICU was restricted, even with a visitor's pass, but the woman evidently presumed he had come to see the child. "Such a tragedy to be left all alone like that," she said as Thomas followed her to Christina's room. "Were you a friend of her mother?"

"No, really, I just . . ." They reached room 314 and the duty nurse pushed through the door. Thomas was not sure what to expect and he didn't expect what he saw. Susan Cassidy was holding the hand of a little girl wrapped in bandages and connected by wires and tubes to monitors, machines and bags of fluid. A nurse's aide was tidying up in the background.

He hoped the surprised look on Susan Cassidy's face did not give him away. Allowing the duty nurse to believe he was there for the child was not the same as telling a lie. If it was, he was sure that lie was pearl white. The duty nurse took a moment to stroke Christina's shoulder. She leaned close and uttered soothing words of love and encouragement. She patted Cass on the shoulder, smiled at Thomas and left the room.

"Hi," Thomas whispered.

"Hi." Cass held his eyes a few seconds longer than allowed by the law of intervals.

He held up the roll of drawings. "Your sketches. Sorry I'm late." It was hardly the place to talk about the attempted suicide. He tried to read her expression. *She has already signed the woman from Europe.*

She waved him closer and turned to the child in the bed. "Christina, this is Thomas Hall. He came to see how you were doing. Mr. Hall, this is Christina, my very best friend." Christina smiled. The left corner of her mouth disappeared beneath the bandages that covered the whole side of her face. Plastic tubes protruded from the right. An IV was taped to her frail little arm.

"I'm happy to meet you," Christina said. Her voice was weak; it sounded as if speaking caused her pain. She raised her right hand. Thomas glanced at Cass, uncertain if touching the wounded child was okay. Cass nodded and Thomas shook Christina's hand as gently as he could.

"I'm very happy to meet you too," he said.

"Thomas is an artist," Cass said, brushing a thin blonde lock from Christina's face.

"Will you draw me a picture?"

"Sure. What would you like?" He plucked a yellow Ticonderoga from the inside pocket of his sport coat and rolled out a few blank inches from his roll of drawings.

"Not there. On my leg." Christina squirmed to pull the bedding aside. Cass turned back the sheet. There were heavy plaster casts on both the child's legs. They began with platforms below her feet, engulfing everything but her tiny toes, and covered the legs like thick white logs until they disappeared beneath the sheet just below her hips. *Too massive for such little legs,* Thomas thought.

"I'll get a Sharpie," the nurse's aide said and pushed through the door to a canister of pens and pencils at the nurse's station.

"What's wrong with your hand?" Christina asked.

"Oh, nothing, just a cut." Cass took his hand and turned it palm side up. The skin on either side of the ragged scab was puffy red.

"You should have someone look at that."

"It'll be fine." The nurse's aide returned and handed Thomas a Sharpie.

"What you like me to draw?"

Christina pursed her lips in serious consideration.

"Do you like dragons?" he prompted.

"No."

"Spiderman?"

The girl shook her head.

"Just think of something that makes you happy every time you see it," Thomas said.

"Can you draw a picture of my mom?"

"Yup. I can do that, but to make sure it looks exactly like her I need to see a picture, or meeting her would be even better, so—" Cass squeezed his arm in a way that made it impossible to misunderstand the signal. *SHUT UP!*

"Mr. Hall isn't very good at drawing people, sweetheart. What about Muffin? I'll bet he could draw a picture of your kitten."

Christina turned her head as if looking for something on a distant horizon that only she could see. "I want to sleep now," she said and closed her eyes. Tears trickled across her cheek and over the bridge of her nose.

Cass kissed the child on the cheek and lingered there. "I'll be back later, okay?"

Christina nodded.

Thomas returned the Sharpie to the nurse's assistant. Observing his upturned palm, she said, "You should have someone look at that." Cass punctuated the comment with a "told you so" look.

CHAPTER

42

THE BEST-LAID SCHEMES OF MICE *and men go oft awry.* Thomas recited the familiar line to himself as he walked with Cass to the new Children's Wing where she said she wanted to look at his drawings.

His well-rehearsed dialogue had been preempted. He wanted to ask about the woman artist from Europe. He wanted to be reassured he was still in the running for the project. He wanted to apologize for being too hasty. He wanted to explain why he'd changed his mind. He wanted to know how much time he had to show Cass his drawings and sell her on his new idea. He wanted to get back to where he had been five minutes before he'd foolishly turned this woman down. The opportunity to discuss his anxious questions never presented itself. Being late, meeting Cass in the ICU instead of her office and meeting Christina had—what was it Berger always said?—"changed the dynamic."

• • •

As a favor to Cass, the duty nurse looked at Thomas's infected hand. She lanced it, scrubbed it clean, bandaged it and gave him a shot of antibiotics. It was throbbing and his Red Bull wings were wilted.

Cass dominated the walk with the story of Christina. The accident. The medical prognosis. What she knew of the child.

Christina was an only child. Her mother had been killed in the crash and no immediate family had come forward. The police were unable to locate her father, who, as far as they could tell, had not been a part of the girl's life almost from the time she was born.

Cass did not share with Thomas the fact she had signed on as the responsible party for the girl or that her interest in Christina had become deeply personal. It was inevitable. Cass had endured anxious moments when the doctors were not sure Christina would survive. She had been there when Christina had awakened to the paralyzing reality that her mother was gone and she was alone in the world. Prayer and faith were a private part of Susan Cassidy's life.

On their walk to the Healing Place she did not share with Thomas that she prayed every day with a plea for God to preserve the precious child.

· · ·

"You still need to wear one of these." Cass plucked two fluorescent orange safety helmets from their pegs.

"I never wear a color that doesn't occur in nature," Thomas quipped. It was not the first time he'd used the line. It usually got a laugh, and laughter lessened tension. The fact that she didn't laugh made him worry.

"Oh, I know, they're awful, but I'm afraid that—"

"I'm only kidding." Thomas put the ugly hard hat on his head. The inner band was too small, so it rode high. He looked more like a peasant woman carrying a clay pot to the well for water than an artist being introduced to the project intended to change lives. Standing there looking ridiculous with a bright orange helmet teetering on his head, it never occurred to Thomas that the life that might be changed the most was one he knew the best—or least—of all.

Thomas followed Cass into a narrow corridor created by scaffolds and construction plastic. They emerged in the spacious new addition on the north side. It was still under construction.

"This is the Healing Place," Cass said in an almost reverent tone. It was not what Thomas had imagined. He turned all the way around as he walked to the center of the chamber. The room was circular. The ceiling was a dome that swept upward from an ornate cornice that crowned the top of twelve-foot walls. Thomas estimated the apex of the dome at twenty-five feet. Maybe higher. A large span of the wall was punctured by large portals that opened to separate hallways. The halls stretched away from the sanctuary like spokes from the hub of a massive wheel. The walls between the portals were glass, etched in the corners with intricate floral motifs that seemed touched by a gentle breeze.

"Wow!" Thomas whispered. He didn't know what else to say. The artistic splendor of the design resonated with whatever it was inside that made him who he was.

"This is the center of the new Children's Wing," Cass said. The earlier intonation of a tour guide was gone, replaced by an eager zeal.

"Be hard not to feel better taking your medicine in a place like this."

She walked to where Thomas was standing beneath the vertex of the dome. "The mural goes there. On that wall." The wall opposite the portals was void of glass. It was all white and crowned by a cornice molding of Victorian design. Thomas scanned it left to right. It was ninety feet wide and twelve feet high, flanked on either side by double doors. Thomas noted how the sculpted wood circled the entire room to form an ornate demarcation between the wall and the dome.

Thomas brushed his hand across the surface. The tips of his fingers read the texture like those of a blind man reading Braille. *Pure Belgian linen. Somebody did their homework.* Cass must have divined his thoughts because when she spoke it was an echo of his own inner voice.

"One hundred percent pure Belgian linen."

"You did your homework. Very impressive."

"The people from Fredrix Artist Canvas wanted to add acrylic titanium double-primed with acid-free smooth ground." *Berger talked to the woman and now she's showing off.* "I wanted that to be your choice." His heart leapt, then fell as a quick smile covered her slip of the tongue: "The choice of the artist. Whoever."

They were both thinking the same thing, but neither was willing to break the ice. Cass concluded the tour. "It's the largest single addition ever made to St. Mark's. It's connected to the old building, as you can see, but designed to stand completely alone."

"Amazing. Truly."

"It is exclusively for the care and recovery of children. The emphasis will be on those with critical conditions."

"Like Christina."

"Exactly! This is what I wanted to show you before you turned us down."

There was no need to feign humility. Eating crow was never easy. For guys with swollen egos, choking was painful. He picked his words carefully. *You'll do better if you call her Cass. She does not like* Susan. *Little heads-up?* The voice of the fairy godmother.

"Look, Cass," he made the sound of her name musical and let it hang in the air, "I made a mistake." The words tasted bitter on his tongue. "You were right. It is a great project. Of course it has to be about Jesus." He waited for her to respond. She didn't. "Once I caught your vision I got excited. I know you've got a nine o'clock but I'd love to show you a few ideas."

"I'm all right for a few minutes," she said and folded her arms. She wasn't going to make it easy.

Thomas taped the end of the roll to the wall of Belgian linen. "I worked up some sketches based on Miss Von Horn's suggestions, like Frank promised when you guys talked." He unrolled the mini-mural and fastened it to the canvas with masking tape.

"I've not spoken with Mr. Berger since our last conversation." *Shot in the chest with a marshmallow gun.* He had no idea why such a curious image popped into his head but that was the way it felt. He taped the last corner in place.

"He didn't call you?" Cass shook her head but her attention had moved to the wall. She walked slowly past the drawings that flowed from one end to the other. Light from the walls of glass bouncing off white linen cast a glow on Cass's face. He tried to discern her reaction. She was more stunning than he remembered. He confessed to himself there was more to his interest in the St. Mark's mural than his dire financial straits.

CHAPTER

43

THE IMAGES ON THE WALL affirmed the impression Cass had experienced the day she'd discovered the art of Thomas Hall. A few of the sketches felt almost complete. Most of them were rough and unrefined. Some were little more than vague indications but linked by notes and arrows. In some places Thomas had included scriptural references. Cass couldn't visualize everything that Thomas had in mind. There was nothing in the center but a few graceful lines. Then she saw it. The name JESUS, printed in the midst of the swirling lines.

For all his hubris, arrogance, insecurity, cynicism, disbelief in God and lack of faith in anything as far as Cass could tell, Thomas Hall was the one thing she had been sure about. He was an artist of extraordinary talent. Maybe even a genius.

"What do you think?" Thomas asked. The question dangled between hope and fear.

Cass scrutinized the mock-up. The delay in answering his question exceeded the interval of expectation. Thomas had put her in a prickly position. "Why didn't you just agree in the first place?" She was angry.

"I should have," he admitted. "Better late than never, though, right?"

"Not always. In this case *late* may mean *never.*"

"I was hoping we could get past my stupidity and focus on how fantastic this can be." He moved to the sketches taped on the canvas. "Do you see where I'm going with this? The symmetry is both visual and thematic. I thought it would be great to include the biblical passage below each of the vignettes. Some of it is rough and may not make sense at first. Let me walk you through it. Do you have time?"

Cass cut him off. "We've signed a letter of intent with another artist." She couldn't hide the bitterness in her voice. "She was on the short list before I found out about you. One of those friends of a friend of a relative of Clinton Carver."

"Who is it?"

"Alexis Bouvier."

"The woman from Europe?"

Cass was surprised that Thomas was privy to that confidential information. She let it slide. "She works in Europe. She's from New Jersey."

"I'm sure she's very good if you liked her work," he said.

"She does restorations for the Rijksmuseum in Amsterdam."

Thomas removed the tape from the mock-up, letting it sag toward the floor. "You think she'll be able to give you what you want?" Cass glared at him. "What Miss Von Horn wants," he amended.

She stopped his hand from pulling more tape away. "Not even close." Cass raised the loose end of the drawing and taped it back in place. "You have put me in a very difficult position. I hope you know that!"

"I'm sorry. Truly."

"I'm not sure there is any way out of it, but I want Miss Von Horn to see this before . . ." She saw Carver's predictable reaction in her mind and lost the thought. "I want to make sure I understand everything you have imagined. I recognize most of the stories but I don't see Jesus anywhere."

The iPhone buzzed in his pocket, but she could see that he was going to ignore the call. Whoever it was would have to wait. Thomas had some explaining to do.

• • •

It took most of an hour to describe his ideas to Cass. He began by describing his discussion with the Chinese woman and the man with the snake tattoo. The mural took shape as he read the stories of the New Testament for himself. It blossomed into a series of vignettes as the people touched by the hand of Jesus became real to him.

It slammed into a stone wall when he tried to draw the face of Jesus. That familiar place he went to find inspiration was closed and the lights were out. There were hours of darkness. He felt abandoned by his gifts.

That's when the idea had come. Once he set aside his prideful passion to create the "all-new-and-improved Jesus of Thomas Hall," the light came on again. The muse set him free. A madman. An angel flying in the rarified atmosphere of his inexhaustible imagination.

By the time Thomas fed the composition to the printer, Jesus was indicated by a swirl of lines but not truly present. When he rolled up the scroll at 6:45 A.M., he printed the name of Jesus at the center of the piece. He was confident he would "see" Jesus at the right moment and bring him to life.

The stories of the miracles depicted the people who had been blessed and not The Blessed himself. That was the idea!

"It portrays Jesus healing the sick in the broader context of all His miracles," Thomas explained. He talked about the four categories of miracles. He explained the reasons for his choices. Jing-Wei's voice was so loud in his head he wondered if Cass couldn't hear it.

In the spots where the drawings were little more than graceful lines, he painted with words. His vision of the mural expanded as he explained it to Cass.

The mural included fourteen vignettes divided evenly on either side of the swirls in the center labeled *JESUS*. Even before Thomas explained the logic of the layout, Cass recognized the thematic symmetry balanced visually by the number and arrangement of figures in each illustration.

Miracles of healing were separated by other miracles of Jesus. Casting out evil spirits. Calming the storm-tossed sea. Feeding the multitudes. Raising the dead. Jesus appeared in none of them. The impact was visceral.

In every piece of Christian art depicting the healing miracles that Cass remembered, Jesus was the main figure. Spreading mud on a blind man's eyes. Touching the leper's rotted skin. Commanding the lame to rise and walk. Touching ears and tongues and withered limbs. Forgiving sins with an iconic gesture of his hand replicated seven times seventy thousand.

Thomas's creation featured the men and women and children healed by Jesus not in the moment of the miracle, but in the minutes, hours or days *after* the blessed event.

"The only thing more powerful than action is reaction," Thomas explained. "A painting is a frozen instant in time," he went on. "The artist must select the fraction of a single second and then stop time. That frozen instant must depict what is, what was and what comes after and give each meaning. If I choose to paint the story of Jesus healing the leper and stop time in the moment the Lord touches him, the man is a leper still.

"In the middle of the night it came to me that the untold story, the best part of Jesus' healing, was not the moment of the act itself, great as it was. It was the consequences. It was what came after." He watched Cass closely, hoping to read her reactions. Encouraged, he continued:

"I want to capture the minutes and hours and days after Jesus performed the miracles. What happened to a deaf-mute man who could hear and talk and laugh? A blind man who could see? The nobleman who found his little son alive when he got home? The sisters of the man dead and four days buried when he returned to their arms? The father of the little girl who died when he threw his arms around her and carried her to the lap of her mother as they laughed and wept together."

Thomas pointed to each of the stories. "The first question I asked was, Which story? The next, In which moment? Jesus was the cause of incredible joy, but in everything I read, he never lingered to gloat over his marvelous achievements or waited around for the adulation of the blessed."

Cass stood with her arms snugged over her chest and fingers steepled over her nose and mouth, hiding her emotions. Thomas went on: "It seemed to me the message for your kids isn't so much the miracle itself as what came after. What the healing means to them for the rest of their lives. That's the part of the story they care about. The relief. The happiness. Hanging out with their friends again. To me, that's hope. The promise of being happy again." He paused.

"I've not forgotten what Miss Von Horn said to me." *How could I?* he said under his breath and Cass laughed. "It is ALL about Jesus." Thomas walked the length of the mural to make sure Cass saw what he was talking about. "They all look to him. I made sure no one forgot the source of their joy. Made sure they all remembered."

He could tell from her eyes that Cass saw it. Every part of the composition conformed to a graceful, undulating curve that flowed toward the center from either side. Every figure was looking, gesturing, pointing or moving toward the center of the piece . . . toward the swirling lines called "Jesus."

"I'm surprised you didn't draw Jesus first," Cass smiled. "I would think he would be the easiest of all. He's so well-known."

The iPhone buzzed. It was on vibrate but echoed softly in the hollow dome. He ignored it. It buzzed again.

"You need to get that?"

"Excuse me a second." He pulled it out and checked text messages.
????????????

HAWKER!

44

D<small>R. H</small>AWKER IS NOT happy with you," the plumpish older woman scolded Thomas when he arrived at Hawker's office a little after eleven o'clock. Maxine was not as old as Hawker had described but unattractive in an angry sort of way. He had a vague recollection of having seen her when he met with Hamilton.

"I got here as quick as I could. You're Maxine? Right?"

"The meeting was at nine!"

"What meeting?"

"I put a note on the painting you're doing upstairs to make sure you didn't miss it."

"I haven't worked much upstairs since Dr. Hawker took over. I've been in and out a lot mostly and . . ." She cocked her head and raised her painted brows to make sure "the hireling" understood that his schedule was also a sore point with Hawker.

She cut him off. "Well, they waited over an hour."

"Who? What meeting?"

"Dr. Hawker does not have the patience Dr. Hamilton had. The other two were rude about it."

"What other two?

"From Walters, Johnson, Lewis & Arlington."

"Lawyers?" he asked and she affirmed it with a nod.

"They had to leave for another appointment and Dr. Hawker couldn't wait any longer because of the press conference."

"What time will he be back?"

She might as well have said *Are you a complete idiot?* out loud because her look barked her thoughts. "He's upstairs at the press conference." Thomas considered his options. *Leave. Wait in Hawker's office. Go upstairs.* Maxine made it easy. "You were supposed to be there!"

Thomas climbed the grand staircase rather than taking the elevator. He was in no hurry to meet Hawker in a foul mood.

Thomas had been awake for thirty hours. The last few minutes of his meeting with Susan Cassidy had not gone the way he'd hoped. She had left him hanging and uncertain. *There's a good chance I'll never hear from her again,* he worried. He was not accustomed to the feeling. Maybe it was her way of paying him back for being a jackass. That was Frank's articulate assessment of the way he'd handled his first meeting with Susan Cassidy. Maybe it was a ploy to get him cheap. *Cheap* spiked his anxiety. Without Frank he was on his own to work out the money himself. If it happened at all!

Cass had seemed impressed by the sketches. She thought Miss Von Horn might like the idea of depicting reactions to the miracles rather than the miracles themselves. Would she put herself in a bind with the board and a difficult situation with the woman from the Rijksmuseum? Would she?

His meeting with her ended with a text message from Hawker. Cass asked him to leave the drawings and dashed away to her other meeting. "I'll call you when we decide what we're doing." Those were not her final words. She yelled, "Don't forget to leave your safety helmet," as she disappeared. As if he would steal a fluorescent orange hard hat even if the band were stuffed with hundred-dollar bills. The thought amused him. *For a hat full of hundred-dollar bills I'd wear the helmet to the opera.* His only motive in trying to salvage the St. Mark's project was money, after all.

On the way up the grand staircase he decided to confront Hawker about getting paid the money he was owed and to talk about a budget for the changes. *More than changes. Starting over.*

Somewhere in the spacious caverns above him he could hear the resonant rumbling of Hawker's voice.

CHAPTER

45

THE DARWIN PAVILION WILL BE something beyond what you've come to expect from the passive exhibits of science. When we're finished, this hall will celebrate the greatest naturalist who ever lived, perhaps indeed the greatest mind—well, that ever evolved." His deliberate quip caused a ripple of laughter from thirty attendees facing him on folding chairs. Members of the press, museum patrons, a congregation of special interests and the inevitable activists who gathered like carrion fowl on a roadkill.

Hawker's remarks were taped by video crews from KGO and KSFX. The heroic, bearded bronze of Charles Darwin looked down on his disciple with unblinking eyes. "It will be much more than a monument to a man . . ."

Hawker's prepared speech was amplified by the narrow hallway as Thomas crossed the third-level atrium and passed through the arch that led to the Darwin Pavilion.

"It will be more than a shrine to *Origin of Species* and *Descent of Man,* his great masterworks. The most important books ever written. The Darwin Pavilion will be what science should be but too often isn't: an aggressive indictment of religion for the deception that it is."

Half a dozen people applauded, one with an audible "bravo." Some laughed nervously. Others were incredulous. Most of them traded derisive comments, unable to believe a man of Hawker's distinction would make such an incendiary remark at a press conference. He obviously took courage from San Francisco's extreme liberalism on most issues. A few sat stupefied.

Thomas stopped beside a gothic column at the end of the trefoil arches. His mural was covered by an opaque plastic shroud. It was disquieting. He folded his arms and listened as the murmurous quake ended and Hawker continued.

"The celebration of Charles Darwin begs the hard question, the question only the intellectually honest dare answer: Does God exist?" Another stir. "Every religious argument simply assumes there is such a thing and moves on from there. Here the question of God, and the endless 'religions' that delusion has created, will be subjected to the same level of intellectual scrutiny that every scientific theory must survive on its way to becoming fact.

"The discovery of natural selection and the brilliant insights of Charles Darwin have been mercilessly scrutinized by the finest minds of science for over a hundred and fifty years. The fact of evolution has been confirmed by overwhelming evidence."

Hawker set his prepared statement aside with a bit of theatrics and said in a tone of confidentiality, "I confess atheism appeals primarily to intellectuals and those well educated, but even so, how it is that so many reasonably intelligent people persist in believing that man was created out of dirt by some mystical power who 'breathed' him into being is frankly beyond my comprehension." He shook his head as if it were his singular responsibility to mourn the ignorant masses of the believing world. He milked the moment, then resumed reading his prepared statement.

"Science encourages curiosity, research, knowledge, progress. It encourages an open and independent mind. Religion demands compliance, acceptance, ignorance and denial. It encourages narrow thinking and close-mindedness. Science looks forward. Religion looks back. Science has given us Charles Darwin, Sigmund Freud, Albert Einstein, Friedrich Nietzsche, James Watson, Stephen Hawking and Ernst Mayr. All of them atheists. Religion has given us Jerry Falwell, Pat Robertson, Ted Haggard and Jim Jones." He paused again for emphasis. "Religion has given us Osama bin Laden and the Ayatollah Khomeini."

Thomas could hardly stay awake. Hawker's voice retreated into the muted gray of a distant twilight. He dozed off standing up. His head lopped forward and cracked his neck. He wanted to sit down but was reluctant to enter the hall and cross the thirty yards of open ground to the nearest chair. The shrouded mural worried him. He was not looking forward to his meeting with Hawker, who continued to charm the media.

"In *Lila*, Robert Pirsig put it all in perspective. 'When one person suffers from a delusion it is called insanity. When many people suffer from a delusion it is called religion.'" A wave of light laughter rippled across the audience.

"Religious frauds, fanatics and even passionate believers present a frightening hindrance to the betterment of humankind. The rationalists among us who know the truth of science must have the courage to openly challenge the traditions of fallacious faith and irrational beliefs that have brought such misery in the world.

"The Bible says, 'by their fruits ye shall know them.' Consider the 'fruits' of religion. September eleventh. Burning women as witches. Muslim massacres in Serbia and Croatia. Persecution of the Jews as 'Christ-killers.' Teenagers who strap bombs to their bodies and cause death and destruction in the name of their God. The endless insanity of Israel and Palestine. The Crusades. The Inquisition. The atrocities committed in the name of God are endless, and sadly, they define the history of the world."

Hawker paused to take a swallow of water from a frosted container labeled Bling H_2O. He ignored a woman on the second row waving her hand with a question.

"The Darwin Pavilion is a temple of science where the only gods are the immutable laws of nature. We intend for it to be a breakwater against the frothing tides of religious superstition that threaten to drown yet another generation. There is, I am sorry to say, no way we can prevent parents from imposing religious ideas upon their children before they are old enough to know what their opinion ought to be. At the Darwin Pavilion we will endeavor to unscramble irrational religious indoctrination wherever we can. Your press packet outlines the curriculum program being prepared for public education throughout northern California. These materials will take the message of the museum to the schools and, I am proud to announce today, we have worked out an agreement with the California

Department of Education for every fourth grader in the public system to spend a day with us and be taught the facts of evolution.

"Richard Dawkins, noted author and scientist, is an example of the caliber of speakers we have signed for the Charles Darwin Lecture Series. To quote one review of Dawkins's spirited presentation, 'His thoughtful engaging thesis on atheism cajoles, bullies, persuades and dazzles. Some of it is hard to disagree with. Some of it will make you hopping mad.'

"I had the delight of attending one of Dawkins's lectures. His marvelous castigation of God may end up here on display: 'The God of the Old Testament is arguably the most unpleasant character in all fiction: jealous and proud of it; a petty, unjust, unforgiving control-freak; a vindictive, bloodthirsty ethnic cleanser; a misogynistic, homophobic, racist, infanticidal, genocidal, filicidal, pestilential, megalomaniacal, sadomasochistic, capriciously malevolent bully.'"

Once again the reactions of those gathered were mixed and the schism between them would, in Hawker's way of thinking, be a perfect illustration of how the question of God was divisive.

"Carl Sagan asked 'how it was that hardly any major religion has looked at science and concluded, "This is better than we thought. The universe is much bigger than our prophets said, grander, more subtle and more elegant." Instead they say, "No, no, no! My god is a little god and I want him to say that way."'"

Hawker looked up from his notes and spoke with endearing confidentiality. "I confess a portion of the inspiration for this place has come from Mr. Sagan. He also said, 'A religion, old or new, that stressed the magnificence of the Universe as revealed by modern science might be able to draw forth reserves of reverence and awe hardly tapped by the conventional faiths.' That is the vision to which we aspire.

"Catholic Cardinal Schönborn has condemned those of us who challenge faith with science as followers of a new religion he calls 'evolutionism' or 'scientism.' Thank you, Cardinal, for giving us a name. It is, as he fears, our hope that science will go beyond being a mere measure of truth and replace religion altogether as a worldview and touchstone for generations to come. It is my commitment that the Darwin Pavilion become a temple of that new religion."

Hawker concluded his prepared statement and opened the floor to questions. It amused Thomas that Hawker looked and sounded like the Christian televangelists he so despised. Hawker fielded the questions with the mental dexterity of a duplicitous politician. Whatever the question, his answer came back to a point in the prepared text.

"Do you believe Darwin's theory rules out a universal consciousness?" It was the woman on the second row who had been wriggling her fingers for several minutes.

"If the comfort you hope for in some 'universal consciousness' requires the neurologically preposterous premise that you will survive the death of your brain, are you sure you even want to ask that question?" A sprinkle of laughter embarrassed the woman. Hawker pointed to a clean-shaven man in a blue blazer with a media tag. "Yes, sir?"

"Dick Hart, *Oakland Tribune.* Two questions. Do you think being so aggressively antireligion is in the best interest of the museum, since it is supported by public funds, the majority of which likely come from people who don't share that view?"

"Like you?"

"Exactly. Like me."

"I already answered that question. Write it down this time." Another smattering of chuckles. Hawker defused his brusqueness with humor. "Rationalists must challenge irrational beliefs. If people want fairy tales they can go to Disneyland. What's your second question?"

Thomas expected the reporter to snap back with an equally sarcastic retort. Instead he wrote a note and asked his second question. "Men of good will can disagree without calling names. Do you think using words like *imbecilic, irrational, idiotic* and *stupid* to describe people who disagree with you is constructive?" Before Hawker could answer, the reporter stood up. "Quoting Dawkins's infamous rebuke of Jehovah is blasphemy to people of faith."

"That's not a question and this is my press conference." More laughs.

"The question is, how do you justify such disrespect and insensitivity in the name of science?"

"Blasphemy is speaking sacrilege against God. If I profane *you,* then I've truly offended. If I profane God, there is none to take offense. I've a bumper sticker on my car that says it perfectly, 'Blasphemy is a victimless crime.'" Hawker's smile was condescending. He took another long swallow of the purified water.

The thought amused Thomas in passing but he found himself offended by Hawker's arrogance. He desperately wanted to be asleep.

Hawker called on the woman who had moved her chair close to the podium and recorded the press conference on her iPhone. "You talk about open-mindedness but it sounds like you've rejected any possibility of a power in the universe beyond ourselves. Any possibility of . . . intelligent design?"

"Possibility? Of course. Unlike fundamentalists who would remain creationists even if all the evidence turned against them, I am a scientist." Hawker paused as if time itself stopped to pay him homage. "I rely on evidence, but I agree with Dawkins: 'If all the evidence in the universe turned in favor of creationism, I would be the first to admit it, and I would immediately change my mind.'" His laugh was condescending as he said, "of course," and continued quoting Dawkins: "'As things stand, however, all available evidence—and there is a vast amount of it—favors evolution. It is for this reason and this reason alone that I argue for evolution with a passion that matches the passion of those who argue against it. My passion is based on evidence, however, while theirs flies in the face of the evidence.'"

"What about miracles?" The question was hurled at Hawker by a man in his fifties in a leather jacket and San Francisco Giants baseball cap. It woke Thomas up. Miracles had kept him up all night.

"What is a miracle?" Hawker asked, the look in his eyes like that of a coiled snake that had killed mice before.

"A miracle is a person who discovers she has terminal cancer and the doctors tell her she has three weeks to live, but she has faith that God can heal her and so she asks her family to pray. And we do."

Thomas looked at the woman on the chair next to him. She looked up at her husband and slipped her hand into his. The man paused a moment to control his emotions. "We pray as a family and the tumor disappears. Gone. Vanished. Doctors can't explain it. They're the ones who call it a miracle. Doctors. Intellectuals. Educated men. A miracle, sir, is 'evidence' of things that are true that you and Mr. Darwin can't explain."

Miracles had never been a part of Thomas Hall's life. In the last thirty-six hours he'd been immersed in miracles—and here it was again. He hoped Hawker had some measure of grace and sensitivity.

"Many people find comfort and base their faith on events they consider to be 'miraculous.' Unfortunately an intensely personal experience is inscrutable by scientific methods, so regardless of what a person believes has taken place, it simply does not constitute 'evidence' in a scientific sense."

Standing in the Darwin Pavilion, listening to Silas Hawker eviscerating *miraculous* from miracles, Thomas felt suddenly defensive. Almost offended.

"By definition, a miracle is 'an event that cannot be explained by natural or scientific law,'" Hawker said, slipping into professor mode. "Over time, inexplicable occurrences achieved mysterious status and were credited to God. Serious men have applied scientific methods to an evaluation of miracles and come up short. There simply is no evidence."

The man in the Giants cap raised the woman by the hand to stand beside him. "I brought the evidence, sir." He put his arm around his wife. "She's had perfect health for twenty-six years. Gave birth to our three kids and volunteers three days a week at the hospital to help terminally ill patients find the faith to get well." Media attention shifted from Hawker to the unexpected couple at the end of the third row. "You can see the hand of God without a microscope."

"Last question." Hawker looked away from the miracle couple. "Yes, there in the back." Thomas thought Hawker was looking at him. A fist grabbed his gut. Hawker wasn't.

A woman between them in the last row stood up. Her hair was thin, wrapped in a ponytail that fell untrimmed a few inches below her shoulders. Her ensemble included jeans, hiking boots, a plaid shirt and a synthetic down vest. Her arms were covered but folded across her chest in protective body language. "My name is Ada Kanster," the woman said.

The fist twisted. He imagined what she was going to say before she ever spoke, . . . *and if you don't get rid of Thomas Hall and get someone else to do the mural for Descent of Man we are going to burn down the museum and put a thousand dead fish in your bed.*

"*Kanster* is spelled with a *K*," she said for the benefit of the press. "I'm here on behalf of SAVE THE SEALS. Your former director was not at all supportive of our efforts to protect the rights of the original inhabitants of the bay. We want to know your position on animal rights."

Hawker was nodding with confidence before Kanster finished her question. "Thank you for being here, Ada. We are all 'animals,' but I know what you mean. I think the best way to answer your question is to show you this." He held up his membership card to SAVE THE SEALS.

The applause continued until Thomas reached the end of the corridor and passed the double doors. He would wait for Hawker in his office. Maybe he should hope for a miracle.

CHAPTER

46

THE PRESS CONFERENCE ENDED half an hour before Hawker returned to his office. When he finally broke away from the press, a female reporter followed him to the foyer of the executive offices where Thomas was waiting. She gushed over Hawker's declaration of war on God, her flattering words dipped in honey. *How to Win Friends and Influence People,* Thomas thought. *Right out of Berger's Bible.* Thomas suspected that Hawker was granting the woman an exclusive interview partly because of her physical abundance.

Hawker acknowledged Thomas with a sarcastic remark about his missing their meeting and told Maxine to call the lawyers. "We'll start when they get here," he said and disappeared into his office. The obsequious reporter cast Thomas a flirtatious smile and followed.

Hawker smoked in his office even though it was illegal. San Francisco had adopted additional tobacco control ordinances that tightened section 7597 of the California Code. Hawker ignored them. The odor was obnoxious but there was soon more for Thomas to worry about than the smell of Hawker's cigar.

When Hawker had replaced Dennis Hamilton as head of the Science Museum he had moved the director's office from the Victorian splendor of Hamilton's old spot in the original building to the ultramodern annex. Glass, steel and plastic. Finally admitted to the inner office, Thomas saw the walls were covered with photographs of Hawker with celebrities and politicians. Prominent among them was Hawker with former U.S. president Bill Clinton—smoking cigars!

Hawker introduced lawyers Lia Chu and Vince Sadereck from the San Francisco firm of Walters, Johnson, Lewis & Arlington. "Lia and Vince keep us out of trouble," Hawker smirked, as if the rules of law were nothing more than speed bumps. Thomas shook hands and wrestled the desire to curl up on the couch in the corner of Hawker's office and go to sleep. The sofa was a Gus Modern Trudeau in Urban Tweed. It did not look comfortable. That helped him resist the urge.

Thomas had drunk a twelve-ounce Red Bull while he was waiting in the outer office. It gave him jitters instead of wings.

Without sleep it was hard to concentrate. Little annoyances, like the stench of Hawker's cigar, blossomed like Audrey II into man-eating plants. The metaphor came easily to mind; Thomas had seen *Little Shop of Horrors* at the Orpheum a couple of weeks before. He'd ended up taking Catrina Lindley since his first pick for a downtown date, Patricia Livingston, had said she had to go to Oakland for her mother's birthday. It was a lie. He was drifting. Catrina morphed into Susan Cassidy. *Wonder if she's seen the show? Wonder if she'd like to go.* It was difficult to focus with the jitters.

Little annoyances. Hawker's sarcasm nagged at him. Missing the meeting. Coming in late. No regular schedule. *It is none of his business when I come in. Berger would never approve a contract that requires me to jump at Hawker's beck and call.*

Frank was a good agent. A tough negotiator. He always got Thomas what Thomas wanted. The agreement with Hamilton gave the artist full discretion over when and how he worked. The only obligation was to finish "on or before October 10."

Then Hawker showed up and changed everything. Told him to start over. Told him to create murals for both sides of the pavilion. No way he could finish by October 10. They had to push the date of completion but Hawker said nothing during the press conference about a delayed opening.

Hawker's bellyaching rumbled around in the sleepless fog. Thomas was irritated that Hawker expected him to work on the revised design for the Descent of Man mural in the Darwin Pavilion rather than his studio. The director had no understanding of the creative process. Reading

The Descent of Man curled up at the feet of a twelve-foot statue was no more inspirational to Thomas than reading the book on his boat. The thought of his boat reminded Thomas that Ada Kanster had showed up at the press conference and that Hawker was a card-carrying member of the enemy.

Hawker finished his castigation of the lowly artisan with an appeal for Thomas to "be inspired by the spirit of Charles Darwin." Thomas found it curious that a man who scoffed at the idea of consciousness beyond the grave talked about "the spirit of Darwin permeating the pavilion" and "Darwin's presence and influence" being somehow mystically accessible from the statue itself.

The ghost of Darwin? Thomas quivered at the thought as Hawker caused a crack in the dam of atheist dogma: no such thing as ghosts or spirits or the influence of the dead other than what they left behind. *Or is there?*

Lia Chu asked Thomas a question and he realized he had retreated into his own thoughts. Daydreams were impossible to avoid when his body was exhausted and his mind demanded sleep.

"I'm sorry?"

"Do you have a different number for Frank Berger? We've been trying to get a hold of him."

Frank hasn't talked to them? He didn't work out additional compensation for Hawker's changes and the expanded scope of the project? He felt a sudden rush of panic. *Before I fired him?*

"We need to work a few things out," she said.

So that's what this meeting is about. I can work this out without Frank. Who needs him? The knot in his stomach argued with his brain. He hated the business side of his business. He had given no thought to the numbers. How much more should he ask for? *Double at least. Maybe more. It would be good to have Frank here. I need to make amends with Frank.* Then pride ejected the temptation.

"His cell phone is the only number he ever uses," he said aloud.

"That's the one we've got. Can you have him call us?"

"Yeah, sure, no problem." Maybe he *would* have Frank do the deal. What mattered in the moment was keeping Hawker happy. Thomas could ignore his condescending comments and breathe the smoke—at least until Hawker agreed on the extra compensation and signed a revised letter of intent.

His discouraging morning at St. Mark's put getting more money from the museum at the top of his list. The angst over cash flow returned. *Do they really need two lawyers at four hundred an hour to make a simple change in my contract?* For a passing moment Thomas felt appreciated.

"Hamilton is being an ass!" Hawker made the statement sound more significant than *The Eagle has landed.* "I need you to fix it!" He nodded at the woman and sat down. The meeting was not about more money after all.

Lia Chu was short of five foot four, even in three-inch heels. She wore a tailored navy blue pantsuit, a white no-nonsense blouse and a wool Pashmina scarf. She put the middle finger of her left hand on the silicon wing bridge of her glasses and pushed them half an inch up the flat ridge of her nose.

"You understand, of course," she said, taking a step toward Thomas, "this conversation is completely confidential. Do we have your word on that?"

"Yeah. Okay." Thomas moved his shoulders with a wary shrug.

"How well do you know Dr. Dennis Hamilton?" she asked.

"Dr. Hamilton? You mean personally?"

"Is that how you would describe your relationship?" Her tone was seditious. Somewhere in the back of his mind a red flag went up.

"Well, I like him personally, if that's what you mean. I wouldn't say I know him all that well." He glanced at Hawker for a clue. There was none.

"How well is that?"

"Dr. Hamilton was the one who hired me to paint the mural. The Descent of Man." Chu's nod affirmed she was familiar with his project. "We met several times to talk about what he wanted and he came upstairs a few times once I started to see how it was going. You know, before he . . ." Thomas let his comment dangle.

Hawker's face was stern. Inscrutable. *Resigned to spend more time with family and pursue personal projects* was the way Hawker had described Hamilton's dismissal.

"What's going on?" Thomas asked.

Over the next twenty-five minutes Chu and Sadereck elucidated Hawker's opening expletive in a game of tag-team legalese. They could have explained it in five minutes or less. Frank was right: *Lawyers love to hear themselves talk because they get paid by the hour.* Even though it took longer than needed, Thomas found the story intriguing. But what Hawker expected of him was troubling.

CHAPTER

47

D<small>R. DENNIS HAMILTON HAD</small> filed a lawsuit against the Science Museum for wrongful dismissal. He had a strong case under the statute provisions of the employment laws of California. A member of the city council, sympathetic to Hamilton, had kept copious notes during the infamous midnight hearing that had resulted in Hamilton's "resignation." The suit contended that Hamilton did not resign of his own free will and choice but was "forced to retire," that he was "terminated, and discriminated against, because of his religious beliefs."

Even before Chu and Sadereck filed the defendant's response to the complaint, Hawker insisted they meet with Hamilton's lawyer and work out a quick and quiet settlement. His instructions were clear: "Find out what Hamilton wants. Pay him off. Double his retirement. Whatever it takes, but I want it to go away!"

Hawker evidently dreaded a storm of negative publicity and wanted nothing in the media to distract from the grand opening of his Darwin Pavilion, nothing to diminish the importance of the shrine to his great god of natural selection.

The attorney representing Hamilton was Darrin Colt. Colt ran a small private practice in Berkeley that specialized in wrongful termination. He and two paralegals worked out of a remodeled Victorian house three blocks from the Berkeley campus of the University of California. He and Sadereck had known each other as law students at Boalt Hall. That was twelve years ago. They had not been friends then and were not friendly now.

Colt was over six feet tall and lanky in a James Coburn sort of way. He had broad shoulders and kept himself in excellent shape. He wore Izod polos to the office and Calvin Klein suits in court.

When Chu called to set an appointment, he said his client had "zero interest" in settlement. It wasn't true, of course, but practicing law was not about the truth, it was about winning the case. In this case it was about settling for a boatload of money.

"Why should he settle?" Colt asked. "We've got them in a corner and you know it." Chu scoffed but her mouth was dry. Chu and Sadereck worried that the notes from the midnight meeting would be admitted into evidence. If that happened, the truth would flash like a pink neon sign for a topless bar on Broadway.

Hamilton had no interest in becoming entangled in a lawsuit. Life was too short. He had not gone to Colt about the legality of his dismissal. He'd wanted to find out if there were a way to stop Hawker from changing the Descent of Man exhibit, the showpiece he considered to be his legacy at the historic Science Museum.

Colt listened to Hamilton's story. He recorded their conversation but also took notes. From time to time he stopped to clarify a fact or get the spelling of a person's name. Mostly he listened. He read a copy of Hamilton's employment contract and highlighted what he called "a bushel of low-hanging fruit, ripe and ready to pick."

Colt gave Hamilton a short course on California employment law and offered to take his case on 30 percent contingency. "You've got a slam-dunk case of discrimination and wrongful dismissal," Colt chortled, unable to suppress a wolfish grin. Colt urged Hamilton to allow him to forge ahead with the filing of the suit. The attorney outlined seven claims he proposed to make. "That's after reading it once," he added.

Hamilton was reluctant. He explained he didn't want to create problems for the new director or negative publicity for the museum. "I just want them to finish the Descent of Man exhibit the way we planned and not turn it into some big deal for Darwin. They are very different things."

"We'd all be out of business if everyone thought like you do," Colt laughed. "Let's go to lunch."

Cafe Rouge was within walking distance of the old residential section of Berkeley where Colt had his office. Colt talked Hamilton into the mesquite-grilled steak with red wine shallot butter and a mound of the skinniest crispy *pommes frites* Hamilton had ever eaten. Colt ordered the organic salad and oysters on the half shell. He offered an oyster to Hamilton and winked. "Aphrodisiac, you know."

"Take a lot more than one," Hamilton smiled. He always regretted making jokes about his age when he felt so young inside, but sometimes it was irresistible. They laughed like a couple of frat boys in college. Colt was hard not to like. He had a ruggedness about him that made him seem more like a tight end for the Oakland Raiders than a smart attorney.

By the time they finished lunch and walked back to the office, Hamilton understood that the only way to keep Hawker from spoiling his legacy was a formal lawsuit—the more onerous, the better.

There was no provision in Hamilton's employment contract that could be twisted by legal logic to prevent Hawker from doing whatever he wanted as director of the museum. He could change everything Hamilton had done or turn the whole place into a Charles Darwin memorial if he wanted. The board had effectively anointed him czar. But even a czar could be brought to his knees with the right battle plan.

48

CHU PROWLED BACK AND forth in Hawker's office like an old-time lawyer making closing arguments in a movie from 1960. "Vince and I drove to Berkeley and met with Dr. Hamilton's attorney in his office. Darrin Colt specializes in wrongful dismissals."

"I knew him in college," Vince volunteered, adding some less than flattering comments under his breath.

"He is very good at twisting the smallest . . ." Chu paused. "I'm reluctant to say 'infraction,' but the smallest oversight or misunderstanding. It's easy to do in a case like this where the line between resignation and dismissal is so easily blurred."

"Get to the point!" Hawker stood up. Chu cowered a bit, then stopped in front of Thomas as if he were judge and jury.

"I just wanted to make sure Mr. Hall had sufficient background so he understands the importance of what you need him to do."

Hawker cut her off impatiently. "The crux of it is that Hamilton will settle on the issues of wrongful termination without an admission of guilt if . . ." His face flushed and a squiggle of a blue vein on his forehead bulged against the skin.

"So that's good, right?" Thomas ventured.

"No! In exchange he's demanded that I make no changes to his original plan for the whole Descent of Man exhibit—or to your mural, for that matter."

"I can do that. I'm excited to finish." He had a sudden sick feeling when he remembered the mural was covered. *If the mural is still there.* The last word had barely crossed his lips when Hawker erupted.

"You're missing the point! I'll be damned if I am going to allow Hamilton to dictate what I can and cannot do here!"

Damned? By whom? By God? Who is it that damns an atheist? From whence the thought came and why it came so suddenly in this unlikely moment Thomas had no idea, but there it was and it made him smile. Smiling was a bad choice.

"You think there is something funny about this?"

"No, no, of course not, I just . . . never mind."

"His attorney claims it is nonnegotiable," Chu said.

"What about the other side? The Origin of Species mural?" Thomas asked.

"Exactly!"

"We still need to talk about that, by the way. The expanded scope of the project. Additional compensation. Not right now, but . . ." Even before he finished, Thomas knew his timing stank.

Hawker's hands flew up. "If he persists, there won't be anything to talk about. You're done!"

"The court will order you to 'cease and desist' on any further work until the matter is adjudicated," Chu explained in legal terms.

"Everything stops!" Hawker slapped the desk with his hand. Thomas's hope of doubling his fee changed to the prospect of getting nothing in two words.

"In my experience, Dr. Hamilton is a reasonable guy. I'm sure if you just talked to him and—" Thomas spoke to Hawker but Chu cut him off.

"Too late for that. Mr. Hawker is named in the suit and Colt won't allow it."

"YOU have to talk him out of it!" Hawker expelled a mouthful of fetid smoke and wagged a finger in Thomas's face. "I want you to get Hamilton to drop his ridiculous demands and let us finish the pavilion!"

Thomas imagined a maniacal lieutenant ordering a private to charge a machine-gun nest. Hawker's changes to the mural obliterated every trace of Hamilton's original vision.

"I'm not sure that's in my job description," Thomas quipped, attempting to lighten the moment.

"If you can't get him to back down, talk some sense into him, there won't be any job."

Thomas wanted to argue in favor of the original design but recognized that supporting Hamilton—while the right thing to do if life were a movie and he were a superhero—under the circumstances would be stupid.

"I'm not sure what I could say that would—"

"His whole precious plan is your design. Isn't it? He respects you." Hawker made it sound easy. "Tell him you've changed your mind."

"Tell him you've 'evolved.'" Sadereck intended the comment to be humorous. Hawker's glare skewered the lawyer with an evil eye like a priest punishing a deacon for muttered blasphemies.

CHAPTER

49

Y OUR CALL HAS BEEN FORWARDED to an automatic voice-messaging system. Four one five, six seven three, nine nine seven two is not available. At the tone, please record your message. When you are finished recording, please hang up or press one for more options." The default recording from AT&T was always obnoxious. In 5.1 surround sound it was almost unbearable.

The traffic light turned green and Thomas accelerated his Mercedes north past the Presidio golf course. The long, shrill tone ended, inviting Thomas to leave a message for Dr. Hamilton. He glanced at the number Chu had written on the back of her business card and checked it against the iPhone. He had dialed correctly.

"Hi, Doctor Hamilton, it's Thomas Hall. Say, listen, I—uh . . ." There was no good way to explain in a voice message why he was calling. "If you get a minute, could you please give me a call?" He left his telephone number and ended the call. He took a deep breath and headed for the bridge. His thoughts were cluttered by the endless day of unexpected troubles. *Of all my troubles great and small . . .* Without sleep nothing worked right. *Stay awake. Get home. Crash.*

. . .

Sleep did not come easily. His legs twitched and his nerves felt raw. Exposed. He never imagined one could be too tired to fall asleep, but that was how it seemed. He had been up forty-four hours. His body was exhausted. His mind was aflame.

Hawker's order to go after Hamilton had given him a jolt of adrenaline. He hadn't left the museum immediately. He'd gone upstairs, curious to find out why Hawker had covered the mural.

He guessed Hawker's plan to change everything made letting the press see anything a bad idea. *The nearly completed vignette of Cro-Magnon hunters could work for both.* Hawker's ego was going to be a problem. Maybe it was an issue of his own ego.

He climbed the 170 steps of the grand staircase two at a time. The chairs and podium were gone. The lights were off. A shaft of natural light from the stained-glass skylights illuminated Darwin from above. His eyes were lost in the shadows of a thick bronze brow.

The visage gave Thomas pause. The faint echo of Hawker's words seemed to hover in the air. As he thought of the press conference, he half expected Ada Kanster to smack him with a dead baby seal or attack with a Shenzhen fishing knife. Disjointed images fluttered through his mind. Adrenaline and second wind notwithstanding, he really needed to get some sleep.

He turned on the work lights and lifted the semi-opaque polyethylene. The light through the shroud of plastic illuminated the tunnel in a murky gray-green glow. He probed his way along the mural to where once upon a time a party of Cro-Magnon hunters had stolen the carcass of a mammoth calf from an outraged feline beast. They were gone. Only a vague sense of the artwork was visible. A thick coat of sizing, the gelatinous solution used to stiffen textiles and prepare walls for decorative painting, had been applied with a roller that lay dry and crusted in a pan at his feet.

Curiously, all that was left was the pool of purple blood the workers had somehow missed.

Thomas felt sick. For a moment he thought he was going to retch. Hawker had hired someone to obliterate seven weeks of work without so much as an e-mail. He could hear Hawker scolding him for not working on the new designs in the shadow of Darwin. *If you're not here, you forfeit the right to be part of the decisions.*

In a rush of anger he decided to storm Hawker's office, express his contempt and tell the arrogant atheist to go to hell just in case there was such a place. The fantasy of revenge was stopped by the reality of debt. He had to have the money from this project.

The heavy plastic pressing against his back accentuated the painful astonishment pressing against the right side of his brain. He felt trapped.

CHAPTER

50

AT 11:15 P.M. THOMAS WAS still awake. He struggled to shut off his brain and disappear in slumber. He got up, took two Tylenol PM and went back to bed. He regretted the inevitable sluggish morning to come but knew of no other way to deactivate his brain and get some rest.

. . .

The hunters clawed their way through the gelatinous white and found him in the dark dreams that finally came. Their arms and legs dripped with dirty white sludge, making it hard for them to move. Reverend Mike was one of them. He wore a covering of fur over the clothes he'd worn on the houseboat. He was carrying a brass bell that was also a loaf of bread with which he fed fishes to the clowder of cats that swirled about his legs. He had a tattered Bible on a leather thong strapped to his neck. Red-and-black snake tattoos started on the bottom of the hunters' feet, slithered up their bodies and protruded from the top of their heads and then the snakes were real and the monster came and the monster was the statue of Darwin. His beard writhed like the tentacles of an octopus and then he distended and blocked out the sun and shadows fell over him and the hunters tried to run but their legs were immersed in the gelatinous mud. The monster crushed the Cro-Magnon men with a bronze fist and Reverend Mike put his arms around all of them and Thomas understood he was trying to bring them back to life but couldn't, and then it wasn't Reverend Mike but Jing-Wei and she raised the hunters from the ground and they laughed and it wasn't Jing-Wei, it was Jesus, but he had no face and a wall of white rain obliterated the faceless man, and it was Hawker painting over the mural and the pavilion filled up with gelatinous glue and Thomas sank and it was a putrid swamp and his head went under and a watery darkness enveloped him and from the darkness there was fire and the fire was a flare in the mouth of a wounded seal and then there were hundreds of them with flares in their mouths and the water was on fire and he swam to the top of the bridge and ran along the walkway and saw a man on the railing about to jump and ran to him and put his arms around his legs to stop him, but the man was the beggar and pushed him over the railing and he fell in terror.

Thomas woke with a start just before he hit the water. His heart was thumping hard. His pulse was 121. He took two swallows of water from the bottle of water on the nightstand, fluffed his pillow and rolled over. He settled at last into a sleep so deep his dreams had no place to play.

51

ANYBODY HOME?"

Was that a voice or my imagination? Thomas leaned his head through the tiled arch of the walk-in shower. It was 9:22 A.M. He'd slept two and a half hours longer than normal and was still groggy from the sleeping pills.

"Hello? Mr. Hall?"

Who is that? he wondered. *Oh, the housecleaner. No, wait! She comes on Friday. It's not Friday. Ada Kanster with a mob of SAVE THE SEALers!* He stepped from the shower and wrapped himself in a towel.

He crossed to the circular stairs that connected the loft to the lower level, splitting the cavernous space into two floors. Through the burned-out hole in the wall Thomas could see the legs of a woman wearing high heels. *Excellent legs.* He sketched them in his mind and tried to get a glimpse of her face, but she was hidden from the waist up by the shards of shredded plastic. *Why didn't she use the door?* A thought jolted him: *SAVE THE SEALS arsonist returning to the scene of the crime. Not Ada Kanster. Not with THOSE legs.*

"Anybody home? Hello?" The lovely legs walked away.

"Who's there?" Thomas crossed to the corner of the loft and looked down. High heels picked their way through rubble. A hand slipped through a gash in the plastic and pushed it aside. Susan Cassidy stepped into the room and looked up at him.

Thomas was not modest by nature. When he ran, he wore only enough to keep from being arrested. But when he saw who it was, immodesty failed him. He felt exposed.

"Oh. Sorry," Cass laughed, averting her eyes. "I knocked at the front but nobody answered."

"I was in the shower. It's hard to hear." She glanced at him again and looked quickly away.

"I'm usually up and running by six, but this morning I . . ." He stretched the truth by half an hour. He felt the need to explain being undressed in the middle of the morning. "Don't try to walk through there; you might step on a nail. Go back around and I'll open the door. Just give me a second."

"Did you get my message?" Cass asked, looking up at him again. This time she did not look away.

"Didn't check yet," he said. The towel and wrought-iron railing covered him from the waist down. His body was wet and rimmed by a shimmer of sunlight that spiked across the loft from the east windows. He leaned forward on the wooden balustrade, bulging slightly the sculpted muscles of his arms.

Thomas watched his weight, ran from Sausalito harbor to the base of the Golden Gate Bridge four times a week with Bill Conti's classic theme from *Rocky* setting the pace at 96 beats a minute. "Gonna Fly Now." He worked out with Nautilus hand weights and kept his body trim, tanned and reasonably cut. Cass stood there looking up at him. He looked back, exceeding the interval of expectation. The awkward moment came. He smiled, threw a modest salute and headed for his closet.

What to wear? There were days Thomas never changed out of his shorts, T-shirt and running shoes. When ideas came on his morning run—and they almost always did—he would stop at the easel on the way to the shower to sketch the impression and still be there six hours later.

On other days—the days of creative seclusion—he would slip on khaki cargo shorts, a black golf shirt and Birkenstocks. He'd read somewhere that Albert Einstein wore the same clothes every day to avoid wasting time to think. It was exaggerated folklore but Thomas found creative kinship in the idea and hung a photo of Albert on the door of his closet. It was the famous shot of the quirky genius sticking out his tongue at the hounding paparazzi. It went up the third time Berger castigated him for wearing the same outfit four days in a row.

For his unexpected meeting with Susan Cassidy, Thomas pulled out a pair of off-white Nautica slacks, a double-knit deck shirt, classic blue blazer and Sperry Top-Siders. Kinship with Einstein or not, Thomas was not in creative isolation today.

Thomas unlocked the door and let Cass in. Following a brief exchange of explanations, apologies and predictable cordialities, Cass told Thomas that Miss Von Horn found his ideas "interesting."

"Interesting?" Thomas shuddered a smile. "Don't you know that to an artist holding his breath and waiting for the world to pass judgment on his work, *interesting* is the most terrifying euphemism in the English language?"

Cass responded with a throaty laugh. Sensuous and musical. "Okay," she said and smiled broadly. "Hmmm. Her exact words were *thought-provoking* and she said she *might* be willing to reconsider the selection of the artist."

"Thought-provoking?" Thomas repeated it slowly. Cass looked at him with large, bright eyes obviously intending to divine his thoughts.

"Have you had breakfast?" Thomas asked.

"I get up at six," she teased and raised her eyes to the studio loft above. "How about a tour?"

"Give away all my secrets?"

"Exactly."

The east wall of the studio was covered with paintings, movie posters, lithographs and drawings. A corkboard in a wormwood frame ran the full length of the south wall. A collection of sketches, tear sheets, comic book covers and fantasy art was pinned, tacked or taped into a collage that was itself a work of art.

Some of the pieces were Thomas's. Some came from fellow artists. Some were collectible classics. The art of Boris Vallejo was prominent. Erotic warrior women saving the universe from fire-breathing dragons. By the look on Cass's face, Thomas assumed it was her first exposure to the genre. He touched her arm and ushered her forward lest she presume it was the erotic and not the artistic that had earned them their place here.

The wall at the far end was covered by paintings of the great masters. Rembrandt, da Vinci, Michelangelo, Raphael, Caravaggio, Vermeer and some that only museum mavens had ever heard of. They were re-productions, souvenir posters or lithographs from the bookstores of the Louvre, Uffizi, Rijksmuseum, the Academy of Florence and even the Vatican. *Night Watch, Militia, Mona Lisa,* ceiling sections of the Sistine chapel. *Transfiguration. The Astronomer. David with the Head of Goliath.*

The centerpiece was a ten-scale reproduction of *Vitruvian Man,* the pen-and-ink drawing created by Leonardo da Vinci in 1487. Superimposed positions of a male figure were simultaneously inscribed in a circle and square. The original was less than fourteen inches high. On the dominant wall of Thomas Hall's studio the perfectly proportioned man was life-sized.

The collection manifested a curious evolution in Thomas's artistic tastes. Only that rare connoisseur of fantasy art who was also familiar with art history could easily see the influence of the old masters in his work, but the influence was clearly there. His mastery of light was inspired by Rembrandt, his anatomy from making a painstaking copy of every sketch or drawing ever made by Michelangelo and the great Leonardo da Vinci.

The exaggerated anatomy of his fantasy art, while inspired by Boris Vallejo, increasingly showed the influence of George Bridgman. Professor Andrus lamented that Thomas's art had not advanced from the simple to the complex, as he had hoped. His art had not "evolved," in the usual meaning of the word, but rather—in the opinion of the professor—"devolved," beginning with Thomas's decision to focus his enormous talent on the extreme end of artistic expression. In private, Andrus referred to Thomas's entry into fantasy art as "selling out."

It was Andrus who had given Cass photographs of Thomas's pencil studies and unfinished painting of the crucifixion of Christ, which now lay partly covered on the floor against the wall. "May I?" she asked as she pulled it out without waiting for an answer. As breathtaking as the photo-graph in her presentation had been, it did not capture the magnificence of the painting. Thomas had all but forgotten the piece, but seeing Cass's reaction he recognized its value in landing him the St. Mark's contract.

"Yes, of course," he said and stepped forward to help her place it on the easel.

"Are you ever going to finish it?" Cass asked, touching a finger to the faceless figure on the cross.

Thomas shrugged. "Maybe. It was a student project."

"You need to finish it."

"Are we negotiating?" He definitely twinkled when he smiled.

Cass shrugged. "Maybe."

"Want to know my deep dark secret?" Thomas held out his hand. She took it and followed him past a wall of costumes, under an unused wooden staircase and through a portal framed by original timbers. It opened to an alcove obviously dedicated to sculpture. The room was il-luminated by tall mullioned windows with the original blown glass. The modeling stand was an old European design and appeared to have gone through the Crimea-Prussian war. A lump of clay covered by a moistened cloth waited patiently. Armatures stood about on the floor. Shelves were cluttered with gargoyles, dragons, warriors and indistinguishable lumps, well-intended as quick sketches but never finished. All of them the color of toasted cinnamon. When Thomas stopped, Cass took her hand away.

"Google doesn't know you sculpt," Cass quipped.

"Shhhh." He put a finger to his lips as if even whispering his secret were forbidden. "I play with clay to relax," Thomas said, pulling off the cloth. "To think and imagine." He was no longer selling, and Cass showed genuine interest. "I took a sculpting class at Art Institute from a woman who was into what she called 'tactile perceptions.' She was from Argentina—Madame Persell. Her English was so broken I'm not sure I ever understood what she was talking about." Another luscious laugh from Cass encouraged him. "She had this theory that working the clay blindfolded allowed an 'unselfconscious expression of affection.' She be-lieved it allowed you to find the object 'living' within the medium."

"Living? That was the word she used?" Cass asked.

He nodded. "Leeeving." He murdered the word with a twisted Latin accent from the soundtrack of a B movie.

"This is what I missed by not taking art classes?" Cass grinned and touched the clump of unshaped clay.

"Never too late," Thomas said and before she could protest, he cov-ered her eyes with his fingers. "Find the 'living thing' inside," he said in his faux accent. She rewarded him with her laugh and pushed her hands into the clay.

He knew what she felt. With his eyes closed and his fingers shaping the soft, cool substance, Thomas could imagine things not otherwise discovered. His secret room was filled with fanciful creatures created in three dimensions. Playing with clay allowed him to create weird new characters and creatures and strange worlds for them to inhabit. The freakish, frightening, fascinating realms of fantasy and fiction. This was the artistic universe of Thomas Hall. It was about as far from the real world of Jesus and the miracles as one could get, and yet . . .

Cass prodded the clay. Thomas enjoyed holding his hands over her eyes. She didn't find a "living thing" but brought forth a lumpy creature with a long, twisted nose. *"Loxodonta Pachydermus,"* Thomas proclaimed and added her creation to a shelf of other unearthly creatures. Cass told Thomas he needed to find Madame Persell and find out what in blue blazes the woman was talking about. Thomas loved the way Cass laughed.

The tour continued through canyons of costumes, past walls of weapons and a march of mannequin warriors, clad in armor and festooned with the flamboyant accoutrements of ancient warfare. "This is overwhelming," Cass confessed.

They stopped at a wall covered with photographs of live models in a variety of poses, costumes and accessories. "You work from photographs?" she asked.

"Sometimes. For the finished art," Thomas said, moving beside her. Looking through her eyes he saw the staged photos again for the first time.

"That's why the finished art is so realistic?"

"Partly. Not exactly."

"Compared to the design sketches?"

"It's a collision between reality and imagination. What comes from here," he touched his temple, then pointed to the photos, "and what they inspire."

"So in doing our mural you will use—"

He cut her off. "Am I doing *'our'* mural?" *Gotcha!*

Cass scolded him with her eyes but smiled as she exhaled slowly and began again. "IF you end up doing the mural, are you saying that the people in the finished painting, the people blessed by Jesus, will be real people?"

"IF I am lucky enough to be picked to do the finest mural of Jesus and the healing miracles ever created," his smile said *touché,* "the faces and fine detail will be based on living, breathing human beings."

She turned to the wall of photos. "Where do you find the models?"

"Kragen Agency in the city."

"Professionals?" She sounded skeptical.

"Working with amateurs is tough."

Cass studied the array of practically perfect human beings. "The people who followed Jesus were common folks. Have you ever used 'normal' people?"

"Only when I find an incredibly beautiful, undiscovered talent. In such a case, I can make an exception." He tugged a silken fabric from the arm of a mannequin and swirled it over Cass's head, around her neck and across her shoulders. "Hiring the right models is the secret of genius." He winked and turned her around to face the full-length mirror behind her.

She lifted the trailing end of the fabric and settled it over her right shoulder. Her hair was hidden. Her face was framed by an oval of silk. Light from the window ignited the fabric with an opalescent shimmer. In a twinkling Cass had been transformed; a faithful disciple of Jesus stared back at her from the mirror.

"Now that you know my secrets I can never let you leave." Thomas took her picture with his iPhone. She turned and studied his face before she spoke. Framed in soft silk she was exquisite.

"Where will you find a man who can be Jesus?"

• • •

They finished the tour. Cass confided that it was Miss Van Horn who had suggested she visit Thomas in his world and get a better sense of who he really was. "Who he is in his heart," she had advised Cass, "is more important than what he does with his hands."

"She left the final decision up to me," Cass said as she picked up the case she had left by the door when she came in and put it on the plank table.

"No board approval?" Thomas asked with hopeful expectation.

"None," Cass said as she opened the case and removed a heavy package. She slid the bundle across the table. Thomas felt like a mouse being batted about by a playful cat.

"For me?"

She nodded. "Open it." The package was bigger than a book, wrapped in brown paper and bound up with twine. He untied the string and pulled the paper away. It was a book after all. As large as any he had seen. It was bound in dark leather with the title embossed in gilded gold. THE HOLY BIBLE.

"It's the famous Bible illustrated by Gustave Doré," Cass beamed, "printed in France in 1865. This one's in English, a replica, of course. Look inside."

He opened the thick cover and turned a few pages. He stopped at the first illustration. "Incredible," he said. It was the creation of Eve. God stood in a blaze of light with his right hand raised. His eyes looked down with fondness on the woman. She hovered over Adam, who lay at her feet in a deep sleep. It was magnificent, the more so because Thomas understood the original was a wood engraving. *Unimaginable to get such detail,* he thought. He read the ornate script aloud. Perhaps it was a show of appreciation to Cass. Perhaps something more.

> God said, Let us make man in our image, after our likeness: and let them have dominion over the fish of the sea, and over the fowl of the air, and over the cattle, and over all the earth, and over every creeping thing that creepeth upon the earth. And the Lord God said, it is not good that the man should be alone; I will make him an help meet for him. And the Lord God caused a deep sleep to fall upon Adam, and he slept: and he took one of his ribs, and closed up the flesh instead thereof; and the rib, which the Lord God had taken from man, made he a woman, and brought her unto the man. And Adam said, This is now bone of my bones,

and flesh of my flesh: she shall be called Woman, because
she was taken out of Man.

"There are more than 245 illustrations altogether," Cass enthused.
"Almost fifty in the New Testament showing the life of Jesus. Many of
them depicting the miracles."

"We studied Doré briefly," Thomas said, "but only his illustrations
for *Don Quixote* and *Paradise Lost*." He hefted the prodigious volume.
"Thank you."

"I just thought it might be helpful in making *our* mural perfect." Cass
put emphasis on *our* and he knew what it meant. He looked up from the
Garden of Eden. With dappled sunlight falling on her hair, Cass looked
radiant as Eve. She smiled and extended her hand. "Congratulations."

Thomas felt a strong and sudden urge to leap into the air and shout
his thanks to all gods past and present. The impulsive thought left him
oddly befuddled.

He gushed instead. "Thank you! That is so great. I'm excited. Thanks.
Really. Thank you very much." He shook her proffered hand in cadence
as relief rushed out in a river of words. "I won't let you down," he said
finally, then bowed like a knight and kissed her hand. "I promise."

Cass blushed and slipped her hand away. "Why don't you show me
that boat?"

CHAPTER

52

THOMAS HAD SPENT FEWER THAN half a dozen days on the Marin coast since graduating from Art Institute. He had never been farther north than Stewarts Point. Professor Andrus took selected students to the dot on the map for a three-day watercolor safari every spring. For a student, a drive across the Golden Gate Bridge and over the coastal mountains was not about the scenery. It was about a weekend party at Stinson Beach or surfing at Bodega Bay.

Memories returned as Thomas drove north on Route 1. He convinced himself he was taking the Shoreline Highway to the village of Mendocino to explore a stretch of the California coast he had never seen. A chance to revisit the picturesque places of Stewarts Point. In truth, he was putting off his face-to-face confrontation with Dr. Dennis Hamilton as long as he could.

. . .

Thomas was with Cass at the boat when the call came. *Eragon* played and the caller ID announced, D. HAMILTON. "Excuse me a second," Thomas said, "I need to take this," and he walked to the bow, trying not to make it obvious he did not want Cass to hear the conversation.

Cass had just given him the deadline for completion of the St. Mark's mural. *Impossible!* It had to be finished for the grand opening of the Children's Wing on Christmas Eve. Five months away! The last thing he wanted Cass to discover was his commitment to the Science Museum project with an even more aggressive deadline. Having lost Vegas, he had to answer yes; the worries about impossible deadlines would have to come later.

Hamilton did not sound the way Thomas remembered. He was hesitant. Guarded. Suspicious. He asked Thomas what he wanted to talk about. Thomas's evasive answer must have sounded illiterate to a man with two PhDs. There was a long silence. Thomas cringed. "Is it regarding the lawsuit?" Hamilton finally asked.

"Hmmm, indirectly," Thomas fumbled, grossly understating his purpose. "Half an hour should be plenty. Besides, I would love to see you again. Truly." He meant it, but the rush of his affection for Hamilton was bushwhacked by an unpleasant sensation of deception.

"Me too, Thomas." Hamilton explained he was staying at his cousin's cabin not far from the coastal town of Mendocino. "It's near a place called Russian Gulch," Hamilton said and the otherwise unpleasant mission was touched with a sense of adventure.

Cass's two-dollar tour of the boat ended with a dollar fifty in change. Thomas expressed appreciation for the opportunity to do the St. Mark's mural and promised brilliance. He gushed another apology for running off and half an hour later was headed west across the Golden Gate Recreational Area on his way to Pacific Coast Highway One.

• • •

It was four hours before Thomas reached Stewarts Point and stopped at General Merchandise. The classic old store was established right after the Civil War and had been owned and operated by the same family ever since. As a student, Thomas had made several watercolor sketches of the old store and sent the best of them to the Stewart family. It was hanging in a prominent place behind the counter.

He ordered a homemade turkey sandwich on whole wheat bread and a cherry Coke. Mrs. Stewart gave him a sly look and did a silly impersonation of Thomas as a student. "Light on the mayo and avocado if you happen to have any," she laughed.

"You remember me?"

"Of course," she grinned and glanced at his watercolor on the wall. "We still laugh about you thinking we could be here since 1868 and not have avocados." She made him a turkey sandwich that could have been destined to compete at the state fair. She refused to let him pay for the food.

. . .

The road snaked north from Stewarts Point and followed the coast, a hundred miles of winding, two-lane blacktop to where Dr. Dennis Hamilton was waiting.

Under different circumstances, the spectacle of nature on all sides would have put Thomas in a state of creative levitation. Rocky headlands. Groves of coastal redwoods. An explosion of waves on sharp black boulders. Here and there a pod of seals and far offshore a gam of gray whales heading south. Coarse sand beaches littered with curious treasures washed ashore and riptides reminding him of crazy, carefree student days. He saw tidal pools begging for explorers and long stretches of coastal marsh animated by a dissimulation of fowls.

Thomas enjoyed none of it. The Bausch and Lomb binoculars never left the glove compartment and the Canon SLR never left its bag.

"Have Frank Berger call me," Cass had said. Frank was persona non grata in his life at the moment and the thought of crawling back was galling. His search for a solution had him thinking in circles like a fugitive lost in a winter wood who runs until he's exhausted only to discover his own tracks in the snow.

The closest cash was the mural of miracles and the only way to get it was to close the deal. *Humble pie! Frank may be the only answer.* More money from Hawker was a possibility but only if he succeeded in persuading Hamilton to change his mind. That unpleasant thought shifted his focus from Jesus to the former director hiding out in the Mendocino woods. He wondered what it would take, what he needed to say. None of the lines he came up with sounded persuasive. The source of his anxiety was not difficult to ferret out. Thomas did not agree with Hawker.

It was dark by the time Thomas reached the village of Mendocino.

The day's descent into dusk was bleak until the sun slumped below a rampart of gray that scudded across the horizon. God rays from the yellow ball kissed everything they touched with a celestial blaze of light. It was glorious. *And never two the same,* Thomas reminded himself, allowing the spectacle to lift his spirits.

Thomas drove to a bed-and-breakfast perched on a bluff overlooking the ocean on the north end of Mendocino Village. The Agate Cove Inn was surrounded by stately hundred-year-old cypress trees and a colorful garden aglow under landscaping lights.

His room was uncomfortably warm. Thomas opened the door to catch the cool breeze that wafted ashore. There was a rocking chair on the porch. He sat for a time with the leather-bound Bible. He turned to the New Testament and rediscovered the miracles one by one. The illustrations of Gustave Doré. The captions of scriptural verse.

It was a welcome distraction from the worrisome expectations of his meeting on the morrow. The arrangements with Dr. Hamilton had been casual. "Anytime in the morning," the former director had said, "just give me a call."

. . .

Dr. Hamilton was standing on the porch when Thomas arrived. The cabin was at the end of a narrow gravel track that twisted through a grove of new-growth redwoods. Swirls of morning fog languished among the ferns still in shadow. Broken sunlight created hot patches of light in an otherwise dense green. By the time he got there Thomas felt like he was in the middle of a Mercedes-Benz commercial.

Cabin was a misnomer. None of the images of weathered, one-room log shelters that had come to Thomas's mind when Hamilton had called his retreat "my cousin's cabin" were remotely accurate. It was made of logs but not the kind hacked from the forest with a pioneer axe. The perfectly shaped logs were custom cut and cost more than conventional construction materials. Logs were the only component that categorized the secluded manor as a cabin. The main section rose two stories from a rock foundation, adding ten feet to the height. The western wall was mostly glass, divided into windows by thick timbers. The roof was oxidized copper. The house sat on a low knoll in a dense forest of evergreens that included coastal redwoods, Douglas fir, madrone chaparral and giant chinquapin.

"Some 'cabin,'" Thomas grinned as he climbed the stone steps to the spacious porch where Hamilton was waiting.

"A testament to education," Hamilton smiled. "I went to college and got a PhD. My cousin dropped out to create video games."

"Life isn't fair."

"Good to see you, Thomas."

. . .

The small talk was finished by the time they settled in the library. It was an intimate space, separated from the vaulted great room by double doors on the north side. The walls were bookshelves punctuated by a stone fireplace and a pair of boxed French windows.

"So," Hamilton began, "since I didn't hear from you following my 'scandalous retirement,'" four fingers punctuated the air with quotation marks, "may I assume this isn't a social call?" Thomas's well-rehearsed opening lines disintegrated like magnesium flash powder touched by a match. He stammered to recover from Hamilton's sardonic salvo.

"I was going to call, and then . . . I'm sorry, you know . . ." He blathered in search of a plausible excuse.

"So what does Hawker expect you to accomplish? Get me to drop the lawsuit?"

Thomas shook his head. "No, no, I think they're agreed on a settlement but . . ."

Hamilton stood up and fluttered his hand to stop Thomas and fast-forward the conversation. "I'm sorry, Thomas. I'm supposed to act like a dolt. My attorney told me exactly what to say, what to ask, how to answer your questions and how to trap you in your words so we can use this conversation against Hawker, but . . ." he laughed softly. "I've no patience with legal shenanigans."

He stood by the window and looked into the dark woods that

stretched away from the house. "I know exactly what Hawker wants. I know the damage he's already done to what you and I created." Thomas was dumbfounded; it was as if the man had read his mind. "Espionage is alive and well at the museum," Hamilton smiled. "Hawker is too arrogant to consider that maybe not everyone agrees with him. He's forgotten some of his people were with me for fifteen years." Thomas was struck by the absence of malice or anger. "Loyalty is a wonderful thing." The comment struck like a double-edged sword. Thomas floundered.

"Look, Dr. Hamilton, if there is any way that . . . Hawker's put me in a very difficult spot."

"I need to finish what I started. If I'm to have a legacy at all, I want it to be a truly enlightened exhibit depicting the Origins of Man."

Movement in the shadows of the woods caught Hamilton's eye. He motioned for Thomas to join him at the window. A family of black-tailed deer moved cautiously through a shimmer of graceful lady ferns. "You like to hike?" he asked.

Thomas had no time to wrap his head around the meaning of the question. *Perhaps there is no other meaning.*

"There's a waterfall three miles up. We should go there after lunch." Thomas's expectation for his meeting with Hamilton was not unfolding the way he had imagined. The deer stopped and stood motionless, their eyes fixed on the window.

"That would be good," Thomas said. Hamilton smiled and put his arm on Thomas's shoulder. The movement caused the deer to bound into motion and disappear.

"Before you carry out your 'secret mission,' I want you to under-stand what has really happened. See the entire composition, as it were." Hamilton's choice of artist's parlance reminded Thomas how much he liked this man.

Mrs. Hamilton brought coffee. Thomas and Dr. Hamilton settled in the plush leather chairs facing the fireplace. As Hamilton recounted the incidents that had brought them to their meeting in the woods, Thomas could see the events and hear the conversations as though he had been there himself.

CHAPTER

53

MUSEUM DIRECTOR RESIGNS. It was a headline in the San Francisco Chronicle. "Pacific Science Museum Director Dr. Dennis Hamilton announced his resignation Thursday following a closed-door hearing at an undisclosed location." For Hamilton to retire in the wake of approval for his long-sought-after renovation of the museum pointed to one conclusion. Scandal!

Thomas had watched the press conference on the late news. He remembered the look of the spokeswoman more than what she said. The pouch of skin below her chin waggled like the engorged caruncle of a trotting turkey.

"The retirement of Dr. Hamilton," she read from a prepared statement, "is in the best interest of the museum and the city. Details pertaining to the board's discussions shall remain confidential. Suffice it to say, Dr. Hamilton wanted to spend more time with his family and a chance to pursue personal projects." *There it was again. Memorized. Word for word from Hawker's mouth.*

Nobody believed a euphemism like *pursue personal projects*. Rumorous tittle-tattle ran from incompetence to a list of heinous suspicions. Embezzlement. Sexual harassment. Alzheimer's.

But Hamilton's dismissal was far more ludicrous than that. He was forced to resign for the sake of a word: *THEORY*. A sensible, appropriate word with only two syllables ended the distinguished career of Dennis Hamilton.

The board called Hamilton to an emergency meeting on a Saturday night. The gravity of the request made him feel like a heretic being summoned to appear before the ecclesiastical tribunal of the Spanish Inquisition. Hamilton was not likely to be burned at the stake but the intolerance of his inquisitors was no less zealous.

Hamilton had started at the museum out of college and earned his PhD in the years that followed. He became director in 1995 and began his quest for a much-needed overhaul. It took fifteen years but was finally approved and funded. When his contract was renewed he was given control over the design, scholarship and presentation of exhibits.

Hamilton's plan included major changes to the Descent of Man Pavilion. He changed the name to Origins of Man and left space for several new unnamed exhibits. The original depictions of the primary stages in the evolution of humans were being replaced by the Thomas Hall mural and expanded to include the history, scientific context and paleo-anthropology of each.

A podium at each, called a "Knowledge Station," was to include audio, printed information and a computer screen that enabled visitors to ask questions and interact with the exhibit in various ways.

Hamilton was honest, open and, as scientists go, modest in his intellect and more teachable than most. He loved learning and trusted the experience and wisdom of the scientists, historians and consultants to whom he gave the task of preparing the audio scripts and writing the text that would appear on information placards.

The strange chain of events began on Wednesday. Hamilton finished his review of the content written for the information placards. He made a few notes, but no changes of any consequence were needed. He initialed the stamped box and scribbled the date and time.

"Ta-dum!" A cute staffer named Megen celebrated the event, picked up the approved text and headed out the door.

The impression came uninvited but the idea was not new. He described it to Thomas as "a voice in my head." As a kid Denny Hamilton had poked a hornet's nest with a short stick. The memory came to mind and made him smile. He could almost feel the burning points of pain but the voice kept saying, "Do it."

"Megen!" The girl turned. "One more thing." He scribbled four lines on a lime-green Post-it note and, when Megen returned, stuck it above his initials. "Make sure this is added in prominent letters to the bottom of each placard." Megen read the note and puckered her face in a quizzical look. Hamilton's handwritten note said simply:

> Evolution is a supposition of ideas
> Intended to explain the origins of species,
> Primarily based on
> The theory of Charles Darwin

The lime-green Post-it note was clutched between the thumb and forefinger of the woman with the turkey-wattle chin as if it were coated with anthrax. She refused to disclose how she had come by the "damning evidence" but held it high for all to see. "Evolution a theory? A supposition of ideas?" she gobbled.

Hamilton was astonished to learn that the addition to the placard had precipitated an emergency meeting of the board in a secret location. Criticisms, arguments and expletives were hurled back and forth in a flurry of exhortation, warnings and final injunction.

"Rethink your position!"

"You're committing professional suicide."

"The exhibit will be a scientific laughingstock."

A caterer arrived with a tray of hors d'oeuvres and two bottles of private reserve cabernet from Beringer Vineyards. It was a timely interruption to the escalating tension. Most shuffled toward the wine.

Louisa Herder, vice chair of the board, rapped on the table with her gavel. "Hold on a minute!" she said and struck the table again. "Before we break for food, I hope I speak on behalf of all of you in thanking Dr. Hamilton for missing his wife's birthday party to meet with us tonight. I think most of you will probably agree we've been a bit overreactive."

"We're either a science museum or we're not," intoned a paunchy man who looked out of character in his Armani suit. He was already pouring a glass of wine and plucking finger food with the other hand.

Herder continued, "Dr. Hamilton, I'm sure you agree a science museum is no place for personal opinions. Everything in our museum needs to be about science and, well, truth!"

Hamilton resisted a response to such naiveté.

"All we are saying here, Dennis," the woman next to Herder used his first name in a way that was both intimate and deliberate, "is you need to reassure us that nothing in the new Descent of Man Exhibit—"

The woman with the turkey-wattle chin interrupted. "He changed the name to Origins of Man!"

"Well, whatever the exhibit of evolution is called, it must not equivocate with established scientific fact."

Hamilton stepped to the hors d'oeuvres and began spearing petite squares of Gruyère with a toothpick and putting them on a napkin. He used the action to collect his thoughts.

"Science is a systematic practice of gathering knowledge." Hamilton spoke with respect and moved to where everyone could see him. He was calm and confident. "It's a process that enables a predictable outcome. *Fact* is the outcome, established not beyond a reasonable doubt but beyond *all* doubt. Science is the journey. True knowledge is the destination. You all know history well enough to know that what we have so often mistaken as the end of the journey has been nothing more than a new threshold of the undiscovered."

"What's the deal, doc? Are you going to drop the word *theory* or not?" It was the fleshy man on his second glass of wine.

"Do you happen to know the etymology of the word *theory,* Mr. Hugo?" Hugo didn't even know what *etymology* was. He put more in his mouth to avoid admitting his ignorance. Too late. It was obvious in his blank expression.

"The Greek root of *theory* is *theoria.* It means 'to look at. To contemplate. And to SPECULATE.'" He annunciated the last word slowly, then smiled as he continued, "*Theory* is a word of science. We describe the brilliant work of Albert Einstein as 'the theory' of relativity. Have you ever heard it called anything else?" He let the question hang and the murmuring settle.

"We accept as 'fact' the notion that the earth revolves around the sun, and yet we still refer to the idea of a heliocentric universe as the

Copernican Theory. And don't miss the significance of the fact that before Copernicus, everyone accepted Ptolemy's geocentric universe—the sun revolving around the earth—as 'fact.' The point, of course, is that theories are not always correct and thus not always fact. Is that why you're so troubled by calling evolution a theory?"

"Just tell us you're going to make the changes we've asked for," Hugo said.

Hamilton put a little chunk of Gruyère in his mouth and finished it before he continued.

"Do continents drift?" An involuntary stir of affirmation wafted through the room. "It is a theory," Hamilton smiled, "and as certain as we are that they drift, no one has a problem calling the phenomenon the 'theory of continental drift.' What do we call the structure and existence of that tiny, mystical wonder we call an atom?" He smiled triumphantly as he added, "Which no one has ever seen, by the way."

"Atomic theory." It was Samuel Taylor, one of the two people on the board who supported Hamilton.

Hamilton smiled and nodded. "Exactly! 'Atomic *theory*.' Are you troubled by that?" He let the question hover just above their heads and allowed time for a response. None came. "Making reasonable predictions based on knowledge is what science is about. But even reasonable predictions remain speculation. *Theory* is the word we use to describe those speculative predictions."

"Dr. Hamilton, I think that—" It was Ms. Herder. Hamilton cut her off.

"Why are you so afraid to use the word *theory* when it comes to Darwin's *Origin of Species*?" A discomforting chill seemed to settle on the room. "Is it because 'theory' leaves the door open to the possibility we might be wrong?" He waited and the pause was discomforting. "That's my 'theory,' and I'll tell you why. If it turns out we're wrong about continental drift, it changes nothing. If it turns out we're wrong about evolution, it changes everything."

"We're getting way off track here," turkey chin grumbled and looked at her watch.

"What's your point, doc?" It was the man straining the buttons on his Armani.

Hamilton moved slightly and stepped into a shaft of light. "To be a bit prosaic: If we slithered from the slime of a primordial sea, then nothing matters. If we walked from the Garden of Eden in the blazing light of cherubim and a flaming sword, then everything matters."

"Am I seriously hearing this? You're the director of a science museum and you're talking about Adam and Eve?" Hugo barked.

"You asked for the point and it's sharper than you imagined." Hamilton shrugged and, unable to resist the delicious irony, added, "I find it curious you call out 'my god' in your moment of stress."

"We're not here to screw with semantics, Hamilton. You think this is inconsequential or something!"

"It is precisely consequences I am talking about, Mr. Hugo. I don't presume to have the answers but I know the questions."

The man made no response. That surprised Hamilton.

Ideas Hamilton was careful to exclude from public lectures at the museum tumbled from the black box to his tongue. "Since Darwin published *Origin of Species,* the idea of evolution itself has 'evolved' from a theory to a broad level of general acceptance. In spite of formidable flaws, evolution has become one of life's certainties among 'educated people.' Why is that? Why do you suppose a theory has evolved into a 'truth' in spite of mathematical improbability, irreducible complexity and the pivotal mystery of spontaneous generation?"

"Because every time you people dig up a bone, it proves Darwin was right." Hugo intended a laugh and got it but it was too weak to fracture the rising tension as Hamilton continued.

"I believe men are drawn to Darwin's ideas because, as frightening as it is to live in a world without meaning—a world in which we are nothing more than creatures of accident and evolution—it is even more frightening to imagine a power or intelligence beyond ourselves. It is daunting to contemplate a 'cause' and thus a purpose. It's terrifying because in spite of extraordinary advancements and escalating knowledge, that possibility remains. And thus our fears are well founded because we don't have a clue what that might mean. What—*or who*—that might be."

"Are you telling this board that the director of our science museum doesn't believe in evolution?" Hugo blurted.

"I believe there is compelling evidence for evolution of species, each within its own sphere. I believe the theory of evolution invites enormous possibility for continued exploration. If you are asking whether I believe in evolution as the one great unifying truth of life, the answer is no. I believe it is premature to extinguish every other possibility for the origin of human beings. I believe the evidence argues against the theory of a common ancestor for every living thing. I don't have the answer but I simply can't believe that you and I, the plant in the corner and the fly on the window all came from the same bacterium. I no longer believe life is accidental and organized itself by some inexplicable cosmic coincidence. But this meeting is not about I believe or don't believe. It's only about a word."

"You're wrong. This meeting is exactly about what you believe!"

"Or don't believe," Hugo blurted.

"Are you really advocating intelligent design or the ridiculous notion of creation?" Ms. Herder rose from her chair.

"The only thing I am advocating, Ms. Herder, is scientific and intellectual integrity. What I 'believe' is . . . well, 'evolving.' Darwin was aware of gaps in his theory—or his presentation of facts, if you prefer. The problem is, they're not 'facts.' That's my only point. Even Darwin recognized his life's work as a theory and left the door ajar."

"That's ridiculous!" It was Hugo again.

"Have you read Darwin, Mr. Hugo?" Hugo deflected the question by looking at Herder. Hamilton followed the fat man's gaze and asked Herder the same question by lifting his thick brows. She looked away. He moved his eyes face to face around the room. Their apparent ignorance amused him. A woman who until this moment had said nothing ended the awkward silence.

"I've read parts of it," she said. Hamilton acknowledged her modest achievement in the otherwise total vacuum. From memory he recited the final paragraph in Darwin's classic work as if it had been written by Ralph Waldo Emerson or Robert Frost.

From the war of nature, from famine and death, the
most exalted object which we are capable of conceiving,
namely the production of the higher animals, directly follows. There is grandeur in this view of life, with its several
powers, having been originally breathed by the Creator into
a few forms or into one and that, whilst this planet has gone
cycling on according to the fixed law of gravity, from so
simple a beginning endless forms most beautiful and most
wonderful have been and are being evolved.

"This is getting senseless." Hugo poured another glass of wine. "Look,
we agreed before he got here he drops the word *theory* and the other. . . ."

"*Supposition*," Herder helped him.

"*Supposition* also or he's out."

An icy chill swept through the room as if it were a polar ice station
and someone had opened a door. Hamilton walked to the window. The
view from the thirteenth floor looked east to where Market Street disappeared behind the Hyatt Regency before colliding with Embarcadero
Plaza. Mercury vapor lamps created fuzzy orange balls beneath a thin
layer of fog rolling in from the north. Wet, black streets were mirrors that
stretched the headlights of late taxies into long, colorful dragons.

Hamilton both loved and hated the city of San Francisco. The clock's
hand on the tower of the Ferry Building jerked forward a minute to
11:46. Ms. Herder joined him at the window. "This has gotten way out of
hand, Dennis, I'm sorry." She spoke quietly. Confidentially. "You've done
a fine job as director, we all know that. This is just a, well, a tempest in a
teapot but there are strong feelings about all of this. They just need to be
reassured. That's all." Her choice of the third-person plural rather than
"we" was not lost on Hamilton. Good cop bad cop.

"I have spent my life as a scientist," Hamilton said. "On the first day
of biology class the professor asked us to stand and recite what he had
written on the chalkboard in large, bold letters: 'Natural science does not
involve issues of philosophy, politics or religion.' He had nine different
photographs of Charles Darwin in his office. I've spent my life supporting
our most hallowed hypothesis." He took a long slow breath and smiled.

"The longer I've searched for 'the truth' about the origins of mankind, the more I've come to realize I've been blind to the very things that define us."

Hugo, turkey chin, and the woman who had read parts of Darwin formed a semicircle around Hamilton. The others joined in. "That is not the reassurance we need, Dennis," Herder warned.

"So what's it going to be, doc? We all on the same page here?" Hugo's voice was slurred from the wine.

Hamilton scanned the circle of faces. The human mind never ceased to amaze him. Their reflections off the black glass doubled their numbers and surrounded him. He saw himself in the final scene from *Man of La Mancha:* family and friends surrounding a decrepit old idealist with a circle of mirrors in hopes he will come to his senses.

Hamilton stepped from the circle, passed between Hugo and Herder and walked from the room.

CHAPTER

54

I<small>T WAS AFTER ONE O'CLOCK BY</small> the time Hamilton finished his story in the library. His obvious delight in talking, coupled with his memory of detail and dialogue, kept Thomas enthralled.

Of greater interest than the pending legal action and closed-door intrigue of Hamilton's "unlawful dismissal"—Thomas concluded without question that that was what it was—were the old scientist's personal confessions. "A shift in my paradigm of meaning," Hamilton called it. A realization that he might be wrong about certain important things.

Mrs. Hamilton served lunch in the sunroom on the south side of the house: an organic salad created from two kinds of lettuce, arugula, avocado, dandelion leaves, chopped seaweed, sprouts, almonds and cranberries. She tossed it at the table in a pomegranate dressing, forked out a pile to each plate and added a shake of rust-colored powder with a pungent aroma Thomas could not identify—ground fenugreek, she told him when he asked about it. The salad was served with homemade whole wheat bread, unsalted butter and jelly made from wild blackberries picked the day before.

They left on their hike for the falls the moment the dishes were cleared and piled in the sink. Hamilton handed Thomas a bottle of water and slipped into the straps of a day pack, forest green and charcoal brown.

They passed through the dense woods behind the house, crossed a broad meadow and picked up the well-marked trail at the edge of old growth redwoods. They walked tandem, speaking very little, conserving their wind as the trail was steep in places and rose quickly. The silence allowed Thomas to ponder Hawker's demands and try to decide what to do.

Just before they entered the green twilight of Fern Canyon they stood on a bluff and took in the spectacular view. The Russian Gulch headlands to the north marched to the ocean in receding ranks, each a softer, cooler blue than the one before it. A fishing trawler headed west across Mendocino Bay. On the farthest rocky point a wave crashed and a geyser of white erupted from a blowhole.

The walls of the narrow canyon were an exaltation of ferns. Thomas followed Hamilton on a path that crossed the stream a dozen times on its way to the waterfall. The sound of falling water was dampened by the tangle of sandbar willows, wild berries and deciduous trees whose canopy allowed only splashes of sunlight to reach the canyon floor.

The sound of the waterfall made it seem bigger than it was. The drop from the rocky ledge to the pool was less than thirty feet and the water was at the summer low.

Thomas took pictures. He asked Hamilton to pose in the foreground. One foot on a boulder. Leaning forward with an arm across his leg. The confident grin of an intrepid explorer. Thomas was reminded what it had been like working with Hamilton in the early days of the project. How much had changed. He regretted he hadn't made an effort to know Hamilton on a more personal basis. He hadn't climbed out of his own head long enough to appreciate Hamilton for the exceptional human being he was. Thomas regretted the anxious circumstances that brought them together again.

"I think I blinked," Hamilton laughed when Thomas took the picture. "Better take another." As Hamilton came into focus on the ground glass, Hawker's angry warning jolted his thoughts. *If you can't get him to back down, there won't be any job. Tell him you've changed your mind! Tell him you've "evolved."*

CHAPTER

55

THE HIKERS STOPPED IN A grove of redwoods on the back side of the trail that looped from Fern Canyon to the Mendocino headlands. They sat on a decaying log that was soft with moss and split a Snickers bar. Hamilton threw bits to a yellow-cheeked chipmunk.

"I was an atheist in college," Hamilton said as he tantalized the chipmunk by dropping bits of bar steadily closer to his hand. "That meant me and this little guy had the same great-great-grandpa." Thomas wasn't sure how to react. "What do you think, Thomas? Some inexplicable event? A single-celled organism? Three and a half billion years. Every living thing on the planet, every incredibly complex living thing began with that one bacterium?" He crushed moss from the log and let it fall through his fingers. "The chipmunk, me, the moss and you," he laughed softly. "Incredible that I ever believed that." The chipmunk mustered courage, darted in and plucked a peanut from Hamilton's fingers. Thomas stood up and the chipmunk vanished. He shrugged an apology.

"When I was a teenager," Hamilton went on, "I had an incredible butterfly collection. I was so excited by the beauty of nature and loved music. The feelings, you know. It made me wonder from time to time about the meaning of life. About God.

"When I discovered the universe was made out of atoms and molecules and organized in some grand scheme of mathematical order, I concluded the meaning of life was biology. I didn't abandon faith per se but I was not prepared for the aggressive attitude of the atheists who populated science. When I read Einstein's biography and discovered he didn't believe in Judaism's Yahweh, I decided you couldn't be a scientist and believe in God without committing intellectual suicide. So that was it. Question asked: 'Is there a God?' Question answered: 'No.' Case closed.

"Then, ten years ago, I decided to renovate the museum. Another question: What had we learned, if anything, about the important questions? There isn't a more important question than 'Is there a God?' I asked myself whether I had honestly considered the evidence. What kind of scientist was I? My wife gave me this."

Hamilton pulled a book from his backpack. "I want to read you something." Thomas settled on a smaller log and saw the title of the book: *Mere Christianity,* by C. S. Lewis.

He felt like an initiate who had climbed to the top of a mountain to seek wisdom at the feet of a wizened sage and was about to learn the secret of life. Hamilton turned to a section called *Right and Wrong as a Clue to the Meaning of the Universe.*

Perhaps "an initiate" was exactly what Thomas was.

CHAPTER

56

THOMAS LEFT THE AGATE COVE INN so early he missed their famous homemade muffins. Breakfast was Red Bull and a banana in the car. He'd hardly slept at all.

Hamilton's comments in the redwood grove flooded his head. The intellectual arguments of C. S. Lewis filled his dreams. Hamilton had read a few passages from the book, marked the pages and given the book to Thomas. It was after 3:00 A.M. before he finally fell asleep. Clothes on. Book open across his chest.

The sun topped the eastern hills. The thoughts of the night fluttered through Thomas's mind like the sunlight through the canopy of trees, flavescent yellow.

The philosophies of postmodern men: "There are no absolutes. No such thing as 'right' or 'wrong.' Morality is relative," collided with the inspired ideas of Hamilton as he had paraphrased C. S. Lewis and his treasured book: "There is a law or rule of fair play and decent behavior and morality, that is as much a law of the universe as gravity itself, THE moral law. Human beings, all over the earth, have the sense they ought to behave in a certain way, and they cannot get rid of it. They know this 'Law of Nature' and break it. These two facts are the foundation of all clear thinking about ourselves and the universe we live in."

Hamilton had confessed that his erudite assumptions about God and the universe were the musings of an ignorant adolescent compared to the intellectual arguments of the brilliant Oxford scholar whose own journey from atheism to faith in Christ had set Hamilton on his own quest for faith.

By the time they had hiked the final mile home, it was dark and the absence of city light made the night sky spectacular. They stopped to stare into the heavens and laughed about the limitations of mortal minds.

"It was the idea of the Moral Law," Hamilton said. "Our sense that some things are right and some things are wrong affirms a standard of morality beyond ourselves." He paused to point out a falling star. Thomas couldn't remember the last time he had seen the night sky so completely.

"Evolution has a lot of holes filled with Silly Putty," Hamilton continued, "but the one gaping wound they cannot hide is the Moral Law. The whole idea of evolution, the whole idea of natural selection relies on a 'selfish gene' that drives every individual within every species to perpetuate itself. That seems true for every species but one. Us." He paused again, lost in his own thoughts.

"Love, altruism and our inborn instinct to help the underdog, to sacrifice for others, to show selfless concern even at the risk of our own lives flushes evolution as the singular explanation of life on earth down the proverbial toilet."

• • •

Thomas had failed Hawker completely, and that left his future with the museum, the Origins of Man mural project and the money still owed on the contract in a volatile state of uncertainty. It left paying for the boat a crisis.

His failure to persuade Hamilton to relinquish his demands was more than defeat. It was treachery. That was how Hawker would see it. Thomas strained his imagination for a way to tell Hawker the truth about his "confrontation" with Hamilton. He rehearsed the dialogue but nothing sounded right.

The truth was, there had been no confrontation, no skirmish, no battle, no hostility. It was one thing to lose; it was another to never even engage. He had never talked to Hamilton about Hawker's demands, never asked him to reconsider. Hamilton had known what Hawker wanted before Thomas ever got there. Once that was clear, it hadn't come up again.

How Thomas had ended up in a quiet woods talking about God instead of trying to reason with Hamilton, he had no idea. He could already hear Hawker spewing anger in a cloud of cigar smoke. *Dummy! Defector! Derelict!* Thomas knew he was headed for disaster.

Thomas took the Comptche Ukiah Road across the coastal range, turned south on Highway 101 and headed for San Francisco. In spite of his angst over the impossibility of explaining the last thirty-six hours to Hawker, his conversation with Hamilton, his night with C. S. Lewis and the St. Mark's project wrestled for attention. They were somehow connected. For one thing, St. Mark's was suddenly the single certain source of income. Thomas knew that the only hope of finishing the mural in the Healing Place by Christmas was to have started two months ago.

He rehearsed a dialogue with Cass about money and drove directly to the hospital. *A small retainer? Good faith deposit? The normal down payment? Advance on materials?* He wasn't sure what Berger would call it and how he would get it, but Berger always did. *Damn Berger for getting himself fired!*

CHAPTER

57

GOOD MORNING, MR. HALL." The crusty receptionist stood with a smile and open arms. Susan Cassidy had paved the way and was good at what she did.

She pulled out an ID badge marked *STAFF* with his picture encased in plastic. "Cute," she said as she glanced at the photo and put the lanyard around his neck.

The photo was the one Cass had snapped by the boat. His mouth was open in a cheesy grin. His eyebrows were raised in a way that erased any hint of intelligence. His hair was caught lopsided in a gust of wind.

"The minute I'm finished, it gets shredded. Okay?" he said, salving vanity with humor. She laughed.

Construction on the Healing Place was nearly finished. It was more stunning than Thomas remembered. Cass had followed his instructions. The mural was cordoned off by a transparent plastic barrier. A ten-foot table on casters was in place. Eight halogen work lights were spaced at twelve-foot intervals. A six-foot Gillis rolling stairway with safety-lock wheels was parked just inside the barrier. The polished granite floor was covered by construction plastic. A worker was taping the last of the edges on the far right side. *The woman is amazing.*

"So what are you waiting for?" Thomas was adjusting the distance of the lights from the canvas and hadn't seen Cass come in. He turned.

"This is perfect," he said. "Just great. Thank you."

"Acrylic titanium double-primed," she grinned, "so here you go. Get started." She offered him her twenty-dollar ballpoint pen. He laughed and sketched a fat short arrow on the canvas pointing to the words *START HERE.* "So when do you start?"

"That doesn't count?" Thomas jerked a thumb at his arrow. Cass was laughing softly.

Thomas felt an eagerness about the project he hadn't expected. During the grueling hours of the all-night ordeal there were moments of creative rapture, but they'd been different from what he felt today.

Sunlight streamed through the windows of the Healing Place and kissed Cass on the cheek. His imagination was in turbo drive. He experienced a strange sense of bliss and felt a sudden rush of affection for the woman standing next to him. His impulse was to put his arms around her. He didn't—but he flushed at the thought.

"Miss Von Horn may be expecting a bit more," Cass smiled and it seemed to Thomas she was also caught up in whatever was enchanting this place in this moment. "Just so you know," she said, "Carver is very unhappy with my decision and Miss Von Horn is your new best friend."

"She thinks I'm 'interesting'?"

Cass laughed. "She is bypassing the board altogether, so . . . "

"I'll start blocking first thing tomorrow. I need to get over to Art Institute and buy all the stuff I need."

"Art Institute?"

"I guest-lecture now and then so they give me the faculty discount on supplies."

"Which you pass on to us, of course," Cass said half seriously. Her comment kicked open the door to the awkward money conversation that had to happen. Thomas's pulse quickened and he stepped through.

"Which reminds me, I usually get, you know . . ." *Why is this so awkward?* "An upfront payment." *Like I don't trust them?* "A down payment, an advance, you know, for art supplies, paint, brushes." He said it offhandedly lest Cass suspect he was desperate for cash. He had learned she could divine his thoughts. "So, however you want to handle that—"

She cut him off. "If it's okay, I'd prefer it if you and I don't get into that side of it." Thomas blanched and hoped it didn't show. "I still haven't heard from Frank," she said.

CHAPTER

58

THE DUTY NURSE TOOK Thomas to Christina's room. She had been moved from ICU to Pediatrics Burn Recovery Center. He had almost forgotten about the little girl—certainly given her no thought—until Cass asked him if he was going to visit her before he left the hospital. It was a suggestion, not a question.

Christina lay in bed, her legs still rigid in their casts. The color of her skin looked better than Thomas remembered. The granulation of new tissue on her burned limbs was a good sign of healing.

Christina's eyes were closed when Thomas came in. She opened them when the nurse stroked her arm. "How ya doin,' hon?" she asked. There was nothing unusual about the tender tone and gentle touch, but Hamilton's words seem to echo like thunder in Thomas's mind: *Our human instinct to help others and to give selflessly without motive is evidence of moral law, and moral law is evidence of God.*

"You remember Mr. Hall, sweetheart?" Christina's eyes shifted from the nurse to Thomas. There was a confused expression on her bandaged face. "He's the artist," the nurse said. "The man who is painting Jesus in our wonderful new room upstairs." *One of 44 figures,* Thomas thought and wondered if everybody in the hospital knew who he was and what he was doing.

"Is your hand better?" Christina asked. Thomas was startled that the child remembered. He held it up with a bandage still in place.

"Yup! Cass fixed me up good. They gave me a shot and bingo! Good as new."

"Did you thank Heavenly Father?" Thomas glanced at the nurse, who raised her eyebrows and waited with Christina for an answer. "I asked him to make it better," the child added.

"Thank you."

"Did you draw a picture of my mother?"

"I'm working on it," Thomas said. The nurse sent him an uncertain signal. "I want to make sure it's perfect."

"She's very beautiful," the child said, wincing from the pain of speaking, then asked, "Is your mother dead?"

Thomas nodded. "She died a long time ago."

"When you were little?"

"About your age."

Christina gave Thomas a grown-up look that conveyed her understanding of such things. "Do you have a father?" she asked.

"I do," Thomas said.

"I've never had a father. You're very lucky."

"Lucky."

"Do you say 'I love you' every day?"

"Hmmmm. Not every day." Thomas shuddered the thought away before it spiraled out of control.

"You should," she said.

"I'll get going on that picture of your mom, okay? Is there anything else I can do for you?"

She looked away as if the answer were a butterfly she needed to catch with her eyes. The little finger on her ruined hand twitched. The ring finger moved a fraction. Thomas glanced from the hand to the face and her eyes held him there.

"Would you bring me my violin?"

"Okay, sure." He ignored the subtle signals from the nurse, who was frowning and shaking her head.

"It has my name on it," Christina said with a surge of joyous energy, as if that were all Thomas needed to find the most precious thing in her life.

59

Thomas turned on the windshield wipers. The fog rolling landward was wet as rain. It was an hour before sundown but everything was twilight gray.

The Mercedes Navigator showed 1.6 miles to his destination, Cliff House on Point Lobos Avenue, where California Highway Patrol Sergeant Ray Evans had agreed to meet him in the parking lot at six o'clock.

. . .

Thomas had asked the duty nurse about the violin. "It was the first thing she asked for when she regained consciousness," she told him. "They were on their way to her violin lesson when they were hit by the truck."

"The violin was in the car." It wasn't a question, but the nurse nodded. Thomas assumed her signal had been to keep him from making a promise he couldn't keep. It wasn't.

"The thing is," she said, "her left hand is so badly burned that it won't be possible for her to ever play the violin again."

"Does she know that?"

The nurse shook her head. "Dr. Namkung wants to tell her, but no one agrees with him. Not for now, at least. Makes you wonder what God has in mind for a child who loses the two things she loved the most." Thomas looked up from the accident report. She elaborated, "Her mother and her music."

"If there's a God, why do such horrible things happen at all?" Thomas said. He copied the investigating officer's name from the report and returned it to the nurse.

. . .

Thomas sat in his car. Frail fingers of fog crept across the asphalt. The ring tone from *Eragon* invited him to fly. It was a call from Hawker. Flying away on a dragon seemed suddenly an enticing idea. He let the call go to message. He would need Red Bull in his blood when he had the inevitable conversation.

It was the third missed call from Hawker. There was also one missed call from Hamilton, along with two from Susan Cassidy and one from Oakridge Manor. He wasn't sure which to handle first. He had to talk to Hawker. He was curious why Hamilton had called. Susan Cassidy was a priority. The St. Mark's mural was the bailout. He had to start now or never get it done. The deal had not been made, though. Frank was missing and a little girl who would never play again wanted him to find her violin. Sitting in the St. Mark's parking lot with a stomachache was not where he'd expected to be.

He called the California Highway Patrol. "For English, push one." He tapped the numeral and waited while the system repeated the language option in Spanish. An artificial voice offered him a long list of options before finally defaulting to a live human. "Push one for emergency, two to report an accident." It went on: crime in progress, traffic collision, "fix-it" ticket, road conditions, weather, bail, employment or "stay on the line." He did.

The dispatcher was not as well-spoken or articulate as the computer, but a real live person. Thomas left his number and the name of the officer he needed to reach. Evans called him back before he reached the bookstore at Art Institute. He turned around, followed Forty-eighth to Balboa and headed west to Coast Highway.

Thomas slowed to pass a line of cyclists bundled in bright nylon against the wet and cold. He wondered if Christina would ever ride a bike. Or walk. Or play her violin.

It was six thirty by the time Evans arrived. Thomas saw the black-and-white Crown Vic pull in and stop in front of a sign for tourists that told the history of Cliff House and celebrated the ecology of Seal Rocks a hundred yards offshore. He was already walking across the parking lot when Evans stepped from his car.

When they had talked on the phone, Thomas had explained the reason he wanted to visit the scene of Christina's accident. Evans had been surprisingly willing to help but gave Thomas no hope of finding the violin.

"The car burned completely and ended up in the ocean." Evans was too modest to explain he had pushed it into the surf. No one but his wife had heard about the miraculous burst of strength that had enabled him to roll the car and put the fire out.

"The only possibility," Evans said, "would be if the violin was thrown out before the car exploded."

"If it's still there we can take a look, at least."

"Gotta be tonight. DOT finally got the big crane in and are pulling what's left of the vehicle out tomorrow. I can't be there before six o'clock so bring a good light, but don't get your hopes up. The chances of finding what you're looking for are zero to none."

Improbable as the venture was, Thomas felt a curious optimism. He had made a promise to a little girl whose soulful, trusting eyes were watching. *It is our human instinct to help others.* The thought caused him to smile but it also made him think.

Evans drove south from Cliff House and parked the cruiser on the narrow shoulder on the east side of the Pacific Coast Highway. Dusk was darkening the site and the damp had turned to drizzle.

When Evans saw Thomas's cheap LED flashlight, he swapped him for a spare 3D-cell Maglite. They crossed to the temporary railing that marked the spot where Gloria's car had gone over the cliff. Thomas had hoped Evans would show him the scene of the accident. He had not expected the officer would wait until his shift ended and go with him. Evans's personal interest in the accident and child were unexpected.

The landscape was changing into shapes and shadows but still visible in the twilight. Evans used the 22,000-candlepower beam of his torch to trace the ragged course the Windstar had taken to the bottom of the rockfall.

Evans swung his leg over the railing. "Come on. We'll take a look. Be careful," he warned, "the rocks are deceptively slick when they're wet."

Evans picked his way over the boulders. Thomas followed. Where rocks were scarred by the impact of the minivan the men stopped to search for any sign of the lost violin. They worked their way to the bottom of the cliff. Their lights found broken glass, a shattered section of windshield, fragments of metal and twisted pieces of the undercarriage. Clumps of soggy paper, ragged cloth, detritus and other debris were pounded into cracks and crevices, but it was impossible to distinguish trash and flotsam from remnants of the crash.

They reached the rock where Evans had bandaged Christina and waited for Life Flight. The sergeant stepped over and down the last few stones to the edge of the water. The tide was out. The ocean calm. The charred frame of the vehicle had been pushed into the rocks and half buried by the sand. It marked the spot like a twisted hand thrust up from a grave in agony.

Evans stood there a long time. The torch hung limp in his right hand. The glow illuminated the foam that swirled around his boots before being sucked back out to sea. Thomas knew instinctively that the patrolman was reliving the horrendous events of that night.

"Might as well take a look since we're here," Thomas said, bringing Evans back from his harrowing memory. He looked up at Thomas and nodded.

Darkness seemed to come all at once and the drizzle turned to rain. Thomas probed the dark hole in the van's side. A slime of kelp was tangled in the skeleton of charred and twisted steel. The tentacles of brown algae hung like macabre dreadlocks over gaping holes where eyes might have been.

Thomas pushed the slippery snarl aside and crouched low to get inside. He gripped the frame of the door. A stab of pain. He jerked his hand away. The alien intruder was already encrusted by creatures of the deep come to claim the spoils.

A wave washed over the sand and filled the cavity to the depth of

Thomas's thighs. It was cold but the chill that prickled his spine was not cause by temperature. His light found the ragged seatbelt. It was sawed and shredded. *Maybe ripped partway by sheer force,* he thought and shuddered. When he touched the frayed ends he could see the little girl from St. Mark's hanging upside down in soaring heat and he sensed for a fleeting instant the terror she must have endured.

"Lucky I carry this." Evans squatted at the open hole in the side of the frame. He lifted a red Buck Knife from a black leather scabbard on the hip of his utility belt and handed it to Thomas. "My dad gave it to me when I earned my Eagle Scout. Never been without it and now I know why."

On their climb down from the road Evans had responded patiently to Thomas's insatiable curiosity about the accident and described the ordeal in detail. Questions that implied any heroism on his part were deflected by a change of subject and left unanswered.

Neptune pulled a rubber stopper at the bottom of the ocean and the water rushed back out to sea. Thomas hurriedly searched the burned-out pockets in the steel before the next wave came. He willfully ignored the obvious. Nothing burnable could have survived the fire. He dropped to his knees and began to claw the wet sand with his fingers. The Maglite rolled away and cast eerie shadows on the floor above.

"It takes a day or so for the sand to build up," Evans said. "Anything light as a violin would have floated away before it got buried." Thomas didn't need to be told. Or maybe he did. He stopped digging and swept the interior again as the next wave came in. *It's not here. Impossible that it could be.* He accepted the reality but couldn't shake the odd sensation that he was going to find the child's violin. A miracle? *No such thing. Sixth sense. Natural law. Of course.* But there was nothing natural about the tingling on his body and the teasing in his mind.

"May I ask you a personal question?" he said to the officer.

Evans looked up at Thomas and nodded. "Shoot."

"How did you know the child survived the explosion?"

"I didn't."

"How do you make a decision like that?"

Evans glanced back at the skeleton from hell. He postponed answering the question by making his way up and across the rocks and posing a question of his own. "Why are you so interested in this girl?"

"I don't know. She asked me to find her violin. Yeah, I know. It doesn't make sense. But she doesn't have anybody, you know, and . . ." Even as he tried to explain, he realized he didn't understand his curious feelings about Christina.

Evans studied Thomas's face as he listened. Finally he said, "She didn't survive the explosion."

"Didn't survive? What do you mean?"

"She was not alive when I carried her out." He said it softly, soberly and as a matter of fact. "Her heart had stopped and she wasn't breathing."

Thomas's incredulous expression asked a hundred questions. "I'm not sure I understand what you're saying, do you mean that—"

Evans interrupted. "I'm not sure I can explain," he said. "Are you a religious man?"

Thomas worried the wrong answer would end the conversation. He nodded slightly and hoped Evans construed it as affirmative.

"You ask me why I took such an extreme risk to save a girl who, as it turned out, had already died. At least by the criteria of medical science," he added. "I'm not sure I had a choice. Call it what you like: destiny, divine intervention. It was like a voice inside telling me I needed to get to her and bring her out, so I did."

"But how did you . . . ?"

"Get her breathing again? Her heart working? CPR, emergency procedures, everything I'm trained to do, but I think that . . ." Evans stopped himself.

"What?" Thomas asked. His drawing of Jairus and his wife embracing their daughter entered his mind's eye without a beckon.

"I prayed," Evans said and paused for a moment to measure Thomas's reaction. "I prayed and begged God to save her life."

Conflicting thoughts collided in Thomas's head.

The patrolman patted the artist on the shoulder and resumed the ascent. He paused and looked back. "Obviously God has something special in mind for that little girl, so make sure you look after her."

Evans turned back up the hill. The beam of his torch swung in a wide arc to the right and flashed on something that was brighter than the black rocks around it. Then it was gone.

Thomas climbed to the spot and probed the wet boulders with the beam of his light. A shattered mirror from the Windstar was wedged into the rock. It reflected the light. He sighed with disappointment and started to climb again. His foot slipped and he tumbled sideways. He caught himself with his injured hand. A spike of pain lanced through his arm and the light tumbled into a jumble of pocked rock.

"You okay?" Evans called.

"I'm good," Thomas shouted back. He lay on his belly, stretched his arms and wriggled his fingers until he reached the light. There it was. The violin, or half a violin, at least. The brown case was buried in the sand a foot below high tide. They'd missed it coming down because it had been washed under a ledge and wedged into the narrow fissure.

"Found it!" Thomas shouted. Evans stopped and turned his light on the violin as Thomas dug it from its muddy grave. The case was crushed and tangled in seaweed but there was no question about its owner. Just below the handle there was a name painted in graceful script.

60

Thomas changed into basketball shorts, took two Advil and went to bed. The Red Bull he had gulped on the bridge was a bad idea. His body begged for sleep but his mind was sparking through the events of an insanely complex day.

He inhaled deeply, held it a beat, and breathed out slowly, hoping his brain would let him go. *The violin is soaking wet.* The thought kicked him out of bed. He clicked on the light and headed for the kitchen.

The case was crushed beyond repair but had done its duty and saved the violin. He ripped the hinges away with a hammer and used a screwdriver to pry away the lid. He cut off the piece with the name and set it aside to dry.

The instrument was swamped in a slurry of brine and mud. Water sloshed inside. He emptied the seawater in the sink, wiped the violin clean and dried it with a towel. He dried the inside with an old Conair hair dryer left over from the days before fame and vanity had superseded utility.

The chin rest was cracked and there was a deep scratch beside the F-hole. Otherwise there was no apparent damage. Thomas plucked the strings for the same reason a man kicks the tires on a used car without having a clue how to evaluate its condition. It just seemed like the thing to do.

He laid the instrument on a cushion and headed for bed. The bulb on the answering machine blinked red. He'd seen it when he first came in but, thinking it was Hawker, shoved it from his mind to be put off until morning. Resurrecting the violin had given him a second wind.

There was a missed call from Oakridge Manor. *Too late to call Alex back tonight.* For the first time in a long time Thomas was genuinely inclined to call his father back. *Be sure to tell him you love him every day.*

He'd been right to expect a call from Hawker. Maxine had left a message. She sounded younger and thinner on the phone. "This message is for Thomas Hall. Mr. Hawker wants you to call him immediately!" *"Immediately" does not include the middle of the night.* The conversation with Hawker would be tough enough without getting him out of bed at two o'clock in the morning to tell him the mission had failed and Hamilton was coming after him with a pack of legal pit bulls.

61

Damn Hamilton!" Hawker scowled. "If he wants to sue me, let him! I'll bury the . . . " The sentence scrolled away in a string of obscenities. He rolled the cigar in the corner of pursed lips and sucked in a mouthful of smoke. The irrational similarity between the Hawker in front of Thomas and the Hawker he had seen in his head was strangely surrealistic.

Hawker paced for a moment, then wagged a finger at Thomas and let foul-smelling smoke blow out with the words. "You just make sure your born-again buddy understands where this will go and where he'll end up."

"The judge could order a reinstatement," Lia Chu warned.

"Only if he wins," Vince Sadereck added quickly, lest his colleague acknowledge the weakness of the museum's position—or worse, risk losing the lucrative retainer. "I think we can build a good case."

• • •

Thomas had called Maxine at 8:01 A.M. and set up a meeting. A face-to-face confrontation with Hawker was miserable under any circumstance. This morning's collision could be lethal.

Of all my troubles great and small, the things that never happened were the greatest of them all. The axiom on the bathroom mirror came to mind. The debriefing by Hawker was not what Thomas had expected. It lasted less than a minute. Thomas walked in. Hawker yelled, "Where the hell you been for two days?"

Two days? Sick. No phone. None of the white lies worked. Hawker cut him off before he could answer. "So what's he going to do?"

Thomas had imagined their conversation as a drawn-out dialogue: *I said, he said, then I said, then he said, then I said.* Hawker was impatient. Cut to the chase. Get to the point. Bottom line.

"I don't think I changed his mind."

"What was his attitude?" Lia Chu asked.

Thomas had not anticipated the lawyers. "Friendly. Reflective. He talked a lot."

"And?" Vince asked with his hands as well as his voice.

"Like I said, I don't think I changed his mind."

"He was friendly?" Chu confirmed. Thomas nodded. She opened her laptop. "I want you to remember everything he said to you. Any behavior. Mannerism? Body language? Did he seem worried or nervous? Did he talk at all about the case? What he is thinking?"

Thomas wondered how much he should say and how to say it. *Will I end up a traitor to both sides?* Hawker spat a trace of tobacco into his fingers.

"It is all very personal for him," Thomas said finally. "He's changed his mind about many things."

"What things?" Chu typed at sixty-five words a minute without looking down.

"No new information. Same issues. Reason he was fired. The exhibit, the origins of life, his feeling that—"

"This is rubbish!" Hawker said, lurching through a cloud of smoke like an evil wraith. The eruption ended the conversation about what had happened in Mendocino. *There are moments of wonderful irony in the universe. Hawker is the one who saved me from confessing that I never did what he asked.* Thomas let out a long, slow breath but his relief was short-lived. Chu's look sent a prickle scampering up his spine. The inquisition was not over.

Hawker yanked the discussion from friendly settlement to aggressive legal offensive. He was determined to punish Hamilton for his "insolence and stupidity." His demands blew out like shrapnel from a faulty grenade.

"Sue him back. Find his enemies. Dig up dirt. Discredit him. Personal defamation. Charge him with fraud. Ruin his life."

Thomas had low expectations for Hawker's civility but he found the man's rancorous outburst alarming.

"Make him sorry he ever screwed with me!" Hawker demanded.

The lawyers struggled to keep their balance. They reminded Thomas of wild beings lusting for a hunk of flesh inside a trap. It was easy for Hawker to bluster but the best and brightest of Walters, Johnson, Lewis & Arlington knew they were the boots on the ground and Hawker's ego was a serious liability.

The slosh between Hawker's hubris and ultimate results was the legal equivalent of an alligator-invested swamp. Statutes, legal precedents, two unimpeachable witnesses and Hamilton's implacable lawyer, Darrin Colt. All of them had teeth!

Sadereck calmed Hawker down with optimistic assurances. Chu ruffled him again with a recitation of potential consequences. She had the reputation of starting with "the worst thing that could happen" and digging the client out from there.

"Worst case," she said flatly, "Hamilton ends up doing the exhibit and getting damages and you lose your job."

Hawker crushed the stub of his cigar in a cut-glass ashtray and glared at Chu like it was all her fault. "Maybe I've got the wrong law firm!" he threatened.

"Whoa, whoa, whoa! Lia's 'worst case' is never going to happen," Sadereck promised.

Chu shrugged. "I think it's foolish not to pursue the settlement." She turned to Thomas and said, "What if you met with him again?"

Hawker waved Chu's suggestion away like a bothersome fly. "We've done that! We gave Hamilton a chance to do the right thing. The smart thing. I'm sure Thomas all but broke his arm." The assumption hung in the air. They looked at Thomas. He swallowed hard and waited for the hammer to fall.

"What if you go back to Hamilton again and we, how shall I put it, make it very worth your while IF you persuade Hamilton to back off?"

"It's a waste of time!" Hawker snapped, then glared at Thomas. "You pushed him as hard as you could, didn't you?"

Chu spared Thomas an answer. "Of course he didn't! Thomas and Hamilton are friends." She spoke to Hawker as if Thomas were suddenly missing from the conversation. "Sorry for always being the skeptic, but I suspect if there was any twisting of arms it was not very painful." She indicted Thomas with a look that brought him back. "Obviously not painful enough." She paused to let the accusation fester. "That's why Thomas needs a second chance, only this time with enough incentive to make sure 'old friendships' don't get in the way."

"How much 'incentive' are we talking about?" Hawker grumbled.

Demonstrating her infamous bluntness, Chu looked Thomas in the eye. "How much do you need, Thomas?" Then, lest it not be perfectly clear, she added, "To do whatever it takes. To tell him whatever you have to tell him."

"Sell the weasel out?" Hawker grinned. "Remember, you've got a big stake in this. Like your whole future depends on this!"

Thomas longed for Berger. He resolved to make that right. He thought about the boat, the bills, and wondered if the modest front money might be the only cash he'd ever see for his work on the museum mural.

He remembered the day in the quiet woods. He tried to imagine what he would say if they met again. What Hamilton would say. Thomas paused a few seconds but it seemed longer, and the longer Hamilton's ideas had time to ruminate, the more sensible they seemed. *Heresy,* Thomas mused as thoughts of moral law filled his head in the office of Dr. Silas Hawker, the champion of atheistic Darwinism.

"Think about it," Chu said. "Be less pressure to have the boat paid off, hmmm?" It went through him like a bolt just barely missing bone. "We'll make a plan and get back to you."

CHAPTER

62

THE VIOLIN WAS IN THE middle of the worktable. It was the first thing Cass saw when she came into the Healing Place on Friday morning. Thomas was at the far end of the wall scribing the canvas into twelve-inch squares.

She glanced at the antique clock above the door: 8:04 A.M. It was evident by the amount of canvas already blocked that Thomas had been working for a while. He bounded up and down the portable stairs setting pins and snapping lines. He broke the tedium with an occasional surge of creativity and a swirl of charcoal lines. He was too absorbed to notice Cass when she came in.

Cass crossed to the table and picked up the violin as if were the Red Mendelssohn handcrafted by Antonio Stradivari. "I can't believe you found it," she said. He turned around, surprised by the sound of her voice.

"Hey!"

"Is this really hers?" she asked. Thomas shrugged with a sense of wonder and stepped down.

"I know. Amazing it survived."

"When the nurse told me Christina asked you to find it, I didn't think that . . ."

"Yeah. Crazy, huh?"

"I can't believe you really went looking for it." Thomas wasn't sure if it was a compliment or a confession. "You just didn't strike me as someone who would . . ."

Confession. "Ouch!"

"No, no. Sorry . . . I didn't mean . . . I just . . ." She sighed. "When are you going to give it to her?"

"I want to get a new case for it." He picked up the shard of broken plastic with Christina's name in a nest of painted flowers. "Put her name on it."

"You're a softy." Her smile was so sweet it felt like the nicest compliment anyone had ever given him.

"Ya think?"

"Yeah." There was an awkward lapse in conversation. "Anyway. I didn't mean to interrupt, I just . . . can I get you anything?"

"I'm good."

"See you later, then."

Thomas watched Cass walk away from him and cross the Healing Place. Her three-inch heels followed one another in a graceful arc, each stepping forward on a single line. The muscles in her calves were defined by every step. His eyes floated with notable appreciation from her legs to where her hair flowed around her shoulders in slow motion. *Beauty queen. Got to get this girl on my boat.*

"Unless you got a little time to help," he called after her, hoping the pragmatic tone concealed his real intent. "Scribing goes faster with two people if . . . uh . . . I'm hoping to get into the city for the paint in time to get a new case for the violin."

She looked at him silently, as if justifying in her mind the time it would take. After a long pause, she smiled and said, "What do you want me to do?"

• • •

Scribing the canvas was faster with Cass holding the end of the snap-line rather than Thomas pinning it each time. They fell into a rhythm and the grid moved swiftly across the wall.

"Have you ever talked to Christina about the accident?" Thomas asked.

"Hmm? Not really."

"She hasn't brought it up?"

"So far she hasn't wanted to talk about it and Dr. Namkung said we should wait until it comes from her. Why?"

Thomas told Cass about his conversation with Evans during their search for the violin. The details of the accident. Evans's part in the rescue of the girl. The officer's statement that the girl was dead for several minutes and came back to life sounded absurd in the cold light of morning. Even repeating it made Thomas feel foolish, and yet . . . He mentioned the CPR but left out what Evans had told him about the prayer. He praised the patrolman's heroism and told Cass what Evans had said about the "voice" that had given him faith to plunge into the fire. Then, almost as an apology, Thomas added, "That's the way he described it, like a voice telling him to risk his life to save the child. An *inner voice.*"

Thomas was still sorting out Evans's courage, his selfless act and the lingering presence of the moral law that was starting to color every other thought. *What is the color of a miracle?* Thomas wondered.

"You've never heard your 'inner voice'?" she asked.

"I wish there was only one," he laughed. "It's pandemonium up here most of the time." He touched his forehead. "A constant ruckus. Babel."

"I don't mean your thoughts."

"My ideas yell so loud for attention, if there's another 'voice' in there, I'd never hear it."

"In your life. In your art. Don't you ever feel some sense of clarity? That a single impression is being channeled through you from another source?" He had been lighthearted to this point, but Cass asked with such earnestness it brought him up short. He paused to think about it.

"Sometimes. Yeah, probably."

"Where did the idea for the mural come from, for example?" she asked. He looked puzzled. "This one, not the first one," she grinned. "Your idea to depict the consequences of the miracles. The aftermath, the repercussions, the joyous ramifications of the miracles in the minutes, hours and days following Jesus' blessed acts rather than the miracles themselves?"

"You want the truth?" Thomas was about to confess, *Because I wanted to create my own personalized version of the classic icon, a sort of "all-new-and-improved-uniquely-Thomas-Hall-Jesus."* He restrained admitting his vain motivations—partly because he would seem flippant and disingenuous, but partly because that was no longer the whole truth and nothing but the truth.

His mind flashed back to the moment the idea had come in the middle of the night. He remembered it with clarity. It had not come in fragments. It had arrived whole and finished. A surge of reassuring warmth, a sense of clarity had seemed to swell up inside.

Ideas came in many ways. Not always the same. Only on a few occasions had one come like this. He had never thought of it until now, but in the context of what has happening he had a sense it had come from a source outside himself. He was not the artist after all. He was merely the brush.

CHAPTER

63

THE BOOKSTORE WAS ON THE ground floor of the original building of Art Institute. Art supplies were in the wing once used as the atrium for the entrance on the south side. Sandstone pillars connected by graceful arches in what might seem an ancient temple transformed brushes, paints and palettes into sacred relics. Thomas made it to the bookstore with time to spare.

Thomas began every major project with a new set of brushes. Selecting the perfect brushes for the exact requirements of the piece was a ritual. He never bought brushes online. He had to hold them. Touch them. Feel the bristles with his fingers. He compared Kolinsky sable to Siberian squirrel. Goat hair to hair from the ears of an ox. Synthetic to natural blend. It was part of the ritual. Intuitive. Inspiring.

For the ninety-foot mural at St. Mark's even the largest tubes of oil paint available from the bookstore were too small and too expensive. He had already ordered the paint in quantity from RGH Artists' Oil Paints in Albany.

The bill for brushes came to $1,280. He signed on his credit account and worried about how he might pay the bill when it came. He needed a contract with St. Mark's. It always came back to Berger.

In the two hours he and Cass had worked on the grid, neither Berger nor money had come up. Thomas knew why. *I'd prefer you and I don't get into that side of it.* That's what Cass had said. *Or maybe,* Thomas thought suddenly, *Berger called and they're talking? Why would he do that?* The hopeful notion ejected the instant it hit his brain.

The day turned warm. By late afternoon the damp chill so familiar to residents of San Francisco was gone. Thomas walked the length of the covered corridor known as the Spanish Porch on his way to the parking garage. Everywhere he looked there were memories of his years at Art Institute. Mostly good. A few great.

He glanced at the classroom on the second floor where he'd spent so much time with Professor Andrus. They had spoken on the phone a few times and swapped a dozen e-mails over the last several months but had not spoken face-to-face in over a year. He checked the time and wondered if the professor might still be there.

• • •

The robust physique and twisted posture of the model posed nude on the riser reminded Thomas of a Peter Paul Rubens painting. He felt a fleeting moment of nostalgia for the clarity of creating art for art's sake instead of for money.

Professor Andrus strolled among a dozen students at academy easels. His hands were clasped behind his back. He paused to torture each student with thoughtful scrutiny, an abstruse expression or silence, the most painful reaction of all. He wore a black crewneck under a coarse beige frock with a history written in crusted smears of color. Faded Levi's and Finn Comfort Pretoria Walking Shoes completed the ensemble that never changed. *Perhaps,* Thomas mused, *I got it from him, not Einstein.*

Thomas peered through a broken pane in the opaque French window separating the studio and hall. It was purified déjà vu to watch Andrus move easel to easel with his familiar frown. For a time Thomas had imagined the imposing old professor would be his mentor for life, but everything changes.

Thomas knew better than to disrupt the class so he wandered the building until the break at ten before the hour. He glanced into familiar places. He looked at artwork in the student gallery, pleased to discover two of his award-winning student pieces still hanging there. He was surprised by a third painting from his student days that looked recently hung.

It was a study that had never been finished. That was why he was surprised it was hanging here. It was large for a student project. Had it been finished, some believed it could hang at the Rijksmuseum Amsterdam in the hall of Flemish masters and not seem out of place. Thomas had almost forgotten he ever did it.

It seemed strangely fortuitous it would be hanging here now. Serendipitous that he would be reminded of his one other excursion into classic Christian motifs.

Roman soldiers dragged Jesus to the cross. An officer in armor and plume sat astride a dapple-gray Arabian stallion. Each soldier symbolized a facet of the horrid event. He who mocked. He who laughed. He who pointed with shame. He who implanted the crown of thorns. He with the scourging whip. He who stole the robe. He with the implements of death. All of them were frozen in a moment of graceful form and brutal deed. Curiously there were neither friends nor family nor any to mourn.

The mounted centurion and several brutish soldiers were finished to a remarkable degree of detail. Portions of the painting were blocks of color. In places the original drawing could still be seen. Jesus was well drawn and partially finished but it seemed that was where the work had ended. The face was unfinished.

Thomas studied it a long time. His technique had gotten better, in his opinion, but the sublime design of the piece, the movement, the sense of being, the angst spawned by the reality of the characters all seemed to have been something Thomas had left beside the road on his way to the slick graphic look of fantasy art. Standing there waiting for a buzzer to go off, he couldn't be sure but thought he felt a strange sense of loss.

• • •

Students hurried from the class, most with their large drawing tablets under one arm. Thomas moved against traffic and stood grinning with expectation. He was not disappointed. The critical frown of Andrus's at-rest countenance erupted into a smile that exposed every well-earned wrinkle on his face.

"Thomas Hall!" Thomas extended his hand. Professor Andrus enveloped him in a fatherly embrace.

Of all the possible things Andrus might have said to him after a year, what he did say was the least expected. "I'm really glad you didn't end up doing that horrible project in Las Vegas. You are so much better than—" and before Thomas could interrupt and justify himself, Andrus waved his hand, "I know, I know, I know, but let's not dwell on that."

Professor Andrus seemed to know what was going on in Thomas's life. It surprised and delighted Thomas that he was watching from afar.

Andrus didn't ask about Hawker, Hamilton, SAVE THE SEALS, the fire or the new boat. He did say he had intended to get over to the museum and see the mural, "Before that idiot painted it over."

Thomas's first impression that Professor Andrus was clairvoyant was exaggerated. A little celebrity often leads to the assumption other people know and care what you're doing. Only rarely is it true. On the other hand . . .

"Tell me about St. Mark's," Professor Andrus said.

"How do you know about that?"

"If you're doing their mural, you know Susan Cassidy." An image of Cass rippled through his mind. *Backlight. Sweet face. Dazzling eyes. Coy smile. Great legs.*

"Yeah, Susan Cassidy is . . ." A froth of clichés continued the cascade. *Awesome, gorgeous, cool, bodacious, the kind of woman who sends men to war.* " . . . in charge of the project."

"Well, Ms. Cassidy sat right there and asked for the names of the top three students who ever came out of Art Institute." Thomas experienced a moment of gratitude. Almost humility. "I wrote your name three times."

• • •

Thomas's intention had been to drop in, say hello to his former professor, head downtown for the violin case, get home early, sleep fast and get a jump start on the day. It was after 8:00 P.M. by the time he left Art Institute.

Professor Andrus suggested they grab an early dinner in the student union cafeteria. Afterward they settled in a plush sectional sofa tucked away in the corner of a student hangout called the Da Vinci Lounge. *Appropriate,* Thomas thought.

It was the most candid conversation Thomas had ever had with Professor Andrus. Giving Susan Cassidy his name three times was a compliment he blubbered over until the hamburgers arrived. Just in time to save him from himself, Professor Andrus told him the rest of the story.

Susan Cassidy had called the day Thomas turned her down. "She was very upset with me," Professor Andrus said. "She called to let me know what an egotistical ass you were. She suggested I amend my earlier recommendation and give her the two missing names."

"Same word Frank used."

"Why did you turn her down?" Professor Andrus asked.

"How honest do you want me to be?"

Professor Andrus leaned forward, rested his elbow on the overstuffed arm of the sofa and waited. Thomas felt an unexpected sense of relief in talking with such candor about what had happened and, more than that, what was going on in his head.

He laughed as he explained his first proposal and Miss Van Horn's pointed challenge. He confessed his lack of belief in God and the fact that developing a mural based on Jesus and religious themes was easy to discard with the Vegas project pending. "To be honest," Thomas said, "I've been living in the comfortable ambiguity of agnosticism for so long I just didn't want to mess with the 'big questions.' It was bad enough dealing with Hawker and Charles Darwin."

The irony of being suspended between Silas Hawker, the outspoken atheist, and Miss Von Horn, the Christian benefactor of St. Mark's, was not lost on Thomas. It seemed even more amusing as he tried to explain it to Andrus.

In the eight years Thomas had known Professor Andrus, they had never had a religious conversation. They had come close his freshman year. It was following one of Andrus's popular Art Forum Lectures, *Art, Space and Nature.* Andrus had referred to "God-given talent" a couple of times and "divine beauty of creation" in describing the artist's challenge to capture beauty and translate meaning.

Thomas had waited for the hall to clear, then approached the professor with three other equally bumptious students. "What do you mean when you say, 'God-given talent' and 'divine beauty of creation'? Are you using them as poetic expressions or do you believe in some nonsense that suggests our talents are somehow outside ourselves and a mystical power beyond nature is responsible for beauty?"

Professor Andrus had smiled. "It means precisely what I said, and I said precisely what I meant. What it means to you is whatever you want it to mean, though you need to remember that what you want it to mean does not necessarily make it so." He had slipped a rubber band around the three-by-five cards he used for notes and walked away. It was the only answer he ever gave.

Professor Andrus asked Thomas if he remembered the incident. Thomas remembered it too well. He blushed slightly over the reminder of his youthful arrogance.

"I would like to finally answer your question," he said, "as a friend, not your professor."

"You've always been more than a professor," Thomas said. "You've always made me feel like your friend."

Andrus was pleased. "I'm glad." He paused, then began.

"Most of my colleagues who breathe the rarified air of academia believe they have not only the right but the obligation to disgorge their personal opinions. Rather than 'teach' students a range of possibilities, they feel the need to 'convert' them to their own way of thinking. Their conclusions. Their view of the society, the world and indeed the universe and God." He paused and raised his eyebrows at Thomas, then added, "Or the absence of anything beyond themselves, as so many of them suppose."

Hawker and Hamilton were at war in Thomas's head. The professor continued.

"I've made an effort to teach art and keep politics, religion and personal opinions to myself. In fairness, if I were teaching philosophy or political science at Berkeley that would be more difficult, but . . ." his gaze drifted through the large windows in the west wall, where he seemed to see things Thomas couldn't. A blaze of orange sun caught the rim of his face and ignited his generous mustache. For a moment he was a viking warrior in a kingdom far away. Thomas was mesmerized by the power of the image and intimacy of the conversation.

"So. To answer your first question. I believe talent, whatever form it takes, is a gift from God. In that regard we may all have the right to life, liberty and the pursuit of happiness, but we are definitely NOT created equal. You had your talent when you arrived. You brought the gift with you. End of story.

"You may wonder why I encouraged some of your classmates to find their way in commercial illustration and chastised you for wasting your talent in that same pursuit." A familiar frown punctuated the point. "Easy answer. Whatever God gives us comes with an obligation to use it well and wisely. Where much is given, much is required."

Andrus ran the fingers and thumb of his left hand over his mustache in a habit that most often heralded a conclusive point. "I believe the mural at St. Mark's has the potential to be your masterwork. I don't mean to say your life won't include other excellent works." He cleared his throat for emphasis and added offhandedly, "Even if you persist in pursuing the commercial fringe."

Thomas grinned and pulled out his credit card, saying, "The commercial fringe allows me to buy you dinner." *Such a lie,* he thought and financial worries shrieked through his head.

"Thank you," Andrus said.

"So the answer to the second question is the same as the first," Thomas said. "If you believe talent comes from God," the word sounded awkward and inarticulate in his mouth, "then obviously there is something more to beauty than nature."

"*Beauty* is a word we use, or more often abuse, in our discussion of art and aesthetics. I've a whole lecture on the topic I would love to use in a forum one day. We use the word *beautiful* to describe roses, rainbows and rockets. We say *beautiful* when we really mean *alluring, awe-inspiring, magnificent, exquisite, drop-dead gorgeous* or a hundred other words. Even *sexy.* It's become a kind of go-to cliché for anything *awesome.*" He laughed at his emphasis on current slang. "For anything that we lack the vocabulary to describe or that transcends our day-to-day experience.

"The list is endless, of course, anything from a three-pointer that wins a championship game to a six-second ride on a bucking bull. When I talk about the beauty of divine creation it obviously embraces all of it—even bull riding, if you happen to have seen the slow motion in that wonderful documentary film *The Great American Cowboy*—but I intended much more."

Whatever movie Andrus was talking about was obviously before Thomas's time.

"Do you remember the second law of thermodynamics?" Andrus asked. "What entropy is?" As he spoke he unscrewed the lids from the salt and pepper shakers and poured a small mound of each on a napkin. There was a sense of order and design in the size and placement.

"I'm all right brain, remember?" Thomas smiled and tapped his head. *Second law of thermodynamics? Lucky it's not a final in physics.*

"I've a few cells left on the left," Andrus said. "Of course, that explains why you're a better artist than I am," he smiled and continued. "I don't pretend to understand it like Stephen Hawking, but, oversimplified, the law predicts that in a closed system, like our universe, matter will become increasingly disorganized over time."

He lifted the corners of the napkin and shook it softly. He opened it again to reveal a unified mixture of salt and pepper. "From order to chaos. That's what the law states. The process is irreversible. No matter how many times I shake the napkin it will never return to this. He poured another pair of salt and pepper mounds on a second napkin and placed it next to the first. "Life is highly ordered and incomprehensibly complex." He touched the neatly ordered piles. "Science defines the law and the law says matter will decline into an increasing condition of disorder.

"The beauty of the earth—the beauty of creation—is exactly the opposite. It does not become increasingly disorganized over time. It becomes more organized. More beautiful. That is what I mean when I speak of the beauty of divine creation.

"It goes beyond the beauty of a raindrop on a blood-red rose refracting a ray of sunlight, incredibly beautiful as that is. Divine beauty is the beauty of order, the beauty of design, the incomprehensible beauty of a million crimson roses in the first light of dawn. It is the beauty each holds in a genetic code of instructions to develop a single seed or a slip into the complexity of roots, stems, thorns, leaves, colors and blooms akin to one another and yet unique unto itself.

"The beauty of the earth did not result from a gradual and irreversible decline into a state of randomness and disorder. Beauty is more than some ubiquitous word describing creation. Divine beauty shatters the idea of entropy and is itself the evidence of creation. The evidence of a Supreme Creator."

The old professor seemed suddenly weary. He closed his eyes as if it helped him see more clearly and stroked his mustache again. Slowly. Thoughtfully. From memory he quoted ancient words.

> Question the beauty of the earth, the beauty of the sea, the beauty of the wide air around you, the beauty of the sky. Question the order of the stars, the sun whose brightness lights the day, the moon whose splendor softens the gloom of night. Question the living creatures that move in the waters, that roam upon the earth, that fly through the air; the spirit that lies hidden, the matter that is made manifest; the visible things that are ruled, the invisible things that rule them. Question all these. They will answer you: "Behold and see, we are beautiful." Their beauty is their confession to God. Who made these beautiful changing things, if not one who is beautiful and changeth not?

Andrus let his testimony of God, expressed in the words of St. Augustine fifteen hundred years before, hang in the air until it glistened in the last long streaks of sunlight. Thomas sat spellbound.

"When you are my age," Andrus said after a time, "you'll look back and realize your professional life was defined by a few significant projects, by a dozen pieces of art that mattered—perhaps, in the end, only one. The opportunity you have at St. Mark's to adorn the walls of a sanctuary dedicated to healing with the miracles of Jesus will never come again. Make it the most important painting of your life. Most of all, do it for the right reason."

Thomas responded with an affirmative nod and wrestled with his conscience.

"Where much is given, much is required," Professor Andrus repeated, "and I've one more suggestion." Thomas imagined him opening the last door in a long hallway, revealing at last where he really lived.

"Believe beyond your doubts. What was it you used to say to me all the time about your fanciful creations?"

"I can paint whatever I imagine and believe whatever I paint."

"How much more powerful might it be if belief came before imagination? I appreciate that may be difficult, given 'the comfortable ambiguity of agnosticism'?" He repeated the expression Thomas had used.

"Acknowledge that your talent is a gift from God and thank him for it. Ask for his help so you can perform at the extreme edge of your ability." His appeal had the power of a Baptist preacher, but his tone was quiet and his manner calm. Here was a man who had that elusive something called faith. A man who truly believed.

"Even if you are unable to believe," Andrus said finally, "at least open yourself to the possibility of the divine beauty your masterwork deserves."

The rim of golden light on the old man's face, the quiet resonance of his voice, the dark pools of his eyes and unguarded sharing of things most personal caused a stirring within Thomas. *A swelling warmth. The inner voice. A quiet grove.*

What was happening?

64

THERE WERE TWO MISSED CALLS AND a text message waiting. Thomas punched up his voice mail as he pulled from the parking lot and headed west on Bay.

"Hello, Thomas. It's your father. Just wondering how you're doing. I know you're busy. I hope it's all right that I called." The call came as a surprise. He felt guilty he'd not thought of Alex at all. *Tell him you love him every day.* The child's words in his thoughts. He was about to touch *CALL BACK* when he saw that the other voice mail was from Cass.

"Hi, Thomas, it's Susan Cassidy." *Why is she being so formal? Why doesn't she say* Cass? "Something has happened and it's important we talk when you get to the hospital in the morning, okay? Before you talk to anybody else. Gotta run."

The stomachache arrived the same instant the call ended. *Cass changed her mind? Miss Von Horn decided she hated the sketches? Berger sabotaged me?* As his demons fought for attention he was struck by the darkest thought of all. *Christina is dead!* As quickly as she died in his imagination she returned to life as he flushed the dark thought and reminded himself he was on his way to buy a case for Christina's violin. He turned onto Van Ness and headed south into the city.

Google stuck pins in half a dozen music stores. The closest was a place called Guitar House on Van Ness near California. Union Music on Market was farther away but had an icon with string instruments and a five-star customer rating. He settled into the flow of traffic and checked the text from Hawker: *You die????* Was that a warning or a question?

On a sudden impulse Thomas called Berger. He urgently longed for
the emotional oblivion possible when Berger handled problems. In the
game of art Berger was more than a left guard protecting his blind side.
He was offense and defense wrapped together and with or without helmet
and pads was the proverbial ten-thousand-pound gorilla.

Amplified in 5.1 surround the broken *BURRRUP, BURRRUP* of the
ring sounding on the speakerphone was unusually grating. It rang five
times before it went to record. A sweet, sexy female voice filled the cockpit
of the SLK.

"You've reached Apogee Artists Agency. Please leave your name, number and the purpose of the call. Have a nice day." The greeting had been
changed since his fallout with Berger. Thomas wondered who belonged
to the voice. Thomas inferred a squall of trouble as he mused about the
change and what it meant. He was about to leave a message but pride
shoved him aside and pushed *CANCEL CALL.*

In the twenty minutes it took to reach Market Street, Thomas envisioned himself face-to-face with Andrus and the feelings returned. *O
God, if there is a God and you know what I'm thinking,* Thomas thought to
himself, *this would be a really good time for you to let me know.*

There was no sign from heaven. There *was* a blast from an illegal air
horn bolted under the bumper of the Chevy truck behind him when the
light turned green. Two point two nanoseconds!

• • •

A petite Asian woman who introduced herself as Mia Ling greeted
Thomas at the door of Union Music. Thomas told her about Christina
and asked her to show him cases for the violin. Mia Ling promised she
would help him select the perfect case. *No wonder Union Music had a
five-star customer rating.*

"What size is violin?" Mia Ling asked.

"Is there more than one size?"

"Oh my goodness," she giggled. "Violin in seven different sizes." She
was so endearing it was not embarrassing for Thomas to admit he was
completely 'out of his tree.' He hadn't used the expression since college,

and by the look on Mia Ling's face the metaphor did not translate very well.

"How long her arm?" she asked.

Thomas measured with his hands like he was bragging about a fish. "About so, I'd guess." She giggled again.

"How old Christina?"

"I think she's ten."

"How well she play?"

Thomas didn't know. "I'm not sure. Pretty good, I think." After a few minutes they agreed that Christina's violin was most likely a three-quarter-size instrument for children ages nine through eleven with an arm length of twenty to twenty-two inches.

Once Mia Ling began showing him cases, he decided size only mattered if he stayed with a shaped student case similar to the original. There were scores of other choices. Professional cases were rectangular or oblong semielliptical. Most of them cost more than Thomas would have expected to pay for a whole violin.

Thomas had just opened a beautiful case when Mia Ling returned with samples of student cases under one hundred dollars. "You rather have very nice case?" she asked, with unusual emphasis on *very*.

"Maybe," Thomas said. "How much is something like this?"

"Ohhh! That Enigma Aureum made by Musafia Cremona. Come from Italy," she said as if both her level of respect and her interest in the sale had gone up. "Very fine case." Mia Ling found the tag tucked under one end. She discreetly turned it over. On the back: *Custom Made in Italy $2,250.00.* Thomas blanched.

"You out of tree?" Mia Ling grinned.

Optimism always had the same result for Thomas. He bought better than needed and spent more than allowed. Most of the thermoplastic cases like the one crushed in the crash were under a hundred bucks. *Not good enough.* He imagined Christina's delight when her violin arrived in a professional case worthy of the concert stage.

He selected a Heritage Challenger Double case with an elegant plush pink interior. There was space for two bows. Mia Ling suggested he wait until Christina was well enough to come in and pick her own. "Bow very personal part of music," Mia Ling explained.

"Art is all about presentation," he quipped, adding an $89 Glaesel Brazilwood bow and handing Mia Ling his American Express card. He removed the tag and fitted the bow into the case. He closed the lid and considered the best place to paint her name and flowers.

"So sorry, Mr. Hall, but credit card no good." The warmth of her welcome remained but a chill wind blew in. The excuses Thomas mumbled in the rush of humiliation resulted in an agreement to hold the case for a couple of days.

"Until I straighten out their mistake," Thomas said, putting the emphasis on *their* and realizing that with Berger out of his life his bills were going unpaid.

"I hope child not so sad," Mia Ling said as Thomas nodded good-bye and crossed to the door knowing every person in the place was watching. Unanimous conclusion: *LOSER!*

CHAPTER

65

YOU'VE REACHED APOGEE ARTISTS Agency. Please leave your name, number and the purpose of the call. Have a nice day."

Panic pushed pride aside and this time Thomas left a message. "Frank, it's Thomas." He thought he'd known exactly what he was going to say when he called. He was wrong. He breathed out. "I'd like a chance to talk to you about a couple of things." *Don't crawl. No humble pie.* The thoughts rasped on his ego at the back of his brain. "Would you give me a call when you get a second?"

He was about to hang up when he was struck by an impression. *Apologize,* a quiet voice whispered. *Saying "I'm sorry" isn't crawling, it's flying.*

"Hey, and Frank . . ." the words formed slowly. "I'm . . . uh . . . I'm sorry, man. I got a little . . . just want to make it right. I'd appreciate a call if you get a minute."

Thomas always drove fast and laughed about "flying low," but it wasn't the speed of the car that let him fly all the way back to Sausalito. It was a lightness of heart and sense of calm.

• • •

As Thomas pulled the Mercedes onto the approach ramp to the Golden Gate Bridge he called Oakridge Manor and asked them to put Alexander Hall on the phone.

"Hello?"

"Alex? It's Thomas."

"Thomas?"

"Tommy."

"Are you all right? Has something happened?"

"Everything's fine. Look, I want to get over there and see you if that's okay."

"You're coming here? Okay. Yes. Okay! That's wonderful. Wonderful. When?"

"Not real sure. Maybe Saturday?"

"I can hardly wait."

"Yeah, me too. A belated birthday, okay?"

Alex's laugh was hardly audible. "Wonderful, Tommy."

"See you then . . . Dad."

CHAPTER

66

A FISHING BOAT MOTORED through the estuary as Thomas turned onto Harbor Road and headed for his studio. Her running lights glittered on the swells of black water like an explosion of tiny fireworks.

Thomas parked the SLK and walked to the edge of his wharf to watch the cluttered craft glide by. A grizzled man in a yellow slicker looked at Thomas through the open door of the pilot house. *Captain Ahab,* Thomas thought. He threw him a casual salute as if they were old friends and the captain waved back. It was the way of the sea. Being at the harbor made him one of them.

Thomas relished the thought and thought about his boat. He had intended to take her out on Saturday. *Saturday!* The feeling that had invaded his life in the car coming home—whatever it was—had faded. He wished he had not told Alex he was coming. *Not hard to get out of. He'll understand.*

A crash on the far side of the house riveted his attention. It sounded like heavy lumber falling. *Maybe a gunshot?* There was a dark car in the shadows on the abandoned road that had once provided access to the Fish Cannery from the back. He strained his eyes against the darkness but couldn't make it out. He moved slowly toward the phantom vehicle. His angst escalated.

A light flashed across the front window from the inside out. A piece of construction plastic was as great an invitation for breaking and entering as a revolving door with *ENTER HERE* taped to the glass. His heart rate pounded past 110 and he struggled to keep his wits. *A burglar? Unlikely.*

The wrecking crew returned? SAVE THE SEALS? Or—he shuddered at the thought—*the arsonist is back to finish his botched job.* His imagination went into turbo drive.

He sprinted in a crouched position to where he had left the Mercedes without taking his eyes off the intruder's light. He grabbed his iPhone and dialed 911. The windows went dark for a moment before the light appeared again. This time at the hole in the wall.

"911 Emergency. May I have your name, please?"

"Thomas."

"What is the emergency?"

"Someone broke into my house."

"Are they in the house now?"

"No, they just went outside."

"What is your address?" Thomas gave the dispatcher his address and continued the conversation as he crouch-sprinted to the corner nearest the water and circled the building on the other side.

"You sound like you're moving. Are you in the house?"

"I'm outside."

"Stay where you are! Do not approach the intruder."

"I'm just moving to where I can see who it is."

"Sir. I advise you to stay where you are."

"Just get the police out here, okay?"

"Do not approach the intruder."

"They broke a hole in my wall, they set my place on fire and they threatened my life. Just get someone out here now!"

"Stay on the phone, sir! Sir?"

"Shhhh. Okay. But just listen."

"Do not approach the intruder."

"Hurry!" Thomas whispered, climbing over the railing and making his way along the wooden walkway that clung to the building on the bay side. His foot broke through. The ragged edge scraped his shin and a curlicue of skin peeled off and rolled up his leg in spite of the denim.

The water side of the Fish Cannery had not been renovated when Thomas had made improvements. Not even minor repairs. Remembering that, he moved more cautiously.

The glow of the iPhone was sufficient to help him pick his way to where a catwalk ran across the back. It was rusted and rickety. The bandage on his hand snagged on the edge of the broken railing. The spike of rusted metal jabbed the wound and sent a bolt of pain up his arm.

Thomas slipped off his shoes to silence his movement on the rattling catwalk. In a strange way he was outside himself. He was a drawing, a superhero in a fantasy adventure. The illusion diminished the level of potential danger. He assumed the intruder was someone like Chastity or Ada Kanster or some other hippie activist from SAVE THE SEALS. They did not pose a serious physical threat.

"Police are on their way," his iPhone reported.

"Thanks," he whispered and hit *END CALL* before Ms. 911 finished her script: "Stay on the phone."

From the end of the catwalk he dropped easily to the ground. The intruder's flashlight swung a wide arc that reached beyond the corner of the old factory. He held his breath and wondered if the trespasser had heard the phone.

The circle of light found a brown pelican on a piling put there fifty years before. The bird looked clumsy but Thomas had drawn them in flight and knew they were graceful elegance.

A bird-watching burglar, Thomas thought as he moved the last few feet to the corner of the building. He crouched as low as he could and was about to peer around the corner when—CLANK!—the sound stopped him. He dropped to his belly, held his breath and slithered forward. A dozen two-by-tens against the return wall blocked his view but also provided cover. He pushed slightly forward.

The beam of the housebreaker's torch flickered as it moved past the dark shapes of the wood. Thomas stretched forward a few inches and raised his head slowly. The light stopped moving and so did Thomas's lungs. He had a good view of the intruder from the waist down. It was not a wimpy hippie woman avenging wounded seals. It was a man. Sturdy. The light came from a heavy-duty lantern in his right hand.

Thomas craned his neck forward for an angle on the man's face. He bumped a board. It shifted with a dull thump. The light jerked around and pointed directly at Thomas. He ducked. A sliver of blinding light from the krypton bulb sliced between the planks and hit him square in the eye, or that was how it seemed. After a few seconds the light went back to work.

The man turned and Thomas could see his other hand and what had caused the clank. A red five-gallon gas can. The man poured the pungent liquid on the ground. The arsonist was back!

The intruder set the gas can inside the plastic barrier. *Hiding the evidence,* Thomas thought. The man took several minutes to examine the recent repairs with the flashlight. *Wants to make sure he doesn't make the same mistake twice,* Thomas reasoned.

The man kept his back toward Thomas. The wooden obstructions and harsh contrast between the krypton bulb and black shadows made it impossible to see his face. Then he walked away.

He's leaving. Where are the police? We're out of time. He strikes a match and the whole end of the building blows away. Thomas's worries were no longer fantasies.

He gripped a four-foot length of charred two-by-four. He was not going to be burned out again. His blood was 90-proof adrenaline.

It seemed like an hour since he'd called 911, though it had really been less than eight minutes. Jack Bauer could move five SUVs full of FBI agents across Manhattan in a less than a minute. Thomas wondered how long it really took police to respond to a 911 break-in call. The sound of a siren reached him. There was a glimmer of flashing red and blue at the far end of the harbor.

The arsonist glanced toward the sound but showed remarkable calm. He was more of a professional than Thomas had imagined. The man scanned his target a final time and reached into his pocket for a match.

Thomas cocked the burned bat over his shoulder and sprang from the woodpile like a jack-in-the-box on steroids. The arsonist whirled so fast he stumbled backward and dropped the light. Thomas swung the club. It cracked across the man's shoulder; he stumbled and whirled toward Thomas with an arm up to shield his face. Thomas swung again and caught the perpetrator on the side of his head. The man staggered backward, fell and curled into a protective ball.

Two police cars with every light flashing vaulted over the speed bump and skidded to a stop.

Thomas picked up the light and shone it on the pathetic, groveling bad guy on the ground. The man's arms and hands formed a protective hood around his head. Blood flowed from the gash above his temple. He slowly uncovered his face. Thomas gasped.

"Frank?"

"Thomas?"

"What the hell are you doing?"

"Keep those hands where I can see them!" Both officers advanced, guns drawn.

CHAPTER

67

THE COPS WERE CONFUSED. It was not immediately apparent who was the good guy and who was the bad guy and which one should be arrested, cuffed and hauled away. They covered both with Glocks, each officer in a two-handed stance, and listened to the guy on the ground with the bleeding head who was angry, and the guy kneeling over him with a club who was embarrassed, sputter mostly incoherent explanations about who they were, what they were doing and how they happened to be in what they admitted must seem like a compromising situation.

They blathered about friendship and fighting, artists and agents, arson and saving the seals. It was all connected somehow with a thread of misunderstanding and mistaken identity. Their stories tumbled one on top of the other and neither seemed able to keep from interrupting the other.

In spite of the way they were yelling abuses at each other, the senior officer concluded they were "friends" and telling the truth, convoluted as it sounded. He put his gun away. The younger officer, a woman who looked like she'd just gotten out of high school, did likewise.

They all went inside. The female officer patched Frank's head and closed the laceration with a pair of butterfly bandages. She suggested he have a doctor pull it tight with stitches in the morning. "Unless you think scars are macho," she smiled and wiped the last of the crusted blood from his cheek. For twenty-five seconds Frank was in love. "If you don't fall in love every day," he'd told Thomas once, "it's been a bad day."

By the time the officers left there was no good reason to rehash the circumstances. Each had repeated his version of the story three different ways and each understood what had happened. In spite of their falling out and his being fired *again,* Frank had followed through with getting the hole in the studio repaired. When Thomas had stopped the work because of no money, Frank had paid the contractor and told him to work on it when Thomas wasn't around.

Frank had gotten the voice mail message from Thomas and decided to drive to his place rather than return the call. Thomas wasn't there when he arrived so he took a look at the repairs. He discovered water in the can of chain-saw mix nearby and dumped it out.

Saying "I'm sorry" to Frank face-to-face was easy, considering Thomas had just cracked him in the head with a charred two-by-four. He wrapped his overreaction, stupidity and embarrassment into one tidy package, laid it on the table with honest humility and asked Frank to forgive him. More than forgive him. He asked Frank to resume the management of his career and life. Frank grinned.

"I never stopped." Berger delivered the line with a swagger that made it sound like dialogue from a James Bond movie. Thomas was surprised to learn that Frank was in active negotiation with the lawyer from St. Mark's and "close to a very good deal," as he described it.

Frank listened with apparent acute interest, in spite of what must have been an acute headache, as Thomas recited his conversations with Hawker and explain the expanded scope of the museum mural. If Hawker expected Thomas to redesign the mural and essentially start over, Frank said, he thought it odd he had not heard from Lia Chu or Vince Sadereck.

"That's not the biggest problem." Thomas described the meeting with Hawker and Hawker's request that he persuade Hamilton to drop the conditions of the settlement. "*Request* is the wrong word," Thomas added. "It was an ultimatum."

Neither of them brought up the skirmish that had ruptured their friendship. In a curious way, whacking Frank in the head with a board, then pleading for forgiveness with genuine humility, was a welcomed catharsis. For Thomas, at least. Once they had embraced and expressed renewed affections, they focused on immediate problems. As he passed his worries to Berger and Berger took them on, a feeling of unburdening relief rippled through Thomas.

"You don't see any way to persuade Hamilton to take the money and let Hawker have his way?" Berger said.

"I don't think so." Thomas remembered the fervor when Hamilton talked about the importance of his legacy.

"Either way, you've got a project," Berger concluded. "Hamilton backs down, you do what Hawker wants. Hamilton gets his way, you finish what you started."

"That's the other thing," Thomas said. "Hawker had it painted out."

"Then it costs them even more," Frank said. "I'll negotiate a deal with Hawker for you to work on the designs while they get things sorted out. Maybe even do some finish art in your studio."

The excitement Thomas usually experienced was absent. He had not told Berger about the conversation in the redwood grove, but it came to mind and for a moment the feelings returned. While Berger schemed to salvage the mural of human descent, Thomas's mind was on moral law and Jesus performing miracles.

"Do you believe in God?" Thomas asked.

"What?"

"You don't have to answer, I just . . ."

"Hey! God made the Jews his chosen people, so heck yes. He's the man!" Frank said, his tone deflecting the seriousness of Thomas's question.

"We joke about you being Jewish and me being agnostic but we've never had a serious conversation about it."

"Hamilton get to you?"

"Maybe. That and the mural at St. Mark's. Lot of things getting to me, I guess."

"You know I'm not particularly religious, right?" Berger asked.

"I don't know. Maybe. Yeah, I guess I knew that." Thomas shrugged.

He didn't know Berger's feelings about such things but he saw an expression on Berger's face he hadn't seen before.

"When I was in law school," Berger said, "I roomed for two semesters with a guy named Bobby Overman. The guy was a flat-out, breakaway genius. Unbelievable. His undergraduate degree was mathematics and he went on to medical school after he nailed his Juris Doctorate. He was fascinated by the questions nobody could answer. Relished the unfathomable, you know. All the stuff science couldn't explain. So God was at the top of his list. He used to keep me up all night talking about it." Berger paused to let old memories work their way forward.

"Whatever smidgen of belief in Yahweh—you know, the God of the Jewish people—whatever belief I inherited from our traditions or had whupped into me by my dear mother getting me ready for Bar Mitzvah, I'd have to say it was staying up all night with Overman that made a believer out of me.

"Most of us grow up reading about Yahweh in the Torah or Jehovah in the Bible or, for you guys, learning about Jesus in Sunday school. Overman came at the question of God from a completely nonreligious point of view. He was convinced that life erupting into being as an accident was statistically impossible. He loved to bend his brain around statistical probabilities. That begged the old question, if not an accident, then WHAT? For him the even more exciting question was WHO? Overman concluded that God was in all probability what could only be described as a 'person.'

"That was back when the whole mother earth thing was in and being atheist was cool. Maybe he enjoyed the attention he got by being so outspoken about his belief in a Supreme Creator.

"One of our professors went after him in class one day. Very pointed. Comments like 'Only fools believe in God' and 'Intellectuals have no need of God.' I'll never forget what Overman did—and remember, this is in a freshman law class. He was sitting next to me. He stood up and said, 'May I ask you a question, sir?' The professor licked his chops, he was so eager to devour the whippersnapper.

"'Go ahead,' he said.

"So my friend says, 'Suppose a computer has two thousand separate components and the components are given to two thousand different people and the people live in two thousand separate places on the planet and none of them know about the others or the use and purpose of their components, but we have confidence they will all get together by sheer happenstance and assemble our computer. What—in the opinion of an intellectual—is the statistical probability that without direction or instruction, all two thousand of them will meet in exactly the same place, at exactly the same time, with exactly all of the critical conditions required for assembly and intuitively work together in perfect harmony to build us our working computer?'" Berger had obviously told the story before but never to Thomas.

"The professor was no dummy," he continued, "and thought he knew where Overman was headed. 'Since you've merely concocted another version of the infinite monkey theorem and the answer is the same,' he postured, 'I will state it properly for the benefit of your freshman colleagues who watch football on the weekends instead of reading Cicero's *De Natura Deorum:* "Will a monkey hitting keys at random on a typewriter keyboard for an infinite amount of time ultimately type the complete works of William Shakespeare?" Given in mathematical terms, the answer is "almost surely."'"

Berger continued the story with such vivid recollection Thomas realized it had been a turning point in his life. He also had a new appreciation of Berger as storyteller.

"The class is laughing," Berger continued. "Overman just stands there until they're finished, then he says, 'The infinite monkey theorem is only a metaphor of an abstraction, a theoretical model. If you're distracted by my use of metaphor, let me ask it a different way.

"'Two thousand enzymes are required to form a single bacterium. Each of them must perform a specific task. The probability of all of them being in one place at one time was calculated by Sir Fred Hoyle as being 1 in 10 to the 40,000th power. "Almost surely" may be a mathematical expression, but every mathematician on earth will agree that Sir Hoyle's number is so vast that probability transcends "almost surely" and becomes impossible.'

"Then the cheeky freshman blew us all away," Berger laughed. "'To put the number in some perspective,' Overman said, 'remember that the total number of atoms in the known universe is estimated to be only 10 to the 80,000th power. You may shudder at the thought there is an intelligence in the universe greater than your own, sir, but you can be positive life is not an accident that organized itself, and thus the fool is the one who tries to argue that it was and did.'"

Berger walked to a mirror and examined the bandage on his head. He was weary in a way Thomas had never seen him. "That's a long answer to a simple question. Maybe it's the bump on the head. That would make it your fault."

"I am so sorry about that. Truly."

"Sorry enough to let me hit you in the head with a hot poker?"

Thomas laughed. "I deserve it."

"The longer I live," said Berger, "the less I know, and the less I know, the more I realize that even the brightest people are still a pallor of pea brains when it comes to understanding God."

68

Y ELLOW BACKLIGHT FROM THE morning sun ignited her hair, creating the illusion that she was floating from the dark blue shadows of
the building in slow motion. "Good morning," she said. It was musical.
Thomas had sent her a text when he exited the bridge so she would know
when to expect him. She had come out to meet him before he reached
the front door of the hospital. His delight in seeing her was more than an
artistic appreciation of the vision she created floating toward him.

"Good morning," he said.

• • •

It was a good morning. Frank had left at midnight. On the way out
the door, he had assured Thomas that the contract with St. Mark's should
be wrapped up by the end of the week and the money . . .

"Looks good?" Thomas asked about cash flow.

Frank said, "Working on it."

Thomas followed him to his car and apologized again. "One last time,
bro, I'm sorry about your head." It came easy and felt good to say it again.
"Sorry for being such a jerk before." Frank pulled him in for a hug.

They had man-hugged before. Special occasions. Celebrating a new
contract. When the Forty-Niners beat the Dallas Cowboys. This hug was
different. Genuine. Heartfelt. He wasn't sure. *Did talking about God take
our friendship to a different place?* Thomas wondered.

Berger let him go, slapped him softly on the cheek and got into his car. The window came down almost immediately. "By the way. On the St. Mark's deal, I agreed to a holdback, a sort of 'performance guarantee.' You'd think Christmas Eve was the Second Coming or something, they're so determined to have it finished for the grand opening that night. I told them not to worry. You can make it okay, can't you?"

"Probably not."

"Hmm. Too bad. If you don't finish on time, they keep half the money. That happens, the boat is . . . " he made a strange croaking sound and drew a finger blade across his throat. The tires kicked up gravel as the car drove away.

• • •

Cass shook Thomas's hand. There was nothing in her demeanor that suggested she was the bearer of bad news. "Everything okay?" Thomas asked hopefully. He had replayed the voice mail on the drive into the city and arrived unsettled.

"You want to grab some orange juice or something?"

"I'm good. What's up?"

"I wanted to talk to you about Christina," Cass began. The tension he had felt a few minutes before drained away. Cass reported that the infection in the girl's left arm had flared up again. The skin graft had gone badly.

"Dr. Namkung said that severed peripheral nerves can take months or even years to grow back IF they grow back at all. The nerves should be innervating the muscles, but most of the muscles on her hand were seriously damaged."

"She going to be okay?"

"Dr. Namkung thinks they can save her hand, but the overlying skin is so badly burned the doctors pretty much agree she'll never have proper sensation in her fingers, which means . . ." Cass caught her breath and touched her lips. They were quivering. "She'll have no way of knowing where her fingers are on the strings."

"So she'll never be able to play the violin again?"

Cass shook her head. The bad news seemed unexpectedly personal.

"Does she know?"

"They told her last night."

"Are they sure about her hand?" Thomas asked. "Why couldn't they wait to tell her? Man, I mean, as if the poor kid didn't have enough trouble in her life."

"That's what I thought, but Dr. Namkung was adamant. He believes it is less traumatic for a patient to get the hard facts and bad news in one big bundle rather than parceled out over time. Particularly for a child."

"Seems brutal."

"That's what I said when I heard the prognosis and found out they were going to break her heart."

"Were you there? How did she take it?"

"I was with her but I couldn't tell what was going on inside. She listened to the whole thing with almost no expression at all."

"The whole thing?"

"Namkung was very methodical. He ticked down a whole list of 'irreversible damage.' He's good at what he does but has zero bedside manner. He explained precisely how each one of her injuries would change her life. What she could do and couldn't do. He explained the fusion of the fingers on her left hand like he was talking to a medical student on rotation and why she would never be able to play the violin again." Her lip trembled.

"You think giving her the violin is a bad idea?"

"I don't know, but that's why I wanted to make sure we had a chance to talk about it."

"What does Namkung think?"

"I don't even want to ask him, to be honest." She grimaced. "He'll probably tell you to smash it in front of her so she gets the message she will never play again!"

"What do *you* think we should do about the violin?" Thomas questioned.

"Wait a little while? Let her talk about it? I don't know?" She caught his eyes and held them for a moment, then gently touched his chest. "Listen to your inner voice?"

Thomas was distracted as Cass continued. "I'm not sure what's right, but I don't agree with Dr. Namkung's hard-core, 'face the facts' approach. Not for Christina. He may think he's helping, forcing her to accept the tragedy of her life. I think what she needs is hope." Her eyes were swimming with unshed tears.

Thomas patted her shoulder softly and allowed his hand to remain there. "Impossibilities are impossible only as thinking makes them so," Thomas quoted a favorite axiom. "Henry Kaiser," he said. "Got him taped on the mirror in my bathroom."

It had a visible effect on Cass.

CHAPTER

69

Thomas sat beside Christina's bed for half an hour watching her sleep. For no apparent reason her eyes fluttered open and she looked at him. A smile appeared on her pale gray lips. "Did you find my violin?"

Coloring the truth was harder than coloring an illustration. "Hmmm, sort of. Not exactly." The puzzling answer wrinkled her nose.

"Will you keep looking?"

"I will."

"Promise?"

"Promise."

"Cross your heart and hope to die?"

"Cross my heart and hope to die." Thomas drew an X across the left side of his chest.

He had sworn the same oath with Ronny Assenberg a hundred times when they were kids. They had crossed their hearts and hoped to die over just about everything. The rest of the pledge, the part adolescent boys snickered about, came to mind. *Cross my heart and hope to die, stick a needle in my eye, stab a knife into my thigh and eat a horse manure pie.*

"When?" she asked.

"There's plenty of time."

"No, because I need to practice."

His eyes darted to her hand and back. Not quickly enough for her to miss it. Her crippled hand retreated under the sheet like the head of a frightened turtle pulling into its shell. The clump of ruined fingers in a wrap of grafted skin looked more like the head of a turtle than a hand.

"If I can't find it, maybe I can get you another one later, or—"

She cut him off. "No. It's the one my mother gave me. You need to find it. You promised."

"Cross my heart," he said again, charmed and amused by her strong-mindedness.

"My mother plays the violin," the child said. Her pride brought color to her face. Her use of the present tense sent a spike of sorrow through Thomas's heart. "She plays at Symphony Hall all the time."

Thomas was suspended between the impulse to say, "and you will play there as well," and a desire to change the subject. *Or retreat into creative oblivion, where none of this would matter.* Perhaps it was the hesitation in his voice, or his look of discomfort. Perhaps Christina had intended what came next from the moment she had opened her eyes.

"They told you I can never play the violin again, didn't they?"

Thomas tried to think of something reassuring to say. Nothing came. "Cass said something about that, but—"

"Is that why you don't want to look for my violin anymore?"

"No. I want to give it to you. Find it."

"Dr. Namkung is wrong, you know."

"Well, he's a doctor, and I'm sure he thinks that—"

"He only says my hand will never be all right because he doesn't be-lieve in Jesus." It was a child's voice with the conviction of a wizened sage. "I don't think he knows about Jesus and how he healed people with a miracle if they believed in him."

"I'm painting a picture of Jesus and his miracles upstairs."

"I know. Cass told me," she informed him with smug little smile. "That's how come I know you know the doctors made a mistake." She scrutinized Thomas a long moment, then lifted the clump of flesh and bandage as if it were a divine scepter granting him entrance into her life.

"Jesus made a man named Lazarus alive even after he was dead, so I know he can make my hand better if he wants to. Are you putting Lazarus in your picture?"

"I am."

"I'm glad. His sister was the one who asked Jesus to bless him, and Jesus said if we ask him for something and believe in him and have faith,

he will give it to us. He really will. It's right there. Cass showed me."
She waved the crippled hand toward the Bible lying open on the bedside
stand. "You can read it." The passages were marked and the pages tagged
with colored paper. *Cass knows the Bible. No wonder,* Thomas thought.

"Ask, and it shall be given you; seek, and ye shall find; knock, and it
shall be opened unto you." He finished the passage from Matthew 7 and
added, "Cass loves you a lot."

"She prays for me. You have to pray if you want Jesus to do a miracle."

"Jesus did some amazing things, that's for sure."

"Will you pray for me?"

He hesitated a moment before he said, "Yeah, sure."

"You don't need to kneel down or anything. You can just say it sitting
right there." Christina closed her eyes and folded her one good arm across
her body.

"You mean right now?" She opened her eyes. Puzzled. "Uh . . . God
and I have not spent . . . uh . . . 'quality time' together for a while. I mean
for a long time, so would it be okay if I sort a few things out before I
pray?"

"Do you believe in Jesus?"

Thomas wanted to respond with the simple answer she needed to
hear, but the gravity of it thundered in his head to the point of pain. *If
there is no God, then what I think of Jesus doesn't matter. He cannot be the
son of something which is not.* Then suddenly a sense of calm and clarity
of thought swept over him. *There is beauty. Complexity. Inexplicable begin-
nings. A power and purpose beyond ourselves.*

Thomas crossed the chasm of dubiety, the gulf between those who believed in creation and those who didn't. The bottomless pit between atheism and the profound faith of a child. It was confusing. Jesus remained an
enigma, but in that moment he knew he had crossed a line in his life. *The
God-line.* He did not know what else to call it.

"I will pray for you," he said finally. She narrowed her eyes. "Know
what a rain check is?" he asked.

"Yup." She smiled and they had a bargain.

CHAPTER

70

THOMAS THREW HIMSELF INTO the St. Mark's mural with creative abandon. With Berger back, he was immunized from the interruptions of reality that so easily distracted him.

The Healing Place had swiftly transformed into an art studio. The table was cluttered with brushes, paints and palettes. Sketches were strewn about or hung on the wall. The easel and mirror were brought from the loft along with three mannequins, yards of drapery and a rack of costumes. The pungent scent of linseed oil and distilled turpentine scented the air. A sting of Damar varnish reminded Thomas of a summer of art in Florence.

The stories of Jesus and the miracles were cut from Reverend Mike's Bible and mounted with sketches like storyboards on the set of a Hollywood movie. The Bible with the illustrations of Gustave Doré was opened on an antique wooden stand that would eventually be used in the children's library.

Berger finished the contract with St. Mark's. It was less money than Thomas had expected but rescued him from the humiliation of no cash. He swallowed his pride and trusted Frank.

By his fourth full day working on the canvas, he felt a sense of attachment to the project he hadn't anticipated. Perhaps it was an increasing fondness for his imposing, irrepressible and always turned out and stunning boss, Susan 'Cass' Cassidy. Of course it was.

Cass came every day, sometimes more than once. She discovered that Thomas often worked all day with nothing to eat but Red Bull and peanut butter Power Bars. "Perfect for the purpose," Thomas explained. "They sustain life and provide energy without interrupting momentum."

By the second week Cass was bringing him lunch if she happened to get there by early afternoon. Sometimes she stayed to munch a sandwich, eat a salad or share a pizza. These interludes could hardly be called "lunch breaks" since they often lasted twelve minutes or less. There were days Cass stood at the canvas and fed him bite-sized bits of hospital cafeteria cuisine.

On a day they spent half an hour sharing a pepperoni pizza, Thomas tried to explain "the zone." Cass observed that he was not always "present" when he was working. When he was wandering through imaginary time and space he mumbled under his breath a lot, and it didn't make much sense. He described the strange sensation of time warp but recognized that it was more amusing than enlightening to her. That was the day he kissed his finger, touched her forehead and went back to work.

Cass had put the Healing Place off-limits. Her memo to the staff blamed "the eccentric peculiarities of the artist." Thomas had not expected Cass to be so interested. In most projects the client showing up all the time—and always unexpectedly—would become a problem. In this case it was a delicious paradox. On the one hand, Thomas preferred isolation and relished solitude. On the other, he liked seeing Cass.

Jesus was a persistent point of contention. He was still missing. When Thomas finished the rough blocking, Jesus remained nothing but a few swirling lines. "I would think," Cass said, "if for no other reason than first things first, you should start with Jesus and work your way to the least of the miracles rather than the other way around."

"Which is 'the least of the miracles'?" Thomas asked without hiding his annoyance. Cass flushed and was about to rephrase her awkward question, but Thomas continued. "Regaining use of a withered hand may seem less important than a child brought back to life, except to the man who was crippled."

Cass marked an invisible scorecard with her finger. "One for the artist," she smiled.

"I understand Jesus is the most important figure in the total piece. In the total hospital," Thomas said. "Certainly for Miss Von Horn. I want him to be perfect."

"He was," Cass smiled.

"I want him to be as he must have seemed to them. I'm still looking." He tapped his temple.

"Are you listening?" She touched his temple then moved her hand to her heart. He followed it with his eyes. *How beautiful her hand looks over her heart. How beautiful the heart beneath her hand.*

· · ·

Professor Andrus visited Thomas with a list of students to consider as apprentices. A mural of this size would require extra hands. Andrus also brought the collection of Carl Bloch prints from the wall of the Old Masters classroom. "On loan," Andrus said, "in case you're looking for inspiration. Some ideas about Jesus." Clearly Cass and Andrus were still in touch. More than in touch—in cahoots.

Thomas interrogated Cass about the coincidental arrival of the professor with what many considered the finest collection of paintings on the life and times of Jesus Christ ever created. She covered her eyes and ears and sealed her lips, miming the famous monkey trio as if they were part of a St. Mark's conspiracy known only to Andrus and her. See no evil. Hear no evil. Speak no evil. They laughed about that.

Thomas admitted that while he was intent on seeing Jesus through the eyes of the figures being created, the presence of Carl Bloch was an inspiration. "Maybe he'll whisper to me," he teased.

"How's your Danish?" she laughed.

Two Saturdays had come and gone and his promise to visit Alex had been set aside with easy excuses. A sense of guilt finally found him.

He was still working when Cass came by for a moment to say good-bye for the weekend. Thomas invited her to go with him to visit his father. She took a breath and let it out slowly. "I never thought of you as having parents."

CHAPTER

71

EVERYTHING OKAY IN HERE, Mr. Hall?" Aki Loki was a St. Mark's security guard on the all-night shift. He stood just inside the main entrance. Thomas gave him a thumbs-up from the rolling stairs at the far end of the canvas without looking up.

He was somewhere in Decapolis two thousand years before with a deaf man healed by Jesus. The man wept as he spoke without impediment to his family and friends. He rejoiced as he heard their laughter for the first time. The almost finished figure looked toward the center of the mural where Thomas had refined the swirl of lines into a rough sketch of a man wearing a robe, but Jesus was still missing.

The exchange with Loki was a predictable ritual on the nights Thomas worked late. He assumed security was exempt from Susan Cassidy's "off-limits" memo. Thomas suspected that Loki and his night-watch buddies invaded his domain and commented on his work during the nights he wasn't there. He never brought it up. Loki was a six-two Samoan who weighed 327 pounds without his lavalava. He carried a nightstick, TASER and 9mm Glock. Loki could look at the mural anytime he wanted. Thomas knew without looking at the antique clock that it was 10:10 P.M.

"You got a visitor," Loki called across the room. Thomas left the rejoicing man of Decapolis and looked up as Loki walked toward him. A nurse with a wheelchair followed. His view of the occupant was blocked by the breadth of the Samoan, but even before the entourage reached the pool of light Thomas could see that the person in the wheelchair was

Christina. Her casted legs poked straight out and rested on a horizontal support covered with soft cotton.

"Hello," Christina smiled.

"Cass said it was okay," the duty nurse apologized as she adjusted the IV connected to Christina's arm and checked the oxygen device in her nose.

"Past your bedtime, isn't it?" Thomas smiled.

"I sleep all day," the child said and turned her head as far as her pain allowed. "Thank you," she said to the nurse and Loki.

"I'll be back in half an hour. Is that okay?" The nurse spoke to Christina, but the question was for Thomas. He nodded.

"That's fine," he said. But it was not fine. The interruption had taken him out of the zone and violated his concentration. He preferred to keep working.

"Cass said you needed help," Christina said.

"She did, huh?" The nurse gave Thomas a look that included unmistakable instructions for him to look after the child. Thomas understood and nodded. The woman left the room and Loki followed.

It was impossible for Christina to manage the wheelchair by herself. She tried anyway, the moment the nurse and Loki walked away, to get closer to the mural.

"Want a tour?" Thomas asked as he gripped the chair and wheeled her to the far left side. She was going to get a guided tour of Thomas Hall's mural whether she liked it or not. She smiled and said nothing.

"Do you know the stories of the miracles?" Thomas asked as he spun Christina's chair to face the man born blind at the pool of Siloam.

"Some of them," Christina said. Thomas rolled her slowly along the mural. He paused at each roughed-in illustration to explain what she was looking at and describe the finished art only he could see. He felt like a tour guide in an art museum assigned to school kids on a field trip.

"They don't have faces," Christina said.

"Not yet," Thomas explained.

"Is that why Cass wants me to help you?" she asked in all seriousness.

He laughed. "These are only layout drawings to get a sense of the overall composition. Do you know that word? How it all flows together?

You see, this way I sort of get to know them and what they should be doing before I bring them to life."

"You bring them to life?"

"I'll start using models with faces, personalities, emotions." He gestured to the next vignette. "Can you see what this is?"

"Jesus feeding the multitude with five loaves of bread and a few fishes," she said, distracted by her counting. "There are supposed to be five thousand," she pointed out, evidently taking seriously her assignment to help Thomas. "You only have thirteen—and there are no kids."

Thomas was about to explain symbols, limited space, consistent scale and other elements of his design. But her statement stopped him short. "Hmmm? Good point. I'll have to figure out a way to get a few more in there," he said.

"There were quite a few children," she informed him.

They rolled past the figure of a man on his knees who a short time before had been a leper. Others of his kind, still infected, were astounded and looked after the rabbi who healed their friend with a miracle.

As they passed, Pharisees conspired in the shadows of a synagogue in a composition anchored by a man in a shaft of light. His once-withered hand was held high above his head in praise to God. Two of the Pharisees turned toward where the troublesome man of miracles had gone.

"I know who that is," Christina beamed. She pointed to the unfinished figure of a girl sitting on the edge of her bed. Her countenance was radiant. Her mother knelt to embrace the child, her face streaked with tears. "It's the girl who died and Jesus brought her back to life again."

"The daughter of Jairus," he affirmed. Christina leaned forward and Thomas pushed her close enough to touch the canvas. Thomas sensed the curious kinship between the child in the wheelchair and the girl transformed by a miracle who might easily have been her friend two thousand years before.

"Who is that?" she asked, pointing to the man faint against a pillar with humility and gratitude, his face covered to hide his tears and deep emotions.

"Her father."

Three disciples comforted others in the house, all weak from wailing.

The daughter's eyes gazed toward the center of the painting to where the man of miracles had gone.

They pushed by the gratitude of the royal official whose son was healed and rolled past the centerpiece toward the seven miracles on the other side. Christina gripped the chrome push rim with her right hand and stopped the chair. She turned herself toward the swirling lines and roughed-in figure that would eventually be Jesus. The word *JESUS,* put there for Cass's benefit, was still prominent.

"That's not what Jesus looks like."

"It's not finished."

"I can tell already, though."

"Now, that's where I need your help."

"What's he doing?"

"He's standing with his arms stretched out to those he's healed and—"

"You're drawing him like he was a rock star or something."

He laughed and was about to be glib. *Any guy who went around healing people would be bigger than a rock star.* Then he looked at his rudimentary sketch through the child's eyes instead.

Like most of the other figures, the face was without detail, but even without looking in the mirror or squinting, Thomas saw what the ten-year-old was saying. The posture of the figure was pompous, condescending and arrogant.

"He should be blessing the children," she said. "You don't have very many children in your picture."

A shiver dashed up his spine and tickled the back of his skull. Something in his chest seemed to burst. The epiphany was not whispered in a still, small voice; it arrived in a bolt of lightning.

"I love that idea!" Thomas said. Christina turned her chair and smiled. The halogen light made a halo from her tousle of blonde-white hair. The glow from the canvas made her skin translucent. His exuberant response to her inspiration gave her a sudden rush of kinship and trust.

"Did you find my violin?"

He shook his head. "Do you want to see the rest of the mural?"

"Not now. I'll wait until you change Jesus. Did you look again?"

"You know I've been so busy with this—"

She cut him off. "You believe the doctors, don't you?" Thomas pretended not to know what she meant. She studied him a long time, then looked at the place where Jesus was now destined to bless the children. She pulled the push rim. The chair turned and she faced him again. "If I tell you something, will you promise not to tell?"

"I love secrets."

"I know my hand is going to get better because my mother told me it would."

"Your mother?"

"She came to my room and told me everything was going to be all right." Thomas stopped breathing without being conscious of doing so. "I saw her when I died, but we didn't talk about the violin so that's why she came back to tell me." It was possible Thomas would never breathe again. "I don't have any money, so that's why you have to find it." The child's eyes filled with tears.

Thomas had no practical experience with children. Kids who came with agents or stage moms to model for him were not really kids. Nothing like the angelic visage sitting in the wheelchair. What happened next was intuitive. DNA? Inherent tendency? Genetic instinct? Inspiration? He wasn't sure.

Thomas crossed to where the violin lay hidden beneath a shroud of drapery and brought it to Christina. She did not seem surprised. Her smile conveyed a curious foreknowledge of the events taking place. Thomas handed her the violin and hunkered down until his eyes were level with hers.

"I'm sorry I waited," he said. "I did believe the doctor, so I wasn't sure if I should give it to you or not." She examined it with a wandering hand, then laid it across her chest and hugged it gently.

Thomas picked his way carefully. "Who told you that you died?" Evans's voice pounded in the back of his head. *She didn't survive the explosion.*

She looked at him as if he should know the answer.

"Did you ever talk to Officer Evans?" he pressed. *She was dead when I carried her from the car.*

Christina shook her head. It was clear she didn't know who Officer

Evans was. "I just knew when I saw my mom and she told me I needed to go back."

The pounding was deafening.

"I've never told anyone."

"It's okay. I'm sorry, I didn't mean to . . ."

"Will you believe me if I tell you about it?" She stared into his eyes unblinking. Innocent. Guileless.

"I'll try."

Christina closed her eyes and spoke softly. "There was a really awful noise," she began.

Using simple words, Christina described the darkness, the fear, the car falling down the cliff, the crushing pain in her leg, the blade of a knife in her side, the heat, the horrid smell, the man coming through the fire upside down, freezing water, gasping for air, the burst of pain and blackness. Her recollection of events was remarkably consistent with Evans's description of the accident. Thomas found it unnerving. The girl continued.

" . . . and then it was like I left my body and floated away, like above where I was and I could see everything. A man came into the water. He tried to undo my seatbelt but he couldn't. He had a red knife that he opened and starting cutting the seatbelt."

A shiver pimpled the nape of his neck with goose bumps. He could see the red handle of Evans's Buck Knife as clearly as if he were holding it in his hand.

"I was watching him but I was, like, above him looking down," she explained. "I could see myself hanging upside down in the seatbelt but it didn't seem like it was really me because I was not down there. It's sort of hard to explain. I tried to tell him I was okay, but he couldn't hear me."

Thomas felt paralyzed. The child told the story as if she were describing a visit to the zoo and not . . . Thomas refused the thought. It came anyway . . . *and not life after death. You don't survive the death of your brain.* Hawker's pronouncement invaded his thoughts.

"I watched him carry me to a rock," Christina continued. "He put his jacket over me. It had holes burned in it from the fire, and he was trying really hard to help me and then he shook his head and I . . ."

Thomas found it unnerving to hear the child describe the details of the rescue with detail she couldn't have known unless . . . unless she had been able by some inexplicable phenomenon to watch "from above" as a passive observer. Whatever had actually happened, there was no doubt about the reality of it in the child's mind.

"That's when I saw my mother," Christina said, thrusting an already unbelievable conversation into a stratosphere of wonder and sending another sizzling spike up Thomas's spine.

"You saw her?" Thomas asked. Christina nodded and smiled. "Where was she?" Thomas felt anxious about upsetting the child. At the same time, he felt an obligation to bring her back to reality. His question seemed to focus the child. Seemed to bring a sudden clarity. She no longer spoke from fragmented recollections. She described the supernatural reality of her experience with clarity. She was increasingly animated and joyful.

"There was a beautiful light that was really bright. Bright like the sun only there were all these wonderful colors," she enthused, "but we were not at the ocean anymore and I was so happy that she was all right and I started to cry, but it wasn't crying like cry-crying, it was like I was laughing or floating or . . ." She evidently couldn't find the words to describe what she remembered. What she seemed to be feeling again.

"I was just so happy and my mother put her arms around me and it was like we still had bodies but they were different and like really hard to explain, but she told me she loved me only it was more like I could hear what she was thinking without saying anything and we could talk with our minds and she told me that I needed to go back, but I didn't want to go back. I wanted to go with her and with the other woman who was there that looked a lot like her and they were friends or maybe sisters and I wondered who she was and then I could hear what she was thinking and she was my grandmother that I never saw before and she had come to take care of my mother and she told me everything was going to be all right but that I needed to go back and that someone was calling me back, but I didn't know why or what that meant, and then the light moved away and the other people came and . . ."

Thomas caught himself staring. Wide-eyed. Incredulous. And yet his doubts were tempered by the tingling at the nape of his neck and the swelling. The swelling inside had come again.

Christina looked away. Tears were tumbling down her cheeks. She clutched her violin. "I felt a horrible pain and it was dark again." The joy passed and tears dribbled from her eyes.

I should pray with her. He had not sorted things out with God as he had promised. He wanted to put his arms around Christina and comfort her. Offer to pray with her. Something.

"You about ready for bed, young lady?" It was the duty nurse. Her arrival spared Thomas from trying to express the thoughts bombarding his brain. He patted Christina on the shoulder as he stood to greet the nurse.

"He found your violin!" the nurse exclaimed with a look to Thomas that said, *Are you out of your mind?*

"I need to start practicing again," Christina said.

"So, did you two have a good visit?" the nurse asked as she adjusted the pillows supporting Christina's legs. Christina looked at Thomas, her expression a reminder that she trusted him. He nodded to seal their private pact.

"She was unbelievably helpful," he said truthfully. "Gave me some great ideas."

She didn't survive the explosion. Evans's words echoed in his thoughts as the child was wheeled from the Healing Place.

CHAPTER

72

Y OU TALK TO CHRISTINA LATELY?"

"Almost every day." Cass smiled at Thomas from the sculpted seat of the SLK through a pair of Kate Spade designer sunglasses. He had never seen her looking this casual. She wore jeans, a layered top and a hooded sweater tied around her shoulders. He was getting attached to this woman. He liked the feeling but it worried him.

"She talk about the accident yet?"

"Not really. Why?"

"Just curious." Thomas changed his mind about sharing his conversation with Christina.

It was Saturday. They were headed east across the bay to visit Thomas's father. The water was the color of old tin. A convocation of low clouds perched on the Oakland hills with lumpy talons. A hole in the overcast permitted a patch of sunlight to creep across the estuary as a formation of phantom fighter jets took off from the naval air station at Alameda and flew low over the Bay Bridge.

Thomas and Cass shuddered, then laughed as the shock wave of sound chasing the war birds pounded them. They exited the Bay Bridge, swung north onto the Nimitz Freeway, then east on 24 through the Caldecott Tunnel.

. . .

The majestic old buildings of Oakridge Manor were tucked in a wooded canyon on the east side of the Berkeley hills. They were among the few authentic Victorian structures from the first half of the nineteenth century still standing in the East Bay.

The cluster of buildings had originally been constructed as a sanatorium back when tuberculosis was wasting so many lives. The "creeping monster," as it was called back then, was finally caged by the discovery of streptomycin, which made treatment and cure possible. When the last of the patients left, the sanatorium was closed and fell into a cycle of revolving ownerships, grand schemes and real-estate speculation.

When Briones Regional Park was established in 1969, the twenty-six-acre property was engulfed by five thousand acres of open land and forever isolated. It was bought by a group of local entrepreneurs and transformed into the Oakridge Manor assisted living facility. The restoration accentuated the authentic architecture that gave the secluded cloister a gothic flavor.

• • •

Mrs. Benning was playing her violin when Thomas and Cass entered the dayroom of the main building. They waited by the door and watched as she bowed her way through the Sibelius Violin Concerto in D minor. Her eyes were closed. Frail fingers blurred across the strings. The joyous look on her face made her seem ageless. She was accompanied on the piano by a girl whose dress and tag identified her as a member of the Oakridge staff. She played well but struggled to keep up with the elegant virtuoso.

While escorting Thomas and Cass from the front desk to the dayroom, the perky young caregiver had told them Saturday was family day at Oakridge Manor. That explained why the room was crowded. Most of the senior residents had visitors: adult children, teenage grandkids, even a few great-grandbabies. The overstuffed sofas in bright floral slips were occupied and folding chairs had been set up for the program.

Thomas looked for his father. Cass watched Thomas. During the drive from the city he had talked a little about his father, opening just a small window into his childhood. He hadn't said much but allowed a few insights.

. . .

His father was old when Thomas was born. He saw very little of the man growing up. Thomas left home at seventeen and didn't see his father again for several years. The last time was when his father had a stroke and his half-sister, Andrea, called from Florida.

Andrea had left home when Thomas was six. The difference in their ages precluded a relationship as sister and brother. Andrea married a midshipman and ended up at the naval base in Key West. Thomas had a vague memory of seeing her once or twice after that, but when she called to tell him their father had had a stroke, she was a stranger.

The telephone conversation was their first real connection as siblings. As half-siblings. It was also their last. Neither of them was prepared to take the old man in so they agreed to find a facility and share the costs. Andrea's husband had a sister who lived in Concord and recommended Oakridge Manor.

The split invoice arrived monthly. Berger paid it along with Thomas's other bills. There was never a need to discuss it further. A year ago Alex began to call and leave messages.

. . .

Thomas loved the kind of music that made him want to fly with dragons. The music of Sibelius was complex, dark and depressing. He wondered if anyone in the room was really enjoying it or if life here was so boring that anything sounded good. *Maybe on family day they feature culture.*

From the back of the room it was difficult to pick out his father. He'd not seen him in over a year. He had just whispered to Cass that he couldn't find him when a portly caregiver blocking his view moved away.

There was an old man by the bay window that looked out on the garden. It was Alexander Hall. He sat alone. Sunlight streaming through the antique glass rimmed his hair with silver. He made small movements in cadence to the music. He seemed unable to take his eyes off the woman with the violin.

He was thinner than Thomas remembered. Older. More frail. The man in the dusty shaft of sunlight did not look like the villain he had locked away for most of his life.

Something changed. Was it the music? The piano abandoned the brooding backdrop and the violin rose like a phoenix into the brightness of a shining melody. It was hardly a flight on a dragon, but the music moved Thomas. Staring at the old stranger at the window in a room filled with music and memories that tumbled into mind, he felt none of the anger he had so carefully nurtured for most of his life. The place reserved for resentment felt empty. He wasn't sure why. For a moment he felt foolish. What was the value of resentment? What retribution was deserved by a weary old man sitting silently by the window? What made Thomas worthy to judge and punish him? The decisions of his life had been punishment enough.

Dark recollections danced do-si-dos with an unexpected flurry of good memories. *Was there any good? Did the man try his best? The past is the past. What difference does it make?* The only reality was the moment he was in. "Live in the moment," was Professor Andrus's pointed advice. So easily said. So nearly impossible.

A cloud passed over the sun. The rim of silver in Alexander's hair turned gray. He shivered. A staffer put a shawl around his shoulders. He thanked the woman with a nodding glance and pulled it up around his neck.

When the sunlight came again it brought with it a vision. The old man's hair ignited in a halo of light. The shawl shrouded him from time. He was anyman. His eyes were lifted to beautiful Mrs. Benning. His face filled with affection. *He is the leper healed by the hand of God.* The thought frightened Thomas. *The hand of God?* The vision inspired him. *Was Jesus God? Is that really what I want to ask myself?*

The idea came in a rush. Inspiration? Mere creativity? Cass would surely wonder if he could hear the voices in his head. His eyes moved methodically about the room as the idea settled and the fullness of the vision opened to him.

A man with both eyes bandaged touched the face of a child to *see* her with his fingers. *A man born blind?*

A middle-aged man sat with his arm around the shoulder of his elderly mother. She held his hand. Her face glowed with youthful beauty. *The woman who touched the hem of Jesus' robe.*

A teenage girl entered with her grandfather in a wheelchair and rolled him to where he had a perfect view. She kissed him on the cheek. *The angel came down and stirred the waters of Bethesda and he was healed.*

In the alcove off the kitchen a woman fed a man unable to feed himself. She wiped his chin and moved a tuft of hair that fell across his face. *And he said to the sick of the palsy, Son, thy sins be forgiven thee. Arise, take up thy bed.*

An adolescent child spoke to a grandmother whose hearing was gone by signing with her hands. A woman with hands writhing one upon the other as if digging for a memory of happiness was interrupted by a small child, apparently not one she knew, who brought her a cookie and a paper cup of punch. For a moment she had found what was lost.

Words bubbled up from the left brain to help Thomas describe as well as see the images he was etching in visual memory. *Gratitude. Compassion. Patience. Kindness. Devotion. Affection. Unselfishness. Goodness. Hope. Faith.*

The epiphany came painted in fire-engine red. *These are the models for the St. Mark's mural! These are the kind of people Jesus touched.*

He got excited about the beggar in the park. The man on the bridge. The girl named Chastity painting *Da Vinci* on his boat. Even Reverend Mike and Jing-Wei were more like the people touched by the miracles of Jesus than were professional models who got paid for the serendipity of flawless DNA.

Even Berger would be better than the usual hunks from the agency with their perfect beards and bodies. He smiled at the thought. Wrapping Berger in a disciple's robe and posing him for the camera might be good for black comedy, but a mural about Jesus? On the other hand, Berger was Jewish and so were most of Jesus' followers.

The remainder of Mrs. Benning's concert played as background. Thomas was absorbed by his study of the faces, expressions, posture, gestures and relationships between seniors and their families. *Seniors,* of course, was the politically correct word for "old people," and it was curious to Thomas that it was in the "oldness" that the ennobling characteristics manifested themselves.

When the concert ended there was gracious applause. Most of the visitors stood to appreciate the talent and tenacity of an eighty-eight-year-old woman who refused to stop living. Thomas ushered Cass across the back of the room to where Alex was on his feet clapping.

"Hello, Pop," Thomas said. The old man turned. His face brightened.

"Hello, Tommy!" There was an awkward beat of silence before Alex extended his hand but none of the unpleasantness Thomas had imagined. He clasped the outstretched hand with both of his and shook it warmly. A wave of emotion passed over Cass's face. There were tears in Alex's eyes.

"Good to see you," Thomas said. "Sorry I missed your birthday and have been so lame about getting over here, I just . . ."

"I understand. Thank you for coming. Thank you." Alex wrapped both arms around him in an embrace that was surprisingly sturdy, given the old man's frail appearance.

Thomas introduced Cass and explained the mural at St. Mark's with a few terse comments. Small talk followed. Thomas said, "I feel very lucky that I am able to combine who I am with what I do." Cass's wry smile left him certain she was divining his thoughts again. It was true. *I know what you do, but who are you?*

It took Mrs. Benning a few minutes to thread her way through a throng of admirers to where Alexander was talking to his son. Cass had seen a woman she knew and stepped away. Alex introduced Thomas to Mrs. Benning.

"Your father has told me marvelous things about you," she said as she shook the artist's hand. "So nice to meet you." Her words were a worn-out cliché but she endowed them with new life and made them genuine.

"Very nice to meet you too," Thomas said. He glanced at Alex and wondered what "marvelous things" his estranged father could have said. *What does Alex even know about my life?*

"Is that marvelous woman you came in with your . . . ?" She completed the question by raising her well-drawn brows, pointing to Cass with her eyes and giving Thomas a knowing look.

"No, no. We're just . . ." *What are we?* Thomas mused for an instant then continued, "Just business associates. I want you to meet her, though. Excuse me just a second." Thomas crossed to where Cass was talking to a woman about her age with a baby over her arm.

Mrs. Benning studied Cass. She whispered to Alex that nothing would heal old wounds quicker than Thomas making him a grandfather. A boy, of course. In those few seconds she hooked them up, married them off, gave them a baby and picked out a name.

"Thomas Alexander Hall," she said. "It's a perfect way to connect the generations while there's still time."

. . .

The food at Oakridge Manor was always good. The Saturday buffet rivaled Sunday brunch at the Fairmont. Thomas was no match for Mrs. Benning's mastery of conversation. Neither was Cass. By the time they finished lunch the woman had wrested from them more information about the St. Mark's project than existed. Not to mention personal details about each of them that were likewise a surprise.

"Anybody ready for a wild idea?" Thomas spoke to everyone but directed the question at Cass. Thomas explained his epiphany in simple terms. He wanted to photograph residents and guests of Oakridge Manor as models for the mural at St. Mark's. "More than models," he added, "archetypes."

"I love that idea," Cass said. "You think they might allow it?" she asked Mrs. Benning. The moment Cass said, *I love the idea,* Thomas was determined.

"Your music inspired the idea," Thomas said. It was only marginally true, but he hoped for Mrs. Benning's obvious influence.

. . .

The manager of Oakridge Manor, Silvia Johnson, listened thoughtfully as Thomas presented the request with the skill of the seasoned pitchman. Johnson was a long jump over fifty but an expensive nip and tuck made her ageless in a pinched sort of way. She wore slacks with a tailored blazer that fit her soft figure perfectly. Thomas was encouraged by the silver cross on a delicate chain around her neck.

Cass described the mural and the goals of the Healing Place. They were hardly finished before Silvia Johnson stood up all excited. The challenge of any senior care facility was minimizing tedious repetition, creating variety and stimulating interest in new things. Dressing people up as Bible characters to have their pictures taken qualified.

Johnson invited everyone interested in dressing up as Jesus' disciples and having their pictures taken, or helping with costumes and props, or just watching the fun to gather in the dayroom.

She introduced Thomas as "one of the most famous artists in the world." Susan Cassidy was "the woman who runs the St. Mark's Hospital in San Francisco." Her description of the Healing Place and the mural of Jesus' miracles rivaled the spiel of a Vatican guide in the Sistine Chapel.

Thomas assembled his camera equipment while Cass organized participants. Johnson mobilized her staff and a surprising collection of drapery, sandals, towels, turbans and odd bits of clothing was assembled in the costume corner.

Thomas set his Canon SLR on a tripod and with the help of an enthusiastic crew, including eight-year-olds on one end and eighty-year-olds on the other, transformed the dayroom into a studio. The wraparound bay windows provided excellent light.

A number of seniors preferred not to participate. Some were too shy or too feeble. A handful were offended by a reenactment of Jesus' miracles in a facility the brochure described as "nondenominational."

Thomas admired Cass for several reasons, not all of them professional. Artistic creativity had not been on the list. That changed as they spent the afternoon scrambling together. The longer it took, the more difficult it became. Thomas was increasingly willing to admit that his idea had been more than crazy. He selected people, suggested costumes, arranged ensembles and pushed his way through fourteen separate setups. Cass made it possible. She was incredibly clever in creating costumes from the mound of materials gathered by the staff. She was invaluable in placing and adjusting people in accord with his design.

In the burst of enthusiasm that followed Silvia Johnson's invitation, none of the participants really understood the demands of what they were being asked to do. Old folks got tired. Others got grumpy—grumpier than usual—and others were simply impatient. Adult children became anxious for their aged loved ones and youngsters became restless.

Susan Cassidy saved the day with help from Mrs. Benning and Alex. Thomas marveled at the way Cass handled people. Mrs. Benning and Alex became willing extensions of Cass, enabling her to manage the galli-maufry and keep it all organized. It was startling. They handled complaints with humor and understanding. They kept everyone calm, comfortable and cooperative. Cass coached the people through the setups, coaxing them when needed, but always with consideration, kindness and respect.

Thomas was used to yelling. Professionals expected it. There was no yelling here. Cass's affection for each person was genuine and it showed. She demanded nothing more than they were able to give, and when they were finished she gushed with genuine appreciation for their every effort.

In the midst of creating his living paintings, Thomas posed his father as the royal official receiving word his son has been healed. The young man selected as the son was not the child inferred by most artists. He was a handsome fellow in his twenties. Whether Thomas thought of it or not, Cass and Mrs. Benning whispered together of the symbolism of the healing taking place between another father and son.

Mrs. Benning told Alexander he needed to make sure Thomas married this girl. The old man told her he had no influence or right to presume he might. When it was apparent Alex was not going to say anything, Mrs. Benning picked a moment when Cass was particularly dazzling and whispered to Thomas, "You should marry this girl." He laughed but her suggestion stuck on his heart like a smiley-face decal on the window of his car.

Silvia Johnson and her staff worked until the sun dropped behind the Berkeley hills and daylight from the windows was no longer bright enough for good exposures. By then only a few members of the original throng were left. Happily, Cass had foreseen the course of the afternoon and urged Thomas to shoot the oldest models first, the youngest next, and save the younger seniors and visiting adults for setups toward the end.

Not all the vignettes were what Thomas had originally imagined.

Most of what happened during the afternoon gave him new ideas and changed his mind about earlier assumptions. The potency and power of the faces exceeded his expectation. Many of them were photographed in close-up, from different angles and, with Cass's gentle persuasion, in a variety of expressions: rapture, wonder, gratitude, exaltation.

"What do you think?" Cass asked as the last of the marvelous models thanked them and left the hall.

"Incredible!" Thomas exclaimed. "You were unbelievable." Alex, Mrs. Benning and Silvia Johnson huddled around him as he put away the camera. "All of you," he added. "This was great. Thank you."

"Did you get what you wanted?" Johnson asked.

He checked the count on the digital display. "Eleven hundred and twenty-five images. Bound to be something I can use."

"You shot over a thousand pictures?"

"The blessing and curse of digital."

73

T HEY HAD SPENT SIX HOURS turning residents and guests into followers of Jesus. The event was certain to become a legend at Oakridge Manor.

Silvia Johnson invited Cass and Thomas to stay for dinner and spend
the night. Cass was shaking her head before the director finished propos-
ing that they "stay in *one* of our guest rooms." Her presumptions about
their relationship were obviously mistaken.

Thomas smiled at the misperception and avoided eye contact with
Cass. "I need to get Cass back," he said halfheartedly.

"Can't you at least stay for dinner, dear?" Mrs. Benning asked Cass
as if no one else were there. She whispered coyly, "He'd like you to stay."
Cass blushed slightly. "Wouldn't you, Mr. Hall?" Thomas gulped, grinned
and nodded.

"I've been trying to get her on a date since I met her," Thomas
quipped without losing the grin. Cass fired an eye-bullet but it came with
a twinkle.

"I teach a Sunday school class so I do need to get home tonight," she
stipulated.

"Just dinner and we'll drive back late?" Thomas offered.

"We'd love it if you could," Silvia Johnson said.

"You've already done so much," Cass argued but her smile accepted
the invitation. "Dinner would be great, thank you, but only if 'Mr. Hall'
agrees it's NOT a date."

. . .

Dinner was served in the boardroom next to Silvia Johnson's office. Her husband, Alan, joined them for what she called "a glorious and momentous occasion."

"Does anyone mind if I say grace?" Silvia's question was rhetorical since she clasped her husband's hand and reached for Mrs. Benning without the slightest chance for anyone to object. Alan and Mrs. Benning did likewise, taking Cass and Alex by the hand. Cass offered her hand to Thomas on his left and his father reached out from his right. Thomas took their hands and completed the circle. He glanced from Cass's hand in his to her face. She smiled and closed her eyes. They all bowed their heads.

"Dear Lord, we thank thee for the abundance of thy gifts and for the bounties of life thou hast given us. We thank thee for the food before us." Thomas opened his eyes and scanned the circle of bowed heads and reverent faces. The woman's prayer was so forthright and personal he half expected to see the Lord listening.

"As we partake may we be mindful of those in need and willing to impart of our substance. Wilt thou bless this food to give us strength in thy service."

Silvia Johnson opened her eyes a slit and caught Thomas watching her. He twitched an apologetic smile and crunched his eyes closed. "We ask a special blessing upon Thomas and Susan in their project that they may truly celebrate the miracles of thy Son. May they be inspired and blessed to do thy will." Thomas stole another quick glance at Silvia. Her eyes were closed and her face gazed upward. "We acknowledge thy hand in all things, dear God, and ask these favors and blessings in Jesus' name, amen."

A unison of "amens" purred around the table like a tiny choir. Thomas couldn't be sure but it seemed Cass allowed her hand to linger a little longer than everyone else.

Alan Johnson was an interesting guy. Not the first suspect Thomas would pick from a lineup of men accused of being Silvia Johnson's husband. He was shorter than she and a bit overweight. His strong point was a cherubic face forged by good humor into a persistent smile. *He must grin in his sleep,* Thomas mused to himself.

The food was excellent. The service attentive. The conversation wandered from the afternoon's momentous event to everything but politics and religion. Alan found out Alexander had been a corpsman in the army and began swapping stories. To all but Thomas their friendly prattle was inconsequential. As Alexander shared stories with Alan Johnson, Thomas was meeting his father for the first time. He listened more than he ate.

Eventually, the conversation found its way back to the mural at St. Mark's. Mrs. Benning volunteered to play a concert for the children. Thomas was suddenly telling her about Christina. The accident. The search for the lost violin. He asked Cass to describe the child's injuries since she knew the proper terminology. Going forward, they tag-teamed the telling of the story.

Thomas didn't even consider talking about Evans, his belief that the child had died or Christina's secret about seeing her mother, but it was impossible to keep the thoughts from flooding his mind.

Thomas made a humorous story out of trying to buy a violin case but twisted the tale so the humor was about a twenty-two-hundred-dollar custom-made Italian Musafia Enigma Aureum case instead of a maxed-out credit card. Mrs. Benning's laugh revealed a lovely gusto unexpected from her otherwise demure demeanor.

"Unfortunately," Cass broke in, changing the mood of the moment, "the damage to the median nerve, the intrinsic muscles and the overlying skin on Christina's left arm is so severe, the doctor said she will never regain the use of her fingers." The strange look on Mrs. Benning's face was the opposite of what Thomas had expected.

"I would love to meet Christina," Mrs. Benning said.

"Anytime. It's easily arranged," Cass said. Thomas worried as she spoke that meeting the woman she aspired to be might be a devastating experience for Christina, given the reality she would never play the violin like Mrs. Benning.

CHAPTER

74

I T WAS TWENTY DEGREES COOLER on the bay side of the Caldecott Tunnel. The top was down and a shiver passed through Cass as they entered the colder air. She glanced across at Thomas. He'd been unusually quiet since they had left Oakridge Manor.

• • •

When dinner was finished, Thomas walked his father to his room. It was on the third floor. They took the elevator. Thanks to OSHA and ADA—Occupational Safety and Health Administration and Americans with Disabilities Act—the intimate charm of the original narrow hallways and quaint staircases had been gutted and replaced by railings, ramps, stairlifts and elevators. Thomas felt a sense of loss at the destruction of such architectural elegance. Providing easy access made sense since the sanatorium was now a home for older people, Thomas allowed, but he still concluded that the bureaucrats who came up with regulations requiring the destruction of such beauty were idiots.

Alexander's room was halfway down the hall. It was the first time Thomas had seen where his father lived—the first time he saw the room he had ordered. When Thomas had been in a cash crunch a year ago, he'd called Andrea and told her he wanted to pay less than the half of Alexander's care they had agreed upon. She said it was impossible. It was an unpleasant conversation. He felt taken advantage of, abused and put upon. When the anger and insults ended, the solution was to put Alex on the least expensive plan available.

"He doesn't need a nurse to come by his room twice a day and tell him to take his damn pills, and he can make his own bed," Thomas had argued.

The basic plan included a single room, very small, no phone, limited access to facilities and minimum services. The room made Motel 6 look like the Marriott. Calling it "basic" was generous. A window, bed, desk with wooden chair, small light, upholstered chair in the corner and a floor lamp. To the right was a closet, to the left, a bathroom. There was no way to regulate the temperature in the room except by opening and closing the window. *Or taking the truck elevator down to the main floor and asking someone at the desk to turn it up or down,* he thought. Like a cuff up the side of the head, he wondered if the "basic package" allowed his father to complain about anything.

"Home sweet home," Alexander smiled and sat down on the bed. It was unmade. Thomas stared down at the frail old man for a long while, then sat down beside him and put his arm around his shoulder. He felt ashamed.

• • •

Thomas stayed in the right lane and followed the connector to the Grove Shafter Freeway. Cass glanced at him occasionally but he was still with his father in the small room on the third floor reciting the things he'd said. Thinking of other things he wished he'd said.

"You okay?" Cass's voice brought him back to the moment. He glanced across at her. Her faced morphed in and out of silhouette as they passed through the pools of mercury vapor light that marked the road into Berkeley. The light was interesting. Her face was bewitching.

"Yeah, yeah, I'm good." Thomas laid his hand on top of hers and shook it softly. "Sorry I stayed so late. I appreciate your patience."

"You're welcome." He expected Cass to take her hand away. She didn't.

"It was good to spend the extra time with my dad," he said.

"You ought to visit him every week!" It was as if allowing him to hold her hand gave her the right to be his mom. She was right, of course. He nodded.

"I know. I'm going to." He exceeded the boundaries of expectation for casual contact by at least five seconds and let go of her hand.

"Silvia said you moved your dad to a different room."

"Yeah. I had never seen the room I put him in. It's too small. They have different plans. I bumped it up a little, that's all."

. . .

Thomas had said good night to his father and gone straight to Silvia Johnson to have Alex moved to a bigger room. He didn't bother looking at the brochure. "I want him to have one of the large corner rooms on the first floor with windows on two walls and a bedroom separate from the living area," he said. "And his own phone. Just make sure he has the best of everything you offer."

"Is cost a consideration?" Silvia asked.

Artists are not logical where emotions are involved. The feelings of the day, the tears in the privacy of Alex's room, the liberation of forgiving and being forgiven overpowered any sense of practical reality.

"He doesn't need caviar and a private chauffeur, if that's what you mean, but no, cost is not a consideration." Optimism reigned eternal. The universal law allowing artists to be artists.

As they walked to the car, Mrs. Benning took Thomas by the arm. Maybe Cass could hear, maybe not. "Susan Cassidy is an outstanding woman, Mr. Hall. You'll be a fool if you let her get away."

"Come visit us at the hospital," Thomas said, then added in a clandestine whisper, "I could use your help with that."

"I will come," she promised. "I am most eager to meet your Christina."

CHAPTER

75

THEY PASSED THE COLLEGE OF St. Albert and drove south through the heart of Berkeley to the MacArthur Interchange. *I am most eager to meet your Christina.* Mrs. Benning's parting comment stayed with Thomas.

He made a decision. It had nagged at him since yesterday and gotten worse when they told Christina's story at dinner. "Has Christina ever talked to you about her mother?" he asked.

"Not really. Dr. Namkung said to wait for her to bring it up. Why?"

Thomas measured his responsibility to keep a secret against the possibility that Christina needed help. *Counseling? A reality check?* He was out of his tree again.

"She told me . . ." He searched for the right words. There weren't any. "She told me some kind of crazy stuff that happened to her."

"Crazy stuff?"

"Yeah. I promised to keep it a secret."

"So are you crossing your fingers?" Cass teased.

Thomas remained serious. "It's not that kind of secret. It's the kind of thing that makes me worry that she might . . . I don't know. It was very real to her. Totally real."

"I'm sorry. I didn't mean to make light of it."

"I wanted to get your opinion in case she needs to talk to somebody besides me, but you have to agree not to say anything for now. Okay?"

"You hope I'm better at keeping secrets than you?"

"Exactly."

Thomas began by telling Cass what Christina had said about her the night he had promised to find her violin. How much the girl liked Cass. That Cass prayed for her.

"Her mother said prayers with her every night," Cass said.

Thomas looked at Cass a long time. "She said her mother came to her in the hospital and told her she was going to be all right." Cass's untroubled reaction was not what Thomas expected. "She said she knew her hand would get better because her mother told her that it would."

"That was her secret?"

"Not quite. Some of what she told me gets way out there. A little weird."

Thomas pulled left to avoid the *CREDIT CARD ONLY* lane at the toll plaza of the Bay Bridge. He put four dollars into the rubber hand and accelerated onto the bridge.

"So I'm waiting for *way out there*," Cass said, but her smile became serious. "Discussing it is the right thing to do for Christina's sake, by the way, and I'm . . ." Now was not the right moment to tell Thomas about the papers she'd signed in the hospital.

The traffic over the Bay Bridge was slow. Thomas settled into the outside lane to give them a view of the San Francisco skyline and returned to his story. He described Christina's late-night visit to the Healing Place and their conversation at the mural. Thomas punctuated the story with personal comments, clever quips and ingratiating behavior. "She said you said I needed help, by the way."

"And did she help?"

"She did."

"You're welcome," Cass grinned.

Thomas recited Christina's memory of the accident. The noise, the darkness, falling, fear, the crushing pain and a man coming through the fire. Darkness.

"Christina's memory of the accident and what Officer Evans told me were the pretty much the same."

The story progressed from the accident to Christina's vision. Thomas did not know what else to call it. Some things you don't forget, and every word of the child's story was tattooed in memory. He described it for Cass the way Christina had described it to him. How she'd left her body and watched from above as the highway patrolman cut her out of her seatbelt, carried her to the rock and attempted to revive her.

"She described it in detail," Thomas said. "Evans's red Buck Knife, the holes burned in his jacket, his efforts to save her." He let the unsettling fact hang in the air. "That was when she saw her mother the first time." Thomas looked at Cass, expecting her to comment. She didn't. She nodded and listened, her face serene.

"They were somewhere else," Thomas continued as he described the bright light, the splendid colors, her mother's arms around her, meeting her grandmother, communicating mind to mind, being happy and being told she needed to go back and that everything was going to be okay. He recited what Christina had said about the sudden darkness, cold and horrible pain.

• • •

Thomas stopped the car in front of Cass's apartment on the north side of Nob Hill. "What do you suggest?" Thomas asked.

"What do you think?" Cass said.

Thomas felt an affinity with Cass—and it felt good. "I don't know. I just . . . is it worrisome when a child has these delusions?"

"Nothing she said rang true to you?"

"Everything was true in her mind," he said. Cass studied Thomas until he worried there must be something on his face. "You think we should talk to Dr. Namkung?"

Cass shook her head. "Let me sleep on it." She put her hand on the door.

"Hold it." He jumped out, circled the back of the SLK and opened her door. He offered his hand. She took it.

"Where did that come from?" she asked.

"Illustrations for a graphic novel set in the fifties. The chivalry stuff was cool."

"Then I thank you, sir knight." She made a modest curtsy and was still holding his hand.

"My lady."

"Thomas?" Her use of his name riveted his attention. "Do you believe it's possible that what Christina says she experienced really happened?"

"Leaving her body?" His effort to appear incredulous was sabotaged by the one nagging fact he had not yet disclosed.

Cass answered his question with a nod. That was exactly what she meant. "Were you aware that a large number of people have had similar experiences?"

He nodded. A girl in his watercolor class at Art Institute was a big *Life after Life* advocate and gave him a copy of Raymond Moody's book. He read a few pages but set it aside lest it upset the comfortable cowardice of agnosticism. *Why does Hawker keep showing up in my head?* The thought got tangled with the question.

The nagging fact tugged his pant leg. "There is one thing I didn't tell you." He lifted her hand and held it in both of his as if it were a tether to sanity that allowed him to say what he was going to say without putting his disbelief in danger.

"Officer Evans told me she was dead when he carried her from the car."

CHAPTER

76

SUNDAY MORNING. By the time Thomas finished his run to the base of the bridge and back, the fog was gone. He stepped from the shower and stood in the sunlight that fell through the wall of glass. He closed his eyes and sorted visual memories from the photo shoot on Saturday. Hard to believe that was only yesterday.

The conversation with Cass about Christina's bizarre experience seemed part of a different day, a different life. *Do you believe it's possible that what Christina says she experienced really happened?*

Berger broke the reverie with flying dragons. "Didn't catch you on your way to church, did I?" he said, sardonic grin apparent even through the cell phone. Berger was an odd contradiction between pushing St. Mark's and making sarcastic cracks about Thomas turning religious.

The call was not about church. Berger had a buyer for the boat and told Thomas he needed to sell. They argued for fifteen minutes, raised voices for ten and shouted for the final five. The tranquillity of forgive and forget never lasted long with an agent on one end and an ego on the other.

Berger acquiesced after pushing his point until Thomas was bare heinie on hard brick. "It's your boat, it's your life. I'm just telling you unless Vegas changes their mind or you win the lottery, something's gotta give." Once Berger backed down, Thomas agreed to think about it.

• • •

Thomas threw on a pair of cargo shorts the color of blanched almond, a black cotton golf shirt with a PowerSchool logo that he'd gotten from his buddy Greg Porter before Porter sold his company to Apple for $60 million. There were days when Thomas wondered what his life might have been if nature had balanced his abundant right lobe with a bit more on the left.

He blended a banana, blueberries, egg, raw oatmeal and muscle milk with water and ice and used the thick elixir to chase a peanut butter Power Bar.

Thomas downloaded 1125 images from the Canon to his Mac and spent the day sorting, selecting and refining images in Aperture 3. "Pro performance with iPhoto simplicity" was Apple's promise. Thomas had found it to be true once he learned the software.

In the commotion of the Oakridge shoot he was unaware how many pictures he had taken of his father. How many close-ups of his face. As he sorted through them, he saw—really for the first time in his life—the likeness of himself in the face of the man who had given him life but whom he'd never known.

By five o'clock the images were organized by category and labeled with descriptive words for type, gender, age, quality, rank and of course the miracle to which they belonged. There were more great images than he could possibly use. The more he studied the collection of authentic faces, the more anxious he became. He was tempted to drive into the city that night and work on the canvas. For once reason prevailed.

Berger called again. Thomas didn't want another round of Berger ragging on him about selling the boat. He let it go to voice mail and deleted the message. Berger was gone. That left the boat.

Thomas walked from the studio to slip 64 where *Da Vinci* was moored. The sloop looked the same as the last time he'd seen it. *Gorgeous. Unbelievable I've yet to take her out.*

There was a note taped to the mast. He felt a stab of adrenaline. *Who's been here? Berger? SAVE THE SEALS? They wouldn't dare to burn my boat like they burned my studio! Would they? The check bounced! Repossession?* Thoughts tumbled through his head like marbles spilling down the cellar stairs. He recognized his life was out of kilter. He stepped aboard and read the note.

Dear Thomas,

I must have misunderstood which day you asked me to go sailing. Did I get the date wrong? Sorry! I waited a couple of hours. Tried to reach you. Do you have a new cell? Hope we can make it a rain check. Love to see you again. It is a beautiful boat.

Much love,
Catrina

Saturday. He'd completely forgotten. He had invited his trophy girl-friend to go sailing. Impress the old boys fishing for perch off the end of the dock. He called to apologize. Happily, she didn't pick up. That made it easier, but he wasn't worried. Catrina would crawl on broken glass to go out with him. He left a convoluted message that included the first excuses that popped to mind: The fire. A day with Dad. A guy jumping off the Golden Gate Bridge.

He was tempted to take the boat out for an hour but worried he would run out of daylight. Besides monthly payments, slip fees and the cost of maintenance, Berger had given him the other reason he needed to sell the boat: "You don't have time!" Berger was right. Thomas would never admit it out loud, and the thought depressed him, but Berger's joke made him smile. *See if you enjoy standing in a cold shower with a leaky slicker stuffing hundred-dollar bills down the drain as fast as you can.*

Chastity was on a ladder on the deck of Reverend Mike's houseboat. Thomas saw her when he knelt on the T-dock to tighten the mooring line. She was working and had no cause to look up as he crossed to the houseboat.

"Hey," Thomas said when he was close enough for the girl to hear his voice if not the clomp of footsteps on the dock. She turned with a curious smile and blocked the sun with her arm so she could see. "How ya do-ing?" Thomas waved. Her smile faded.

"Oh. Hello. I'm good," she said and went back to work. Chastity was painting on the large flat wall above the window. Thomas moved to where he had a better view.

The letters were beautifully ornate and looked like an illuminated manuscript from the tenth century. Large letters in the center announced the new name of the houseboat:

GOD'S PLACE

Below, in smaller decorated script, was the message:

The Sacred Circle of Life Is Green

The margin was an intricate lattice of floral symbols. The corners were miniature icons that might have been created by monastic scribes of late antiquity except the otherwise classic religious motif was tainted by a twenty-first century environmental bias. Saints of antiquity hugging redwood trees. The anachronism was amusing. The quality of the art sensational.

"Your design?" Thomas asked. The underlying drawings were still visible where artwork was unfinished. She nodded. "You're even better than I thought," he said, chipping away at the ice, "and I already thought you were very good."

She turned on the ladder, relaxed her brush arm across the top and scolded him with a look that said, *I know I'm good. I don't need you to tell me.*

"Mind if I come aboard?"

"It's not my boat." Her focus went back to her painting. Thomas made the short jump from the dock to the deck. Chastity was working on a floral detail. The boat rocked when Thomas landed. Her brush slipped. She threw up her hands in a way that yelled *IDIOT!*

"I am so sorry," he said. "You'd think that I of all people would know better."

"Yeah, right. You of all people!" She wiped away the smudge of asparagus green.

The swells died quickly in the heavy pilings. Chastity resumed

working. Thomas stood close enough to examine the detail of the miniatures and appreciate the vibrant mix of colors.

Thomas supposed the impulse came from nowhere. It wasn't the
"voice in his head" that Susan Cassidy talked about. At least he didn't
think it was.

"How would you like to work for me as an apprentice on a huge
mural I'm doing for St. Mark's Hospital?" For an instant it seemed she
hadn't heard. She continued to work but the question clearly affected
everything. Her hands slowed. Her breathing increased. She lost focus
and mixed a new color she didn't need. She turned and looked down at
him. "Michelangelo used twelve apprentices to paint the Sistine Chapel,"
he said. She backed down the ladder and when she reached the bottom
turned to face him.

"What does your apprentice do?"

"Help. Mix paint. Block in. Clean up. Just about everything except
the finished art." He poked his chin at the miniatures. "Might even have
you try your hand at some of that."

"I know who you are," she said.

"I gave you my card."

"I know about the mural at St. Mark's."

"Really?"

"Do you know who I am?"

"A young woman with too much talent to be painting *Da Vinci* on
my boat," he glanced up again, "or *God's Place,* though I've got to say
what you've done here is amazing." He rejected the rest of the thought,
*You want to save the poor seals decaled on your bumper and might even be the
girl who torched my studio.*

"I'll think about it."

CHAPTER

77

THE PHOTOGRAPHS INSPIRED changes to the mural that were both troubling and exciting. Thomas had intended to make the St. Mark's mural the way he always did. Work up sketches. Block the canvas. Pose models with props and costumes. Add the details and paint the faces.

Some considered his approach backwards, but he never liked to begin with the constraints of reality. He preferred giving his imagination a first pass of unbridled freedom. He would rather torque human anatomy with the sweep of his hand than push a model to contortions. Not many artists could draw perfect anatomy from memory. Another of the gifts that set Thomas apart.

The pathos of the models, the power of their faces, even the curious fall of the draperies inspired positions, postures and compositions that improved the original sketches. There were bursts of creative rapture that left Thomas believing it would be what Cass and Andrus and even Berger had imagined. His masterwork.

It was Tuesday afternoon. Thomas had begun to paint over sections of the preliminary drawings when someone knocked. It was security. "There's a woman here who says she works for you."

Chastity stepped into the Healing Place. When Thomas saw her he realized he had not expected her to show up. The invitation had ignored the conflict both understood but neither acknowledged. Thomas's decision to focus on her talent instead of her misguided zeal for animal rights had made the difference.

"Do I get paid?" She was standing just inside the portal.

"Of course."

"How much?"

"What are you worth?" Thomas smiled.

She thought carefully about her answer. "Twenty dollars an hour?" It was a question, not a demand. Archie Granger paid her less, charged clients more and took a fat margin for himself.

"How about twenty-five an hour to start and we'll see how it goes."

Chastity crossed the room. She seemed unable to take her eyes from the canvas. Each setting was adorned with the photos Thomas had selected on Sunday. He extended his hand. "Glad to see you."

She remained tentative. "I tried to get here earlier but I needed to finish Reverend Mike's boat."

"No worries," Thomas said. "Wouldn't want him to miss his tax deduction." Chastity furrowed her brow. "No, no. I like Reverend Mike," he laughed and added sheepishly, "Judge not that ye be not judged."

The curious change in Chastity's expression reminded him that the saying came from the Bible. She smiled and absently touched the silver cross at her throat.

Thomas gave Chastity a quick tour of the project and described her duties. What he needed and what he expected. He was in the middle of demonstrating the way he liked his brushes cleaned when Susan Cassidy came in.

Thomas introduced Cass to Chastity, calling one "the big boss" and the other "our talented apprentice." Both of them seemed to enjoy their titles. Cass apologized for the interruption and took a few minutes to walk the wall and look at the selected photos. The apology was a courteous ritual since Cass was "the big boss" and could interrupt anytime for any reason. Thomas looked forward to her interruptions.

The collage of photos, arrows and sketches made sense to Thomas. He was never sure whether Cass could see what he intended. He watched her for subtle signals. A nod. A smile. Body language. Every artist lives his life with one foot on the banana peel of criticism. Thomas was no different. In this circumstance it was more than artistic fragility. Susan Cassidy's approval had become important to him on a personal level.

"How do you feel about our 'models' now you've got them here?" Cass asked. Her signals of approval were tainted by a glimmer of uncertainty.

"They're going to be great," he assured her.

That was apparently all she had needed to hear before moving to the real reason she had come. "If you have time later, there is someone I would like you to meet."

CHAPTER

78

JANIS AHLSTROM LOOKED FAMILIAR. Thomas tried to place her face as Cass introduced them in the foyer of ICU. It was a face people remembered. Janis was in her late fifties but had a glow that made her younger. Her high cheekbones were held in place by a perpetual smile. Her eyes were a pale, glaucous blue like the coating on grapes of fine wine. They were framed by happy wrinkles. An abundance of flaxen blonde hair was piled and pinned on top of her head. The color came from Swedish DNA, not a spray bottle of hydrogen peroxide.

"Janis is one of our volunteers," Cass said after introducing Thomas as "the gifted artist working on the mural at the Healing Place." Janis Ahsltrom seemed honored and impressed. "She spends three days a week with a special group of patients."

"You were at the Science Museum!" Thomas realized as the words from the left lobe collided with an image on the right. For a moment she looked confused. "For the press conference," Thomas clarified.

"Oh, yes. You were there?"

"I was, I . . ." Thomas stopped short of finishing the thought: *I am painting a mural for the Descent of Man exhibit, or was, or should be or maybe I wish I wasn't.* So far he had kept the projects separate and, as far as he knew, Susan Cassidy did not know about his commitment to the museum.

Thomas remembered the woman's husband in the Giants baseball cap. He had stood and challenged Hawker. *What about miracles? Cancer.*

358

Perfect health for twenty-six years. Gave birth to our three kids. That was Janis Ahlstrom.

"Janis helps in remarkable ways," Cass said.

The woman waved the praise away. "Cass told me you've become interested in life-after-life experiences," she said. Thomas was taken aback. He glanced at Cass to be reassured she had not divulged Christina's secret. She hadn't. "Officially, of course, they're called 'near death experiences,' or NDEs, but I prefer life after life."

It was getting dark outside. Cass and Thomas waited while Janis Ahlstrom checked on the last of her patients; then the three gathered in Cass's office. Jessica served hot tea and ginger snaps.

"I died of cancer but was given a choice to come back because of prayers and faith." That was her opening line. Thomas stopped breathing. The woman's frankness was disquieting but left no doubt that the experience was completely real to her. Thomas felt a rush of confidence that the woman was telling the truth. "I kept it to myself," she said. "I've never talked much about it, except with Jim, of course."

"The Giants fan."

"How did you know?"

"He wore his hat." They laughed and any lingering discomfort disappeared.

"My cure was a miracle. My life is a gift," she said. "I volunteer as a way of expressing gratitude. In working with patients, their families and sometimes the terminally ill, I discovered that my experience was not unique. Far from it. I began collecting similar stories from other people."

She presented Thomas with a three-ring binder thick with plastic sheet protectors stuffed with typed pages, letters and clippings. One sleeve held a note written on the back of an envelope. "My first thought was to give people faith to live or courage to die, but as it turned out, gathering these experiences and sharing them with others has blessed my life more than anyone else's. What is it they say? 'What you do for others you are truly doing for yourself.'"

Thomas let his eyes run over snippets of a cursive letter protected under plastic.

The paramedics were rushing around . . .

I felt sorry for my body . . .
It was the strangest thing I've ever experienced . . .
Thomas turned the page.
I know we do not die . . .
I have no fear of death . . .
My mother told me she was looking down watching us . . .
There was a brilliant light and marvelous colors . . .

Thomas turned over a dozen pages and leafed forward through the sheets. He glanced at a line here and a passage there.

I experienced the most wonderful feelings of peace . . .
I heard music, majestic, beautiful . . .
I moved at fantastic speed through a tunnel . . .
There was a being of light waiting for me . . .

Thomas paused to read a note attached to a letter. *I recognized my grandmother and saw my sister who was still alive but much later I was told she had died while I was ill but they kept the bad news from me . . .*

Cass studied Thomas as he turned the pages. He stopped to read a story that had been typed and printed out. "Read it out loud," Cass said.

Thomas glanced up at her and realized she had believed Christina's story was true from the first time he had told it to her. His eyes were drawn to a passage underlined in red. He cleared his throat and read aloud.

"It is almost impossible to describe what happened next. It was so amazing. I was looking down at my body. Then all of a sudden I was someplace else. A beautiful place. It was stunning. So many colors I had never imagined. Truly magnificent and yet it was familiar. There were others there. I can only describe them as beings of light. They embraced me. They knew me somehow and filled me with love and brilliant light. I never felt such happiness. I was laughing. I understood the importance of my life and that life had meaning and purpose. Then I was back in my body and the pain and struggle of mortal life returned, but my life has never been the same. I have no fear of death."

He turned the page slowly and leafed his way through another dozen pages in silence.

"Interesting stuff," Thomas finally said to the women who were watching for his reaction.

"'The most terrifying euphemism in the English language,'" Cass quoted.

"What makes them remarkable is that they're all the same," Janis said. "Individually they are, as you say, 'interesting,'" she made it his word rather than her own. "A whisper of hope, you might say. But taken all together, they are . . ." she paused in search of a worthy metaphor, "they are a thunderous choir."

"I have a question," Thomas said.

"Of course."

"Are most of these people religious?"

"Not really. Many had no religious belief at all. A few of them were atheist . . ."

He stopped her. "Atheist? Really?"

She nodded with none of his surprise. "Yes, even atheists, and yet their experiences were very similar to those of the deeply spiritual. In some cases, identical." And then she laughed softly. "Well, except of course people with no belief in God were more baffled and confused by the reality that death is not the end of life."

"So you don't think their experiences could have been shaped by what they already believed? Some previous idea or expectation?"

She ran her fingers over the open pages as if doing so enlightened her memory. "It doesn't seem so. What I do find *fascinating* is that not one of those people, not even those from a strong Christian background, ever referred to 'heaven or hell.' Not one described an experience that conformed in any way to the traditional ideas about such places."

Is it a fear of the unknown that makes me want to believe the ultimate answers are unknowable? He could hear Hawker spewing his *cop-out cowardice of agnosticism* speech and was thinking about hell when the cell phone went off in his pocket.

It was Hawker. He excused himself and touched *ANSWER.*

CHAPTER

79

Hawker was unusually cordial on the phone and invited Thomas to meet him for dinner at the French Laundry Restaurant in Yountville. His first reaction was relief but a rodent of suspicion gnawed on his nerves. French Laundry was the most expensive restaurant in California and Hawker was not a friendly guy.

Thomas called Berger. Berger was already in the loop since the earlier meeting and had made preliminary contact with Walters, Johnson, Lewis & Arlington. He was waiting for a call back from Lia Chu and Vince Sadereck. "Obviously they need you. That's a good thing," Berger said.

"You should be there."

"Hawker will be peeved if you bring a date." They laughed. "Look," Berger said, letting the humor pass, "just remember you're an artist, you paint pictures. That's it. We've got a contract, they owe you money, they want to expand. Don't even talk about the deal. You're there to talk about the art. Period." He chuckled. "That and to find out what two hundred bucks' worth of hors d'oeuvres tastes like. You ever been to French Laundry?"

"No."

"You're in for it, then."

"I'll smuggle some hors d'oeuvres out in my pocket."

"Long as it's not the back one," Berger chuckled.

• • •

362

Yountville was a wide spot in the St. Helena Highway in the middle of the Napa Valley. George Yount had planted a vineyard there in 1831 and it became a town. The sign that said *WELCOME TO YOUNTVILLE* bragged a population of 2,196.

The French Laundry Restaurant occupied an old rock building that was built as a saloon in 1900. When Prohibition hit and booze became illegal, it was converted to a French steam laundry and later a cafe. It had been bought as a struggling eatery in 1996 and turned into one of the world's finest restaurants.

Thomas had heard of it. He had never eaten there. He couldn't imagine who did. With so many excellent restaurants in San Francisco, it made no sense to drive ninety minutes and pay a minimum of $250 per plate—plus the cost of the wine—unless of course you were an irrational connoisseur searching for the meaning of life in the pleasure of food. *Or unless it was not about the food at all.* A meeting with Hawker and his lawyers at the isolated location sixty miles outside the city was obviously the latter.

By the time Thomas arrived, Hawker had already ordered the nine-course chef's tasting menu and a decanter of local wine at $249. In his cash-flow crunch, Thomas had money on his mind. He did the math in his head and wondered who was paying for a dinner and wine tab that would reach $1249. Even before they launched into the business of the evening, Thomas assumed Hawker and his legal carnivores had come up with a slam-dunk plan to make sure their extravagant dinner would come out of Hamilton's hide.

The waiter's accent was so perfect and the atmosphere so French that Thomas promised himself a return trip to draw a series of caricatures.

"No ingredient is repeated," the man promised in his beautifully tainted English. He reminded Thomas of Lumière in *Beauty and the Beast,* and he smiled. When Lumière brought the first of the nine courses, he discovered that none of the guests had been there before. Introducing the wonders of French Laundry to newcomers buoyed the man to a fever of ecstasy. "Each of your courses will be a surprise," he raved. "Each is new. Each so exciting, so comforting, so delicious you will say, 'wow,' and then it will be gone and you will be so sad and say, 'Ah, I wish for one more bite of that,' and then *voila!* the next plate arrives and it happens all over again, but each time in a different way and with each course a whole new flavor and feeling and emotion." He was emotional and excused himself.

Reality usually fell short of hyperbole in Thomas's experience. Not this time. The food was flavorful, mouthwatering, delectable and exquisite. All of Lumiere's adjectives were perfectly precise. Berger would probably say, "lip-smackin' and melt in your mouth," but by any description, Thomas had never tasted food like this. *Whatever Hawker wants this time,* Thomas thought, *he's made it important.*

French restaurants are methodical. The dinner at French Laundry lasted three and half hours. Hawker engaged Thomas with questions about Art Institute, his favorite projects and even the Heavy Metal Hotel and Casino. He left more than enough time for the lawyers to describe their plan to Thomas in hopes of persuading him to cooperate.

Chu moved from the small puffs of choux pastry stuffed with cheese to the business at hand. She reminded Thomas that their meeting and everything discussed was strictly confidential. Like a tag-team partner at WWF, Sadereck pulled a nondisclosure agreement from his briefcase and put it in front of Thomas.

Hawker acted surprised. Whether that was part of the libretto or genuine, Thomas wasn't sure. Either way, in his apparent eagerness to convert Thomas, Hawker snatched up the document and ripped it in half.

"We don't need that," Hawker scolded, smiling at Thomas like a father to a son. Sadereck flushed. Chu looked startled and started to say something. Hawker cut her off. "If we can't trust Thomas, why should he trust us?" The whole event was so smooth and the dialogue so perfect it felt choreographed. *It felt scripted.* Thomas rejected the thought.

"He knows this is sensitive stuff," Hawker assured them. "Don't you, Thomas?" He patted his arm and plucked the last of the melt-in-your-mouth Gougères from the basket.

In the hour that followed Hawker explained the strategy, the timing and the role Thomas would play. Lia Chu and Vince Sadereck punctuated the plan with the legal ramifications and, "in fairness to Thomas," Chu said, "the risks."

Thomas quipped that it sounded like a "sting operation." Sadereck reacted with a babble of legalese and Chu cited legal precedents. Their message was singular. Care would be taken to circumvent the aspects that might be marginally illegal.

Thomas listened and pretended to understand the difference between *admissible* and *not admissible,* the meaning of *injunction* as it pertained to the exhibit, what constituted a *violation of injunction* and what Chu argued might not. He thought he understood their explanation of why Hawker had to distance himself from the plan and avoid personal contact with Hamilton. Why his role as the artist was the key to all of it and essential to make it work and keep it legal.

"Reasonably legal," Chu clarified.

The elements of the plan were straightforward. On the other hand . . . if it was all so on the up-and-up, why was he brought to a clandestine meeting in the middle of the Napa Valley and sworn to secrecy?

Hawker's offhanded use of the word *operations* was disconcerting. Thomas was eating the finest food he would ever consume but felt a dull pain in his stomach that had nothing to do with gastronomy.

The waiter arrived with sashimi of Pacific Kampachi, Akita Komachi rice, pine nuts, Tokyo turnips and a thick sauce of wine, mizuma and sugar. They suspended their covert conversation and sat silent as the large plates and tiny portions were set in place.

The plan in broad strokes: Hawker wanted Thomas to hire a crew of artists and finish the mural in one month. "Apprentices like Michelangelo used," he said. Thomas regretted their earlier conversation on the matter. "I want you to finish it, whatever it takes," Hawker continued. "We'll pay for the extra labor, of course, and . . ." he leaned forward and spoke softly to add emphasis, "we are adding a substantial bonus on top of the expanded contract." Hawker spoke with a glimmer of his trademark smugness.

Or you could start by paying me what you already owe me, he thought and was about to bring it up, but remembered Berger's instructions.

The plan continued. When the mural was finished, Thomas would invite Hamilton to the city and, by whatever deception necessary, entice him into the Darwin Pavilion.

The plan had two presumed results. Result number one: When Hamilton saw the Descent of Man exhibit finished and realized the mural was a fait accompli, he would abandon his demand, accept the financial settlement and go home. "Or drop dead from a heart attack." Hawker said it like a joke but didn't smile.

Result number two: Thomas would persuade Hamilton that if he persisted in his legal action it would damage Thomas personally. Chu had come up with the scenario and had written out the artist's dialogue.

Chu's story was pure fiction: Thomas was to tell Hamilton that he'd had to cooperate with Hawker because he was in financial trouble and needed the money. That he'd signed an agreement that obligated him to pay the money back in the event that Hamilton prevailed and the mural was undone. The message was simple: If Hamilton went forward it could wipe Thomas out. "The leverage you have, of course," Chu spoke like the director of a daytime soap, "is friendship and sympathy."

Just in case Hamilton was more stubborn than they imagined, there was a third element to the operation. Hawker called it "the backup plan." Thomas would wear a concealed microphone and recording device. It made digesting the eighth course impossible. His appetite was gone.

"A wire?" Thomas was incredulous. He'd watched all eight seasons of *24* and knew what Jack Bauer would call it. Chu explained they would make it easy by preparing a script. "More like a guideline of questions," she clarified. The conversation would hopefully catch Hamilton saying something damaging to his claims that they could use in the case. *Or to blackmail him?*

Wearing a wire was illegal, he knew. But before Thomas could object, they explained that the recording was "for informational purposes only" and would be used exclusively to insure Thomas's perfect recollection for his deposition and testimony on the witness stand. The digital recording would be erased. No one else would know. Simple!

No one talked about Chu's assumption that the recording would provide leverage in lowering the amount of the settlement. "A win-win for us," she had said.

There was one other problem. Working on the mural was a violation of the injunction to cease and desist pending resolution of the lawsuit.

"While technically any work in the Darwin Pavilion could be

construed as a violation," Sadereck explained, "you are not named in the injunction so repercussions are unlikely."

"Worst case," Chu said, "a violation of injunction is a first-degree misdemeanor, punishable by up to one year in county jail, twelve months of probation and a $500 fine."

"That'll never happen!" Sadereck scoffed and mapped out the plan. The museum would be closed for a month. Hawker would take a holiday and be "otherwise unavailable," since he could have nothing to do with it. Thomas would "decide on his own" to finish the mural. Chu gave him a short list of ways he could justify his decision to finish the mural in spite of the injunction. He could choose the one he liked.

"You understand Mr. Hawker has no knowledge of your plan?" Chu said. Thomas nodded slowly but his mind was not saying yes. "Dr. Hawker will hold a press conference and be outraged by your stupidity," she added.

"He won't say it like that, exactly," Sadereck hurried to soften Chu's blunt choice of words. Hawker smiled with condescending affection and offered Thomas an unsealed envelope. Thomas didn't take it. Hawker opened the envelope and handed him the check inside. Thomas pinched it between his fingers and took a breath. It was a cashier's check made out to Thomas Hall for $100,000. *Untraceable.*

"Signing bonus." Hawker wrinkled his face with an arrogant wink.

"Wow!" Thomas said and let out a puff of air. "Wow," he said again as he stood up. "I think I need a bathroom break." Hawker laughed. Thomas smiled and walked away. The check stayed on the table.

The ninth course arrived. Dessert selections included candied cashew ice cream with concord grape jam, délice au chocolat et à la menthe, crème brûlée, blackberry panna cotta and cheesecake with raspberry sauce.

Thomas walked through the bar, slipped out the side door and followed a gravel path to the garden behind the restaurant.

Berger answered the phone on the first ring.

CHAPTER

80

Hawker was taking the last bite of the cheesecake with raspberry sauce when Thomas returned to the table. He stood partway, genuflected as if Thomas were the Queen of England and slid the blackberry panna cotta and the crème brûlée toward his plate. "Try both of these. The crème brûlée is wonderful."

Thomas forked a bite of the panna cotta and picked up the check. Hawker patted him on the shoulder. Thomas moved so the man's hand fell away.

"I'm withdrawing from the project," he said.

"You can't mean that!" Hawker gasped.

"No, I do mean it. I don't want to get involved in—"

"You *are* involved!"

"I'll give Maxine the names of some artists you can—"

Hawker cut him off. "Sit down! Let's talk about it."

"There's nothing to talk about." Thomas put the check back in the envelope and offered it to Hawker. Hawker pushed it back. Thomas dropped it on his plate. The paper absorbed the raspberry sauce and turned slowly red as if run through by a sword and bleeding.

"Sit down!" Hawker demanded. The couple at the nearest table turned to look.

"Thanks for dinner." Thomas turned and walked toward the door.

"Thomas!" Hawker's face flushed like the raspberry envelope. He waved at Chu and Sadereck. They left the table.

The Mercedes's headlights swept across a stone wall as Thomas

368

rounded the corner of the building. Chu stood between the rock posts that marked the entrance with her arms folded across her chest. Sadereck waved Thomas to a stop.

"Sorry about that little drama," he apologized, stepping to the passenger side of the open Mercedes. "We told him it was the wrong approach. He never listens. We suggested an exploratory conversation. Hash the whole thing out. Get your ideas. Answer your questions. Make sure you were completely comfortable before we even . . ." He continued with disgust, "Before he started throwing money around like you were the kind of man who could be bought." *Would that have made a difference? No way! Hawker should be shining Dennis Hamilton's shoes.*

"Why don't you come back in and give it another shot? Do it the right way? Hawker is right about one thing—the crème brûlée is to die for."

Thomas was shaking his head before Sadereck finished. "Hawker will obviously do what he wants, but Hamilton is a good man and there is no way I am going to be party to Hawker's—"

Chu cut him off. She was behind Thomas on his side of the car. "Hawker is not a nice man. Fine. He is our client and our job is to make sure he gets what he wants."

"As long as it's legal, of course," Sadereck grinned.

"We understand your reluctance," Chu continued. "The problem is, when Hawker doesn't get his way there are always consequences." If she intended a veiled threat, the dupatta was gossamer thin. Thomas hadn't considered there might be more to it than "I quit."

"I get fired and don't get paid. I got it."

"You've got more to worry about than that." The way Chu said it jammed a rusted spike into his stomach. The light from the lantern hanging over the entrance fell on half her face. The dark side merged with the night. "Your debts. Your enemies from SAVE THE SEALS. Arson!

"Oh, and by the way, the mural at St. Mark's violates a provision in your contract with the museum." He searched her face for some clue as to what she was talking about. "I'm just saying, not getting paid by the museum is the least of your worries." She turned away from the light and became part of the darkness as she walked back to the restaurant. Sadereck shrugged. "Why don't you just come back in and we'll sort it out?"

The Mercedes SLK-350 can accelerate from 0 to 60 in 4.3 seconds. On the loose gravel of the French Laundry Restaurant it took 2.4 seconds longer. Sadereck stumbled back to avoid getting slammed by the fishtailing rear end when Thomas kicked the 350 horses to 5000 RPM. The lawyer was pelted by tiny stones and enveloped in a cloud of dust thicker than the smoke from Hawker's cigar. He was trembling and his face was bleeding.

Michelins screamed when they hit the asphalt, and the car careened left onto Washington.

"You get all that?" Thomas said into the open Parrot microphone.

"Yup. Every word." It was Berger listening in.

"What do you think?"

"You didn't sign the nondisclosure?"

"Hawker ripped it up."

"Perfect! They can cause you some grief, but when push comes to shove and you talk about your thousand-dollar dinner in a deposition, they'll rue the day he ripped it up."

"So we'll be okay?"

"Okay?" Berger laughed. "I've been recording since Hawker pushed the crème brûlée."

"I'm sorry I hit you in the head with a two-by-four."

CHAPTER

81

BERGER TOLD THOMAS TO PUT Hawker out of his mind and ignore the subtle threats from his lawyers. "They're the ones breaking contracts, not you. If they are stupid enough to annoy you after what went on in Napa, well . . ." After the fact Berger wished he had gone to the meeting at French Laundry. *Maybe for the crème brûlée.*

Colt told Berger that Hamilton had a strong case regardless of the recording. "Can't use it, of course, but knowing they're in panic mode is very helpful," Colt said. Berger felt strangely optimistic that his client would eventually end up finishing the museum mural. The engine of optimism needed a quart of irrational lubricant now and again.

Berger knew it was essential to immunize Thomas from Hawker and get the museum project out of his mind. He reassured Thomas that he and Colt would handle everything so he could focus on St. Mark's without looking over his shoulder.

"It's about miracles, so make it miraculous," Berger quipped.

"You believe in miracles, Frank?"

"I believe in you, and I've seen you work miracles, so yeah, maybe I do. Now get your butt back to work!"

• • •

From his earliest days as an artist Thomas had recognized that the joy of creation was the process, not the results. The state of creative consciousness where reality ceased to exist. Once he severed the tentacles that

attached him to the worries of real life and abandoned himself to the process, Thomas was swept away in a euphoric rapture, impossible to explain
to someone who had never been there.

Berger put up the walls, hacked the tentacles in two and nudged
Thomas back into his mystical world. He spent long hours at the canvas
without interruption.

Chastity learned her job with minimal conversation. Thomas did not
talk while he worked. One encroachment and she figured out where the
boundaries were. She complained to Cass that they had worked two days
without a word between them. "He just points," she said.

"We pay more for eccentric," Cass laughed.

"*Eccentric* is a nice way of saying *kooky,*" Chastity grinned. "Of course,
he LOVES to talk to *you.*" Cass's face flushed. "You ever notice he always
stops? Never keeps painting? Wouldn't you hate to be a man and only able
to do one thing at a time?"

For all her woman-to-woman grumbling about Thomas's antisocial
behavior, Chastity had told Cass many times that Thomas was incredible
and she was grateful for the opportunity to work with him. "I learn so
much just watching," she said, "waiting for him to point at me and hope
I understand what he wants. I watch for hours sometimes." She grinned.
"Of course, I don't breathe and I pray my stomach doesn't growl."

"He told me you've been a huge help."

"He said that?"

Cass nodded.

"I could do a lot more for Mr. Da Vinci than block in, clean his
brushes and keep the place from being declared a national disaster area if
he'd let me."

"You call him Da Vinci?"

"Not to his face. I painted it on his boat."

"He might like being called that."

"You try it first, okay?" Chastity paused for a moment. She was suddenly serious. "That's who he would have been, you know."

• • •

Thomas lost track of the days. He measured them by Cass's visits. She came every day. Many days she brought Christina.

The first time Chastity met the injured child, she seemed to take an immediate and personal interest in her. Thomas wasn't sure why it surprised him, but he discovered a side to his apprentice he had not expected. *Why not?* he reasoned. *If she sets my house on fire over a stupid injured seal I should expect her to have empathy for other injured creatures.* Thomas scolded himself for being cynical. A hazy flash. *Cherubim's sword? DOES everything matter?*

"When are you going to put in the children?" Christina demanded again. Every time Christina asked Thomas about the children it became a game that Cass and Chastity found amusing. They were always on Christina's side.

"Soon. Very soon," Thomas said.

"Do you always tell the truth?" she asked, and he pretended to think about it long and hard. Actually, he was pretending to pretend, because he did need a minute to think about how to answer such a question.

"Not always," he finally admitted.

"You don't!" Christina seemed struck by a thunderbolt that left her unable to speak.

"Well, I want to," Thomas reasoned, hoping to help the child recover, "so I thought I should tell the truth, that I don't always tell the truth."

That struck Christina funny and she laughed. "So when are you going to put in the children?"

"When you tell me exactly how to do that." Christina squinted at Thomas. *Did she doubt him?*

"Cross your heart?" she pressed.

"And hope to die."

"Stick a needle in your eye, stab a knife into my thigh, eat a horse—" Thomas cut her off, and regretting that he had confided the way he and Ronny Assenberg used to pledge their lives and sacred honor.

"Shhhhh!" he chuckled.

• • •

Chastity was right. Thomas stopping working the moment Cass came in. Cass had given it no thought until the apprentice brought it up. She was flattered, but decided she needed to minimize her interruptions. On the days she came without Christina she slipped in without notice, watched in silence and left.

Some days she was never discovered. Some days Thomas saw her and they talked. Some days she would leave evidence behind. A sandwich. A Power Bar. A cold Red Bull, which had become a contentious joke between them.

One day she watched without detection, then left a note with a clever verse of admiration and approval:

> *There are strange tales told of the brave and the bold*
> *And the artist who used to draw fiction.*
> *His talent abounds and the word's got around*
> *He can work weeks without any diction.*
> *But silent or loud, under sunshine or cloud,*
> *Sincere or doggone satirical,*
> *For children with ills on crutches and pills,*
> *He's giving them Jesus's miracles.*

Thomas read the note and went looking for Cass.

• • •

Susan Cassidy was not in her office. Jessica was exuberant to see Thomas again. He asked why she hadn't been down to look at the mural. "Oooo," the executive mother laughed, "I'm the one who wrote the 'death to intruders' memo." Thomas assured her she was exempt from being eaten by the lions.

"Is Cass around?"

"I think she's with Christina."

He thanked her and headed out to hunt the pair down.

Christina and Cass were in a room known as the Sun Lounge. It was next to Pediatrics and used for visitors and extended-care patients. The outside wall was mostly windows. The wall separating the room from the main hall was mostly glass. From the nurses' station, Thomas could see Cass and Christina on the divan in the corner by the window.

Christina was cuddled under Cass's arm. Her legs rested on cushions. Her wheelchair was parked so the IV reached her arm without stretching. They were reading from the Bible. The sunlight through the window kissed the tops of their heads and fell on the pages brilliant white. The light bounded onto their faces and chased the shadows away.

Through the glass the woman and child looked like an antique painting. In a curious kind of time warp, a phenomenon he had experienced before but could never quite explain, it was an old master's painting of the daughter of Jairus and her rejoicing mother. Was it only an impression or had the idea come from a still small voice? Thomas took several candid pictures with his iPhone.

It was his turn to watch in silence and slip quietly away.

• • •

Cass came late Thursday night and walked with Thomas to his car. His thoughts were only slowly leaving the leper with whom he'd spent the day. As they exited the building, Cass looped her hand over his arm. Her touch brought him into the moment. It encouraged him, but he realized she was a friend who needed to talk, not a girl looking for a date.

"They're keeping Christina here a while," Cass said.

"They couldn't find her next of kin?"

"We've given up on that, but that's not the reason." Cass paused. "She developed another infection in her hand." They reached the car and Thomas turned to face her even though it meant losing the touch of her arm.

"That can't be good."

Cass shook her head and explained that the child had a resistant infection called MRSA. He looked puzzled, so she quartered the acronym, "Methicillin-resistant *Staphylococcus aureus.*"

"Will she be okay?"

"The initial skin graft didn't hold, so there was no new vasculature penetrating into the skin." Another puzzled look. "No new blood vessels," she clarified, "and without the tissue being vitalized, bacterial infections are hard to contain."

"You sound like a doctor."

"MRSA is a big problem for hospitals and for burn patients especially. A PR nightmare. I've learned a lot about it."

"How serious is it?

"Infections are always dangerous. The doctors are on top of it, of course, and . . . well . . . we pray together every day." *Mother and child in the God rays by the window.*

. . .

The followers of Jesus evolved from ideas to living figures. From black-and-white lines to colorful forms. From spiritual creations to reality.

The family of mannequins from the studio now lived in the Healing Place, adorned with draperies and surrounded by props.

In spite of Jessica's infamous "death to intruders memo," an increasing number of visitors invaded the Healing Place. Some were authorized by Cass; many were not. Eyewitness accounts were swapped in lunchroom prattle, and rumors spread. Sneaking a peak was increasingly enticing for the hospital staff and visitors.

Thomas added "sentinel" to Chastity's other duties. Gatekeeper and protector. For people working in the hospital, getting a glimpse of the mural was worth the risk of Chastity's wrath. The apprentice was not the least bit evenhanded in her enforcement of who got in and who got kicked out. She was as capricious as the doorkeeper of a trendy Ultra Club in the heart of San Francisco's SoMa district.

Thomas didn't always agree with her choices but her reasons seemed thought out, and he was adamant about "control and responsibility." The doctrine was simple: If you made a person responsible, you gave that person control. Thomas was scornful of executives who held underlings responsible for results but gave them no control over the process.

Whoever Chastity let in—visitors, guests or gawkers—they were allowed to look, but she kept them away from Thomas. Thomas seemed oblivious to the parade of curious spectators and Chastity's governance.

He was not. He kept a weather eye on her choices and tuned into her conversations. She countered criticisms, deflected frivolous comments and handled stupidity with brilliance.

If there was a golden key, it was Chastity's assessment of a wanna-look-at-the-mural person's artistic worthiness. She tracked and recorded their comments. She favored those who kept their mouths shut. Those who presumed the role of art critic or asked stupid questions were ejected and branded brain-dead.

Chastity wrote *STUPID QUESTIONS* in giant letters on the whiteboard. Below, she printed out the funniest of them. The "stupidest."

"Are you going to color in the white parts?"

"Why are there so many lines?"

"Why are some of the people bigger than the other ones?"

"Why doesn't the sky have any clouds?"

By the time Kimberly Johnson finished her viewing, seven of the questions were hers. Chastity found her questions so funny she encouraged Kimberly to come back whenever she wanted. Kimberly counted Chastity among her closest friends. Kimberly joined SAVE THE SEALS.

Bradley was impressed by the work. Chastity was impressed by Bradley. Nothing the old doctor asked about came close to her whiteboard of shame.

Cass told Thomas that Miss Von Horn had suggested she give Clinton Carver a personal tour. She suggested a brief rehearsal with Thomas and Chastity. Thomas objected.

"He'll either like it or he won't," Thomas quipped. "Coffee, donuts and good PR can't give the man artistic taste."

"It wouldn't matter if you were Da Vinci," Cass said, "and this were the lost masterwork of *The Battle of Anghiari*. If it isn't his idea, it isn't a good idea."

"So he's the one with the problem, seems to me," Chastity said and Thomas grinned and gave Cass a look that said *so there*.

• • •

On his way out the door from his law office on Montgomery Street, his secretary reminded Carver he was the last member of the hospital board to get the official tour. He arrived with a ninety-pound chip on his shoulder.

Cass and Bradley greeted Carver. The old doc had come to provide moral support. Cass introduced Carver to Chastity, but he mumbled that he had to leave in fifteen minutes and pushed past the barricade to where Thomas was working on the wife of Jairus. The woman in the painting bore a remarkable likeness to what Susan Cassidy would have looked like in 32 c.e.

"So is this what it's going to be, then?" Carver probed. Vast sections of the canvas remained undone.

"Of course it isn't finished," Cass said. Thomas kept working.

Carver raised his voice. "Is what we see more or less what we get, Mr. Hall?" The question had a biting edge to it.

"Not really. Still practicing." Thomas kept working without turning around.

Chastity erased the top line of Stupid Questions and wrote, "Is what we see more or less what we get?" Cass waved at Chastity like a construction worker trying to stop a car on its way to a washed-out bridge and dragged a finger-blade across her throat. In the few beats it took Chastity to realize Carver was somebody important and find the dry eraser, Carver saw what she had written. He stepped to the whiteboard.

"What's this?"

Chastity was halfway through a swipe with the eraser when he stopped her.

"Nothing, it's just something that I—"

"Stupid questions? That people ask?" he asked, getting it in the same moment.

"Yeah, more or less," Chastity said, unintentionally mimicking his idiom.

"That's got to be Kimberly Johnson," he said, pointing to *What if you run out of paint?* Chastity nodded.

"That one too?" Carver asked and read it aloud. "Do they kill the squirrels to make the brushes or only pluck their tails like eyebrows?" He was starting to smile. "May I please withdraw my question?" He was a lawyer addressing the judge after a major faux pas, but laughing out loud.

Then Carver said, loudly enough for Thomas to hear, "What you've accomplished to date is a marvelous indication of what it is you are doing, and I like it very much."

Chastity smiled proudly at Cass, who was breathing again. Thomas turned around. Bradley joined Carver in the laughter. Carver shook Chastity's hand and said, "I'm sorry I missed your name, young lady."

Jessica arrived with coffee and donuts. They took a break. The urgency of Carver's schedule vanished. Cass passed on the coffee and made a cup of herbal tea. Thomas washed down half an apple fritter with a twelve-ounce can of Red Bull and winged his way back to the first century.

• • •

Thomas expanded the role of the apprentice to include creative work on the mural. Not only did Chastity catch the vision of the finished creation, she made it her own.

The following day, a nurse who worked in Pediatrics asked, "Why doesn't Jesus have a face?" Chastity wrote it on the board.

"Not that one," Thomas said. "Fair question."

"He doesn't have a face because you haven't finished," Chastity said to make her point that it qualified as a stupid question.

"Just erase it," Thomas said.

CHAPTER

82

SOFT HANDS COVERED Thomas's eyes from behind. "Guess who?" Cass could sneak up on Thomas in a '56 Ford pickup without a muffler when he was absorbed in his painting and lost in his imaginary world.

Thomas recognized the voice. "Friend or foe?" he teased.

"Hmmm? Friend, I'd say."

"Positive or negative?"

"Very positive."

"Lady Godiva?"

Thomas turned with a mischievous grin as Susan Cassidy's hands fell away. She wasn't alone. Mrs. Benning's face gave away the fact that she had overheard the little flirtation. Cass fired a "bad boy" bullet with a playful scowl.

"This looks wonderful, Tommy." It was Alex. Thomas hadn't seen his father, who was staring at the mural stretching the width of the wall. Mrs. Benning had paid extra for an Oakridge Manor van to drive her and Alex to San Francisco to visit Thomas, see the mural and meet Christina. Thomas introduced Chastity and asked her to give them the grand tour.

Chastity's tour was something to behold. She pointed to her favorite parts, articulated the motifs and explained the visual metaphors with such clarity they could have been her own. She punctuated her narrative with repeated references to "Mr. Hall's vision." Her enthusiasm was contagious.

Thomas and Cass strolled a few steps behind. At each of the miracles, Alex looked back at Thomas and nodded his head with pride.

"Wonderful, just wonderful." He said it over and over. Mrs. Benning's praise was silently reverential.

Thomas was accustomed to adulation. Being idolized normally triggered a pleasurable rush of narcissism affirming his sense of entitlement and destiny. Not today. Their wonder and praise gave him a curious feeling of humility. Privilege. Gratitude.

Mrs. Benning steadied Alex by the arm. Thomas realized how old and fragile his father really was. So much of his life gone. So many years lost. *How sad and selfish that I robbed him of the joy a son can bring. So much simple satisfaction. I've missed what my father could have added to my life.* Remorse shuddered through him.

When they had finished their tour, Cass took Mrs. Benning and Alex to meet Christina. Mrs. Benning explained that she had looked forward to meeting the child since hearing about her from Thomas and Cass the day they visited Oakridge Manor.

Christina had not been to the Healing Place since the latest infection. Thomas had stopped by to see her once when she was asleep, leaving a silly caricature of the duty nurse. The cartoon was taped to the chrome rail at the head of her bed. No wonder the woman glowered when Thomas arrived with the Benning entourage.

Christina sat in a stack of pillows. Her electric bed was cranked all the way up and forward. The violin was on the white sheet next to her thick plaster legs. Her casts were decorated with signatures, notes and colorful doodles. A box of colored Sharpies on the stand next to the water pitcher was a tempting invitation to wannabe taggers.

Cass introduced Christina to her visitors: Chastity, Alex and, saving the best for last, Mrs. Benning. "Mrs. Benning is a musician," Cass said, but before she could surprise the girl with the news that Mrs. Benning played the violin, Christina's eyes brightened.

"Do you play the violin?"

"I do," Mrs. Benning smiled, "and I'm told you are a violinist as well." Christina nodded modestly. "And very good, I understand."

"I was getting better until my accident." Christina smiled with bright optimism. She picked up the instrument with her good hand and held it up by the neck for Mrs. Benning to see. The IV tube drooped in a gentle curve from the liquid in the plastic bag to the needle in her little arm. The dark stains on the violin hurled Thomas's thoughts to his night on the rocks with Officer Evans. *She didn't survive the explosion. She was dead when I carried her from the car.*

"It got sort of ruined." Christina pointed to the crack across the lower bout that ran from the *F* hole to the purfling. "It has a broken string," she shrugged and laid the instrument across her plaster lap. "It used to be really beautiful. It was my mother's."

"It's still beautiful." Mrs. Benning's voice was soft and soothing. Almost musical. " . . . and everything is going to be all right." Christina looked deeply into Mrs. Benning's eyes. A twitch of a smile sealed the unspoken bond between them and the moment was gone.

"Cass helped me tune it," Christina said. The duty nurse frowned at Cass with her well-rehearsed *you should know better* look. Christina reached for the bow. It was on the stand next to the colored Sharpies. Thomas put it in her hand. Half the unbleached hairs of the bow were frayed or broken. He scolded himself for not getting back to Union Music to pick up a case and the Brazilwood bow.

Christina steadied the violin with her bandaged left hand and drew the bow across the strings. It was not a pleasant sound. The child hunched her shoulders playfully and laughed to hide her embarrassment. "I haven't practiced since . . ." She shuddered with the chill of memory. She rolled her injured left hand as if reaching for the strings. There was a tiny twitch in her pinky but her fingers didn't move.

"It's fine, sweetheart." Cass seemed to be searching for the right words of comfort that would not be a total lie. "There's plenty of time, you don't need to—"

"No!" Christina cut her off. "I have to start practicing again so I can play on Christmas Eve when people come to see Mr. Hall's picture of Jesus."

Thomas's gaze moved from the child's face as her words of simple faith tumbled over the clump of her hopelessly ruined hand. A spike went though his heart.

"You better not plan on that, honey!" the duty nurse clucked. "We talked about that, remember?" Christina glared at the woman with disapproval. An awkward pause followed. The child leaned close to Mrs. Benning and spoke quietly.

"She's just saying that because Doctor Namkung told her I won't be able to play anymore." The old woman closed her eyes until there was nothing in the universe but a child whispering her confidence in God. "They don't believe Jesus is going to make my hand better." Then quieter still. "She doesn't go to church, and Dr. Namkung doesn't even believe in Jesus."

Mrs. Benning kissed Christina's forehead. She lifted the violin and nestled it under the child's chin. Christina's hands fell into position. Cass held her breath as if the sound of her lungs might shatter the magic of what was about to happen.

Mrs. Benning slipped her fingers around Christina's ruined hand. She moved the child's fingers with her own until they found their place upon the strings. Slowly. Tenderly. Christina drew the bow across the strings. The sound trembled, but the note was sweet and caused a joyous sense of wonder that was almost tangible. Christina's face brightened with a smile none of them had ever seen. The pallid complexion flushed with a rosy hue and her skin was luminous.

Tears welled up in Cass's eyes. She let them come. When Thomas saw her crying he looked away to quash his own feelings. He stared at his silly cartoon of the duty nurse but the feelings came anyway. He blinked and swiped away the one tear that escaped.

Mrs. Benning guided Christina's fingers. The child tilted the bow and continued the movement over the strings. A new sound blended with the reverberating echo of the first. When *G* repeated itself in the second measure the woman and child became one and *Ode to Joy* filled the room.

The music resonated with the rhythm of Thomas's heart. He felt hypnotized. Entranced. He could not take his eyes off graceful old hands guiding young crippled fingers. *If there is a life beyond death, then surely, however it works and whoever's in charge, God must be smiling and telling Beethoven to have a look.*

The music ended. Chastity clapped her hands. Mrs. Benning acknowledged the young virtuoso with a graceful gesture. Christina grinned and took a little bow. Alex, Cass and Thomas added their applause.

"Will you pray with me?" Christina asked. "I need my hand to get better very soon or I won't be ready to play on Christmas Eve."

"We'd love to pray with you," Cass said. She stood up and offered her hand to Alex. Chastity took his other arm and helped him shuffle from his chair. They gathered around the bed. The duty nurse shook her head, let Cass know she disapproved and slipped quietly into the hall.

"Will you say the prayer, Mr. Hall?" A jolt of epinephrine made Thomas want to run. *I'm such a fraud.* He imagined a circle of aversive stares. It was always about him. He cringed at the thought.

"I'm probably not the best one to . . ." He looked up. No one was looking at him. They were focused on Christina. Thomas Hall was the last thing on anyone's mind.

"Didn't you and God get your stuff worked out?" Christina asked. Her candor was like a mute button on the Thomas Hall remote. The question struck him dumb. Cass put a reassuring hand on his arm. Patted.

"I'll be happy to say the prayer," Cass said, coming to Thomas's rescue. A shaft of sunlight fell through the window and splashed across the bleached white bed. Christina's face was translucent in the strange light. She looked at Cass, then back at Thomas. Her eyes were bright and full of expectation.

"Shall I?" Cass said softly.

"No. It's okay," Thomas said. "There's still a few things, well, a LOT of things, I need to sort out but I'd be honored to say a prayer for you."

Christina's countenance beamed brighter, impossible as that seemed. Thomas used the time it took to glance at each of the faces around the bed to gather his thoughts. He felt exposed. Inadequate. Submissive. He was suddenly desperate for their friendship. If they just liked him, it would be enough. If there *were* a divine being who heard and answered prayers, Thomas knew the only way his words could get out of the room was on the faith of those gathered about the bed.

Thomas reached out his hands the way Silvia Johnson had done. *She believes in God and goes to church so praying the way she prays is probably good.* Cass took Thomas by his left hand. Christina took a hold of his right. Mrs. Benning held the child's hand on the other side. Alex was on her right, Chastity stood between the old man and Cass. The circle was complete.

Christina bowed her head and closed her eyes. Everyone in the circle followed her example except Thomas. He looked heavenward without intending to. Without a reason why. The silent pause between "eyes closed" and "prayer begins" evidently exceeded Christina's interval of expectation. She opened one eye and watched Thomas for a few seconds before he caught her peeking at him. Both of them blushed but for vastly different reasons. Christina mouthed the words, "Close your eyes," then bowed her head in a broad pantomime showing Thomas what to do.

He bowed his head and was about to close his eyes when he felt a gentle squeeze in his left hand. He looked up at Cass. She opened her eyes and gave him a reassuring smile. She closed her eyes again.

"God in heaven," Thomas began. The words sounded hollow and hung in the stillness a foot above his head. He squeezed his eyes tighter and forced the image of the sterile green room from his mind's eye. He struggled through darkness and found God speaking to Eve in Gustave Doré's *Formation of Eve.* He continued as if speaking to the masterfully etched Being of Light.

"Christina is our friend. She asked me to say the words but this prayer is from all of us. She was in an accident and . . ." In his life Thomas had never listened to the sound of his own voice. "She loves to play the violin and needs for her hand to get better. The doctors say that . . ." Cass squeezed his hand again. It wasn't gentle affection. It was a bone crusher that said, *Don't go there.* He changed direction. "In the Bible it says, 'ask and ye shall receive,' so we are asking you. We are *praying* for you to make her hand well again and . . ."

A loud whisper reached him in the darkness of eyes shut tight. "In time to play on Christmas Eve." He opened his eye a slit and caught Christina quickly closing hers.

"In time for her to play her violin on Christmas Eve." Thomas stopped. He opened his eyes. God and the garden were gone. He fought the feeling of foolishness. The others remained in a reverent posture of prayer. Heads down. Eyes closed. He looked at the limp claw of Christina's left hand. He forced the doubt and darkness from his mind and looked up.

"You know I'm not one of your good guys," Thomas started again. Cass opened her eyes. "I don't know you or much about any of this, but I have learned a little about miracles so maybe what we're really doing here is asking for a miracle. Christina told me that faith comes first and then the miracle. Everyone else here has that kind of faith."

"Amen," Mrs. Benning said.

"So please don't keep her hand from getting well just because of me. Thank you."

The loud whisper spoke again. "In the name of Jesus Christ."

"In the name of Jesus Christ," Thomas finished.

"Amen," Christina said and reverent assent was uttered around the circle. Everyone but Thomas opened their eyes and released each other's hands. He squeezed his eyes shut and held on to Cass and Christina. When he finally opened his eyes there were tears on his face.

"Thank you," Christina said.

"No, thank you . . . it was . . . I . . ." In most circumstances Thomas relished attention. Not this time. He felt awkward and embarrassed.

"It's the nicest present anyone could ever give me," she smiled. "Tomorrow is my birthday."

"Happy birthday," Thomas said.

"Not today. Tomorrow," Christina said. Mrs. Benning looked at Cass and smiled.

"So, when are you coming up to help me finish the mural?"

"As soon as you're ready to put in the children."

CHAPTER

83

I T WAS AFTER MIDNIGHT. The work lights were on. Thomas sat on the top of the ladder in the center of the Healing Place. His eyes wandered over the mural. *As soon as you're ready to put in the children.*

The others were gone. Mrs. Benning's invitation to Alex had included a night on the town, with dinner at Paoli's and a room at the Hyatt Regency. As they were leaving, Alex pulled Thomas aside with an awkward blush and whispered, "I'm sure we have separate rooms."

The possibility of a romantic liaison had not occurred to Thomas. He found the confession amusing. *Too bad he couldn't be in love again.* The thought came in a rush of empathy for how lonely his father must be. It had been a long time since Thomas had thought about his mother. He felt a tingling at the nape of his neck and for a moment it was as if she were there. He put his arm around Alex's shoulder and embraced him with the kind of macho hug a fraternity man gives a brother.

"You two have fun," Thomas said. "Behave yourselves." Mrs. Benning took Alex's arm in a little show of mock defiance.

"We're coming back tomorrow for Christina's birthday," she said and touched her lips with a graceful finger to make it a secret. "We might even have a surprise for you," she teased and escorted Alex from the room.

When are you going to put in the children? Christina's question played like the lyric of a country song that gets in your head and refuses to leave. *When are you going to put in the children?* The thought rattled down a chain of associated images. *Children. Christina. The accident. The violin. The hope. The crippled hand. No hope. The music. The prayer. His prayer.* He was at the child's bedside searching for something beyond the acoustical tiles of the ceiling. *What we're really doing here is asking for a miracle.*

. . .

The black water of the harbor reflected orange orbs of light from the mercury vapor lamps that stood like sentinels at the end of the dock. It was after two o'clock by the time Thomas got back to the Fish Cannery. Ever since the arson he had felt a ripple of relief when he turned onto Harbor Drive and saw no flames or ruined buildings.

Thomas got out of his car. A gibbous moon found a hole in the clouds and sent a shimmering slash of silver across the dark water. The beauty of it enticed him to the water's edge. He was weary from long hours at the wall and the relentless pace of the painting as the time to completion grew shorter.

He inhaled the night and closed his eyes. The mural was as vivid in his mind as it was on the wall. His thoughts floated from face to face of those blessed by the miracles of Jesus. Some were friends. Some remained strangers. He came to the unfinished figure of Jesus. Chastity had blocked in a scripture from the Gospel of John, its first letter illuminated like a medieval manuscript: "For God so loved the world, that he gave his only begotten Son, that whosoever believeth in him should not perish, but have everlasting life."

Thomas's mind flooded with the course and conflict that had brought him to this moment. He felt a rush of anguish that spoke in his head as if someone could hear his thoughts. *I'm a pretender. A cowardly agnostic! How foolish. How arrogant to ask for a miracle when I am without faith. How wrong to pray when I don't know who you are or IF you are?* The last thought came with unexpected resentment. Where was his entitlement?

The heavens moved. The light of the moon disappeared and Thomas was left in the gloom. He relished solitude and enjoyed being alone. He often came here at night by himself, but as darkness came he felt a sudden rush of angst and despair. He felt abandoned. Not only alone but cut off, adrift, a vessel with no moorings near a treacherous shore, with no lighthouse or safe harbor. Fear gripped his neck with icy fingers.

He thought of Christina. His promises and prayers. The child's bright hope hung from his conscience like a sack of stones. Shadows of the night came in on a chill wind and troubled the waters. His voice was barely a whisper.

"God? If there is a God, and you can in reality somehow hear our prayers . . ." *Our thoughts.* "If you are ever willing to listen to people like me . . ." He felt vulnerable. In peril. He looked up from the harbor as if the turmoil of the black water were the source of the danger. The moon was a soft halo behind the clouds. "If you are there, please look past my doubts for Christina's sake." *Please make yourself known unto me.* His final silent thought.

The cloud slipped away and a glimmer of cold light splayed out like a silver path to heaven. Thomas didn't see. His eyes were cast downward and he slumped in a pitiful heap.

CHAPTER

84

THE MAN HUDDLED IN THE cleft of a rock and stared at the loaves of bread and fishes passed among the multitude. Thomas darkened his face and turned the robe to a muted chamoisee. The color of goat. The man was a sullen shape in the shadows of the stones.

"Have you been here all night?" It was a few minutes after eight A.M. and Chastity was surprised to see Thomas already at work on the mural. He glanced up and shook his head without losing focus on the figure emerging from the whiskers of his brush.

The man slumped in a pitiful heap by an outcrop of rock between the blind man washing in the pool of Siloam and the multitude. A gaunt and hungry stranger. Suspicious and unwilling to partake of the gifts freely given. Barley loaves and frying fishes.

Chastity persisted. "When did you come in?" The girl's artistic talent was eclipsed by her calloused candor. "You look awful!" *Vanity of vanities, all is vanity.* One of Berger's curious catchphrases bubbled as Thomas ran a finger comb through his hair and stroked his unshaven chin as if it were a well-trimmed beard. *Why do I care what Chastity thinks of the way I look?*

"Couldn't sleep," he shrugged.

Thomas wasn't sure how long he'd stayed at the water's edge or when he had finally gone to bed. It was a short and fitful sleep. He had awakened and driven back to the city.

"Are you okay?"

In the trice it took to nod, "I'm good," the blizzard of questions that had chilled him with an icy grip the night before inquired of him again.

Do we survive the death of our brains? Did you and that chipmunk come from the same single cell? Will you pray for me? Do you believe in Jesus? Do you believe I can play the violin again? Is there such a thing as miracles?

The faceless figure in the center of the canvas waited patiently for Thomas to find the answers, and time was running out.

"I'm good. Fine." Thomas stood up and twisted away a kink between his shoulders. "Find Cass and see if she knows when my dad and Mrs. Benning are coming."

85

HOW MANY TIMES DO you want me to say it?" Namkung asked impatiently. "She will never play the violin."

"I'm sorry to be such a bother, but it just seems to me, Doctor . . . ?" Mrs. Benning paused.

"Namkung!"

"Oh yes, of course. I'm sorry. I have a difficult time remembering names these days. You're a doctor so you know about 'senior moments.'"

"It's normal. I wouldn't worry about it if I was you."

"Namkung. I won't forget."

"Is that it, then?" Doctor Namkung frowned at Cass to make sure she knew he blamed her for Benning's inquisition.

After meeting Christina, Mrs. Benning had asked to speak with the doctor. Cass found Dr. Namkung with a cup of coffee and a pile of patient charts chatting with the duty nurse in the doctor's lounge. Alex watched the confrontation between Mrs. Benning and Dr. Namkung with the same angst he felt when the San Francisco Forty-Niners played the Dallas Cowboys.

"May I ask you one more question?" Mrs. Benning smiled. Namkung folded his arms across his perfectly starched lab coat, inhaled slowly and twisted his face to a scowl. "You said she has lost the use of her fingers." Namkung nodded silently. "Is it never possible in a case like Christina's that the fingers might—"

"Never!" He cut her off.

"If it is an issue of cost, or an expensive special procedure that—"

"Hold up your hand!" His impatience spilled over. Mrs. Benning lifted her left hand with such grace Cass was sure she was cradling an invisible violin. Sweet music, if only imagined, would have been a welcome reprise from the vocal tension.

Mrs. Benning's slender fingers, blue veins, bones and tendons became a hand in a tissue-thin wrap of translucent skin. Namkung used it to illustrate his impatient explanation.

"There are two main nerves that control the palmar surface of the fingers." He drew a line down the pinky side of Benning's palm with a hand-crafted Mont Blanc ballpoint pen. Cass's instinct for public relations made her cringe.

"The ulnar nerve controls sensations on the ring and little fingers." Namkung went on. "The median nerve controls sensation in the rest: thumb, index and middle fingers." He tapped each of Mrs. Benning's long, graceful fingers, then traced the median nerve down the center of her wrist in a line of blue-black ink. He pivoted her hand like a plastic prop on a spindle and traced a finger over the back of it. Ridges of tendons and bulging blue veins made it too bumpy for a drive with the ballpoint.

"The radial nerve, here on the other side, controls sensation on the back of the hand, along with wrist and finger extension." He twirled it back. "Every nerve is critical, of course, but if the ulnar or median nerves are compromised," he tapped the lines with his Mont Blanc, "never mind the violin, the girl is not going to pick up a spoon!"

"Isn't there some possibility that—"

Namkung stopped her short. "When they opened the transverse carpal ligament the median nerve was gone. There was nothing left of the ulnar but a few threads of nerve fiber. If it were just the nerves she had lost, I might say that *maybe,* in several years, she may gain some function, but the flexor digitorum superficialis and flexor digitorum profundus were also badly compromised."

"Flexor digitorum and . . . ?"

"The flexor muscles that control movement of the fingers."

"But over time . . ."

"What you don't appreciate is that anywhere else they would have amputated her hand and half her arm. Dr. Durant found that unacceptable and did everything possible to save it. The bad news is, she'll never play again. The good news is, she still has a hand!" Namkung took a long draught of coffee to punctuate the end of the lecture.

"Thank you. We appreciate all you've done."

"You're going to see her now?"

"I bought her a new violin."

Namkung shook his head. "You're not doing her any favors giving her false hope. The sooner she accepts her limitations and begins to deal with them, the sooner she will become functional."

"You don't believe in hope?"

"I don't believe in miracles."

CHAPTER

86

THOMAS DIDN'T HEAR THEM COME IN. He was still in the shadows with the man who hungered for bread but would not eat. There was nothing subtle in the symbolism. Nothing graceful in the tortured posture. Nothing hopeful in raw umber hues darkened with Payne's gray. *Does the haunted face reveal the artist's gnawing ambivalence? Does the man huddled in the crevice of the rock betray the artist, or does the artist's empathy allow the allegory to deepen his own torment? Can you keep the artist from the art?* Perpetually puzzling questions. Lack of sleep twisted everything.

"Hi, Mr. Hall!" Christina's joyful burst of enthusiasm shattered the darkness like an explosive beam of sunlight. Thomas knew it was her even before he turned around. "We came to help you put in the children."

Cass pushed Christina forward in her wheelchair. Her legs protruded from her waist like a plaster battering ram. The colorful casts, covered with doodles, designs and well-wishes, rested on metal supports wrapped in lambskin. A dozen birthday balloons filled with helium and tied by long strings to the brace made it a parade. Mrs. Benning walked beside her with one hand on the chair and the other looped through Alex's arm. They had not come alone.

Christina's retinue was followed by a passel of children from the Pediatrics wing. A wondrous menagerie of children were entering the Healing Place. They were ushered, trundled, pushed and paraded by every nurse and orderly Thomas had seen and several he had not. They came in wheelchairs, on crutches, walking by themselves or helped by the staff. Chastity held hands with a child on either side. When she caught Thomas's eye she shrugged an innocent smile.

One little girl was carried in the arms of an orderly. There was a young boy with pallid skin whose hair had fallen out. Some of the youngsters were attached to IVs. Others to monitors. The bottles, bandages, dressings, casts, slings, braces and appliances were like pages from a medical school textbook documenting childhood injuries and ailments. All the children were in the white gowns or pastel pajamas of St. Mark's. They glowed in the sunlight streaming through the wall of glass. Thomas was struck by a singular thought: *They are angels.*

It was a grand field day for the children of St. Mark's. Thomas knew Cass was in cahoots with Christina and Mrs. Benning even before he saw the mischievous smiles on their face. He ran his finger-comb again and wished he'd shaved and changed his clothes.

"Wow!" It was all he could say as the end of the parade joined the crowd of children surrounding Christina and staring at the mural.

"I cleared it with Berger," Cass teased.

Berger was invisible when he did his job right. Except for a couple of phone calls—one with the date of a hearing on the complaint filed by SAVE THE SEALS and the other to report "no rumblings from Hawker"—Thomas and Berger had hardly spoken.

Christina rolled close to Thomas. "I told everybody about what a good job you were doing," she confided, "and they were jealous because I got to come here all the time. Some of them won't be here at Christmas so I hope it's okay that I invited them."

Thomas caught himself staring at the bald-headed boy. At Christina's worry, *Some of them won't be here at Christmas,* a wave of sorrow passed through him. *It's not likely the meaning she intended, but not all of them will be going home.* The thought struck him deeply. Lack of sleep drags a person to the edge of his emotions. Tenderizes hearts. Strips pretense.

"It's okay," Thomas said, releasing a breath he'd held too long. "You're welcome here. Really. I'm glad you've come." He glanced at Cass. She always looked good. With a halo of sunlight and surrounded by a host of angelic children, her beauty was transcendent. They held each other's eyes for a moment. "If you have any questions, I'll be happy to answer them."

"How come you haven't painted Jesus?" a little girl with a bandaged eye and residual stain from surgery raised her hand and asked at the same time.

"He's saving Jesus until last," Christina said and glanced at Thomas with a glint of suspicion that said, *I rescued you, and you better not let me down.*

"First the worst, second the same, last the best of all the game," a chubby boy on crutches intoned. Most of the children laughed.

"Jesus is the most important and takes the longest," Christina confirmed.

Thomas thought about the long, dark night. *Waiting for a sign from God.* He thought about Jesus. Not the Jesus in heaven. The Jesus still missing from the mural. He tried to envision an imposing, impressive, distinctive, unique and original *Jesus of Thomas Hall.* In the sleepless hours something had begun to change. Weary and worried, he had rolled out of bed. *I don't expect a sign. I'm embarrassed I asked, but if you're there and if you're willing and if it matters . . . Show me how to paint Jesus.*

"I told them about the children," Christina smiled. "You need models. Right?"

She was right—not only about the models but about how including children magnified the consequences of the miracles. He blocked in nine children to the miracle of bread and fishes. They brought life and pathos. Innocence and joy.

He sketched a boy hiding near the entrance of Lazarus's tomb. He read the story again in the Gospel of John. There was no mention of a child but there was something about Gustave Doré's illustration, *Resurrection of Lazarus,* that put an idea into his head. *Lazarus was a father. The anxious child, hiding and striving to see into the tomb of his father was the oldest son, who had followed his aunt and the man called Jesus to the tomb. There with hope. There to see his father alive again.*

It was only much later that Thomas would understand why, next to the Christ himself, the son of Lazarus was Christina's most cherished creation. Cass wheeled the child closer to the canvas so she could study the sketches. Thomas felt a twinge of anxiety. *Why is what this child thinks of me so all-fired important?* he mused. Christina nodded her approval and turned her attention to her grander purpose.

With help from Cass, Chastity and Mrs. Benning, Thomas posed and photographed every child. Some were little superstars. Most gave what they could. A few only giggled.

Christina took it seriously. Thomas asked for her opinion on every setup. She twisted her face when she concentrated. "What do you think?" she would say, answering his question with a question. Thomas would suggest, the child would agree and the result was her idea. Christina was Queen for a Day.

It was noon by the time Christina and Cass posed the last of the youngsters. It was the boy with no hair. "Zack's got leukemia," Christina announced loudly enough for everyone to hear. Her voice echoed in the dome of the Healing Place. Thomas wanted to protect him, but Zack grinned like leukemia was something every kid wanted and having it was like winning an Olympic medal.

"I'm gonna beat it!" Zack said.

"We pray together all the time," Christina explained. "We're having a race to see who gets better first." And then in case Thomas wondered how she knew, she added, "He's got way more faith than me so winner gets five dollars!"

Thomas dug a twenty-dollar bill from his pocket. "Let's make it twenty." A surge of optimism surprised him. It was a joyous swelling. For an instant he knew they'd both be okay. *Please make yourself known unto me.* The thought was a whisper far away.

CHAPTER

87

WHEN THE PHOTOGRAPHS were finished, Thomas expected the nurses to gather the children and head back to Pediatrics. A quick look at Cass and Mrs. Benning made it clear the event was not over.

Mrs. Benning spoke to the gathering of young patients. "As some of you know, today is Christina's birthday." Thomas had forgotten. "She wanted to have a birthday cake and ice cream, but your doctors said, 'Don't you dare give our patients that awful stuff.' The children twittered at the thought of ignoring doctors' orders. "So instead she wanted to give you each a little gift." Mrs. Benning winked at Christina, who blushed slightly.

An orderly placed three large, lumpy bags next to Alex, who was sitting in a chair nearby. "This is Mr. Hall, the artist's father," Mrs. Benning said. Alex waved his cane and grinned without getting up.

"Call me Alex," he said.

"Christina asked . . . *Alex* to pass them out to you, so gather around." The menagerie swirled forward until each had found a place on Alex's lap, at his side, over his shoulder or spread out on the marble floor around his feet.

"Aren't we going to sing Happy Birthday?" It was Zack, the boy with the Olympic medal for faith. It was the son of Lazarus gazing with wonder as Mary and Martha unloosed the shroud from off his father's face.

"That's such a wonderful idea," Mrs. Benning said. She opened the black leather case she had carried into the room. Children craned their necks to see what it was. She snapped the hinges made of burnished brass.

Nurses and orderlies shuffled for a better view. Cass pushed Christina forward.

Mrs. Benning took out a hand-crafted violin. Musicians share a peculiar kinship and Christina smiled at the wink she got from the elegant woman preparing to play the magnificent instrument. "Perhaps you'll lead us, Susan," Mrs. Benning said.

Cass picked up a paintbrush and raised it small end up as if the kids were the Mormon Tabernacle Choir. She stretched the moment. Children squirmed and giggled with delight. The baton with its wet tail of Russian squirrel hair came down. The music began. Mrs. Benning played a few measures of a jaunty classical concerto as a prelude to the well-known Happy Birthday song. Cass gave the sign and the chorus began.

"Happy birthday to you. Happy birthday to you." The children belted the familiar words at the top of their voices. Thomas sang often with Toby Keith in 5.1 surround so joining the angel choir was easy for him.

Thomas had no memory of birthday celebrations as a kid. He looked at Alex. The old man laughed as he sang. It was the father he had never known. He pushed the past away and relished the moment as if something missing had found its place. *It is never too late to be what you might have been.* George Eliot's pithy wisdom bubbled up without a beckon.

"Happy birthday, dear Christina, Happy birthday to you."

"And many more . . ." Thomas added in his Toby Keith persona without the violin to sweeten his raspy voice. He hung onto the E-flat under *more* for so long, Mrs. Benning came back with a burst of down-home fiddling that might have been Charlie Daniels dueling with the devil.

The children squealed with delight. Nurses and orderlies clapped their hands. Christina blushed and whispered, "Thank you. Thanks, you guys. Thank you." Thomas saw her brush a tear from the outside edge of an eye before anyone else could see.

"Are you ready for your presents?" Mrs. Benning asked the children.

"Yeeeessssss" was a chorus even bigger than "Happy Birthday to You."

"We have a present for Christina. Shall we do that first?" she asked as she walked to the wheelchair and stood in front of Christina hiding something behind her back.

Another wave of "yeesses" included an undercurrent of curiosity. "What is it? What did they get her?" Zack whispered to Thomas. "I shoulda bought her a present."

"Me too," Thomas confided and they punched knuckle bones.

Christina looked up at Mrs. Benning with surprise. Mrs. Benning's hands appeared from hiding. The magnificent violin floated on the tips of her long fingers. She laid it on Christina's lap. Gasps of amazement inhaled the room into breathless silence. Christina stared at the instrument in disbelief. Mrs. Benning leaned down and kissed her gently on the forehead.

"I thought we should frame your mother's violin so you will always have it," she confided softly, "and this old thing, well . . . you can play it until the strings fall off."

"What's wrong with that woman?" The question was a harsh half whisper in Cass's ear. "Didn't she hear a thing Doctor Namkung said?" It was the duty nurse. "She may think she's doing the child a favor with all this violin nonsense, but that child will end up in therapy because of it. It's pathetic. Mark my words." Before Cass could respond, the woman pushed past and barked at the staff: "Okay, everybody, time to get the sick folks back to bed!"

Cass upstaged the woman before anybody moved. "Not until we pass out the presents for our young models, though. Right?" The staff just clapped and no one moved. The duty nurse scowled at Cass.

"Get it done and get them back!" She stomped from the room, muttering as she passed Cass, "Picking a fight with Doctor Namkung is a big mistake!"

• • •

Alex put his hand into the lumpy bag. "Oh, my!" He dropped his jaw, stretched his eyes wide and gasped. "What's this?" he exclaimed as if he clasped the Holy Grail. Children squirmed and giggled with anticipation. This was a man Thomas didn't know. He picked up his camera, switched to the 70–300 zoom and drifted to the back of the gathering.

Alex pulled the first of the gifts from the bag. A stuffed elephant, fluffy pink, the color of amaranth flowers, with a royal purple bow around its neck. There was a flutter of outstretched hands. He handed it to the little girl with a bandage over her eye. She squealed with delight and hugged it to her with both hands.

Mrs. Benning had brought enough stuffed animals, fluffy toys and Puffalumps to fill Noah's Ark. Each child ended up with two or more. Alex made a production out of giving them away: digging in the bag, discovering a treasure, looking surprised and, just before the kids burst with anticipation, pulling out a fuzzy, furry, funny something like a magician popping rabbits from a hat.

Thomas framed the moment on the ground glass of the SLR and clicked off half a dozen shots.

Alex handed the gifts to the children one by one. Thomas continued taking pictures. Mostly close-ups. He crossed to the other side and moved back to include the group at 70 mm. He selected an angle between two orderlies that blurred the edges and gave the scene a sense of both isolation and intimacy. The light changed as an early fog enveloped St. Mark's and softened the sunlight coming through the windows.

Thomas held the camera at his eye and depressed the shutter release button halfway to trigger autofocus. Fuzzy shapes took form. The image on the ground glass was Alex and the patients of St. Mark's . . . in his mind's eye the picture was Jesus blessing the children. The SLR buzzed as it captured the burst of images at 3 frames per second. His sense of the people and things around him merged with the fuzzy darkness at the edge of his frame until the only reality was the surrealistic transformation taking place through his lens.

It was as if the memory of Gustave Doré's etching of Jesus blessing the children had fused into the reality of his father bestowing gifts on the youngsters of St. Mark's. The similarity in composition was startling. The postures and positions were confounding. Jesus of Nazareth. Alex of Oakridge. The children of Jerusalem. The children of St. Mark's. Disciples looking on. Orderlies standing by. Mothers with their little ones. The nurses, Cass and Mrs. Benning.

Thomas could not disjoin the images of his eyes from the perceptions of his mind. Time moved in a different dimension. An errant shaft of sunlight pierced the ashen grey and Alex was a silhouette. Young again. *Lacy leaves and sunshine. A summer together. Sparkling water. His mother was laughing. His father wore a beard. A long and winding road beneath a canopy of orange and yellow-gold.* Memories of a happy time invaded the space.

Alex gave away the last Puffalump, a big soft bear made from parachute silk. He gave it to Chastity. She cried.

Suffer the little children to come unto me, and forbid them not: for of such is the kingdom of God. That was the Jesus he wanted. That was the missing part of the mural. That was the promise and assurance of the Healing Place.

Thomas was surprised he had remembered the passage from the Gospel of Mark. Some other part of him was taking control. A part of him he hardly knew swelled up inside and took his breath away. It burned. It brought joy. It frightened him. His inner sense of self. What was happening?

Thomas could not describe the experience but it was not a flight of fantasy into the place where he went to find creatures and creations of imagination. This was real. His inner self, the part of him that wouldn't die, the part of him he knew standing there in the middle of the Healing Place would survive the death of his brain, told him this Jesus whom he presumed to paint was more than the man history allowed him to be. He was God, and condescending to the flesh, the Son of Man and Son of God.

The man blessing the children with his gifts lifted a little girl to his lap. She had braces on her legs. He brushed a strand of white hair from her face. More light. Changing now. Celestial fire. Burning bush. Brighter than the noonday sun.

Thomas saw it clearly. The images and ideas washed over him and crashed like raging waves upon a rocky headland, and for a fleeting instant he envisioned the face of God made man. He was starting to imagine the face of Jesus and it was not the face he had expected to see.

CHAPTER

88

THOMAS WAS ASLEEP ON THE floor when Cass came into the Healing Place the Friday after Thanksgiving. He was curled on his side with a cushion of folded plastic between his knees. His jacket doubled as blanket and his pillow was the leather Bible with the illustrations of Gustave Doré.

Learning the truth by osmosis, Cass mused. When she was in fourth grade, Leora Hardy, a really smart sixth grader with thick glasses, had told her that her brain could absorb information from a book if she slept with it under her pillow. Cass put her math book in her pillowcase and slept with it for a week. She got a kink in her neck and a B instead of a C. The brain was a mystery.

From the number of empty Red Bull cans tossed toward the garbage can, Cass assumed Thomas had intended a quick nap, not hibernation. He had only hit a couple of two-pointers; most of the cans lay crumpled on the floor.

He wore the same clothes he always wore. His face was grizzled and unshaved, his hair tousled. *He looks soooo good with his hair messed and wild,* Cass thought. She reprimanded herself for being shallow but kept looking at him anyway. *For an artistic guy, he is rather more of a hunk.* She allowed another shallow observation. *Shall I wake him up or let him sleep?* she wondered. *He has to be exhausted.* She decided to let him sleep and walked over to look at the mural.

It was more than empty cans, unchanged clothes and a grizzled face that made it obvious Thomas had been working around the clock. What he had accomplished in the sixty-four hours since Cass had headed home for the holiday was astounding.

On Tuesday evening the center of the canvas had been mostly blank. The central figure was a swirl of lines and the only indication of motif was the word *JESUS* printed in large block letters. Chastity had made of it an archaic illuminated icon.

Cass looked at the new image with reverent awe. Thomas had created a scene of Jesus blessing the children. It was magnificent in scale but modest in its depiction of Jesus. Common people were gathered. Seventeen children. Nine mothers. Five infants in arms and three disciples. It was unlike any painting of Jesus blessing the children Cass had ever seen. Bolder than Bloch. More daring than Doré.

Christina had been right. What finer moment in the life of Christ in a Healing Place for children than Jesus blessing the children? Cass studied the characters and composition. No matter where her eye began, the flow of the lines, the contrast of the light and the movement of the figures brought her back to the face of the Savior.

The face was still unfinished. It was sketched and perfectly proportioned but abandoned and postponed. Christina had asked Thomas about Jesus the first time she came. Cass remembered his answer. *I need to know the people who knew him before I can know him.* The people who knew Jesus were mostly finished. They inhabited the miracles that stretched away on either side. Thomas had imagined them and brought them to life. Surely he knew them. It could no longer be the reason. Cass wondered what was still holding him back. Curled up at the bottom of the painting, Thomas made her imagine he had exhausted himself in his frantic search for the face of Jesus and finally collapsed.

She stood a long time studying the masterful artwork. Thomas Hall had returned to the touchstone of his true brilliance. She wept. She experienced a clarity she had not enjoyed in a long time. She looked down at the artist and considered his influence in her life. She kissed Thomas on the cheek. Softly enough that he not awaken. Strongly enough to be in his dreams. She left him a note and slipped quietly away.

89

MISS VON HORN CAME TO SEE the mural on Sunday. At the scene of Jesus blessing the children, she removed her glasses and dabbed at her eyes with a quivering hand.

"I'm still working on Jesus," Thomas said. "He's not . . . not right." Color and detail had been added but the face remained unfinished. The man with the children looked somewhat like the Jesus of Carl Bloch confronting the rich young ruler, but not the Jesus Thomas knew was *there* but could not quite see. The Jesus he longed to see was hidden as it were behind a gossamer veil in his mind. Present, but obscured. Near, but uncertain. Willing and at hand, knowable, but unknown.

Miss Von Horn nodded as if she might agree but was satisfied it was going to be all right. She motioned for Thomas to help her stand and gave him a long embrace. In spite of all the dabbing and wiping there were still tears in her eyes. "You know what this is?" Her voice trembled in a coarse whisper. Her hand wavered toward the mural.

What is her real question? What is it she wants me to say? "I hope it's the mural you imagined. When I'm finished, of course," he added and looked to Cass for a clue.

Miss Von Horn shook her head. "It is the divine confirmation of your own inspiration. This is what the Lord wanted you to do. He gave you your talent so you could honor him and that is what you've done." She clutched his hands with both of hers. "Thank you, Mr. Hall. Thank you for having the courage to believe beyond your doubts."

"Your approval means a great deal to me."

"It is not my approval that matters." She glanced heavenward with a twinkling smile. "I suspect He is also pleased."

The thought struck like a bolt of lightning. *He is also pleased.* Second-guessing a client's tastes was worse than painting by the numbers, but the expectation of the person writing the checks was an inescapable agony of commercial art. Of all the people Thomas had tried to second-guess in the creation of the mural for St. Mark's, Jesus had never been one of them.

"Assuming you finish Jesus the way you should," Miss Von Horn smiled as she clutched his hands and lowered herself to the wheelchair. "Remember your evil dragons?" She scolded him with smiling eyes. "'Spewing sickness from their noses'?"

"I do," he smiled.

"All those children with clubs on their way to the castle." She laughed in a way that made the original idea sound significantly more ludicrous than it was. Thomas and Cass also laughed.

He stood in front of the mural with his arms crossed for half an hour after Cass had rolled Miss Von Horn away. *Is Jesus really pleased? Does he even know about this?* He glanced in the direction they'd gone and wondered how the old woman could possibly know that Jesus was pleased.

He turned back and saw the unfinished face of Jesus. He was waiting.

90

THE CHRISTMAS TREE WAS SIXTEEN feet tall. Thomas helped Loki and his helpers carry it from the truck to the dome of the Healing Place. He felt a tingle of déjà vu. For him the odd sensation that he had experienced this before was a flash of memory. *A sixteen-foot statue of Darwin placed under the dome at the Pacific Science Museum.*

It felt like another lifetime. The dissimilarity between a bronze statue and a coniferous tree was a puzzling precipitate for déjà vu. Then the connection struck him and the tingle became a shudder. *The semblance was not in the objects but in the opposing ideology each symbolized.*

The Christmas tree was a symbol of Christ, creation and everlasting life. The statue of Darwin was a symbol of godlessness, evolution and the dismal doctrine of oblivion in death.

• • •

The Children's Wing was completed. The opening was nine days away. Rumors about the mural had begun to circulate. Internet blogs, snippets on the news and even Jon Carroll's column in the *San Francisco Chronicle* sprinkled out a few juicy tidbits of both fact and fiction.

Biggest mural ever painted.

Took a dozen artists more than twelve months.

Jesus like no one has ever seen him.

Fantasy art with dragons and children warriors.

Spectacular.

The new showpiece of the San Francisco art community.

The most disconcerting statement was, "The same guy painting the evolution of man at the Science Museum is painting Jesus and the miracles."

The Healing Place had been off-limits to everyone since the day Cass had brought Miss Von Horn to see Jesus blessing the children. The venerable matron and Cass had agreed together to keep the crowning scene of the Savior a secret until the opening on Christmas Eve. Miss Von Horn said people should experience the rush of wonder and awe she had felt when she first saw it. She sent one of her inimitable memos to Clinton Carver and her wish was granted.

Chastity's apprenticeship was over. She stayed around to watch the completion with Thomas's blessing. Finishing touches were mystical. An accent of light. *Unfathomable!* A warm reflection in a cold shadow. *Astounding!* A tiny highlight in a human eye. *Transcendental!* She strained her senses to see the way he saw. It was not about training or technique, devotion or even persistence. Diligence and desire could carry one only so far. Thomas's "gift" was something more. Chastity had her own list of nouns to describe it. *Hypervision. Second sight. Instinct. Imagination. Intuition. Inspiration.* Toward the end she added *revelation.*

In a conversation with Cass, Chastity confessed her deep faith in Jesus and what working on the mural had meant to her. She said some things Cass would not soon forget. "I believe," Chastity said, "artistic gifts are innate to the part of us that is eternal, the part of us that lived before and will continue. They are spiritual gifts and not of this world." Chastity concluded that Thomas Hall's talent was his special gift from God. "His divine appointment," she told Cass. She prayed on her knees that night that she might discover the promise of her own appointment.

• • •

Mrs. Benning came to the hospital every day during December. At least it seemed like every day. She spent long hours with Christina in the expensive private room she had arranged and paid for.

Alex's health was in decline and he came with her only twice. Both times he spent the day watching Thomas while Mrs. Benning kept her private rendezvous with Christina.

Alex's weakening condition was worrisome. Thomas was grateful the money from the St. Mark's project made it possible to afford twenty-four-hour care for his father and the best amenities Oakridge Manor had to offer. He had shocked Berger with the call saying he had sold the boat and wanted to know how much he still owed on the Mercedes.

There was a feeling of urgency. An intuitive sense. A premonition? Whatever it was, Thomas promised his dad they were going to spend some serious time together the moment he finished the mural. They talked about doing some of the things dads and sons do that they had never done. They made a list.

Get perfect tickets to a Giants game and scream at the umpire.

Pan for gold on the American River.

Go fishing for bluegill and black bass in some backwater slough in the Delta.

Go to Disneyland and ride Space Mountain until one of them threw up. That was Alex's addition and he laughed when Thomas confessed he hated roller coasters and *always* threw up.

There was of course an unspoken condition to all of their fanciful plans: *If I'm alive and well enough to go.*

"Whatever happens," Alex promised, "I am coming to the unveiling of your mural, even if Mrs. Benning has to drug me and smuggle me out in one of her giant handbags."

Mrs. Benning's collection of handbags was legend. She had one with her every time she came and was always toting something wonderful, not only for Christina but for other youngsters who came and went in the endless parade of the sick and wounded children. Most of the bags were almost big enough for Alex's purpose.

Cass was gobbled up with finishing details and preparing for the opening. She looked in on Christina every day but was relieved that Mrs. Benning had become a sort of second mom. Neither Cass nor Jessica had sorted out the exact arrangement Mrs. Benning had made with the hospital to prolong Christina's stay and keep her from the ruinous clutches of the California Child Protective Services. Cass was certain Miss Von Horn was involved. The day Cass introduced her to Mrs. Benning they spent the entire afternoon together and had since become close friends.

A horde of government do-gooders from the California Department of Social Services had swarmed Carver's office when the hospital was unable to locate Christina's next of kin, or anyone related to the "orphaned child in B-112." Cass had petitioned to become the child's legal guardian shortly after she had signed the hospital papers making her the responsible financial party, but the legality of that was still in question. She finally told Thomas. He talked to Berger and Berger called Darrin Colt. "Not to worry," Colt had promised, but there was too much at stake not to worry.

The incursion of CDSS meant Christina was headed for a foster home unless Colt prevailed. There were marvelous men and women in the system who provided loving foster homes and honestly cared about the children. There was also a prowl of charlatans who took the taxpayers' $335 a month per kid, overcrowded their houses and skewed the system to their own advantage rather than nurture high-risk children in real need. Cass was sickened by the thought that Christina might end up a victim of a system that allowed such deplorable circumstances by the bad luck of the draw.

The woman from Child Protective Services wore men's clothes. Her name was Angela Russell, but she was the antithesis of *angelic*, the kind of person one would hope not to find in a program to help children. The woman acted more like the witch who wanted to eat Hansel and Gretel than the fairy godmother who wanted to help Cinderella live happily ever after. *Bureaucrats! Maddening! Angela! Such irony in the world,* Cass thought every time she had to endure the horrible woman.

· · ·

Chastity volunteered to help Cass decorate the Healing Place for the opening. Creativity is rarely confined to a single expression, and Chastity brought a splendor to everything she touched. Mrs. Benning was so impressed that she brought in the collection of Christmas ornaments she had accumulated over sixty years. Chastity persuaded Cass to buy three more

Silver Tip pines so she would have a place for every piece. Chastity gave each tree its own expression of a Christmas tradition. One depicted an old-fashioned Christmas with antique ornaments and toys. Another tree was resplendent in crystal and gold. Burgundy bulbs and pink silk ribbons covered a third tree. The final tree was adorned with angel ornaments in every imaginable expression and crowned by a cluster of stars and a choir of angels.

CHAPTER

91

CHRISTMAS EVE.

The celebration of the new Children's Wing was scheduled to begin at six o'clock. Chastity had transformed the Healing Place into a Christmas wonderland without diminishing the elegance of the hall.

Members of the press began arriving around four o'clock. Reporters and photographers hoping for a sneak preview of the mysterious mural were chagrined to discover that it was hidden behind a blue velvet curtain running the length of the wall. Rumors were bandied about. In spite of the perfervid plea from KPIX-TV newswoman Lisa Newman, Cass refused to allow anyone to shoot B-roll before the unveiling. Aki Loki stood guard with two of his friends. Both Polynesian. Both as big as Loki. There was one other enormous disappointment to the news junkies: Miss Von Horn had told Clinton Carver there would be no cocktail hour.

"Have you talked to Thomas?" Cass asked. Chastity was adding ornaments to the garland around the podium.

"He's not here?" It was not her job to keep track of Thomas, but Chastity's tone suggested that the question dismayed her.

"I haven't seen him since last night," Cass said. "He started in again on Jesus' face. 'Final touches,' he said, but it was still not finished when . . ." Worry for Thomas eclipsed her concern for the opening.

"What time did you leave?"

"A little after nine."

• • •

The celebration was by invitation only. Black tie. RSVP. The first of the guests arrived at five thirty.

From the outside it looked as if St. Mark's Hospital were holding a movie premier for a Ridley Scott blockbuster. The effect was Chastity's idea. A pair of rented searchlights sent long, foggy columns sweeping through the night. A red carpet ran from the curb to the double doors of the main entrance. Members of the board welcomed guests and directed them to the new wing. Kimberly Johnson wore a dress guaranteed to make "Top Ten Worst Dressed Women" if a gadfly from the *Hollywood Reporter* happened to show up.

Miss Von Horn arrived in a chauffeured Maybach. Clinton Carver and the board applauded as she was wheeled down the red carpet.

The guest list included the usual odium of politicians, legendary movers and shakers, business leaders, residents with an embarrassment of riches—designated as "potential donors" on the official list—notable physicians and, of course, family and friends of the board. The latter included a mélange of curious characters from professional sports and "celebrities du jour."

Cass thought it ironic that Silas Hawker and Dennis Hamilton were next to each other on the guest list of VIPs. Thomas had never discussed either of them with her, but thanks to Berger she knew most of the story.

Cass had also invited the people at Oakridge Manor who had been photographed for the mural. Many of them couldn't come, but Silvia Johnson and her husband brought a caravan of loaded vans and told Cass how honored everyone was to be invited.

Thomas gave Cass a few names of friends and acquaintances he wanted to invite. She was curious to meet people from Thomas's world. As guests arrived she took particular interest in matching faces with the names on Thomas's list.

It was written with a No. 2 Ticonderoga pencil on a half page of coarse paper ripped off the bottom of a sketch pad. A swooping arrow took her eye to his note: *Jessica will have to find addresses for some of these.* She glanced at his list.

Professor Roman Andrus, Buena Vista Art Institute.

Michael and Jing-Wei Landerman, houseboat, Harbor Road, Sausalito.

Phillip Marston, c/o Sausalito City Council.

Felix Edgers, Pacific Science Museum.

Archie Granger, Blue Marlin Boats.

Mrs. Stewart, General Merchandise, Stewarts Point, California.

Janis Ahlstrom, St. Mark's volunteer.

Catrina Lindley. The name had been scrawled with such artistic flare that Cass suspected it was there to provoke a reaction. It did, but she would make sure she didn't give Thomas the satisfaction he was obviously after.

Ray Evans, c/o California Highway Patrol. *She was dead when I took her from the car.* Recalling her conversation with Thomas about Christina's transcendental experience made her wonder again where he was.

Professor Andrus entered with his wife. Cass had not seen him since they had met to talk about Thomas six months ago. She crossed the room to greet them. Her irritation over Thomas's being late had become anxiety. She pushed her nerves aside and greeted Andrus with an expression of appreciation.

"You will be so pleased," she promised.

"Where's Thomas?" Andrus asked. Her angst came bounding back.

"I'm sure he'll be here right away if he's not off wandering the halls somewhere." Her nonchalant smile lied about the knot in her stomach.

Cass identified Michael Landerman and Jing-Wei immediately. In spite of the visual contradiction of the prefix *Reverend,* she knew who it was. It was hard to miss a bald man with a snake tattoo. When Thomas had finally confessed his crazy, all-night crash to create preliminary sketches and how he'd borrowed a Bible, he had described Reverend Mike in detail and Jing-Wei as a "striking woman of mixed Asian ethnicity." Jing-Wei was likewise impossible to miss.

Thomas's absence was starting to feel like a disappearance.

CHAPTER

92

LADIES AND GENTLEMEN, if I may have your attention, please?" The
acoustics in the Healing Place were perfect and Cass's voice was melodic.
The purr of conversation and little spikes of laughter faded. Guests could
finally hear the Christmas music that had been part of the festive ambi-
ance since their arrival. "If you would be kind enough to find a seat, we
are about to begin." Guests settled into the chairs.

There was new commotion as the children came in. They were all
dressed in white. Gasps of surprise. Exclamations of delight. Every child
in the hospital who could possibly be there walked, hobbled or was
helped, wheeled or carried into the Healing Place. A few were rolled in,
still in their beds. Sounds of gladness filled the dome as the youngsters
took their places opposite the podium.

Christina was rolled into place by the duty nurse. The moment she
cleared the archway she began scanning the room, stopping only when
she locked eyes with Mrs. Benning, who sat by Alex on the front row. The
look between them seemed unusually charged. Cass saw it and wondered.

Clinton Carver welcomed the guests and gave a short history of the
project. He mentioned in an offhanded way how it had all started the year
he became president of the hospital board and what a long and challenging effort it had been. When what amounted to a reelection campaign
speech ended he returned to prepared notes, dazzling guests with amazing
facts about the world-renowned staff, innovative care, cutting-edge treatments and ultramodern medical technology of the new Children's Wing
at St. Mark's.

"And all of it," he concluded, continuing to read from the text Susan Cassidy had written, "has been made possible by the generosity of one person. A person for whom Christianity is not only about believing in Jesus but about doing what she can to do what He did—to heal the sick and afflicted. To bless the lives of children."

The words were spoken with less conviction than had gone into their writing. The difference between Susan Cassidy's heart and Clinton Carver's head. Cass would have been disappointed in Carver's delivery if she had been listening. She was watching the door and thinking about Thomas.

"St. Mark's is not the first institution to benefit from her generosity," he continued and acknowledged the old woman sitting to his right, "but in this place her charity will never end." At last his emotions were genuine.

Miss Von Horn scolded Carver with eyes peeking under the edge of her black veil.

"She prefers anonymity," Carver confided, "but happily we prevailed upon her to cut the ribbon and open the St. Mark's Children's Wing. We thank you with all of our hearts. Ladies and gentlemen, Miss Lucy Von Horn."

The room rose in a standing ovation as Miss Von Horn was rolled to the front by the tall attendant. The old woman took the microphone with a quivering hand. She smiled at Christina and the other children in wheelchairs and talked to them as if no one else was in the room. "Any of you guys want a race?" They giggled gleefully.

She drew a deep breath and looked back. "None of this is about me or any of us." She shot an eye-bullet at Carver. *Bull's-eye!*

"Everything we do here is about the children who are here and those who will come here for hope and healing and faith. Hope they will be healed and well again. Faith that God can still work miracles."

Cass did not recognize the three men and a woman who slipped through the portal and found a place to stand near the Christmas tree.

Miss Von Horn clipped the white ribbon with unsteady hands. The ends floated to the floor like albino butterflies wafting in slow motion. Another wave of applause. Miss Von Horn bowed her head humbly until the clapping stopped. She returned the ceremonial scissors to Cass. "Where's Thomas?" she asked in a whisper.

Cass's face confessed she had no idea, but she whispered back, "He texted he was running late, but that was an hour ago." Miss Von Horn looked at the curtain but seemed to be looking at the painting. She patted Cass's hand.

"He'll be here. Don't worry." Cass believed in the power of positive thinking. Close as she was to Miss Von Horn's dark eyes, she knew the old woman's assurance was more than that.

• • •

"Mr. Hall is a little delayed," Cass stood on the podium with the microphone in her hand, "but we expect that . . ." A movement near the back caught her eye. Thomas was standing by the Christmas tree. He and an older man Cass had never seen had come in during the ribbon ceremony. When Cass started her apology they moved forward into the light.

Seeing Thomas in the colored glow of the tree took her breath away. She laid her arms across her chest and gasped in relief. Their eyes met. He was watching her. She blushed. The part of her that never lied pushed the warning button. The buzzer was going off but now was hardly the time to sort that out! She was sure about one thing: The rush of emotion was more than relief that the man of the hour had showed up in the nick of time to save her perfect presentation.

The stranger with Thomas was rumpled and rough-hewn. Handsome in an unkempt sort of way. His hair was a variegation of sun-bleached auburn and gray swept back over the collar of the silken lapels. His eyes were dark blue-violet, almost black, with tiny flaws of green and gray. In the half light at that distance Cass thought it was Jeff Bridges. *Now, there's a friend to keep to yourself.* The thought vanished as the man turned and she could see it was not the famous star. He wore a classic black tuxedo. *A symphony conductor?* Probably. Then Cass noted that the tuxedo was exactly like the one she had rented for Thomas. *It is the one!*

Thomas was not in black tie. He wore a beau blue open-collared shirt the color of his eyes, a charcoal blazer, jeans and Tony Lama boots.

"Ah, even as we speak. He is here," Cass said. Thomas lingered by the Christmas tree, studying her.

Why aren't you wearing a tuxedo? Cass scolded him affectionately with her eyes. She gestured toward Thomas. "Thomas Hall, ladies and gentlemen. The man who created this . . . marvelous mural of miracles."

Video cameras captured her image. DAT recorders recorded her voice. Ballpoint pens scribbled her words. Cass had just given Thomas Hall's masterwork a name that would endure. *Until Christ himself came to visit?* she mused. *Mural of miracles. Marvelous!*

The room erupted in applause. Guests twisted in their seats and craned their necks to get a glimpse of the artist. Thomas waved politely.

"Come on up here, Mr. Hall," Cass said. She was amused by her own formality. Thomas tried to wave away the invitation.

"It is with a sincere . . ." Cass paused, then dropped the formality of the moment and became herself. "Well, it is in truth with a great sense of relief that he made it here at all." A ripple of laughter. "But, with great appreciation . . ." she was looking at him as if he were the only person in the room. Her hand motioned him forward. Her expression made him obey. She took a breath, " . . . and sincere admiration that I introduce to you the creator of the work you are about to see, Mr. Thomas Hall."

Thomas shouldered his way through a gauntlet of guests. Some shook his hand. Some patted him on the shoulder. A woman with too much rouge on her cheeks kissed him and whispered, "God bless you." She left a lipstick smudge on his face.

Singling out his father next to Mrs. Benning, Thomas dipped his head and crossed his hands over his heart. The sorrows of a lifetime vanished in a smile that cracked Alex's face into a thousand wrinkles.

"Thank you," Thomas began when Cass handed him the microphone. "Thank you very much." He waited for the applause to end. Thomas nodded graciously and waved a hand to quiet them. Cass continued clapping. She looked at the artist, shrugged and smiled. Quiet came.

"A Chinese philosopher once said, 'A picture is worth ten thousand words.' He was only partly right. Words and pictures are very different things and art must speak for itself. For once in my life, I sincerely hope what this art is about speaks louder than the art itself."

Miss Von Horn closed her eyes with a sigh that conveyed supreme satisfaction. The room was perfectly quiet and Thomas held each person present in the palm of his hand.

"Nothing I say can change what you see, and what you see will be unique to you. What you see will tell you more about yourself than about what I've painted on the wall. Maybe more." He smiled at Cass.

"A year ago I would have stood on a box, basked in your applause and let you believe I did this all by myself. It may seem to you an artist sings solo, but we are influenced by a choir and inspired by a symphony. It is our hand and brush laid to the canvas but it is the sound of instruments and the influence of players that allows that hand to move." His eyes darted to Alex, Mrs. Benning, Christina and Cass. Then Cass saw him look to the strangers at the back who had come in late.

"With the old philosopher in mind, I'll not use ten thousand words to thank the players in this symphony. But some must be acknowledged." He held out his hand to Miss Von Horn. "First, of course, is Miss Von Horn." A swell of applause passed through the hall with the Doppler effect of a passing train.

"Thank you, great lady, for your vision and patience." Then, to the guests, "I told her I wanted to paint a fantasy fortress with demons of sickness and kid warriors." Miss Von Horn smiled at the memory. "She looked me in the eye and said something that inspired everything you are about to see. 'Mr. Hall,' she said, 'Jesus healed the sick. He gave us hope. A painting in a Christian Healing Place should be about Jesus. About hope and healing.'" Thomas quoted the grand lady with such reverence that even the nonbelievers in the audience struggling to remain aloof were tempted to applaud.

Thomas pointed to Professor Andrus and his wife on the second row. "Professor Roman Andrus taught me everything I know about art. He tried hard to teach me about myself, but . . ." He paused for effect. "Well, professor, one outta two ain't bad, but don't give up on me just yet." The professor waved a casual salute. His wife squeezed his arm with pride and leaned against him.

"To my dad, Alex Hall." He poked a thumb at the painted wall. "It's your DNA, Pop." A pause. "Thank you for bringing me back into your life. Your influence in all of this has been . . ." He teetered at the edge of an emotion that made his lip quiver. "Awesome! Good times ahead and that's a promise."

Alex wiped his wet face with a trembling palm. Mrs. Benning took his hand and squeezed it softly in both of hers.

"Silvia Johnson and our friends from Oakridge were marvelous." Silvia sat with her husband amidst the residents of Oakridge Manor. "Thank you one and all." Silvia fluttered her fingers in a little wave. The men and women who had posed as models nodded and exchanged proud whispers as soft applause rippled through the hall. "You're in there somewhere," Thomas smiled and glanced at the curtain.

"Artists don't like to admit that their agents and managers have anything to do with their success. That may be because artists don't always know what 'success' really is or how to measure it. Or what is best for them. My agent and manager, Frank Berger, knows." Berger folded his arms in a rare moment of self-consciousness and nodded. "He dragged me to St. Mark's kicking and screaming, and for that, Frank, I will always be grateful. You are a true and loyal friend. Thank you." Berger saluted with both thumbs up.

"To Janis Ahlstrom. Thank you for important insights not easily expressed." He glanced to where he knew the daughter of Jairus was rejoicing with her mother. Even without seeing the image, Janis obviously understood. She steepled long fingers and acknowledged his gratitude with a modest bow. Her husband squeezed her shoulder.

"Superheroes are a big part of our popular culture," Thomas continued. "I've painted a few, as some of you know." Professor Andrus shot him with a finger pistol as Thomas put his lips against the microphone and whispered in a booming voice, "None of them is real, in case you wondered." His antic caused a ripple of laughter.

"There are real heroes among us who don't wear blue tights and red capes. We have the honor of having one of them with us tonight. Where are you, Sergeant?" He pointed toward the back. People twisted in their chairs to see a "real hero" and clapped without knowing why. "Sergeant Ray Evans deserves his own mural. Your influence on this work has been miraculous." Sergeant Evans nodded modestly and remained seated. His wife put an arm around him and waved acknowledgment.

"Michael Landerman and his wife, Jing-Wei, lent me a Bible and told me where to find the miracles of Jesus." There was a ripple of laughter; people thought he was joking. "That's true. This has been an amazing journey for me and it started with you. Thank you, Reverend Mike, and thanks, Jing-Wei."

Thomas looked for Dennis Hamilton. He hadn't come. "There are others," Thomas said. "Some whose courage and influence have been life changing. I'll thank them in person, as I intend we shall remain friends.

"Finally, there are a couple of other people who were kind enough to come with me tonight. I hope they don't mind me calling them my friends." Cass noted the difference in tone as Thomas continued. "They came on short notice. That's because—I'm embarrassed to say—I didn't put them on the guest list." The comment caused a murmur among formally invited VIPs.

"It took me all day to find them and persuade them to be here tonight. Sorry we came in late, but it was midnight last night when I realized—*when I got the word*—that they needed to be here. They have influenced the creation of this painting in ways they still don't understand. In ways I didn't understand until last night."

CHAPTER

93

I T WAS JUST AFTER MIDNIGHT. The Jesus of the unfinished face waited expectantly as children gathered at his feet and other characters came to life. The face of Jesus troubled Thomas. He had never been so unsettled about one of his creations.

In seventeen hours and fifty minutes the blue velvet curtain would open and the world would see the Jesus of Thomas Hall. He had to finish. He sketched a nobleman, changed him to a rabbi, drew him over as a fisherman, then settled on a prince. The drawing evolved from prince to perfect man and then to superhero. The face was strong, majestic, perfectly proportioned, anatomically correct and as lifelike as any face on the wall.

"That's not what Jesus looks like." Christina's assessment was still painfully accurate. Skull, skin, bones and beard were not the essence of Jesus. In spite of acknowledging God, *or indeed perhaps because of it,* Thomas toppled backward into doubt. His questions loomed over him with mocking voices and he grappled with the contradiction. *Mortal man or Son of God?*

A wave of hopelessness crashed over Thomas and he tumbled like driftwood onto the ragged rocks of despair. In a burst of frustration he seized the sponge and scrubbed away the face in a smudge of zinc white. A sense of dread enveloped him like the power of a demon from an unseen world. Oppressive loneliness. Falling backwards. A black and bottomless pit.

Hamilton's words from the quiet woods spoke as if the man were standing in the Healing Place: "Evil in the world is an evidence of God."

Thomas fell to his knees and cried out, "God help me!" He knelt beside the children. He imagined a place beyond the angels he had painted on the ceiling. "Father in heaven. I believe this Jesus is your Son. I want so desperately to know him, to 'see' him, to create an image pleasing to him . . . your image." His words were a hollow echo in the dome. "Please help my unbelief." His prayer swept through the apex and found heaven.

A heavy silence followed. He heard a voice. Small. Quiet. *A voice or only a feeling?* Thomas wasn't sure. There was no sound. There were no words per se but he heard and understood. He opened his eyes and looked to see if someone had come in. He was alone. Thomas continued praying in a whisper. The voice came again. Pierced his mind. Ignited a burning within. He trembled. Whether in words or impressions of the mind, Thomas knew with certainty it was *the voice* Cass had tried to describe. It was the voice Hamilton had said called him on his journey from atheism to faith in God. He had spoken of a "broken heart," a "contrite spirit." It had meant nothing to Thomas in the redwood grove, but now, on his knees in the darkness of the Healing Place, he understood. It was not an idea. It was an experience. There was an explosion of light in the darkness. Like a voice that spoke without a sound, it was a light that illuminated without a gleam.

Thomas understood. There were broken things that needed to be fixed. Offenses to make right. Missed opportunities to salvage if he could. He prayed. He listened. He made promises. He reminded God what he'd learned from Christina. *Knock, and it shall be opened; ask, and ye shall receive.*

Thomas confessed he had no right to ask God for anything, but he bargained anyway. It seemed to him the voice was guiding him in it. Telling him what to do. The voice and explosion of light seemed no less tangible than the marble floor that made his knees ache before he finally finished his pleadings and his promises were done.

Thomas stood and cast his eyes upon Jesus. Not the Jesus on his canvas with the ruined face, but the image of the Lord Jesus Christ that appeared so clearly in his mind.

He painted until dawn. They were wondrous hours. His angels watched from where he had painted them on the ceiling. He felt certain that they were not the only ones looking on.

He closed the curtain and set out to keep his end of the bargain.

CHAPTER

94

THE TRAFFIC WAS HEAVIER THAN Thomas had expected for Christmas
Eve morning. When he crossed the Bay Bridge the memory came back.
*Let the idiot jump if he wants to jump. Big loss. Some manic-depressive loser
living at the edge of society.* Thomas shuddered with remorse and wondered
how he'd been so hard-bitten and without compassion.

By the time he found Walter Richter, the remorse was complete. Jesus
had spoken parables about men like Thomas Hall. Two thousand years
before, on the dusty road to Jericho. Thomas was the priest who had
crossed to the opposite side rather than help the Jewish traveler beaten
and robbed by bandits. He was the Levite who had ignored the stricken
man and hurried on his way. He was nowhere near when the Samaritan
had come.

Walter Richter lived on Underhills Road in Oakland. Thomas got the
name and address with a phone call to Ray Evans. Disclosing the name of
an attempted suicide breached privacy protocols, but Evans bent the rules
in the interest of a "greater good." It was the kind of judgment that made
Evans a superior police officer.

Underhills Road was a narrow residential street that cut east from
Park Boulevard at the 580 overpass and twisted along the base of the
Piedmont Hills. Richter's home was a faux English Tudor from 1949,
cut into the hillside with two stories stacked over a single-car garage that
opened directly onto the street.

Richter was on a ladder replacing a bulb in the string of Christmas
lights draped around the massive juniper that dominated the steep yard.

There were sixty-seven steps from the sidewalk to the porch. By the time Thomas got to the top, Richter had succeeded and come down. The juniper was covered with lights.

"Beautiful," Thomas said. Richter was suspicious. Thomas got straight to the point.

Richter was embarrassed to discover that Thomas knew about the incident on the bridge. That he had actually been there and seen it happen. He was bewildered when Thomas said he had come to apologize.

"For what?" Richter asked.

"For doing nothing," Thomas said. *For crossing to the other side and going on my way.*

Richter didn't know what to say. He confessed he must seem like a basket case.

"Not at all," Thomas said, then asked if there were anything he could do *now* to help Richter or his family. Richter remained wary but invited him inside.

Richter's wife, Vivian, played patty-cake with a toddler whose head was an explosion of dark curls. Richter introduced the stranger and Thomas repeated his name.

Richter remained standoffish. *As much as I deserve,* Thomas thought and tried to imagine the conversation had he been the one rushing to the railing. *What if the angels in white overalls had not appeared and it was left to me to explain that her husband was dead and the father of her children was gone because a man jumping from a bridge was not my problem?* It was a dark and sobering thought.

Richter talked about his life, not as a man speaking to a friend but as a pilgrim unburdening his soul to a stranger. Purging the ignominious mistakes of your life to someone you didn't know and who shouldn't care was easier than confessing your blunders to a friend.

When he paused, Vivian said, "Walter is a good man in spite of . . . He's a wonderful father." As the Richters slowly let him into their lives, Thomas realized he'd been a fool in his rush to judge this man. Richter was not the "manic-depressive loser living at the edge of society" that he had envisioned.

"It's very kind of you to come," Vivian added.

Thomas learned that Walter had married his high school sweetheart. They had three kids. He worked as a mechanic and, from the look of the house, had managed a decent life for his family. Richter remarked that they belonged to a small Christian congregation but didn't attend church very often. "Christmas, Easter, you know how it goes when life gets so busy and the dang ball games are all on Sunday."

He admitted they probably should try to go, "especially because of the kids," and seemed anxious for Thomas to know he believed in God.

It was almost forty minutes before Richter came to the bridge. It was why the stranger had come. Why Richter had invited Thomas to meet his wife. For this welcomed catharsis to be complete he needed to explain the bridge and talk about the cankerous flaw in his life that almost ended it.

"I smoke!" He made the word smell worse than stale tobacco. He'd started when he found a half-smoked Camel. He was thirteen. By age fourteen he was addicted, shoplifting cigarettes and smoking more than a pack a day. He promised to quit so he could play sports. He promised to quit when he got married. He promised to quit when the baby was born. He promised to quit every Christmas. It was always on his list of resolutions for the New Year. He couldn't quit.

He gave up quitting and joked about beating the odds of lung cancer and emphysema. Then a guy from Milpitas who brought his '65 Mustang to the garage for a valve job told him about a highly touted quit-smoking wonder-drug. He didn't tell him about the warning notice or the dangers of serious neuropsychiatric consequences. The pill blocked the parts of the brain that produced the feel-good pleasures from smoking. An unfortunate few experienced a bad reaction to the drug that plunged them into deep depression, suicidal ideation, suicide attempts and, in some cases, completed suicides.

What had almost happened to Walter Richter on the bridge was not about who he was. He was not some schmuck who thought death and obliteration were preferable to life. *Let the idiot jump if he wants to jump and stop holding up traffic.* Remorse returned.

Richter insisted that asking forgiveness was unnecessary. "It's for me, not you," Thomas confessed, and Richter finally accepted Thomas's apology. Afterward Richter thanked him.

Thomas promised Vivian he would paint portraits of her kids. She was thrilled by the promise and articulate in her appreciation.

When Thomas said good-bye and shook Richter's hand, the mechanic said, "I'm glad to meet a Christian who walks the walk." Thomas was taken aback, but before he could respond, Richter patted him on the shoulder. "Because of you we're going back to church."

Vivian put her arm around her husband's waist. "Thank you so much for coming, Mr. Hall. Merry Christmas."

Thomas invited them to attend the opening. They promised to find a sitter if they could.

Thomas left $200 under the windshield wiper of their car with a note: *Hope you can make it. Gas and dinner on me.*

CHAPTER

95

WHEN CASS FIRST MENTIONED the still small voice, Thomas had taken it as a figure of speech, nothing more than an impression of conscience. He laughed when he thought about what Berger would do with it in a contract. *Still Small Voice, Hereinafter SSV, shall be required pursuant to paragraph . . .* He thought of the verse in the Bible Cass read when they spoke of it again. The part he remembered ran through his head. *God passed by and a big wind smashed the rocks but God was not in the wind. Then there was an earthquake but God was not in the earthquake. Then there was a fire but God was not in the fire. Then, after the fire, there was a still small voice. God.*

After Thomas made his bargain with God in the middle of the night, the whispering in his head was unabated. Whether the whispering was from God or all in his own brain, one thing was certain: "SSV" was not always *still* and *small.* On his drive back to the city across the Oakland Bay Bridge, Thomas discovered it was not only persistent but, because it was giving instructions he didn't want to hear, it was downright annoying. Ada Kanster kept coming up.

I'm supposed to kiss and make up with Ada Kanster? With the enemy? She burned down my house! Instructions were imprecise at one level. Unmistakable at another. What was SSV thinking?

Love your enemies; bless them that curse you. He was surprised that the passage he'd read in the Gospel of Matthew returned to his mind with such clarity. It was not exactly what he wanted to hear.

He turned on XM Radio, Channel 16, the Country Highway. Even

Toby Keith was not enough to drown out SSV. Keeping his bargain with God was more difficult than he'd imagined. *Ada Kanster?* A bargain was a bargain, but after what she'd done and what Thomas was feeling. . . . He ejected the thought and resolved to call Ada Kanster.

Silas Hawker was next. *Not Hawker! He's an arrogant, atheist, son of a . . . He's a borderline criminal who bullies people! Hawker hates me!* Thomas was about to let "Judge not, that ye be not judged" swirl out of his mind like a clog kicked loose by Drano. *Do good to them that hate you, and pray for them that despitefully use you and persecute you . . . and coerce you.* Had Matthew said "coerce"? It didn't matter. SSV had made the point.

How can I "do good" to Hawker when he wants Hamilton's head on a platter and a painting of monkeys turning into men? The disdain Thomas felt was a reassuring affirmation of his fledgling faith. He was no longer an agnostic coward. He was persuaded that a person could *know* the reality of things beyond material phenomena. He felt a calm certainty that one could experience—*even know*—about the existence and nature of God.

I can pray for him in the car. The voice was silent and Thomas knew it was a weak rationalization. *Silas Hawker! Pray for them that despitefully use you.* The thought of going to Hawker or Kanster in the spirit of "forgive and be forgiven" was bitter. Thomas wasn't sure he could face either of them without a nap or at least without sprouting wings with the help of a twelve-ounce Red Bull. *Wings? Angels get their wings a different way. Has Red Bull got to go?* He listened. No word from SSV. *Whew!*

The Lord had kept his end of the deal, and whether out of integrity or fear, Thomas would keep his. He resolved to go to Hawker's office right after he found the beggar whom he had turned away. *He brought it on himself.*

CHAPTER

96

THERE WAS NO ADDRESS OR phone number on the card from Staff Sergeant Jake Demeanus. Thomas was surprised that the card was still in the glove box. His recollection of the panhandler who had asked him for something to eat when he had stopped his car at the corner of Lincoln and Seventh five months before was remarkably vivid.

"Just need some bread for some bread, brother," the man had said.

"Get your hand the hell off of my car." *To be a completely contemptible human,* Thomas thought as the memory returned, *I should have said, "my $65,000 car that I just paid $125 dollars to have detailed," and why not add, "Hey, I got a new boat."*

Thomas hadn't expected that the beggar would be part of the bargain. He should have known. He went looking for him where they'd met near Lincoln. *Met? Collided.*

A woman with a black mongrel dog and a Safeway shopping cart piled with lumpy plastic bags sat on the bench for Municipal Transit. The dog had a broken tooth. The cart had a broken wheel. The woman had a broken spirit.

The woman and her dog shared a soggy sandwich from the trash. Thomas asked her if she knew Jake Demeanus. "He fought in Vietnam," he added.

She shook her head and gave the dog another gob of wet bread and bologna. He gave the woman a hundred dollars. "For you and your dog." It was an apology. He knew why.

"God bless," she said and patted the dog. "God bless."

• • •

Google provided Thomas with a list of homeless shelters in San Francisco. A volunteer at Raphael House remembered Staff Sergeant Jake Demeanus.

"He replaced a broken toilet a couple of weeks ago," the volunteer said. "Big guy. Handy. Very sweet." She suggested Thomas check the Thrift Store on Stillman Street.

"Thank you."

"He fought in Vietnam, you know?" she said as he was leaving.

It was three o'clock by the time Thomas found Sergeant Demeanus driving a forklift behind the Thrift Store at St. Vincent de Paul. Thomas waited for Demeanus to unload a freezer and park the forklift.

"Sergeant Demeanus?" The man furrowed his brows and looked at Thomas. His beard was clipped. His faded coveralls were iceberg blue with *Help Us Help Others* stenciled across the back and a St. Vincent de Paul patch over his heart. It was the same man. His eyes were unmistakable.

"Mr. Mercedes man," Demeanus grinned. Thomas was startled that the man remembered him.

What Sergeant Demeanus did next was chiseled in stone on the everlasting walls of Thomas Hall's memory. He dug into a pocket of the coveralls, fished out a thin pad of money and peeled off a five-dollar bill. He offered it to Thomas. "Need a little bread for some bread, brother?"

"I'm so sorry about that." Thomas was shamefaced. Humiliated. "I came to make it right. Apologize for being such a . . ."

"Heartless soul?" Demeanus laughed.

"At least," Thomas agreed, feeling genuine sorrow for the way he had treated the man.

"Just give me the keys to that Mercedes and make it all good." He laughed again and his leather face wrinkled. The sergeant's reaction was unexpected. Thomas had come willing to subject himself to a profane tongue-lashing. Well-deserved. Sergeant Jake Demeanus was not the man Thomas Hall had judged him to be.

"Or dinner at Buffo's be good," he said quickly to rescue Thomas from his obvious discomfort.

• • •

By the time they ate their way through a pair of Buffo bacon burgers with cheese, onion rings, Coca Cola, beer and blackberry tarts with ice cream, they were friends. Thomas listened in marginal disbelief to the painful life story of Staff Sergeant Jake Demeanus, Company D, 38th Infantry. The war. The wounds. Agent Orange. Disability. Depression. Disadvantaged. The doctor's mistakes. Greed. Graft. Government stupidity. Crack in the streets. Cracks in the system. The wife who was killed.

"They say you sometimes gotta hit rock bottom 'fore you can dig yourself out," he concluded without bitterness.

"That's what happened?"

"That's where I was the day we met, man. In the pit!"

"Saying I'm sorry is . . . it just sounds so weak. Lame. If I had had any idea that—" He was cut off.

"Wouldn't a mattered. You were who you were. You're not the same guy. What changed?"

"Long story," Thomas said.

"No worries, man. Wasn't you that put me there." Demeanus continued his story. Rescue. Recovery. Helping hands helping others. Hope.

"You believe in God?" Demeanus asked.

It always comes back to The Question. Thomas nodded. "I didn't, but . . . yeah, I think I do."

"And that's what changed?" Demeanus asked. Thomas nodded again. "Same with me, brother. When I started praying to God instead of looking to the government, everything changed." He twisted in his seat so Thomas could see his back. "Can you see that?"

Thomas read the slogan stenciled there: *Help Us Help Others.*

"It's all it took. Take Jesus at his word. Once I went lookin' for people to help instead of for people to help me, it was like God reached into the pit and took me by the hand." The rush of warm emotion was no longer unfamiliar. Thomas understood. "So, what's your story, Thomas?"

Thomas laughed softly. "What size suit do you wear, Jake?"

CHAPTER

97

M<small>R. H</small>AWKER IS UPSTAIRS in the Darwin Pavilion." The woman in Hawker's office was not plumpish Maxine. Quite the contrary. She was college age, attractive and, judging from buttons left undone, not likely the most qualified replacement.

Thomas was tempted to ask what had happened to Maxine. *Maybe she discovered evolution was only a theory and went back to teaching Sunday school.* The thought amused him but did little to lighten his angst.

"Who shall I tell Mr. Hawker is here to see him?"

"Thomas Hall. I'm the one who . . ." He stopped himself. "Never mind. I'll just go on up. I know the way."

"I don't think that Mr. Hawker will—"

"No worries. We're . . . friends. Old friends."

Thomas climbed the grand staircase. He was in no rush to have what he feared would be an ugly confrontation. He wished he had called Berger to come with him. Protect the blind side. Run interference. Not today. It was a skirmish he must face on his own. Part of the bargain.

The lights were out. Work on the pavilion had been suspended by the court order. Hawker was circling the bronze colossus brooding over something of grave importance. *The fate of the world and future of man,* Thomas mused. The sardonic thought came with the realization, *Wrong day. Bad timing.* The director's hands were clasped behind his back and his eyes cast to the floor. A smudge of dirty smoke from his cigar swirled after him and hung in the gloom.

Thomas's footfalls echoed in the hall but Hawker didn't turn until he spoke. "Doctor Hawker?" The director twisted around and squinted into the dim. Thomas moved to a patch of filtered light. If Hawker was surprised to see Thomas, he didn't show it. Whatever his thoughts, they were shrouded by conspicuous scorn.

"YOU!" His animosity was thicker than the smoke.

"How are you?" Thomas muttered. The dialogue he had rehearsed was woefully inadequate.

"Is this a personal invitation to come and scoff at your ridiculous mural of miracles?"

Thomas wanted to swallow but his throat was dry. "I came to see you because I wanted to . . . I wanted to see if there was a way for us to resolve our differences. Bury the hatchet."

"There is only one place I would like to bury a hatchet!" There was violence in his voice and the implication was chilling.

"Look, I know that . . . I'm sure there is not much we can agree on but on a personal level I wanted to . . ."

"Personal! There is no 'personal' level!"

"I was just hoping that . . ." There was no other way to say it. "I came to ask you to forgive me for whatever you feel I have done to offend you . . ." and, unable to think of a single wrong thing he had done to make Hawker angry, he added, "that was wrong in any way." He tried to get his head around what Jesus was talking about. *Love your enemies? How?*

Hawker strode toward Thomas. The artist's instincts cried out to back away but he stood his ground. Hawker hunched his shoulders. His hands swung forward. In the semidarkness he looked like a Cro-Magnon hunter. "And whether you are willing to forgive me or not . . ." Thomas continued.

Hawker jabbed Thomas in the chest with both hands, arms straight and elbows locked. Thomas fell backward and landed on his behind. Thomas was no fighter but his ego demanded he leap up and pound the older man in the face. *Smash his stinking cigar down his throat.* The quiet *whisper* was louder than the screaming ego and anger was overshadowed by a sudden calm.

Hawker glared down and wagged a threatening finger. He looked much different than Thomas remembered. He was withered. His eyes were sunken in bruised circles. Pallid skin. A tremor in his threatening hand. The robustness gone. No joy.

"You think you're done with me? You have no idea!" Hawker stepped past Thomas and headed for the portal.

Thomas stood up and brushed the dust from his pants. Then it struck him. The difference in Hawker. The change. *He's sick. It is not the "fate of the world" on his shoulders; it is the fate of Silas Hawker. Is he dying? Has he come face-to-face with extinction?*

He called after Hawker. "I also came to forgive you."

Hawker left the Pavilion and disappeared in the shadows of the arched hall. *And to thank you for being such a . . .* The thought stopped short of a profane execration. *For saving me from this.*

He looked up at the brooding face of Charles Darwin. There was no hint of happiness or joy. The dour countenance was the same as Silas Hawker's.

"In one respect my mind has changed." It was as if Thomas could hear the voice of Charles Darwin echoing in the gloom of the chamber intended to celebrate his thoughts. While reading *Origin of Species* he had discovered the life and letters of the famous naturalist assembled by his son Francis in 1887. Alone in the shrine to Charles Darwin, he remembered the old man's lament near the end of his life. He no longer found joy in beauty.

To the age of thirty or beyond, poetry of many kinds, Milton, Byron, Woodsworth and Shelley gave me great pleasure. Even as a schoolboy I took intense delight in Shakespeare. Pictures gave me considerable enjoyment and music very great delight. But now for many years I cannot endure to read a line of poetry. I find Shakespeare so intolerably dull that it nauseates me. I have also lost my taste for pictures or music. Music generally sets me thinking about what I have been at work on, instead of giving me pleasure. I retain some taste for fine scenery, but it does not cause me the exquisite delight which it formerly did. The loss of these tastes is a loss of happiness and may be injurious to the intellect and more probably the moral character by enfeebling the emotional part of our nature.

Whatever other feelings Thomas might have had for Silas Hawker, by the time he descended the grand staircase there was nothing left but sorrow and even—to his astonishment—compassion.

CHAPTER

98

THE DAYDREAM DISAPPEARED. Cass touched him on the arm and brought him back. He was still standing in front of the guests in the Healing Place. Thomas wondered if he had exceeded the limit of expectation for men with microphones.

The brain can review enormous amounts of memory in excruciating detail in a few nanoseconds. A brain that evolved from a simple bacterium and advanced to incomprehensible complexity against impossible odds while contradicting the law of thermodynamics? Not likely. Thomas's complex brain filled with disjointed thoughts in the seconds it took to leave the flashback and resume his introduction. Richter. Demeanus. Hawker. Ada Kanster? Why hadn't she answered her phone? Thomas had called twice from the car on his way to the Science Museum. She didn't pick up. *Did she see it was me on caller ID? What is she planning that makes her not answer?* Creativity came with an unpredictable level of psychosis. Paranoia was unexpected. He shook it off. A different thought jumped in. *What would have happened if she had picked up?* The dialogue that might have been played in his head. *Painful. Stop it!*

• • •

Thomas glanced at Cass and looked for his other invited guests by the tree. He wasn't sure of the last thing he'd said so he rewound just in case. "There are a couple of 'new' friends who influenced all of this in

439

ways they can't imagine." He waved a hand toward the Christmas tree and guests twisted around to see more of those the artist liked best.

"Mr. and Mrs. Walter Richter," Thomas said. Walter looked like a penguin in his rented tux. Vivian was stunning. *So easy to misjudge.* They nodded modestly. Vivian waved and Thomas was certain she'd been homecoming queen at Piedmont High School and had ridden on a float in the parade. "Thank you for coming." He smiled and nodded at them.

"Staff Sergeant Jake Demeanus." The man Cass thought might have been Jeff Bridges stepped forward and came to parade rest. "Sergeant Demeanus is a Vietnam veteran. He did three tours of duty. He received the Medal of Honor twice and a Purple Heart for the wounds that took him out of battle. Wounds that changed his life." All but a few of the guests applauded. "Thank you, Sergeant." Thomas saluted Jake. Jake came to attention and saluted back. Erect, proud and handsome in the tuxedo Cass had rented for Thomas.

"Mrs. Benning," Thomas continued. The elegant old woman smiled and Christina snuggled closer. "Frankly, I think God put you here to help us understand what angels do and what heaven will be like."

He waved a hand toward Cass. "Thank you, Susan Cassidy. For finding me. Persuading me. Trusting me." *Loving me.* He blushed as the thought struck him. "And for putting me in my place."

The alter-ego actor on the backstage of his brain flared up in a wonderfully funny impersonation of Susan Cassidy. Creativity is not confined to a single expression, and Thomas had her down cold. Gestures, voice and tippy-toe high heels. Everything the woman did or said was burned in his brain. "You used to have talent, Mr. Hall—before you sold out to the quick and dirty world of fantasy art," he said in faux Susan Cassidy. People who knew Cass saw her immediately in Thomas's antics. Christina giggled with delight. Even Clinton Carver laughed.

Cass laughed to camouflage her reddening face. Thomas stopped and waited for the chortling to fade, then spoke only to her.

"Most of all, thank you, Cass, for giving me the second chance I didn't deserve." She bowed her head graciously. "You promised me this project would help me find out who I was or at least who I was supposed to be. You were right." Thomas blew her a kiss. She blushed, and whatever it was between them leaped forward to a place it had not been.

"Chastity? Where are you?" Thomas scanned the room for his apprentice and saw a hand wave by the window. There were only remnants of the girl he had met at the dock. Working on the mural had changed many things. Tonight, at least, Chastity was a different girl. *A lovely woman.* She wore a burgundy-pink, floor-length sheath with a modest V-neck and three-inch heels to match.

"Come on up here for a minute," Thomas said. She moved toward the front with unexpected grace. The woman with whom she'd been talking turned as she passed. An icy chill stabbed Thomas in the back of the neck. The born-again hippie had been transformed by an inexpensive evening gown, but there was no mistaking who the woman was. Ada Kanster!

He felt paralyzed. The innate instinct of fight or flight erupted in his head. *Who invited the enemy? Chastity? Cass? Why? Ada Kanster set my house on fire!*

The still small voice spoke softly. *Ada Kanster is on your list. What better place to forgive and be forgiven than here at the mural of miracles?* Chastity threaded her way through the guests. Ada Kanster typed a text message into her phone.

Adrenaline replayed the incident in the parking lot of the French Laundry. Lia Chu spoke over shouts and whispers. *People who oppose Silas Hawker suffer consequences!* That was what Hawker meant! The thought jammed his imagination into turbo drive and their confrontation in the shadow of Darwin smashed into mind. *He put her up to this. They're in cahoots! She's Hawker's stooge! He sent her to disrupt the opening!*

The ice pick was joined by an iron glove with a grip on his gut. Thomas scanned the shadows half expecting to see the arrogant atheist reading the text from Ada Kanster and scowling at Jesus.

Love your enemies; pray for them that despitefully use you and persecute you. The little voice was back. Why was he remembering this stuff? *Let him who is without sin cast the first stone.*

"Hi," Chastity shrugged, retiring and modest. Thomas forced Hawker from his head. He risked a side glance at Kanster. She looked up from her phone and caught his eye. Stared at him. Smiling! *When does she make her move?*

Berger. The positive hope pried away the talons of the iron claw. He scanned the room. The agent was flirting with a well-preserved widow who had graduated from high school the year Berger took the training wheels off his first two-wheeler. *Look up here. Berger. Berger!* The desperate attempt to reach him through mental telepathy didn't work.

He put his arm around Chastity's shoulder. "I hired this young woman as an apprentice. Her job was cleaning brushes. I came early one morning and caught her using those brushes on the mural." There was an audible gasp pregnant with the obvious question: *Why is she still alive?*

"You'll see in a moment what she was doing. This gives you some idea." He held up a poster Chastity had used to work out her illuminated passages of scriptures. First letters were decorated with the pious flare of a medieval monk—who in spite of a cloistered lifetime copying the holy word was never as good as Chastity. The hubbub of disbelief changed to audible *ooh*s and *aah*s. Many applauded.

"You could lock me in here for a year and I could never do what you have done. Thank you, Chastity. Your contribution is enormous."

"That is so not true. You taught me so much." She blushed and started to turn.

"One more thing. We added your name to the plaque and got you a little something to show our appreciation." He handed her an envelope.

"Shall I open it?" It was halfway opened before she finished her question. She looked at the letter, her expression confused at first. Then hopeful. Could it be? She looked at Thomas with skepticism and ecstasy. "A full-ride scholarship to Art Institute? No way!"

"There's the man to thank," Thomas said, pointing.

Professor Andrus gave Chastity a thumbs-up. "See you in the spring," he grinned.

"Congratulations." Thomas reached out to shake her hand. She leaped out of her high heels and flung her arms around his neck. There is no statute of expectation for the duration of a hug and no one was keeping track. Except Ada Kanster. Thomas watched over Chastity's shoulder as Kanster whispered to a frightening woman beside her, then glanced down at a text message coming in.

"I've violated the Chinese edict about yapping when a picture can say it all, but there is one more person you need to meet. She is last on the list but in all ways first and most important. If one person opened the door to where I needed to be to do this painting, it was this young lady and her simple faith." He gestured toward Christina. "Christina Christensen."

Christina waved from her wheelchair on the front row of the children's choir.

"I didn't know Jesus very well at all before I was asked to paint this mural. Christina introduced us, and for that I'm forever grateful. The man who saved her life told me, 'God has something special in mind for Christina.' I believe I know what it was. He suggested I look after her . . ." he fought off a wave of emotion. "And I intend to do just that." A darting glance at Cass made her part of whatever it was Thomas had just promised. It was unconscious and unintended, but Mrs. Benning's face suddenly took on a deep sense of satisfaction. Thomas blew Christina a kiss with both hands.

"This is a place of hope, and I hope this 'mural of miracles' will touch the hearts of those who see it the way it has changed the heart of the man who painted it. I hope the children who spend time in this place will not only find hope in getting better but faith in being healed. I hope their dreams come true and miracles are part of their lives. I hope they will discover, as I have discovered, that there is a God in heaven. I hope you will come to believe, as I have come to believe, that creation is the most miraculous miracle of all."

• • •

The lights went out. Theater lamps suspended from the dome with blue and amber filters faded up on the children. Mrs. Benning tapped her baton and lifted the young singers to their feet with a graceful sweep of her arms. Her hands were suspended by invisible strings. When they moved, bright, clear a cappella voices filled the Healing Place with the strains of "In This Very Room."

Thomas went to the back and stood by the Christmas tree. Cass was suddenly beside him and slipped her arm through his. They spoke without words as the kaleidoscope of colored lights danced across their faces.

No one noticed how the violin got into Christina's hands but when Zack rolled her to the front of the choir everyone saw it. A hand-crafted violin tucked under her chin. The neck cradled in the palm of her ruined hand. The bow poised gently across the strings.

The duty nurse tapped Dr. Namkung and he looked up from something in his lap at the child with the violin.

Christina drew the bow across the strings. It was far from perfect but the fingers of Christina's left hand—*the fingers that would never move again*—touched the strings, then methodically made their way to a new position and pressed again. The children came in on the second verse, adding angelic voices to the sweet sound of strings.

Cass covered her mouth lest joyful tears turn to audible sobs. Thomas put his arm around her and felt her trembling against his body. He blinked away tears. The joy he had felt that wondrous midnight when he saw the face of Jesus came again. The miracles of the Master were no longer old stories painted on a wall. They were tangible and real. A miracle was taking place before his own eyes and he was a witness. Jesus knew this child and God's miracles had not ceased.

Those who knew Christina gazed in absolute wonder. Chastity whispered to Ada Kanster. The duty nurse stared in disbelief. Old Doctor Bradley smiled and closed his eyes. There was a glow about Alex, whose eyes were raised toward heaven. Miss Von Horn wiped her eyes, and the tall man laid a gentle hand on her shoulder. She patted it softly.

Mrs. Benning and Christina had kept the hours of patience, practice, pain and prayers—*so many, many prayers*—a secret. With the sound of her violin accompanying the singing of little angels and fire coursing through their souls, everyone was willing to accept what they were seeing that moment for what it was. A miracle!

No one accepted Christina's miracle with more calm certainty than Thomas Hall. No one experienced a confirmation of the spirit greater than the one that filled his overflowing heart. The truth of it was more luminous than ten thousand lights glimmering from the Christmas trees.

Thomas glanced at Dr. Namkung, who dangled between astonishment and disbelief. *Dr. Namkung said my hand would not get better because he doesn't believe in Heavenly Father. He doesn't know that Jesus can do miracles for people who believe in him.* Christina's expression of simple faith floated to him on the strains of her music.

The useless fingers that would never play again changed positions and the vibrating strings touched by the bow blended with the voices of the children. Mrs. Benning's hands prolonged the final note of Ron Harris's classic piece, sustaining the *A* until there was nothing left but *hmmmmmmm.*

Jesus was in the room called the Healing Place. His spirit was tangible. He was smiling at the children and waiting for the curtain to open. Thomas could not escape the daunting sensation that the real Jesus was also watching and waiting.

• • •

The light on the children faded away. They hummed until no light remained but the luminescence of the trees. The segue from angels humming to the Christ theme from *Ben Hur* was seamless. The curtains opened in the darkness as the sacred anthem set the ancient stage.

Zack wheeled Christina to where Mrs. Benning had taken her seat. Her face seemed to glow in the darkness. Mrs. Benning embraced her and whispered approval and hope. They wept together in each other's arms.

Dr. Namkung stared at the child's fingers as they tightened around the old women's neck. *Inexplicable. Bewildering. The one in a million. Certainly no miracle.* But there was something about her face. Was it possible he was wrong?

Twelve seconds into Miklos Rozsa's marvelous score the curtains began to open. The choir began a succession of *hallelujahs*, each more formidable than the one before. Voices ascending Jacob's ladder.

A bank of Fresnel lights recessed in the dome came on. Like rays of a rising sun, the luster grew brighter as the velvet rolled away and the entire painting glowed in perfect light. The mural was a portal to another world. Life-sized figures, perspective, foreshortening and the depth of diminishing value and hue concealed any sense of a solid surface. At any distance it seemed possible to step into the painting and walk into the past.

Hushed whispers rustled through the audience like an autumn wind of awe through a grove of quaking aspen trees. As they recovered from the initial shock and scanned the broad mosaic, the guests were animated with delight. Seeing the work through so many other eyes left Thomas with a strange sense of detachment. It was as if he were meeting the people of the mural he knew and loved so well for the first time.

A man born blind comes up from the pool of Siloam and looks upon an aged mother's face that he has never seen.

A man deaf and mute for all his life laughs with his wife and children.

Fathers, mothers and children eat bread and fishes with the multitude.

Disciples on the sodden deck of a fishing boat marvel in the peaceful eye of a raging storm.

A father embraces his little son who was lost to mental sickness until the Healer came. Disciples ponder the lesson of the Master.

Two women huddle among the tombs and praise God they are free from the legion of unclean spirits that plunge into the sea with a herd of swine. *My own interpretation of Mark ignoring Matthew,* Thomas thought. *Artistic license. Fair enough.*

A man of the synagogue praises God and holds his once-withered hand, now healed and whole, high for all to see. Pharisees conspire.

A man healed of leprosy makes an offering. Priests ruminate with wonder for the Son of Man who made the miracle.

Nine men are astonished over arms and hands and faces cleansed from leprosy as they show themselves to a piety of priests. A tenth man, also healed of horrible disfigurement, lies prostrate on the ground in humility and gratitude.

A paralytic fellow lowered through the roof in his bed now takes it up and walks. All in the house are dumbfounded. Pharisees murmur.

The daughter of Jairus, whose spirit is returned and life restored, embraces her mother. Her father weeps and those of the house who had wailed her death rejoice.

Lazarus, still wrapped in the shrouds of death, embraces Mary and Martha in the cavity of a rocky tomb. His little son watches from the opening in joyous wonder.

A Roman centurion returns to find his servant healed of a grievous paralysis.

A nobleman of Capernaum is met by servants who have run to tell him that his son recovered from the point of death in the very hour Jesus promised, *Your son will live.*

. . .

Cass invited guests to linger as long as they liked. The formalities were finished. Her duties were done. It was her turn to let the mural take her into the past and allow her to enjoy the miracles of Jesus. She took Thomas by the arm and insisted on a private tour. They started with Jesus and the blessing of the children.

Cass had seen the painting more times than she could count, but there were changes and she could not take her eyes away. Finished. Illuminated. Perfectly displayed. She marveled how the turn of a character's head, the direction of an eye, the movement of a figure and flow of the composition compelled the viewer's eye to go to where Jesus sat with the children.

Cass focused on His face. It was Him and yet not a likeness of the Savior she had ever seen or quite imagined. What was it Thomas had done? What made the Jesus of Thomas Hall so dissimilar and unknown and yet so familiar? *Is it the flicker of mysterious passion behind his eyes?* The eyes were dark blue-violet, almost black, with tiny flaws of green and gray. Gentle yet piercing. And wherever you moved, they followed.

Mastery over light distinguished the old masters from most of the art created since. The fall of the light on Jesus was breathtaking. Had Thomas stumbled upon an undiscovered secret of the old masters?

Angels had been added since she saw it last. They moved among the mothers and the children. There were angels everywhere. The beautiful beings both focused and framed the shaft of light that fell on Jesus and reflected on the children.

Some of the angels ministered to the children as if they were mothers themselves. Others merged with the light that fell from heaven and Cass looked up. There were angels painted on the dome above the canvas! They descended from the concave vertex as if the skylight at the crest of the dome were the gateway into heaven.

Michelangelo painted on the ceiling in the Sistine Chapel. Why not

Thomas? Cass thought and glanced around to see if Miss Von Horn had noticed. The old woman was looking straight up, her eyes full of wonder. There was a smile on her face.

It came to Cass in a rush. She understood what she was seeing and why it was both startling and familiar. *Light of the World is His name.* Thomas gave the idea literal expression in ways other artists hadn't. In ways only a few Old Masters had dared. In the marvelous mural of miracles Jesus was a Being of Light. The source of light. He was God made man. He was man resurrected. He was the Resurrected Christ come again as He promised. *Chastity was right. Thomas Hall would have been Da Vinci.*

. . .

Christina asked Mrs. Benning to park the wheelchair in front of Jesus and the children. She stared at the fingers of her left hand, afraid to expect them to move again. Was it more than she deserved? She wondered if the miracle was over. She had prayed that God would let her play the violin to celebrate the miracles of Jesus. She had forgotten to talk to him about what happened after that. She closed her eyes and thanked him again for answering her prayer. Cautiously she rubbed the hand—*the left hand that would never play the violin again*—and willed her fingers to move. Whether they moved or whether they didn't, she agreed with herself it was going to be okay. She trusted Jesus either way.

Christina saw the angels descending from heaven. She looked at the children and found her friends among them. She looked at the mothers who had brought their precious ones to be blessed by Jesus. She rested her eyes on the face of Jesus. He was who she knew him to be and she smiled.

. . .

Cass and Thomas worked their way slowly along the length of the painting, greeting guests and accepting congratulations. Some asked Thomas to sign their programs. He did so with kindness and modesty.

Berger gave Thomas the predictable compliment: a pat on the back in perfect synchronization with the word *brilliant.* Afterward he hovered within a few feet so he could swoop in on useful VIPs or potential clients who approached *his* artist.

Thomas introduced Cass to the Richters and Sergeant Demeanus. "Along with his other talents," Thomas said as she shook the veteran's leather hand, "Jake is a journeyman carpenter and has agreed to help me finish renovating the other half of the Fish Cannery." Berger gave him the scowl he'd seen a hundred times. "Now that I don't have a boat anymore," Thomas said loudly and tainted with sarcasm for Berger's benefit. "This time we are going to take the old place all the way to her historical splendor." He put a hand on the proud shoulders of Sergeant Demeanus.

Mrs. Benning invited them all to a late dinner and Alex promised her he'd do his best to live that long.

Thomas signed Jessica's program: *To the gorgeous creature who saved me! Warmest personal regards, Tommy.*

He was listening to a woman brag about her forty-four-year-old artist-son who was living in her house and painting in the garage when he saw Silas Hawker. The director was standing alone by the Christmas tree staring at the painting. He stood with his arms folded tightly across his chest. The angst over seeing Hawker again—and here of all places—was replaced by an ache for the man that trembled through him.

Thomas excused himself and shouldered his way through the guests. Hawker moved around the tree and out of view. Whether he had seen Thomas coming toward him was impossible to know. When Thomas got to the other side of the tree Hawker was gone. He caught a glimpse of him at the portal leaving the Healing Place.

Thomas felt a sense of loss he didn't understand. Bittersweet. Standing in the glow of colored lights adorning an ancient symbol of Christian faith, Thomas resolved to leave reconciliation with Silas Hawker on his list. *Part of the bargain. Go forward with faith.* Thomas's collection of pithy aphorisms was changing.

"Thomas?" Chastity tugged on his arm. He turned. The latent image of Hawker was replaced by the face of Ada Kanster. The spider, spike, claw and fist attacked like the A-team. "There is someone I want you to meet," Chastity said.

"We've met," Thomas snapped, flat and icy as a frozen pond. *Chastity invited the enemy? Does she know I'm at war with this woman?* A quick deep breath. *Love your enemies. Love your enemies. Love your enemies.*

"Well, you've *met*," Chastity squabbled, "but you've never really *known* each other," the girl explained. "Aunt Ada, this is Thomas Hall. Thomas, this is my Aunt Ada." *Aunt Ada? Chastity knows everything?* A history of arcane comments over the past few months fell into place like tumblers on a lock. *She's known all along!* Before Thomas could snag one of the retorts cascading through his head, Ada Kanster extended her hand.

"It's a beautiful, beautiful work of art, Mr. Hall. Congratulations." He shook her hand. Dumbfounded. "I wanted to thank you for your kindness to Chastity. Giving her this opportunity."

"She's a talented young woman." His mind was not on Chastity's talent.

Ada smiled at his discomfort. "You and I still have some things to work out, Mr. Hall, but Chastity convinced me you are not the—"

"Monster?"

"Exactly!" She laughed. Thomas had never imagined Ada Kanster capable of such a delightful, lighthearted laugh. "It is obvious you are not the person I thought you were," she said, "or the SAVE THE SEALS folks think you are."

"I should have paid you more," he said to Chastity.

"Just so you know," Ada added, "I had decided you were a good guy before that wonderful scholarship."

"Art Institute is going to be so awesome," Chastity beamed.

"I tried to call you today, Mrs. Kanster," Thomas said, "to apologize for the monster part." Thomas wished now he'd tried harder and been the first with the olive branch.

"Call me Ada, if that's okay. I'd like to do lunch after the holidays. See if we can find some common ground." His nod was wary. "Oh, and never mind the hearing on Monday. I persuaded them to drop the complaint."

"Thanks again," Chastity said and gave Thomas another hug. "I want to thank Professor Andrus before he gets away." She took Aunt Ada by the arm and ushered her away.

. . .

Most of the guests were gone. From the far side of the Healing Place Thomas and Cass could see the full sweep of the mural. Cass slipped her hand over Thomas's arm until their hands touched and she leaned against him. They stood for a long time in silence.

"It's extraordinary," she said finally. "The angels are incredible and the Savior's face is . . . I don't know how to describe it. I knew you were good. I didn't know you were miraculous."

"It wasn't me. Last night . . ." She waited for him to finish but he was caught up in a rush of emotion and just looked at her and shook his head.

"Would you like to come to church with me on Sunday?" Cass asked.

"You asking me for a date?" She cuffed him with her free hand. "I can't think of anything I'd rather do."

Cass kissed him on the cheek. Her face remained close. "Well, almost anything," Thomas said. He brushed an errant lock of hair from her cheek and studied her perfect face. He knew every supple shape and subtle tone. Every line and hue and value. He had drawn it in his mind a thousand times. Cass blushed and moved away but Thomas did what he'd longed to do every time that face had taken form on the sketch pad of his mind. He kissed her. On the forehead. On the cheek. At the corner of her mouth. On the lips. Gently. She closed her eyes and kissed him back and the kiss was not so gentle anymore.

• • •

Christina's eyes moved to the woman who stood very close to Jesus. She was holding the hand of the little girl who sat on Jesus' knee. Her face was radiant in the light coming from the Savior. Christina had never seen a woman so exquisite and full of joy.

Christina raised her crippled hand. "It's going to be all right," she whispered, "just like you promised." She moved her fingers. The miracle had not ended. The beautiful woman smiled. Christina wondered if anyone else could see what she could see so clearly.

She was the child being held by Jesus. The woman holding a hand that would play sweet music for a lifetime was her mother. Jesus had kept his promise and so had Thomas Hall.

EPILOGUE

Hamilton settled his lawsuit. In exchange for dropping his claims of wrongful dismissal, the board gave him full control of the Darwin Pavilion.

The statue of Darwin was moved to Golden Gate Park and placed near a pond clogged with green algae. "So he can contemplate the primordial stew until the Second Coming," Hamilton liked to say.

Hawker resigned. *For personal reasons,* the paper reported. Thomas worried he was ill and had gone to face the death of his brain and the terror of extinction alone.

Hamilton hired Thomas to paint the new murals for the Origins of Man Pavilion. There were three. On the left was a depiction of the theory of Evolution; on the right, a portrayal of the folklore and mythologies of man's origins in the traditions of diverse cultures.

In the center, and by far the most dazzling and unexpected, was Thomas Hall's presentation of Divine Creation. The *Chronicle* called the exhibit "outrageously bold and surprising." The *Christian Science Monitor* said, "inspired."

No one had ever envisioned cherubim the way they emerged from the imagination of Thomas Hall. Who would possibly want to slither in the dark from primordial stew when they could walk from the Garden of Eden in the divine light of angels with flaming swords?

Miss Von Horn opened the Healing Place to the public on Sunday afternoons so everyone could experience the mural of miracles and the resurrected Jesus blessing children in a glorious light and a concourse of angels.

Chastity earned a 3.8 her first semester. She introduced Jake Demeanus to Aunt Ada. Ada had Jake over for dinner on a Sunday. In the very moment she served her delectable blackberry cobbler, the sun struck a skylight near the harbor and filled the room with a dazzling display of light.

Thomas and his dad made it to a Giants game. They ate hot dogs and yelled at the umpire. The Giants won. They made it to Disneyland and rode Space Mountain. Thomas threw up. Alex rode five times. Alex was living with Thomas at the Fish Cannery when he passed away. Thomas was holding his hand.

Mrs. Benning continued violin lessons with Christina and sponsored her first concert at Oakridge Manor. The final piece of her performance was a Hungarian folk tune by Bartok.

Cass won full custody of Christina and legally adopted her. It was a Sunday when she brought her home and gave her the good news. They had been to church and Thomas was with them. Christina leaped into their arms. It is unlikely there was ever a group hug with more love and happiness than happened that day.

When the laughing and crying were over, Christina looked at Thomas and Cass for a long time. She smiled. With the same simple faith that had helped Jesus work his miracle, she said,

"You guys know I'm going to need a dad."

ACKNOWLEDGMENTS

Special thanks to:

Sheri Dew—for asking me to write this book. Nay, for browbeating me ten years until I finally did it. From cub reporter on a snowy mountain to a powerful positive force in publishing. What a journey. What a remarkable person you are. What a cherished friendship we share.

Dagny—the love of my life, for reading the first draft first and sustaining me with your inimitable high praise: "Good, honey," and inevitable perfect balance: "Don't forget to clean the garage."

Our eight children and your quintessential spouses—for filling our cup completely.

Our thirty-three grandkids—for thinking Papa is "cool" for writing a book. But hey, guys, no more treats until you actually read it.

Dr. Jeffrey Hill—for the crash course in emergency medicine and for inspiring one of the good guys in the story.

Emily Watts—now I understand why authors praise their editors. Thank you for your gifts and for guiding my steps through this wondrous yellow woods.

Chris Schoebinger and the team at Shadow Mountain—for bringing your collective creative talents to the project. Your contributions are immeasurable.

Peter Rancie—for encouraging me to write and sharing dreams in my cottage in the woods. I miss you in the leather chair.

Marilyn Faulkner—for being my intelligent, articulate favorite cousin and for making me feel clever even though you're smarter and better.

Thomas Hall—who thanked me for giving him life by giving me my voice.

. . .

I thank the Giver of all good gifts and acknowledge the hand of God in all things. Any portion of this tale that touches your heart was not mine alone. The parts you didn't like . . . I wrote all by myself.

. . .

And a particular thanks to Jack Stone
for waiting in the cottage for me to
write about his astonishing adventures.
*"Be right there, Jack. Still looking
for the missing piece of the map."*